S

BUSTERS

MW01175128

Also by Michael Scofield from Sunstone Press

ACTING BADLY

MAKING CRAZY

WHIRLING BACKWARD INTO THE WORLD

SMUT BUSTERS

GRIT, SANTA FE STYLE

Homeless Heroes Battle
Cocaine, Blackmail,
and Pornography

Third Novel in a Trilogy
Michael Scofield

9-26-13
for Thea,
Friend, inspiring leader,
powerful writer, with love
from Michael
Laguna Woods

SUNSTONE
PRESS

SANTA FE

This book is entirely fictional and may contain views, opinions, premises, depictions, and statements by the author that are not necessarily shared or endorsed by Sunstone Press. The events, people, and incidents in this story are the sole product of the author's imagination. The story is fictional and any resemblance to individuals living or dead is purely coincidental. Sunstone Press assumes no responsibility or liability for the author's views, opinions, premises, depictions and statements in this book.

© 2013 by Michael Scofield
All Rights Reserved.

No part of this book may be reproduced in any form or by any electronic or mechanical means including information storage and retrieval systems without permission in writing from the publisher, except by a reviewer who may quote brief passages in a review.

Sunstone books may be purchased for educational, business, or sales promotional use. For information please write: Special Markets Department, Sunstone Press, P.O. Box 2321, Santa Fe, New Mexico 87504-2321.

Book and Cover design › Vicki Ahl
Body typeface › Palatino Linotype
Printed on acid-free paper

Library of Congress Cataloging-in-Publication Data

Scofield, Michael.
    Smut busters : grit, Santa Fe style : third novel in a trilogy / by Michael Scofield.
        pages cm
    ISBN 978-0-86534-964-3 (softcover : alk. paper)
    1. Homeless persons--Fiction. 2. Santa Fe (N.M.)--Fiction. I. Title.
    PS3619.C63S68 2013
    813'.6--dc23
                                    2013024454

WWW.SUNSTONEPRESS.COM
SUNSTONE PRESS / POST OFFICE BOX 2321 / SANTA FE, NM 87504-2321 /USA
(505) 988-4418 / ORDERS ONLY (800) 243-5644 / FAX (505) 988-1025

ACKNOWLEDGMENTS

Special thanks to my wife, Noreen, my initial editor. She continues to make of our home an ideal writer's retreat.

For two years Michael Pahos helped me get clear on many subjects about which I knew little. Thank you, Michael. This book wouldn't have seen daylight without you.

Added thanks to Dr. Paul B. Donovan for detailing the physical and emotional effects of stress, and to Audacia Ray for helping me set up on paper the Beautiful Tomorrows Web site.

Thanks to Santa Feans Irene Webb and Bill Maloney for their back-cover comments.

I'm grateful to the following friends who served as fact checkers: Jerry Baker, Elizabeth Bradley, Dave Caldwell, Jane Chermayeff, Laura Cooley, Dennis Culhane, Heide York DeGomez, Terry Egbert, Christopher Ford, Ben Glass, Carolyn Gonzales, Hank Hughes, John Kennedy, Elizabeth Lawrence, Chip Lilianthal, Marie Lopez, Rex McCreary, James McGrath, Clint Marshall, Shane Miller, Bruce Pratz, Margaret Robbins, Deborah Rodda, Sandy Schultz, Steve Seifert, Marian Shirin, James Clois Smith, Jr., Gayle Snyder, Jennifer Sprague, Karen Squires, Deborah Tang, Susan Tixier, Brendan Ward, Jerry Williams, Jennifer Wynne, and Dan Yarbrough.

CAST OF CHARACTERS

Jock Gunden—author, Germaine Edmonds's boyfriend

Germaine Edmonds—editor at Bennett Books, Quentin Edmonds's daughter

Quentin (Q) Edmonds—composer, homeless

Byron (Buzzy) Hurd—former Kullman College professor, homeless

Dirk Pellington—former journalist, homeless

Nate (Flasher) Cobb—cocaine dealer, homeless

Tish Earp—Nate's addict companion, homeless

More of the Homeless:

    Chiffon

    Reuben, Wilda, and Hisi Lightningfeather

    Clara

    Universal Cosmic Divinity

    Stormy Weathers

Katherine (Kat) Ulibarri—founder of Kat's Harbor

Beatriz Ulibarri—Kat's granddaughter

Marta Fitzheimer—Kat's former lover

Veronica (Vonnie) Trumble—intern at Kat's Harbor

Fritz Joseph—owner of Beautiful Tomorrows Hacienda, former hedge-fund manager

Arlene Joseph—Fritz's wife

Raven Feldman—cocaine addict, sex facilitator for Beautiful Tomorrows Hacienda

Jimmy Holstein—Miami real estate developer, guest at Beautiful Tomorrows Hacienda

BACKDROP

Monday 30 September 2009

You may recall once reading in the papers about a group of homeless Santa Fe, New Mexicans who exposed an Internet-driven blackmail ring offering weekend sex and cocaine. This was the tip of the iceberg. It took three months of twice-a-week therapy to steady me enough to begin this full account.

The events all may be true, may not. The statistics probably are.

Top Ten Reviews reports that in 2006—the year before this story took place—the Internet contained four-hundred-and-twenty million pornographic pages, and that forty-three percent of all Internet users view porn. By 2006 the pornography industry had grown to ninety-seven billion dollars, larger than the combined revenues of Amazon, Apple, Earthlink, eBay, Google, Microsoft, and Netflix.

The year 2006 saw the street value of cocaine in the United States soar to seventy-five billion dollars, representing three hundred metric tons— or fifty percent of world consumption. According to the US government's *2004 National Survey on Drug Use and Health,* by then thirty-four million Americans over twelve years old had used cocaine at least once. Just last month researchers from the University of Massachusetts found that ninety percent of one-dollar bills studied in seventeen of our major cities bore trace amounts of cocaine.

Stats on the homeless? Hank Hughes, Executive Director for the New Mexico Coalition to End Homelessness, at the time this book was written, estimates that three million women, men, and children are wandering our country's streets or couch-surfing with friends—or lie slumped in doorways or sleeping in shelters or curled up somewhere in the brush. That's one percent of the US. Many suffer from schizophrenia, many from post-traumatic stress disorder. Many are addicted—alcohol, meth, heroin, cocaine. Hughes believes that thirty percent of the homeless are veterans. A small share opts permanently to depend on shelters, soup kitchens, Medicaid, and their wits rather than return to what they consider the living death of a sixty-hour workweek.

Is it any wonder that pornography, street drugs, and homelessness underpin society today? Terror, poverty, desertification, and floods have become the world's norms.

It's now September 2009 and I'm about to submit my manuscript to the woman I'm calling Germaine. She bought my first book; I've gotten used to working with her rather than through an agent. Germaine is west-coast editor for Bennett Books and we've been engaged for two years. Why haven't we tied the knot? A Florida real estate developer she met during her first weekend at the Josephs' sex hacienda continues to make her waffle. The son of a bitch is flying into San Francisco again tomorrow.

Once you finish this saga, you'll probably wonder where some of the participants are today. Tish Earp and Arlene Joseph remain in the women's prison west of Albuquerque, New Mexico. Arlene's husband rots behind bars in one of the prisons in Canyon City, Colorado. Nate "Flasher" Cobb hopes for parole from Santa Fe's state pen.

Sex facilitator Raven Feldman paid a three-hundred-dollar fine and did forty-eight-hours' community service at Kat's shelter, then found work at the rehab center where she got clean. She waitresses weekends while studying for a degree in Applied Science, Film Production, at Santa Fe's community college.

Dirk Pellington died in an arroyo in Taos. Quentin Edwards, Dirk's friend and my fiancée's father, has just finished up his composer-in-residency at the Red River Music Festival. His cello sonata, *Lamentation for Buzzy*, which Germaine and I flew back to hear, got a rave in *The New York Times*. Once a month Germaine sends him enough to live on. He rents an earthship out on the Taos mesa.

Quentin writes that Byron "Buzzy" Hurd, who teaches at Columbia, wishes he could leave Vonnie and return to Quentin's side. But Vonnie's pregnant—Buzzy supposes they'll marry—and he feels responsible for an earlier illegitimate child living in Rhode Island.

FREED

"I can't do this any more, Byron."

"Not listening, Sarah."

"Dude, I'm saying that after you began snoring, I threw up again."

"I thought..."

"Right, right, the test from Walgreens showed negative. It's got to be nerves."

Adjunct Professor Byron Hurd sat on a bench near the lily pond with nineteen-year-old Sarah Chacks on a hot morning two weeks before Kullman College's fall semester began.

He had spent nine years teaching algebra, music, and tennis at Prep a mile from the private college snuggled below Sun and Moon Mountains on the east side of Santa Fe. But three intense evenings at Garrett's Desert Inn bedding a sixteen-year-old student at Prep so frightened Byron that he applied for whatever position at Kullman he could secure. This past spring, teaching music and calculus there, he had left his wife and children and persuaded Sarah, a Kullman freshman, to move into his casita off the Alameda.

Byron and Sarah stopped talking now as a dozen women and men attending the yearly meeting of the Los Vecinos Homeowners Association, representing a cluster of forty-eight high-end condominiums, spilled from the student center. They fanned across the grass with their Styrofoam cups of coffee in sundresses and shorts, khakis, and short-sleeve button-downs.

Byron tried to talk Sarah into abandoning the outdoors for the privacy of his office. But she shook her twin ponytails. So he led her up brick steps—in his jeans that had become too loose—to shade under an elm near Wilkinson Hall.

She folded her legs and stared at him, compressing her lips and straight-arming the grass.

He wrapped his upraised knees. "The landlord's going to kick us out, Sarah. Nine-hundred bucks plus seventy for utilities due last Thursday.

Half my paycheck goes straight home for my kids' school. We've got to start looking around."

"Dude? You really *aren't* listening, are you?"

He raised his wrist to wipe a high, freckled forehead. "I refuse to go back home! You know Val's got a lover. Anyway, I don't want her, I want you. We've been tight since May, haven't we? Shit-and-a-half, I'm about to lose a chunk of change I no got."

"Is that all you can think of?" She flung out her free hand, each of its four fingers ringed, and jerked her chin toward the condo owners below. "God, those freakin' plutocrats talk loud."

"Money does."

"Ha ha ho, Byron, *so* not funny. This morning while you were buying groceries I phoned my folks. They're going to be out a lot of wampum, too—way more than you—but they're letting me crash back east with them a while. Adios, Santa Fe; see ya, sophomore year. Maybe the dean will let me start up in January."

"I'll go crazy on my own, Sarah!" Byron vised his temples. His pink polo dampened his chest. "My kids have probably forgotten me, who knows what Val's been telling them—last night after you and I made love you said you loved me."

"I do, sometimes. Dude, I'm trying to be strong here." She reached forward to cup the back of his neck, breasts wobbling in a flowered, low-cut top.

"It's too damned hot, let's go in."

"Don't want to. After Mom and Dad and I talked, I drove up and walked into Wilkinson. The admin said Dean Wolfe was there so I talked to her."

"You *what*? Without consulting me?"

"You were at Wild Oats and I was afraid I'd chicken out. I'd have to meet with her sometime, wouldn't I?"

"What did you tell her?"

"Everything."

"You Delilah! Just got me fired. You know the rules here."

"Okay, everybody, back inside," called a rawboned woman in a sombrero. "We've got officers to elect."

The condo owners rose from the grass. A man in shorts and country-club cap, scone shoved half into his mouth, gazed up the slope at Sarah and Byron.

Byron leaped up and grabbed her hand.

"That hurts!"

"I don't care." He pulled Sarah along the concrete walkway until they reached De Vargas Hall. They climbed its five stairs. Byron spotted a note tacked on his door opposite the water fountain. *Mr. Hurd—urgent. See envelope slipped inside.*

He released her, ripped the note off the nail, and turned his key.

A white rectangle lay on the rug's maroon.

"Close the fucking door." He picked up the envelope and watched Sarah trudge barefoot, head drooping, to an upholstered chair near the bookcase. Its shelves stretched from the hall wall to a window that looked out at two New Mexican locusts and the elm.

"I know the fourteen years' difference between us doesn't matter a damn and I'm feeling pretty shitty," she said, slouching against the cushion. Her arms, its hairs bleached by the sun, dangled off the chair's arms. "Listen, maybe if I come back..."

"Oh, bag it." He flicked on the ceiling's fluorescent panel, moved behind his desk, tore open the envelope, and read, *Mr. Hurd, Dean Wolfe asks to see you before noon. Roxanne.*

He lifted the receiver and punched two numbers. The drops of perspiration tickled as they ran down his ribs. "Roxanne? Byron Hurd." He listened. "Of course.

"I've got to go right up."

"Oh, dude, I love you, I do, I love you." Sarah bolted from her chair and embraced him on tiptoes, raising her cleft chin to press her lips to his.

The palm clasping his neck felt moist. He pushed her face away. "Make sure the door's locked when you leave."

"I'm going nowhere till you're back." She mopped her eyes with her wrist.

He managed half a smile, wishing he could slit her throat before he slit his own.

The sun heated his bald spot as he passed the elm, trudged up

Wilkinson's slate steps, and onto the porch. The upper and lower quads lay empty, except for the maintenance man in blue overalls who bent to net chip wrappers and cups from the lily pond.

The glass entry door squeaked. Byron stepped inside onto the brick floor. Students wouldn't be lounging on the foyer's two sofas until September.

Roxanne looked up through her interior window as he headed her way. She pulled the door wide. "I think she's ready for you, Byron."

His left eyelid twitched. This was the first time he'd seen the slats covering Dean Wolfe's windows opened.

"Shut the door, will you?" Dean Wolfe asked in a scratchy voice— sometimes he'd seen her smoking on the porch. "Sofa? Chair at the conference table? Take your pick, Mister Hurd."

He settled in one of the rattan-bottom chairs facing her, gray hair as ever knotted behind her head.

"Well, you've screwed up, haven't you, pardon the pun. Unh huh. After following proper grievance procedures—of course we'll give you that—I suspect we'll want to let you find a more suitable position. So sad. During the two years you've been with us, the students seem to have grown fond of you—one rather too much, yes? Tell you what. Why not just resign? It would save us a lot of paperwork. Might you do us all that favor?"

He stared at her glasses. "Fait accompli? Well, why not?" The words burned his throat as he shrugged.

"I'll have Roxanne type up something, though you may want to consult a lawyer before you sign. What reason shall we give for your leaving?"

"Broke the rules?"

"A few of our big donors think them somewhat old-fashioned. How about Adjunct Professor Hurd needs more time to help his wife with their three children?" She narrowed her eyes. "With perhaps a fourth on the way, I understand from little Sarah?"

"It's not mine! Little *Sarah* knows nothing."

"Oh? Then let's add Professor Hurd needs time to practice the cello, hoping soon to start playing professionally. Shall we do that for good measure, pardon the pun?"

"Whatever," Byron growled.

"Should Sarah find she's with child, I fear we can't help you if the girl or her parents decide to sue."

"The test showed negative."

"Unh huh. Or if a doctor finds something worse. The girl *is* vomiting. We're through for now, I believe." Dean Wolfe smoothed the sides of her skirt as she stood.

He rose and grabbed the chair's back to keep it from toppling.

"One thing more." She covered her lips with her fist for a moment. "Aren't you a little bit ashamed?"

Ashamed? The dean had no idea. For years his mother, bedridden with pleurisy, had used him as her nurse before he left Fresno for Dartmouth on a tennis scholarship. How often had she begged to be kissed as though she were his girlfriend? How often had he complied, each time pretending her the beauty in her wedding photos. While his father worked days as a mechanic, nights and weekends restoring pre1940s Fords.

He clenched his teeth, pivoted, and strode out.

Byron threw open the door to De Vargas Hall, ran up the stairs, and tried his own door. Locked. He placed his mouth close to the crack. "Are you in there?"

No answer. He thrust his fingers into a pocket, pulled out his keys, shoved one into the knob, turned, and pushed.

At least she wasn't spread out with a letter opener buried in her chest—here, anyway. He expelled his breath, started to fiddle with the tiny electronic piano that perched on his blotter, abruptly picked up the phone.

"Yes?" Val's voice sounded harried.

"It's me."

"Me?"

"Buzzy."

"Oh? Why? Your check arrived on time."

"I want to come home! If the guy who got you pregnant disappears."

"But, doll, I've applied for a restraining order. On Leroy's advice. You must have expected it. To protect the children."

"I've never hurt the children on visits."

"Me, then."

"You neither!"

"You won't hurt us now? I told the judge differently. They're scared of you, Buzz. Me, too."

"Emotionally, maybe, but that's no basis..."

"You'll need to appear in court. You've hit them."

"Shit-and-a-half, Val. Spanked Michael once. On your suggestion."

"No one wants to see you any more, Byron."

"My cello's there, my music! My books, winter clothes! I want to apologize to Michael and Pooh and Rachel. And help you with the baby, I don't care whose it is."

"Leroy lives here now."

"That's *my* home, I'm their daddy. What a mistake I've made."

"Could be, but it's over, Byron. Thanks to Leroy, I've started composing cowboy songs again."

"The college found out about Sarah and me. Kullman's fucking ethics are twentieth century. Okay, I've resigned. Where am I going to stay?"

"I thought you and your teenager have a casita. No? In any case, you'll need to find work fast because I've also decided to sue for alimony and full child support."

"Val, stop! Sarah's going back to her parents in Rhode Island. We're behind on the rent."

"You poor souls. She's going to have your child back there, then?"

"What?"

"She's throwing up, isn't she?"

"How did you know that?"

"Wild guess. Got to ring off, doll. Hear Pooh and Michael screaming in the bedroom?"

"Valentine! Indian Market starts tonight. All the hotels have got to be booked. Let me stay the weekend, please?"

"Bugger off, Buzzy. Didn't I tell you Leroy's moved in? Sweet-talk your landlord or hole up out of town. And go buy a paper."

"Paper?"

"A *news*paper. For the *want* ads."

Her receiver became a pistol cocked in his ear.

— — —

That afternoon, sixty-two-year-old composer Quentin Edmonds, made jittery from the shower's continuing splash, glanced from the bed into the B and B's bathroom. He pushed back against the pillow and fluttered the silk flaps of his robe to dissipate the steam.

He needed quiet in order to attend the muses—what he called his whores—that had started ruckusing in his head. He took a stave notebook from the bed-table's drawer and jotted down three fragments of music.

The electronic, roll-up keyboard he used for storing and editing lay beside him on the king-size quilt. Would he ever dare compose again? Cave into silence, probably. Like Sibelius. Even having Milt fuck him here after last night's concert hadn't canceled the pain of watching half-a-dozen women stand during his world premiere in the St. Francis Auditorium, edge past patrons still seated, and walk out. One tubby bitch in a sequined dress had jerked her husband along with her.

Hell's broth! They should have waited for the last movement, when the four washboards protesting the oboe's obbligato gave way to an F-major victory proclaimed by cello, viola, and French horn.

His *To My Daughter* was a masterpiece, wasn't it? He leaned sideways, flicked the CD player into *Play*, and stabbed the button until the display read *Track 6*. Clash of symbols—yes! Violin attempting to break into freedom, stopped by the cello. Mastered by brass and morphing into...

"Quent!" A broad-shouldered redhead strode out, hair curling from his chest, towel wrapped around his waist.

"Stop shortening my name."

"Yes sir, Beethoven. But turn that barnyard bedlam off. Wasn't your concert last night enough?"

"You know nothing about music."

"Not your kind, excellency." Milt flicked his already-bent nose with his thumb. "I favor tunes like we danced to when you and I hooked up Wednesday night. Though I think I'm gonna fly the coop—too much gibble-gabble the last forty-eight hours explaining why you wrote that din and pissing over having to kick out your longtime live-in back in the Big Apple for cheating. After the New School for Jazz or whatever fired you for belittling the director. Too much—save the mouth for better things, old daddy."

Quentin punched the player's *Off* button and jerked his chin up. "Hang around, Milt. I may need you again." He pulled his billfold from the bed-table's drawer and extracted a couple of fifties. "These say at least stay put until I find out if Shasky's going to honor his promise to make me composer-in-residence in two-ten."

Half an hour later, Quentin stepped into the heat beneath a string of chiles, decked in a white beret and embroidered guayabera worn over white ducks. He marched along a breast-high wall and turned left, graying hair secured with an elastic band. Wisteria vines, now bare, clung to the stucco between his room's two shuttered windows.

He passed Milt's pickup and his own rental sedan angled in beside the B and B. Beyond lay the lot reserved for the High Mesa Music Festival office. Ragweed and hairy asters choked the base of a phone pole and he veered into the street to avoid them. Already his new white loafers hurt. He turned into the walkway of the Festival's adobe building and passed its iron gate and locust-shaded patio.

He patted his forehead dry with a handkerchief extracted from his back pocket—he must have left his billfold in the bed-table's drawer.

The Music Festival's outreach manager, her eyelids blushed in purple, waved him back along a hall hung with fifteen years of Festival posters. At its end, Rudi Shasky rose in a denim jacket from behind the littered desk he'd placed in the center of his office.

"Look, Rudi," Quentin blurted, "about those walkouts last night…"

Shasky removed his horn-rims. "Take a load off, genius." He indicated one of the Mexican-style bucket chairs facing him. "The CD doesn't do your work justice. That second movement's brilliant."

Quentin laid his arms along the chair's, leaving his beret aslant, as Shasky lowered his bulk.

"You enjoyed last night, then?"

"Made me gnash my teeth, Quentin, but indicative of our country's current self-loathing—like the lead in a Georges Simenon thriller."

"George who?"

"Became the best-selling author in the world after we wiped out Hiroshima and Nagasaki. Simenon's pretty much nobody today though he's never been more pertinent. Could be where you're headed."

"Like where, do you think?"

Shasky stared at him and Quentin looked down. He noticed a Jackalope price label on the chair's leather beside his thigh and scratched it off with an uncut thumbnail, releasing the tiny wad to the carpet. He raised his head. "You asked me to come see you...."

"Right." Shasky pushed his glasses to his nose. "I had thought we might chat about the future but we received some calls this morning."

"About..."

"Your premiere." Shasky spread fingers tufted with hair on his desktop. "Two calls from trustees alone. One said the work had given her tinnitus."

"Too much time on the phone can bring tinnitus on."

"I hope you keep composing in the same vein as *To My Daughter*, Quentin. Our country needs its Cassandra. Get that music performed. But not here."

"Here."

"For us."

A scene from a year ago flashed behind Quentin's eyes. He'd been sipping tea in bed after sex with his live-in, telling him that, to rid himself of shame, he intended to construct for his Festival commission a piece in three movements dedicated to his daughter. "Don't want to dedicate it to me?" the live-in had whined.

"I had hoped our patrons were ready for Georges Simenon," Shasky said. "I'd hoped wrong."

"Then I'm to forget that residency in two-ten?"

Shasky threw his shoulders back and yanked off his horn-rims. He chewed the end of an earpiece. "Can't be done, I'm afraid."

Rage he'd had no clue he harbored propelled Quentin out of his seat. He flung the two bucket chairs against the edge of Shasky's desk, threw up a hand, and began to pace. The beret had tumbled to the carpet. "You chickenshit bureaucrat, don't give me all this merde. You have no idea what inside my head is like. Clamoring far worse than tinnitus, whores running around desperate to be heard. 'Listen to me, no, to *me*,' and I agonize, wanting to let them all become music."

He grabbed the fired base of Shasky's lamp and tilted it off the desktop like a beacon. "Our culture no longer knows devotion to mystery. I long to restore that."

"Washboards'll do it." Shasky edged his hand toward a bell near his out-box and ran his tongue along the inside of his lower lip.

"Whores dressing as goddesses."

"I'm afraid you're way ahead of me, genius."

"Of course I'm way ahead of you! You're the crossing guard for kindergarteners. Screw the jazz and contemporary music scenes. I want out—freedom to turn my pocked-face whores into vestal virgins."

"You deserve a larger audience," Shasky said softly. "Put the lamp down, will you? It's a gift from John Rainer, the flutist." The heel of his hand thumped a knob on the bell twice.

"No need. I'm going." Quentin snatched up his beret and walked out.

Sun seared his eyeballs as he left the shadows of the walkway and turned toward the B and B. He pulled out his handkerchief to blot his neck and cursed to see Milt's truck gone, then figured he'd left to purchase another wedge of cake from Chocolate Maven that Quentin had learned Milt adored. Had the boy toy thought to bring back a treat for *him*? Doubtful.

He turned up the B and B's walk past the cottonwood, nodded to a couple lounging beneath a yellow umbrella on the patio, opened the front entry door, and unlocked his own across the hall, pinched feet burning.

The floor-lamp's moonlike globes were lit. The roll-up keyboard lay on the wrinkled blanket. But no laptop sat near the bed's foot nor CD player on the table. Hell's broth! He spotted his suitcase still standing against the wall and hurried to the bathroom doorway. Milt's kit had vanished. He wheeled, ran to the closet, slid the door open, and saw only wire hangers. Boots, turtlenecks, his sport jacket, robe, pink-and-white dress shirts—gone.

He leapt to the bed table and yanked the drawer out. There lay his notebook, but no billfold.

What a fool! He didn't even know the boy toy's last name.

— — —

Meanwhile, Quentin's daughter, Germaine, an editor at Bennett Books, endured the unknown minutes she'd have to wait for her buzzer to sound. She sat in her New York apartment's bedroom just before sunset, gazing at her monitor while the conditioner her boyfriend had installed in the window pushed cold air at her.

She double-clicked on *Internet Explorer,* still in her office skirt and black flats, then rose and walked to the other window. It offered a full view onto West 8th three stories down. The shoe store's neon flashed *Yo Mama* as a cop on a bicycle chased a dark-skinned woman in ankle-high sneakers into Washington Square West. A couple of youngsters whose T-shirts read *NYU* straddled the bench outside the deli munching sandwiches. A third, standing, was pushing a pickle between his lips.

She returned to her monitor. *U.S. and Israel sign arms deal to give Israel $30 billion in military aid in what officials called a long-term investment in peace.*

Investment in brain damage, Germaine thought, and pressed a pearl to her left earlobe hard enough to make her wince, a trick her mother had taught her for renewing focus. She highlighted *nytimes* between *http://* and *.com,* typed *craigslist,* moved the cursor right, and hit *Enter.*

Last night Jock had asked where she'd most like to spend a weekend if the facility they sought could be found, and without thinking she'd answered Santa Fe. Because her mother had said her father was there now? Germaine snorted. Her father and she had not talked for nineteen years.

She clicked on *New Mexico* on craigslist's home page, and then on *Santa Fe,* as fed up with her frigidity as was Jock. Under *Services* she clicked on *Erotic.*

She pursed her lips, exhaled, and scanned the page, clicking first on *Check out our safer sex forum, courtesy of the folks at San Francisco City Clinic.*

She clicked on *safer sex forums.* Too many choices! She hit the *Back* button and clicked on *San Francisco City Clinic,* then on *STD Basics.* Oh, my God: six sexually transmitted diseases, ending with an ominous *Others.* She hadn't the guts to explore them alone. She chuffed out breath, closed the eye that had started to throb, hit *Back* and *Back* again, hit *Services* and *Erotic,* and—topping a long list—hit *Need partner for fun and games, w4m.* Hi, the posting started, *I'm new to this…recently single, white, 5' 8", 142, auburn, hazel, rather sexxxxy boobs…*

No, no. She clicked on *So just thy face and shape my fancy fitteth,* unable to spot any listings implying a weekend retreat. What popped into view was a woman's ass tagged *for more squirting power.*

She highlighted *santafe.craigslist* and—consulting the scrap of paper Jock had brought to her office this afternoon—typed in *adultfriendfinder*. *Meet people looking for sex, 19,319,758 members.* Jock had promised dinner if she could find a site, but she felt ravaged.

About to click on *New Mexico*, she heard the buzzer, jumped up, hurried out and past the living-room sofa, reached the speaker, and punched *Talk*.

"Yes?"

She punched *Listen*.

"Me, princess."

She thumbed *Door*, unhooked the chain, threw the bolt, and rushed into the galley kitchen to down the half shot of scotch she'd set previously on the counter. She returned to the door, shuddering at the drink's bite, and opened to his footsteps on the third-floor landing.

"You've been drinking," Jock said.

"Needed one."

"Same." Jock stood slope-shouldered in a dress shirt and khakis, an inch shorter and five years older, sleeves rolled above his elbows, thumbs stuck into his pockets. He'd slung a gray, V-necked sweater around his neck.

She raised the dark eyebrows she'd begun tweezing white hairs from every couple of months.

"You're waiting for something?" she asked.

"Your lips."

"Come on in." She leaned down to kiss him.

He turned to secure the bolt and chain. "Still in your work clothes."

"I want that dinner."

He pulled the sweater off and flung it to a chair. His shoulders bulged from lifting weights in his own apartment four blocks away. "Any luck?"

"Not yet. This is nerve-wracking."

He took her bare arms in beefy hands that seemed at odds with so trim a waistline. "I've booked us at Ye Waverly Inn for eight-thirty."

"Well," she sighed, "here's hoping." She pulled from his grip and led him into the bedroom. He brought the wicker armchair, draped with her mother's antimacassars, next to her swivel chair. She lifted her hands, facing the screen saver of winged books.

"Hold it." He pressed her wrists to the pullout shelf, using his forearm. "I just finished a couple of martinis at North Square with a writer pal. He told me about a domain called Beautiful Tomorrows."

"You talked about what we're doing? This is private, Jock!" She clenched the eye that was throbbing.

He removed his arm. "At ease. I said you had an author with a shyness problem. My buddy described the site as discreet and classy. Small groups in a hacienda, guess where. He was going to book for a weekend but his publisher had just finished selling out to Bertelsmann and he lost his advance. Beautiful Tomorrows Institute dot—believe it or not—org. Let's have a look."

Just then the white phone on a table covered with another antimacassar rang.

"Don't answer that!" Jock sucked his thumb. "Broke my nail unpacking those bookshelves I found for your closet."

"Go fix us a scotch-and-soda, will you? It's probably Judy working late to amend your contract. You want that extra ten-grand advance for *Muslim Moderates* and extension until April, don't you?"

She knocked his knee rushing to the bed's far side.

He rubbed it, stood, and left for the kitchen.

"Oh, hi," she blurted.

Germaine pictured her mother perched in her red robe in Queens on the stool near the dishwasher, white hair loosened to her waist, brush and hand mirror laid on the Formica.

"Dad's world premiere? No, I haven't had the chance to look at today's *Times*. Called *To My Daughter*? How do you know he wants to make contact? If he had called it _For My Daughter_ I might be intrigued. Sure, why not, save the review. Panned him? Yes, Mother, I know my father's talented. You've told me often and I've heard some of his pieces. What do you want me to say? No! I don't hate him."

Jock returned with drinks as she jerked the receiver from her ear. He stiffened to hear her mother shout, "Your father never had sexual relations with you, Germaine!"

Jock's jaw clenched. He cracked the other window open, despite the conditioner's struggles to keep the bedroom cool, and walked to the armchair.

Germaine gulped her scotch and brought the receiver close. "Yes, I'm still here. Where's Dad teaching now, anyway? Did he ever get tenure at Mannes? Oh—where? Third Street Music School Settlement? Starts next month? Bit of a comedown, isn't it? Well, yes, I assume he still plays jazz piano when he can get a gig, and still gives private lessons.

"You want *what* when he comes back to New York? To arrange a lunch to celebrate his residency at the Festival three years from now? Is that for sure? You said the reviewer—Mother, for God's sake, you've told me Dad's turned gay. Let him go, find yourself a real boyfriend! Listen," she lied, "Jock and I have to race out of here or cancel dinner plans. I'll be over Sunday."

She gave him a lopsided smile and trudged to the window, swiping her palm across her forehead. Down past the fire escape she watched a white-bearded man Rollerblade to the left, right, and left again, dodging taxis and a limo and the three students from NYU. The odor of exhaust made her cough.

She rolled her chair back to the monitor.

"You want me to take over?" Jock asked.

"It's not your problem. Though I want you here when I search craigslist for tips on side effects."

"Side effects?"

"Diseases." She brought up the *Times* home page and typed in the new URL.

Jock hopped the armchair to a spot beside her.

The *Beautiful Tomorrows Institute* home page, backgrounded in green, showed a wraparound sofa, leather chairs, and ottomans that looked out on a cottonwood and spruce and a long bed of iris. The headline read, *Heal in our Hacienda to get back in touch with you.*

"It looks gorgeous!" Germaine exclaimed.

Jock scratched his scalp between the down-the-center part of brown hair. "No street shots to give away its location, I notice."

Germaine bent to pry off a flat from her heel, then used her stockinged toes to pry off the other. She hit *Click here—please, we work only with those over 18.* The screen darkened, then lit with, *For beautiful tomorrows, rejuvenate your sexuality through group and individual encounters. Led by a facilitator trained in*

Institute-approved techniques. Accepting applications for September and October. Learn more by clicking here.

Germaine did so.

"Maybe I ought to accompany you after all," Jock offered, feeling his penis stiffen against his jockeys.

"You've no good reason, sonny." She swiveled and smiled and patted his unshaved cheek.

"But what if..." He stopped as the new page showed two men and three women fully clothed, drinks in hand, chatting in a large kitchen. A third man in hibiscus-flowered shirt and cargo shorts stood beside a range, hefting a frying pan. A tortilla hovered in midair. A stencil of jackrabbits chasing cottontails lined the wall near the ceiling.

"I want to go!" Jock blurted.

Germaine laughed and, feeling more at ease, undid the top of her blouse. She recited out loud the words running along the left side of the photo. *Groups limited to six. You must bring the report from a SxCheck-affiliated clinic (every major city in every state has at least one) that indicates your blood pressure is between 100/60 and 140/90, your pulse rate is under 60, and you do not have HIV/AIDS, chlamydia, or gonorrhea.*

"What the hell is chlamydia?" Germaine frowned.

"Part of our education. I'm glad the outfit's being careful."

They read on. *Additional STD tests optional—consult sxcheck.com for details. For more information about your Beautiful Tomorrows stay, click here."*

Germaine let out a squeal over the photo on the next page. Yellowing aspen glowed along a two-lane road leading to the ski lift. *Our van will pick you up and return you to Albuquerque's Sunport. You'll spend Saturday night in Santa Fe at our Hacienda, a five-minute ride from the Plaza. Gourmet dinner, Sunday breakfast, and lunch if you wish it are included. All for $750. To apply for a reservation, click here. To learn about optional photo opportunities—for those who choose to sharpen their newly acquired skills later at home—click here.*

"Jock? Photos?"

"I wouldn't. You don't want a stranger to control the negatives or digital files."

"Good point." Germaine clicked on *reservation.*

Circles to check off ran in columns down the page.

I am/We are O *a woman* O *a man* O *two women* O *two men* O *a woman and man. Wish to encounter* O *a woman* O *a man* O *two women* O *two men* O *a woman and man. I am __ years old/We are __ and __ years old. Would like to book* O *first* O *second* O *third* O *fourth* O *fifth weekend in* O *September* O *October.*

E-mail us the following within three days of submitting this application: a) A recent photo of you (and partner) b) One hundred words explaining why you wish to visit us. c) E-mail and phone of whom to contact in unlikely chance of emergency.

"Jock? I just got frightened."

"Want to forget it? We could consult yet another sex therapist here."

"What good has it done?" She bit her lip and checked O *a woman,* typed in [*I am*] 32, drew the cursor down to *first,* then to *September*—and hit *Send.*

She reached for Jock's hand and clamped it. "My father will have left long before then."

"I'm proud of you, princess." He slipped a watch from his watch pocket. "Let's make use of this bed before we go eat."

CHEAP DIGS

Friday 31 August 2007

An overgrown, triangular enclave of perhaps three-fourths of an acre serves in Santa Fe as a refuge for the homeless. It lies wedged between the School for the Deaf and land owned by the Public Service Company of New Mexico. Beer cans have been tossed into the rabbitbrush; bottles and torn jackets peep from tangles of ragweed, cheat grass, and sweet clover. Fifteen years ago, fire blackened the limbs of a copse of Siberian elms.

Early in May, a homeless man known as Flasher, along with his girlfriend, Tish, used hoes and shovels provided by Kat's Harbor homeless shelter to clear three small campsites in the refuge and paths to connect them. Tish stood sentry duty during the day, where two paths branched from an old trail that wound toward Fairview Cemetery off Cerrillos Road.

On this Friday, a mile and a half northeast of the refuge, vendors had set up canvas-roofed booths for the arts-and-crafts market on the Plaza. The evening of Labor Day weekend always launches the annual, nine-day Fiesta.

Quentin, who had begun calling himself Q, was trudging back from Kat's Harbor. Two weeks had passed since Milt had stolen his wallet, laptop, and clothes. A torn sleeping bag and empties of tequila littered the drainage ditch he paused beside, wondering if he could hear trumpeters practicing on the Plaza's bandstand. But the only sounds came from traffic jostling home along Cerrillos and, just beyond the barbed wire, the hum from a substation's transformers. Quentin used his teeth to scrape the last sweetness from the orange he'd pocketed at Wild Oats Market and swallowed the peel's bitterness.

"Halt!" Flasher's girlfriend called out at the refuge's entrance. She jumped from a threadbare sofa and leveled a snub-nosed .38 at Quentin, the left side of its grip gone. Red hair sprung from under her rolled sombrero; a mole on her jaw sprouted red.

Old Glory fluttered from the roof of Kat's Harbor. Kat had created the shelter from a three-bedroom adobe at the street's dead end half-a-block away. The western sun ignited the flag's stars and white stripes. A raven swooped low, its wings sounding like silk rustling.

"Hey!" Tish snapped, exposing a blackening upper gum. "Ho!" The words rattled in her throat. Snuffling, she wagged the revolver's muzzle. "Password, fartface."

"Digs," Quentin said. He'd found his boots and backpack outside St. Elizabeth's shelter less than a mile to the east—far larger than Kat's Harbor. Its thirty-two bunks stayed filled. The brimmed rain hat he kept on no matter what the weather had appeared days later on Kat's own giveaway table. Thunderheads boiling up from the Sangre de Cristos told him he'd need the hat tonight, though the six-pm heat made his head feel like a hot sponge.

"Name?"

"Q."

"Oh, yeah, bow wow wow, Flasher gives me too much to remember."

The secondhand socks were making his ankles itch and he bent to scratch them.

"No funny business, mister."

Quentin shook his head.

"Keep those shoulders back and go on in."

Tish lay the broken-handled .38 across the tuft of cotton that sprouted from a cushion of the sofa. She wiped the cocaine-caused drip from her nose with the back of a hand, sat, and hung her head, the unwashed red sheaves of hair flopping forward.

Quentin pushed aside the branches of rabbitbrush whose not-quite-yellow clusters arched into the path. A grasshopper buzzed and, rubbing its front wings together, leapt out of the way. Startling, the composer lurched against a clump of hairy asters. Puffs clung to the cheap fleece jacket draped over his arm that he'd grabbed from the table at Kat's this morning. He'd rolled up the sleeves of the guayabera worn for the appointment with the Music Festival's director in the middle of August.

The campsite where Quentin had spread his pad and sleeping bag showed through the leaves. He kicked two empties of rum from stones knobbing the dirt, and saw that while he'd been playing the battered upright piano at Kat's, a family of four had moved in.

A mongrel husky started to bark, raising its black-and-white snout, but a girl in a wheelchair slapped its muzzle. The barks turned to whimpers. Even in this heat she wore a stocking cap, the same pink as her lips. She stared in silence at Quentin.

A Native American woman stopped hacking up a chicken under a nylon lean-to and hugged a toddler in yellow-stained diapers to her chest. Nearby, a man in camouflage shorts and muscle shirt knelt beside a fire that heated the grill placed on a ring of rocks. He looked up, grunted, and set his tattooed arms akimbo. A pruning saw and branches cut into foot-long sections lay beside him. Someone seemed to be playing "London Bridge" in the camp further on, invisible through the tangle of New Mexican locusts and shoots of elms. The tinkles sounded electronic.

Quentin turned his attention to the kneeling man. "Isn't that kind of dangerous?" He tossed his jacket to his bag, lowered the pack, and removed his hat.

"Flasher said okay to a fire in daylight because the girl needs hot food. Kat—" he cocked his thumb behind a bare shoulder—"serves Mondays and Thursdays and can't serve more 'n twelve. Can't sleep more 'n six and she's as full up as Saint E's."

Quentin's graying ponytail swished against his neck. "Hell's broth!" He jerked his hand from the dead branch of a locust and squeezed blood from his forefinger. "Stabbed myself."

"I'll cut the mother down." The big man grabbed his saw, lumbered close, and gripped the branch between thorns. The sun, nearing the treetops, turned the sawdust the Native American created into glittering gnats. "Where you from, anyhow?"

"New York."

"Why hanging out here?"

Quentin unzipped his pack and rolled out cans of vegetable soup and white-bean chile. He removed the pouch holding his roll-up keyboard and covered his belongings with his jacket.

"Got sick of my life, friend. And almost everything I flew out here with was stolen."

"Did you mark them?" asked the nine-year-old, crippled by osteoarthritis in her knees—a possible result of early scarlet fever. She hoisted a teddy bear tucked between her thigh and the wheelchair's arm and pressed it to her cheek.

Quentin smiled, remembering his ex-wife long ago sewing labels into the collars of Germaine's shirts and dresses. "None of the clothes were marked," he said.

"No! Slash the robbers!" the girl exclaimed.

"Mind your business," the man growled, returning to his cooking fire and adding the branch he'd just lopped to the pile of wood. The woman resumed swinging her butcher knife.

"Only one robber. Someday I'll find him." Quentin bunched his whitening brows. The whores in his head had started singing fragments. He extracted the spiral book from his pack and scribbled a couple of measures along the staves. "Any of you know who's that playing?"

"Damn sure no Indian," the man said.

Laughing, Quentin started to rise but sank back as a crunching sounded along the path. Limbs creaked from the gust that blew thistledown onto the lean-to's green.

First to appear between two blackened trunks was Nate Cobb—Flasher—a slight man in a T-shirt rolled high up one shoulder to hold a pack of Chesterfields. Three nicks from shaving marred the hatchet face peering beneath a red beret. Twine tied under his boots kept his dungarees taut.

"We found us a new boy," Flasher squeaked. Rings holding a ruby, an opal, and a white sapphire, each gripped by claws of stainless steel, sometimes served as brass knuckles, Kat had warned Quentin.

"C'mere." Flasher twisted to grab an old geezer in a red-flannel shirt and overalls. He hauled him to the front by a strap. While Flasher always smelled spicy, as if he'd just slapped on cologne, this gent smelled of baking soda.

"This here's Dirk, up from Socorro. He's showed me he can handle a thirty-eight. Could be he can relieve Tish some if he decides to stay on."

What was left of Dirk's white hair blew like ricegrass over the grizzled face and jug ears. A screech issued from the hearing aid in his left ear and Dirk reached up to twist the device's stem. He'd tucked a scabbard holding a knife through a denim loop near his hip. Tooled poppies garnished the blue-leather handle; snatches of sun glinted off the guard.

"You 'bout done with that chicken, Wilda?" asked the refuge's self-appointed leader. "I'll need to hang onto your blade until daylight."

She nodded. A tic snatched her lips to the side.

"Don't you get up now, darlin'. Ruben, give it here. Dirk?"

"Mahdi stays with me, sport," the seventy-four-year-old said, his voice a low bass.

"Whoa, there, Dirky Lurky, I'm not noways sport to you."

"You're whatever I say you are. *Sport.*" Dirk arced an arm, freeing his knife—Mahdi—in mid-swing, backed off a step, and thrust it toward Flasher.

"Coming at you, idiot," Reuben snapped. "*Adiós, cojones.*" He had swept his hand behind him, butcher knife gripped by its black handle, point hovering.

The girl's mother hugged the toddler and pressed against the woodpile. The mongrel stood.

"Daddy! Stop it!" The girl hoisted herself up, clutching the wheelchair's arms. A cloth sunflower, pinned to the dress ripped at one shoulder, jiggled. Her face tightened. "You mustn't! Flasher hates noise. You know how I scream. Please, Daddy, I can't help it."

The part-husky began to snarl and pulled at the rope tied to one of the chair's big rear wheels, throwing up dirt.

Dirk licked cracked lips. He pointed the knife down toward foxtails springing around his high-top sneakers. "No more names, Nate, a promise."

"Flasher to you."

"Flasher, okay. Got nowhere else to go. Took a box at the P.O. earlier for my pension, but there's not enough to add rent to food and meds. I'll be cashing in soon, anyway." He stooped to pick up his knife by the point and offered Flasher the handle.

But the wiry little man had bent double to cough—the Legionnaire beret had fallen into a clump of cheat grass. The sinews in his neck quivered. The hacks he made sounded as if he might spit blood.

Flasher retrieved the red beret from the grass and straightened, swallowing before he took Dirk's knife. He'd bitten off all his nails except that of the pinky.

Reuben now gave Flasher the butcher knife. From the camp's edge came the flute-like whistles of a Townsend's solitaire.

"Okeydokey, we're cool," Flasher managed, and paused to hiccup. "Want to issue everbody a reminder of the rules." He cocked his thumb. "Tish controls the thirty-eight; knives come to her or I before dark." He threw up his forefinger. "You're out minglin' by eight with this city's real crackpots, an' back in camp by seven pm." His middle finger straightened. "Nobody bothers the cops so's they don't bother us. No cut fences into the cemetery, substation, deaf school, or computer-annex parkin' lot." His fourth finger lifted. "You need street drugs, you see Tish or I; you need meds, you hoof the half mile to La Familia near Saint E's."

All five digits stood up stiff. "For food you're on your own. I do allow some cookin', as you can see, an' I've stashed lean-tos behind the willows down by the creek bed. Near Tish's sofa there's temporary space in the culvert, where Dirk holed up last night.

"You see girls cruisin' the arroyos with water bottles, steer 'em away. They's case managers from Saint E's an' they make camp life complicated. Kat an' Vonnie are simpler bets for basics when the Harbor's not full up." He raised his cleft chin and sniffed. "Smells like a real dump's gonna hit us soon. Dirky Lurky, you want to meet who's here?"

"Why not?"

Suddenly, a bicycle bounced into the clearing. A woman in flowered bra and chartreuse capris, head shaved, pedaled a beat-up two-wheeler that hauled a three-wheeled garden cart heaped with clothes. "Lo, Nate," she called out. "Bunk's opened up at Kat's, I hear."

"Take it. Come see us again when you can't stand clean livin' no more."

"My daughter claims she wants me down with her."

"Where's down, Clara Bare?"

"Las Cruces. Gonna bust outta here snow-free."

"Mebby."

The woman hunched over her handlebars and disappeared toward the sofa.

Flasher turned to Dirk and pitched his thumb toward Quentin. "The elegant in the embroidery calls hisself Q. Says he writes music. Mebby. That's Wilda Lightninfeather with the baby. Hisi's in the chair—Tish's dizzy busy teachin' her an' Kat's granddaughter readin'. Reuben here,

Wilda's old man, cooked for Wendy's an' he's cooked for Furr's but he does get bored an' goes off his meds an' throws a few pots aroun' an' gets hisself canned like yesterday, don't you, soldier?"

Reuben's grin, three gold teeth flashing, spread under high cheekbones. He squinted at Dirk before turning to toss chicken legs, neck, breast, wings, and all the innards into a frying pan.

"Let's have Dirk squat here tonight," Flasher said.

Reuben clanged the pan onto the grill. "You're the boss man."

"We'll try it."

"Try it?" Dirk twisted the stem in his hearing aid.

"Go on an' get your gear, Dirky."

The electronic tinkling beyond the tangle of elms became *hinky-dinky, parlez-vous*, from the World War I song, "Mademoiselle from Armetieres."

"Who *is* that, Flasher?" Quentin dipped for his rain hat, hoisted his pack, and slung it across his shoulders.

"Calls hisself Buzzy."

"I think I'll go meet him."

"Just so's you keep your distance from Headquarters."

"I know. Your and Tish's sanctum."

"Our what?"

"Off limits."

"Right."

"Tend our own gardens, we stay out of trouble," Dirk muttered, hair blowing. He left, sinking more on his right leg than the other.

Suckers jutting into the path forced Quentin to walk slowly. The turpentine scent of occasional rabbitbrush made him sneeze. Scant light filtered through the elms and locusts. He ducked his head to miss a charred limb, sidestepped an abandoned sleeping bag, and stumbled over a bottle, sending it clanking against another. A pair of shoes, soles half ripped away, hung by their laces over a limb. Ten feet ahead, the dark ends of branches thrust into the second camp's yellow-white glow. The tinkling grew louder.

He first saw not the musician but a form at the clearing's farther edge. A blanket patched with electrical tape rose and fell with snores that seemed the oinks of a pig about to plunge into garbage. The blanket covered all but the man's head, shaved to create a black cap of hair.

"Keep your distance!" came a shout.

Quentin swung his eyes left and discovered, standing in front of a lean-to, a half-naked fellow in camouflage pants brandishing a pair of scissors. The young man's hair hung tied into a ponytail like Quentin's, but dull blond.

"I'm safe!" Quentin shouted back. "Where's that gizmo you've been melodizing with?" Then he spied the tiny keyboard rimmed in pink that lay in a fold of a poncho spread on the ground.

Byron Hurd lowered the scissors and stooped to retrieve the toy. "My son's," he said.

"You play well." Quentin laughed and Byron joined in, one cuff of the dingy shirt that he'd draped across his shoulders lifting in the wind.

— — —

"Dumbfounding!" Quentin exclaimed. He gulped down a mouthful of beans. "Meeting a cellist in the urban wild."

He'd transferred his bag and foam pad to Byron's campsite an hour ago. They sat cross-legged in the dusk on their jackets, under the lean-to the composer had brought up from the creek bed, an open can of beans in each of their crotches. One of the lean-to's aluminum legs was missing, but Quentin had substituted a branch he'd severed from a locust, using the jackknife saw he'd stolen yesterday when buying clippers.

The snorer across the clearing, dragging his blanket, had stumbled into a thicket toward the Santa Fe Southern's abandoned right-of-way that skirted the School for the Deaf.

Between bites, Quentin snapped leaves from a head of iceberg lettuce and fed them to his new friend. The clouds showed scarlet through blackened limbs. Shadows skipped over the men's laps as a grasshopper clicked past.

"I've got some fruit salad," Quentin said. He hauled the rest of its contents from the backpack nestling his hip into the diminishing light. "I'll prune more branches away from the canvas tomorrow." He spotted a price label on a handle of the clippers and coaxed it off with his thumbnail.

"Why bother doing that?" Byron asked. "Afraid they'll be traced?"

"Into this wasteland? Trying to simplify, I guess. Plus I like to pretend my things have been mine forever. And that they'll stay spotless."

"Like those white ducks were once."

"And will be again when my turn comes up at Kat's washer. I've got to get you over there. Why haven't you gone?"

"Admitting I'm homeless feels too degrading."

Quentin shrugged. "Free showers at Kat's. And a lot better food than this. Your can empty?"

"Yeah."

Quentin pulled the tab on the fruit salad and spooned half of it over. "Listen, I've got a favor to ask. Nothing but bad luck for me has come from composing electronically."

"Not much of a worry in the bush, is it?" Byron guffawed while thunder boomed in the north. "Guess we'd better finish up."

"You boys plan to join us for anger management?"

They glanced toward the path that led to the third campsite—that Flasher called Headquarters. The former snorer stood there holding his blanket by a corner. A billed cap on backwards, topped by a sombrero, now hid his black round of hair.

"Anger management?" Quentin asked.

"Class convenes in fifteen minutes in the culvert. Everyone brings a six-pack except"—his mustache rose as he punched his thumb into a hole in his T-shirt—"the organizer, me."

"No beer here," Byron said.

"Nose candy preferred."

"Nose candy?"

The man thrust the end of a pinky into his nostril.

"We're busy," Quentin said, frowning.

"Got a fag for a pal, anyhow?"

Quentin felt his own anger rise. It fell as he understood the vagrant meant cigarette. "Scram," he called out. "We don't smoke. Go see Flasher."

"All that bozo does is embarrass us, unzipping his pants where there's women attending."

"So that's it," Byron said.

"If Flasher's coming, class dismissed." The man pushed a spray of rabbitbrush from his face and headed for the first camp. The bandaged blanket raised a plume of dust behind him.

Quentin rose, bent to extract a blue pouch from the recent pile of socks, water, extra shirts, beans, stave notebooks, and his raincoat.

"You stole all that?"

"The Festival's director cut me a check for a couple of hundred bucks when I told him I'd been had. But look at what I brought from home." He handed the pouch to Byron.

"What is it?"

"Open."

Byron unrolled the neoprene keyboard. "Shit-and-a-half! I've heard about these."

"Two speakers and a volume control and ninety different tones. Chords up to sixteen notes over five octaves. Records and plays back with four AA batteries. Let's see if they're good while we have light. Haven't used it since the plane ride."

Byron spread the keyboard on both of their jackets, gazed at the console at one end, then tapped the button marked *piano*. He ripped off an arpeggio. "Whoa!" he cried as the notes blared through the speakers.

Quentin thrust his hand toward a ribbed knob but Byron was already turning it. The composer's fingers stayed on his camp mate's. Byron's brows lowered and Quentin lifted his fingers. Byron tapped the button marked *cello* and began the prelude from Bach's suite in C major.

Quentin picked up his notebook and opened it. "If I write in this, do you think you can play it?"

"Don't know."

He flipped to the first page where notes darkened a dozen staves. "Take a stab at this lullaby I scribbled out three days ago."

Byron stared at the music a moment, then tapped *piano*. To him the sounded notes directed the wind to rattle the pods of locusts like castanets.

Byron's vision started blurring and he stood. "You told me your music was either harsh or jazzy. Humanity's frenzy hiding the peace that turns the world, you said. There's no frenzy here." He wiped the back of a hand across his nose. "I miss Sarah, damn it all!"

"Your wife?"

"My girlfriend who might be pregnant. I've already given my wife three."

Quentin turned quarter round, leaned toward the man half his age, and gripped his shoulders. Byron fell against his chest. Quentin held him, breathing hard. "I've got a daughter...."

"Whom your music says you miss."

"I haven't seen her in nineteen years." Quentin pressed his temple against the other's neck.

"How come?"

"Can't talk about it," Quentin said.

"That lullaby tells what needs to be done."

"I'm not sure. One night I'd better let you listen to what I wrote for the Festival. Or my jazz piece, *Improv for Piccolo and Prepared Guitar*."

The taller man broke from the composer's embrace. "I can't believe I'm in this weed lot! But Sarah's folks are probably after me, the college's lawyers, too. My wife wants alimony, my landlady wants back rent—"

"I'm going to take care of you," Quentin said.

To Byron the composer seemed more wraithlike than human, though he felt both comforted and agitated that the body heat of the man he'd pulled away from lingered.

In the dusk, the blossoms embroidered on Quentin's guayabera had faded. A rolling drumbeat followed a flash in the north as a gust shook the thistles clumped nearby. Drops spattered the bald top of Byron's head and fuzzed the notes Quentin had penned. He slapped the notebook shut and placed it near Quentin's shirts. "Let's go!"

A light raked the clearing as the two men gathered their belongings. Flasher's high voice pierced the gloom. "Night check, people."

"Darn tootin'," came Tish's phlegm-thickened gutteral. When the next electric zigzag and peal of thunder ended, the beam of the flashlight had gone.

They set their gear and jackets on tarps dragged under their lean-tos, removed their footgear, and, leaving their socks on, wriggled into their sleeping bags.

A burr had lodged in Quentin's. It pricked his calf where the ducks had ridden up. "Hell's broth!" he hissed. Unable to reach far down, he squirmed out and flung the burr away.

Snug at last, he drew in the sweet-sour scent of the raindrops that struck the nylon shelter and pattered against the leaves. A coyote howled. "Us two," he exulted, "free."

— — —

A stinging in his penis woke him a little before midnight. The clouds had disappeared, the wind had stopped, the *whoo* of an owl sounded. He wriggled his torso out into the night and sat up. A white, half moon lit the puffs on the hairy asters. Foxtails glittered. One of the whores started singing in his head, part tune, part screech. He rummaged through cans and socks to find his notebook as the cramping in his bladder built. A branch snapped, then nothing. He startled and slithered back into his bag.

A form in a knit cap stepped into the clearing off the path leading to where the Native Americans slept. It moved closer, avoiding the ragweed and clusters of thistles. White overalls! The old geezer with the poppy-handled knife! Oh, God, Quentin prayed in silence, don't let me pee yet. He tried to shallow his breathing.

Dirk began to tiptoe. He extended his arm and wrapped his fingers around a can of potato soup at the edge of the tarp.

"Buzzy, Buzzy!" Quentin shouted and grabbed Dirk's wrist.

The septuagenarian vised the back of Quentin's neck with his other hand and shoved Quentin's face against the tarp, mashing his nose.

Quentin wrenched his head to the side. "Buzzy!"

Dirk jerked his wrist away and started to rise. But Byron, who had extracted himself from his bag, hurled himself against Dirk's spine and flattened him to the dirt. Quentin clawed his way out of his own bag and sat on the backs of Dirk's knees.

Apparently they'd not wakened Flasher. The only noises were the huffs of the three men trying to catch their breaths.

Dirk's cap hung askew, exposing the disposable hearing aid that plugged a Dumbo ear.

"I thought you had a pension."

"A pittance," Dirk said.

"Go steal from your blind mother."

"Yeah, beat it, fucker," Byron added.

"No point to that."

"Huh?" Byron slapped the dust from his pants.

"Can't even get it up any more. Thanks to a prostate going bad. Roll off me, will you?" Dirk spit into a tuft of grass.

Clutching his crotch, Quentin knuckled the ground to help himself stand. "You can't get yours up and I can't get mine out," he said and, guffawing, scrambled toward a tangle of rabbitbrush.

GETTING IN TOUCH

"**Y**ou want what?" Raven, the Hacienda's sex facilitator, her voice hoarse, asked a guest the following evening. His question had hurt. She'd put an hour into preparing the welcoming dinner's salmon, basmati rice, and asparagus.

Raven had been an escort in New York and, already at age twenty-four, a producer of two pornographic films. Her *You and Me and Everything in Between* had won Best Interracial Release last year at the Adult Entertainment Expo in Vegas.

Raven's large areolas turned her into a nutcase when licked. At the moment their nipples, platinum-ringed, hid under a tunic she'd chosen for its black swirls, to suggest how she moved in bed. They and matching capris contrasted with the pink frames of her glasses, worn instead of contacts to heighten the image she wished to project: smart, sexy, contradictory.

The Hacienda's owners, Fritz and Arlene Joseph, had left after dessert for a sunset walk in their residential neighborhood, a mile east of Kat's Harbor.

"Tell us again what you want," Raven demanded of Pete, who sat with Germaine and a man named Jimmy, facing snifters of brandy around the dining table. A central-conditioning vent above them next to the smoke alarm released cold air into the room.

"I'm still exhausted from the trip out. I want to go home."

Pete's United flight had idled for two hours before lifting off from Portland, Maine. Jimmy's Delta flight from Miami had laid over an hour in Atlanta. And fog had delayed Germaine's six-am American Airlines flight for three hours. So this morning at the Albuquerque Sunport, Raven had been able to leaf through the September issues of *Penthouse* and *Cosmopolitan*—and wolf down a quiche—before Pete, the first weekender to show up, approached the *Beautiful Tomorrows/Hello!* sign she'd started waving. Parking had cost her twelve dollars instead of three. Now Pete wanted to go home?

"You just got here, stud."

Pete reddened and, pinching a wad of flesh, stretched it from his jaw. "I don't know if I can perform." In his early fifties, he wore leather suspenders and black rubber sandals. Germaine thought his checked shirt smelled of camphor. For the mosquitos he'd left behind in Maine, she wondered?

"I've yet to meet the guy who can't give me a money shot," Raven said. "Your SxCheck tests look clean. You're paying mucho to help recapture your sexual sense of self." She snuffled, combed the fingernails of both hands back to the bun she'd made of her black hair, and pushed at the sides of her tunic to build cleavage. "I'm tired of spending hours by myself in the guesthouse, Pete, sweetie. I want to cuddle all night with you." Her penciled brows disappeared behind her glasses's rims as she pouted lips glossed in fuchsia.

Pete gulped, leaving a smear of chocolate-pie dessert on the rim of his snifter. "I'm homesick."

Raven grasped his wrist across the table. "But sweetie, we can't possibly refund. Lots have already been drawn for tonight and tomorrow afternoon." The turquoise ring on her thumb shown under the chandelier. "Okay?"

"I guess."

"Take another nap while I clear up. We'll be enjoying margaritas and doing a little dancing after the boss gets back. Use our room again. Upstairs is the Josephs' hideaway."

Pete started off. His rubber sandals seemed clumsy mismatches to his designer shorts.

"Hold up a sec, Pete," Raven called. "I need to review how tonight and tomorrow are gonna work. You'll miss this evening's Light Night Parade that launches Fiesta, but tomorrow there's mucho arts and crafts. Sunday breakfast's from eight till ten because we may not sleep a lot tonight. Afterward I'll drive whoever wants to the Plaza.

"Back here by one-thirty for the new pairings-off before I drive you down to Albuquerque for your return flights. Oh! Take a gander past the sofa—sunsets are a big part of Santa Fe's magic."

Striations of magenta and pink blazed above the horizon between a cottonwood and spruce towering from the garden. Like paint flung by a cosmic Jackson Pollock, Germaine thought.

"We've got better in Maine." The heels of Pete's sandals slapped the tiles as he headed toward the hallway's entrance and the wire sculpture of a unicorn opposite the stairs. A nude, spine arched, rode the beast. Her arm reached behind to clasp its rump. She cradled a monkey between her thighs that mouthed the tip of its tail.

"Are you as nervous as I am, Jimmy?" Germaine had donned a pleated blouse for tonight's welcoming dinner. Her mother's pearls hung under its linen collar. The editor's skirt was the brightest she could find at Bergdorf Goodman, orange spiraling through a field of mauve.

"All my grown-up life," Jimmy said, "I've fantasized a night like this. After my wife passed, I tried men and I tried women and every morning-after I'd take off. Here's to staying for breakfast."

His bracelet's gold coins clinked as he lifted his glass and drank. Sputtering, he put it down, started to wheeze, and stood, jowls jiggling. "I better go lie down myself," he managed, flattening a palm against the table's top and leaning forward to grasp the snifter's stem. But he knocked it to the slate floor, where the snifter burst.

Raven grabbed a napkin without a word, knelt, and swept the major shards away from the Navajo rugs. The napkin browned with the brandy.

Raven stepped to Jimmy, wrapped an arm around the red silk draping his torso, and kissed one of his cheeks. His wheezing grew worse. "Not a problem, Jimmy Jammy. The altitude can make lots of us light-headed at first. Mucho liquids, remember. Germaine, give him a hand, will you? First room, I think. Arlene's got him later."

"I want to help with the dishes."

"Yeah? Appreciate it." The sex facilitator lowered herself into one of the ladder-back chairs, bit the end of her pinky, and gazed at the woman eight years her senior.

Germaine had cupped Jimmy's elbow. Its skin felt like sandpaper, unlike the seeming softness of his neck. They passed the unicorn and a vase holding cactus dahlias that Fritz had brought home earlier and placed in hot water.

In the hallway Germaine opened the nearest of three doors, twisted on the table lamp, and sat with Jimmy on the bedspread.

"That woman scares me," he wheezed. Hanging his head, he clasped his hands in the lap of his slacks.

"She's only trying to do what she's paid to."

"Raven has soul. I mean Fritz's wife, Arlene."

"Scares you? Why?"

Was she really alone with a stranger, Germaine wondered, in this rough-stuccoed room—varnished ponderosa limbs forming its ceiling— two thousand miles from home? The uplights canistered on the flagstones outside suddenly switched on, seeming to set the trees on fire. While she sat here, was Jock drinking martinis with her assistant at North Square? Was her mother phoning her father to arrange lunch for four if Jock had lost all reason and asked to join them? Germaine jammed the pearl against her earlobe.

"Why Arlene gives me the heebies, you're asking?"

"I am, yes."

"Hidden agendas," Jimmy said. "Like she seems to have the hots for Raven. Well, understandable, who doesn't?" He waited to catch his breath. "But Arlene's mannish. Do this, do that. Fritz just clamps his teeth."

"I feel like I'm in Oz, Jimmy, hoping the wizard can bring some relief."

"From…"

"I've never had an orgasm."

"Oh." His breathing sounded like a warbler with a hole in its throat.

"Maybe Arlene was weaned too soon, Jimmy. I'll let you get some rest."

Pete's snores began to jackhammer through the wall.

"No way I'm gonna sleep."

They laughed together.

Five minutes later, Raven and Germaine had carried the last of the dishes from the table. Pots, plates, silverware, and goblets sat on the granite counter. A mercury lamp overhanging the street corner glowed through the kitchen window. The sky's former streaks had gathered into a purple scrim.

"Thanks for the offer," Raven said, draping a piñon-pine-colored apron over her tunic and handing another to Germaine. "We'll get started as soon as the boss comes back."

"Not Arlene?"

"She never leaves him." Raven bent to flip the lid of the dishwasher down. "You still anxious about tonight?"

"Kinda." Germaine scraped remains of the salmon and rice into a polyethylene bag whose sides Raven had rolled down. "Actually, I'm a mess inside."

"We've got a little surprise that will help," Raven said, kneeling, depositing the bag of garbage into a basket under the sink.

From far away a siren started up.

"What's that?"

"Always extra cops on the prowl during Fiesta."

"No, the surprise."

Raven wagged her forefinger. "You gotta wait half an hour." She brought the back of her hand to her nose and snuffled hard.

"Have you a cold?"

"Allergies," the facilitator lied.

Germaine gave her two empty snifters. "How did you and the Josephs hook up, anyway?"

"Hook up? So far we've kept it strictly business."

Germaine's cheeks flushed. "I meant meet each other."

"Gotcha. Fritz paid a rare visit alone to the Museum of Sex on Fifth and Twenty-Seventh where I was an operations assistant. I paid most of my bills by making DVDs there nights with my boyfriend. A Muslim, believe it or not."

"Why shouldn't I?"

"Yeah? So a week later Fritz brought Arlene in. We went to lunch a few times. Big plans. The three of us left New York nine months ago, November last year. They'd bought this spread two months prior. But what are you doing out here? You've got more smarts than most of the dweebs we see."

"I'm frigid." Germaine laughed and shivered under the cold air blowing from near the smoke detector.

"Fritz can fix that. Or I will tomorrow."

"I'm an incest survivor, Raven."

"Oh yeah?"

"My dad."

"Then you may need to visit us again. How often..."

"Can I afford to?"

"Did your dad..."

"He left me intact."

"Easier to treat. You never took him to court?"

Germaine dropped her eyes and shook her head.

"Most of us don't. My own dad made a play for me but I slugged him in the nuts."

"Mother insists it never happened."

"Typical white-collar response. I got lucky—my old lady came running in and cracked his skull with my boom box. I scrammed out of town for good."

"I was too young." Germaine passed Raven the rest of the dishes and turned on the hot water to rinse the asparagus steamer.

"Leave it be. I'll finish up mañana. That's the front door."

Raven flipped her apron over a towel rack while the footfalls across the living room rugs grew louder.

Fritz's wife, her lips mere lines, appeared in the doorway. "Not dancing yet?"

The facilitator said nothing.

"Hello, there, Germaine." Arlene's streaked ducktails indeed suggested butch. In her mid-fifties, Germaine judged. The tight skin, lack of crow's-feet, and forehead shining under the fluorescent panel indicated face-lifts. The golden ear hoops matched her sneakers.

Arlene lifted her hands to brace herself against the door's jambs. The hem of her blouse of horned toads, cows, snakes, and goats lifted free from her capris. "Where are the other guests?"

"Second nap," Raven said, turning away.

Fritz, about his wife's height, stooped to peer under her upraised arm. He wore his graying hair cropped and a chain around his neck. The points of a handkerchief sprouted from the beige shirt's pocket. He threw a thumbs-up at Germaine and grinned. "Not tired?"

Germaine shook her head. She liked that nose, authoritative, unblemished by capillaries. By contrast, Arlene's nose was snub. Would

Fritz be harder to please tonight than Raven tomorrow afternoon? Germaine couldn't recall ever longing to try woman-to-woman sex, even with her assistant. Hold on! She was paying Raven and the Josephs to heat *her* up, they weren't paying her.

"You into sports?" Arlene asked, stepping into the room. The acrid scent of the hollyhocks that brightened the Hacienda's fencing seemed to cling to her.

"Me?" Germaine's fingers tapped her breastbone.

Nodding, Arlene approached Raven and circled her shoulder. "We follow track and field, don't we, love? Just now up at the Baking Company I read that Randy Mariner, that pussy chaser, last night in Osaka clocked the fifth fastest four-hundred meters in history." She shot an elbow toward the door. "His nibs follows nada except the health of his iris, dead in their bed right now."

"Dormant." Fritz clamped his teeth.

"Dormant, unlike that therapeutic dong of his." She flicked her head, causing the ducktails to flap. "Right, Doctor? But tonight before the main event I want a quick little dance with this one." She dipped to smack her lips against Raven's neck and marched back to where Fritz waited.

"We dance with our bedmates. You know the rules." He spoke mechanistically, as if to the teak-paneled refrigerator, and—stepping forward—reached toward the cupboard above the counter. "Give me a hand, hey?" he said to his wife.

Arlene withdrew her arm from Raven's shoulder to place six glasses on the granite, each a large upturned bell set on a smaller bell set on a stem.

"Official shape endorsed by the Mexican government as of two-oh-oh-two," he told Germaine, folding his arms. "Round up the nappers, Rave, and let's get the music started. It's after eight. The editor can help us carry the drinks in."

Soon Raven sat on the wraparound sofa with Pete, Germaine, Jimmy, and Arlene. They faced the corner windows and the lit, rock-walled garden with its kiva fireplace beyond.

Germaine caught herself focusing on Fritz's crotch as he stood in front of a floor-to-ceiling stack of electronic equipment. Embarrassed, she raised her eyes. The techno heartbeat and remixed voice of rocker Joe Lee from Moby's "Find My Baby, Whew!" pulsed softly out of ceiling-mounted speakers that flanked the vent and smoke alarm.

"A friendly howdy to each of you," Fritz began, gazing directly at Germaine. "Arlene and I regret that crowded runways delayed the start of your adventure. But now you've settled down and are, we hope, ready to learn."

His monotone seemed so unnatural—constructed to block a frightened scream, Germaine wondered?

Fritz lifted one of the Mexican-government-blessed glasses that he and Arlene and Raven had discovered on special at Jackalope. "José Cuervo Sec. *Salud*. Squeeze your lime and drop it in.

"Tonight," he continued, taking a sip, "we're all heterosexual. And be assured there'll be no need for the hottest trends in cosmetic surgery, vaginal or G-spot rejuvenation." He smiled, then knit his brows. "If your heart is broken or your lust is blocked, surgery isn't going to fix that, though technique and tenderness can. It's why Arlene and Raven and I open ourselves up to you. Good, isn't this?" He chugged the iced cocktail and, near him, Raven did the same. The others nursed theirs.

Fritz widened his stance, wearing moccasins slipped on after his walk. His arms straitjacketed his chest. "A little background to reassure you that we're not in this profession for the monetary gain. Arlene and I made a king's ransom on Wall Street as hedge-fund managers. We give a percentage of that each month, plus much of what you've paid us, to charities in Santa Fe. Particularly the Coalition for the Homeless, Salvation Army, Saint Elizabeth's Shelter, and Kat's Harbor. Why? Arlene comes from a dirt-poor family and mine spent a year in an Army-surplus tent in the New Jersey pine barrens."

He flung his arms free. "Our Hacienda's yours for the weekend. We're here to help you explore your sexuality and have a good time. Which brings me to tonight's surprise. On Raven's suggestion we've decided to make cocaine available. Some of you may know that in small doses she's a ladylike aphrodisiac. For those who wish to discover her charms, Raven will lay out a few lines on the coffee table. As with our welcome-to-Santa-Fe margaritas, there's no charge."

He gestured toward a maple table stationed next to the glass vase on the tiles holding the dahlias he'd bought.

"Raven will show those who need instruction how to use the straws."

"Hold it," Pete called out. "No hidden cameras? I got busted six years ago in Portland."

Fritz placed his palms on his buttocks. "Did you not hear my spiel about charities, Pete? We don't need your money. I see none of you signed up for technique-reminder photos, though you're free anytime to tell Raven you're thinking differently. Otherwise, Pete, no cameras, no tape recorders."

"Well then, hell yes, lay 'em out. Better be better than I can get at home."

"Maybe so, maybe not." Raven snuffled and drew one side of her lips toward her cheekbone. She stood, smoothed her tunic against her thighs, and looked down at Germaine. "Ever tried snow?"

"Snow?"

"Coke, hon."

"Oh, no, just pot, a long time ago." This adventure was beginning to feel dangerous. But the cocktail tasted so smooth! She started to shiver. What she needed was the usual manuscript to buy, a text to edit, a marketing conference to attend, Jock to lie back with his hands behind his head and let her give him an orgasm, to doze then in the crook of his arm.

"Are you cold?" Raven asked.

"I'm scared."

"There's no reason to be. You'll like Lady C. She'll speed the end of your troubles."

"'Fore that sun goes down," Moby wailed from above.

"Should I take a little?" Jimmy asked Arlene.

"Not with your asthma, Jimmy Jammy," Raven said.

"I don't have asthma! Listen, no wheezing at all. " He took a deep breath and blew it out, then drank his margarita to the lower bell.

"You're right, can't hear a thing. You and me, kid." Arlene slipped her hand into Jimmy's crotch. Her saffire-encrusted diamond disappeared as she pointed her lips up at Raven and mimed a kiss.

Fritz moved to the black stack of consoles and turned two knobs. The electronica's decibels rose. Arlene took Jimmy's hand off her knee. "Let's rock."

Fritz sauntered close to Germaine. "Want to try it?"

"Just so we don't move too fast. I'm a bit dizzy."

The digitized bells and marimba of Moby's "Down Slow" sounded on a kind of back-and-forth wind.

"I meant try the Lady," Fritz said.

"Are you going to?"

"I teach best by keeping my head clear of cocaine, buttercup. But Raven says you've a clitoral log jam and I think you might want to do a whole line to loosen things up."

"All right." How she wished Jock were here.

Fritz crab-stepped to thumb down the levers on a couple of dimmers. The lights in the living room and garden softened, though an uplight continued silvering the bark of the cottonwood.

Raven had left the living room several minutes earlier to hurry along the flagstones to her backyard casita. Now from a cache beneath the doormat she carried seven bindles in a paper bag and a handful of half-straws. Yesterday she'd sliced off an end of each on the bias.

She headed back to the main house but instead of pulling aside the living-room's slider, she unlocked the outside door of the last bedroom under the portal, entered the closet, and on tiptoes pushed up a switch in its farthest corner.

She padded down the hall, patting the pink comb that held her bun and vowing to ask Fritz for more money tomorrow morning. She worked too hard—their arrangement wasn't fair! She swiped her nose with her forearm.

When Raven reappeared, Germaine felt Fritz's pelvis pull away and his jaw leave her temple. Arlene was rumpling the hair on the back of Jimmy's head as he pressed himself against her, weaving to the music.

"Sweet Pete," Raven said, "come give me a hand." She upended the bag onto the table. The packets Flasher had sold her, a little bigger than credit cards, tumbled out. "Let's get these unwrapped. My street pharmacist cut them twenty percent with talcum."

"Just so it's not laxative or rat poison."

"I'll take the first hit."

They unfolded the corners of the bindles and poured the fourth-grams into two piles, then knelt on opposite sides of the table Raven had grooved.

"You got your wallet with you, daddy-o?"

Pete hauled it from his back pocket. He pinched out a Visa card for himself and handed her another inscribed *Portland, Maine, Public Library.* They started chopping the powder as methodically as if dicing garlic, though the tap-tapping sounded to Raven more like a mating call.

They shoved the powder, fine as flour, into the grooves she'd chiseled into the table's top.

Pete had snatched up one of the candy-striped straws before Raven finished laying them out. He placed the biased end at the start of one line, pressed a nostril, inserted the straw's other end into his open nostril, and inhaled, nudging the straw forward halfway up the line.

He pressed the other nostril, inserted the straw into the nostril now open, and finished the line. He licked the tip of his pinky, drew it toward him along the groove to pick up the residue of coke, and rubbed his fingertip across his upper gum.

"Oh, yeah, it's good."

"Good enough, anyhow?" Raven hooked her thumb with the turquoise ring into his nearest suspender and snapped it. She did her own one-n-one, then moved the straw to a second line and snuffed up that.

"Hey, what's going on with the two-for-one?" Pete asked.

"I'm feeling stressed."

"And I'm paying big time for the weekend." Pete grabbed his straw and dipped his head but she pressed his wrist.

"Barely enough to go around. You'll get what you've paid for, fret not."

Fritz left Germaine and strode over. "There's a problem?"

"Nothing we won't be solving soon, Boss."

"You okay with that, Pete?"

"Gonna wait and see."

After Fritz left, Pete wet his pinky, drew it through the two grooves Raven had emptied, and scrubbed his upper gum. "How much this nose candy cost you?"

"Yesterday, a hundred bucks a gram."

"Take me to your leader!"

The stacked player switched from Moby's *Play,* to Ben Taylor's

Another Run Around the Sun, his guitar and lyrics echoed by the voices of his sister and his mother, Carly Simon.

"You ready to hit the horizontal?" Pete asked.

Raven rounded the table, handed over his Visa card, then bent and French-kissed him. He reached for her but she retreated toward the vase holding the cactus dahlias. She plucked out an orange-and-lavender blossom, walked to where Fritz was kneading Germaine's lower back, and pushed the stem between his teeth. "I love you, Boss."

Never, Germaine thought, had her father said he loved her. Though years ago her mother had whispered, "You're my honeybunch, Germaine." Jock sometimes blurted, "I love you, oh Jesus God," when he ejaculated, but that didn't count, did it? She finished her drink.

Raven sasheyed toward Pete, swinging her buttocks. The tunic's rayon billowed.

He extended his hands and squashed her braless breasts. "Take those glasses off, huh? Let's go make our move, forget this prelim shit."

Raven twisted away. The nails he'd jammed into her flesh had stung. "Patience, little man. Gather round, all." Her pupils dilated. "Lady C needs our attention."

Fritz had spit the dahlia out when he saw his wife watching.

In brocaded slippers Arlene tugged Jimmy to where the blossom lay near the vase, leaned to pluck it up, and crushed it in her fist.

She moved to the table and knelt next to Raven. "If you'd given this to me, love, I'd have pressed it under my pillow." She grabbed a straw, sniffed half the line, plugged the other nostril, snorted the rest, and turned to Jimmy. "What's our room?"

He blinked at her.

"The room where you put your suitcase."

"Second room," Raven said evenly, then polished off her margarita. She blinked at the impact, smiled, and sighed. No need tonight to brood about the goofballs a john three years ago had handed over.

"I'm not asking you," Arlene said.

"Second room," Jimmy said, echoing the sex facilitator.

Arlene made a kissing sound and drew in as much air as she could. "Drag me to your cave."

She followed Jimmy toward the hall, pausing to pat the unicorn's rump.

"The first thing to do is get down here with me," Raven told Germaine. Fritz had brought the editor close to the table and was stroking the side of her thigh.

Ben Taylor, backed by drums and bass guitar, began to strum, "You Must've Fallen Out of the Sky." Germaine braced herself on the table's edge and, kneeling, felt her skirt tightening around her thighs.

Taylor and his sister started singing, "Where did you get those delicate eyes?"

"C'mere, hunk," Raven said to Pete. "You show the editor how, while I play."

"Another line for me?" he asked.

"Just the motions while I rivet your attention elsewhere." She patted a spot for him beside her bare calf.

Germaine's stomach spurted acid up her throat. She winced and swallowed and punched the pearl against her earlobe. Her heart started rapping her breastbone as she followed Pete's pantomime. Coke was sweet! Though Germaine thought she might gag. She lay the straw down. Her head started to buzz.

"Oh, girl!" Pete exclaimed.

Raven had reached into his shorts from behind and was massaging his balls and erection.

Germaine continued snorting while Fritz, rising, mussed her curls and rubbed her neck. She gulped more of the sweet mucus dribbling into her throat.

"It's time, merrymakers," Raven said. "Lesson number two takes place behind the green doors. Remember there's a bathroom on the other side of the hall, next to the den."

Outside, a siren, then another, started wailing.

"Fiesta brings out the gangs. We may hear gunshots, oh, yes. Enjoying the rush?" Raven asked Germaine, circling her waist. Germaine nodded. Fritz seemed cocooned in fog. But she smiled to feel her crotch warming and an unknown tingling there. No wonder Jock's brother had got hooked.

Fritz took the editor's hand.

"Petey, you still wishing you'd not left Maine?" Raven asked.

"Going bye-bye, girl." He sagged against her shoulder.

Fritz paused to twist three knobs in the recessed stack of electronic equipment. The hallway glowed green as indoor and outdoor lights turned off. The cold air and Ben Taylor stopped.

Germaine veered into the bedroom at the hall's far end. Music for meditation—a lute, gongs, and an oboe—drifted from speakers on either side of the window. It looked onto Fritz's long bed of iris she and Jock had seen on the website. The music echoed that at Hot Tub Dreams on 46th where they liked to spend Wednesdays after dinner out, before Jock suggested making love. The only light in the Hacienda's bedroom, beside the half moon's radiance, rose from two pottery jars on the floor that glowed the color of semen.

Fritz drew the green shade. Was that an inch-long beetle clinging to its woven polyester? Who cared? The room's scent—hyacinth? Peppermint? She found she couldn't wait to jettison her clothes, and lugged her suitcase from the spread to the chair. Her trembling hands unbuttoned the blouse and threw it over the chair's arm. As she unzipped her skirt, Fritz unhooked the bra. It dropped to her silver-toned flats.

"Leave that necklace on," he whispered. His fingers traced the pearls from behind her neck to her collarbone. He inscribed circles around breasts that Jock, by massaging and sucking and coming between, had, over the nine months they'd been lovers, made her proud of.

"Oh," she sighed when Fritz rubbed her nipples between forefinger and thumb. The man no longer frightened her—she pretended the hands were Jock's.

He pressed his pelvis to her buttocks and hugged her tummy. No wonder Arlene had called his erection a dong. Hard to pretend it was Jock's. Good Lord.

Her skirt had slipped to her ankles. Fritz pivoted her by the hips and offered his lips. She pushed her tongue between them, but how shaky she felt.

"Undress me," Fritz ordered, stepping back. "After we get those clothes off you."

She hobbled to the edge of the mattress, sat, pried off her flats, kicked off her skirt, and stood. He pulled the bikini she'd bought for the trip down to her knees, and rubbed her black bush with the heel of his hand while she struggled to coax the light-blue lace from her toes.

Through the coke-induced blur she saw him jab his thumb toward his shirt. She reached to unbutton the cotton printed with hibiscus and he shrugged out of it, then pointed to the buckle shaped as the head of a Texas longhorn. She undid it, freed the hook of his khakis, and pulled them down.

The dong, stiff as the ineffective dildo she'd bought on a sex therapist's urging, stretched his undershorts.

"Take them off, Germaine." Fritz pressed his hard-on's head to his belly beneath the shorts' elastic band.

She swayed, then gasped as she jiggled them to his ankles. The heavily veined shaft with its strawberry, a third longer than Jock's, ended above Fritz's navel. She had no memory of what her father's looked like.

"Moccasins."

She removed the beaded leather as he lifted each leg.

He stepped from his shorts, sat beside her, and curled her fingers around his erection. "Stroke it."

She felt what suddenly seemed a peeled, baked zucchini and started pumping the thing. Her thumb couldn't reach her fingertips.

He threw his arms back to brace himself. "Raven will be here any second."

"Raven?" Her fingers flew off.

"Don't stop!" He grabbed her hand. "Partners back home love photos and Raven has an eye. In case you've changed your mind, buttercup. Slower."

"Like that?" She closed her eyes.

"Good."

The prickling beginning in her vagina vanished at two raps on the door. Raven walked in, wrapped in a robe and dangling a camera, pink-framed glasses hugging her nose. The loosened hair hung in black waves past her shoulders.

"Don't think I want pictures," Germaine managed. She started squirming as Fritz pushed his forefinger between the lips of her vulva. "My boyfriend's worried that—"

"He'll love them," Raven said, moving to the jar-lamps and switching on a second bulb in each. "Pete was snoring before I could bring him off, Boss. Head shots first?"

Nodding, he pulled one of the pillows from the headboard to the rug. "Get onto your knees, Germaine."

"I know how to do it."

"Raven can delete the photos tomorrow if you like. Does my finger please you?"

"God, yes." She longed to swallow this man's cum but feared her stomach would cramp, as it so often did with Jock.

"Don't finish me off. I've other treats for you."

Germaine pushed her lips over his strawberry and lowered her face until she gagged—raised and lowered it, picturing the head of an oil-well pump's walking beam.

"Ohhh," Fritz moaned as Raven snapped and saved. "Enough!" he gasped less than a minute later, and thrust Germaine's shoulders back. The glistening shaft sprang free. "Ribbed or smooth?" he panted.

"What?"

"Condom."

"You choose. But hurry!"

FIESTA!

Sunday 2 September 2007

In the gloom of next morning Raven sat bleary-eyed under the kitchen-nook's frieze of jackrabbits chasing cottontails. She unfolded the corners of a bindle brought in from the casita, wiped a paring knife clean of blueberry preserves, and began to chop the snow-white grains.

While the unseen sun fired gray wisps of clouds into rose, she produced a cut straw from her robe, removed her glasses, and set them beside the tumbler of tomato juice, wondering how the photos of Fritz and Germaine would look on her monitor. Not that it mattered so long as the spy cams embedded in smoke alarms had done their jobs.

Shit! A shock of hair tumbled from the bunch held by the silver knitting needle presented by the john who'd insisted they marry and settle down. No way, hon, you were three times my age. But thanks loads for the goofballs in my fridge, the Phenobiconal your sawbones got you off of—to put you onto Librium, less dangerous, oh, yes. The bottle chilling in my casita, never opened, pills to pop in case the cops get wind of the Josephs' scam.

Raven knuckled her breastbone. No bastille for this broad. She managed to tuck most of her black strands back under the john's glistening knitting needle.

A quarter gram of cocaine lay scattered. She formed a line and quickly snuffed up half, thumbed her right nostril closed, and snuffed the rest. Expelling her breath, she pocketed the straw and empty bindle, returned the pink frames to her nose, and watched the clouds change from rose to salmon, pressing the platinum rings against her nipples until they hurt. Goddamned Pete last night.

"Morning, bright eyes."

Raven's head jerked toward the doorway. Fritz stood in his Sunday best, moccasins stitched with thongs, black silk socks, creased khaki shorts, black shirt splashed with peonies. Its pocket displayed the points of a white handkerchief. What a specimen! Nearing sixty and no fillings showed. That grin must mean he'd launched Germaine into her first-ever orgasm.

"You," Raven said and blinked.

"Who'd you expect, Butch Cassidy?" Fritz advanced to the glass pot and poured coffee into one of the mugs inscribed *City Different*. "What a gorgeous sky—those clouds remind me of the coral reef I used to snorkel off Key West." He pried two slices of nine-grain from their polypropylene bag, pushed them into the toaster, and shoved the lever down.

"I'm fed up, Fritz."

"Why's that? Let's have another look at those eyes." He clanked his mug onto the counter and strode to the table half-circled by a cushioned banco. Raven slumped opposite it in one of the caned chairs. He lifted her chin. "Only six-thirty and you've taken your first hit." He thrust her head aside and returned to the sink.

"That hurt, Boss."

"Good." He bent to breathe in the fragrance of the toasting bread.

"Last night I had to slap Pete awake to fellate him—yecch, like tasting aspirin—and two minutes later he was snoring. I hightailed it back to the casita."

"We're paying you to keep clients happy all night, Rave."

"I crept in around five to diddle his cock but he pushed me away." She snuffled phlegm from her nose. "Someday I'm going to diddle you."

"Arlene would cut our throats." He flicked on the fluorescent panel in the ceiling.

"We keep it secret, bro!"

"This is a business, beautiful. And usually, you are."

She thrust her face forward and stuck out her tongue at him. The knitting needle slipped free and bounced on the tiles. Her hair swung past her neck.

Fritz backed against the granite as the toaster dinged.

"Your shorts are bulging, Boss."

He turned from her and extracted the toast, cupping his crotch.

The sun flared between a V formed by the double trunk of a weeping birch and glinted off Raven's plate. "So you succeeded with the editor last night?"

"Incest's no picnic. Best I could do was get her to moan."

"How about you?" Raven asked.

"Came three times." He smiled and spread out margarine and a knifeful of preserves.

"You'd be awash in cum if you'd give me the chance."

Fritz brought his breakfast to the table across from her and settled on the banco. "I wonder if she'll want a CD of your photos last night." He poured half-and-half from the little pitcher Raven had set out.

"Who cares?"

"I'm relying on you to bring her off this afternoon, Rave."

She snuffled again. "Won't be easy."

"Clear your nose, can't you? Jesus."

Tissues sat boxed beside the TV squatting on the side table. She blew into one.

"I need more money, Fritz. You and Arlene have made a lot of jack since jump-starting this operation last November." She stuffed the wadded tissue into her robe. "I've been with you all those nine months and every weekend I bust my ass off."

"No argument there." He snapped off a corner of toast and chewed, gazing into her olive eyes. "I'll talk to Arlene—"

"Who's wearing the pants here? Fuck Arlene."

"Fuck me? Meaning what, love? Sometimes he does that."

Arlene stepped into the kitchen and placed her fists on her hips. She'd stuck a purple aster in one of her ducktails above a tight green sweater and skirt. A butterfly concho belt cinched her waist.

"Or have you decided *you'd* like to bed me, in spite of our rules?" Arlene sucked rouged lips between her teeth.

"Rave's afraid you won't agree to what seems a well-deserved raise," Fritz said.

"Raise?" Arlene moved to the coffee pot. "Better get her to break her little habit first."

"What little habit's that?"

"You're a coke whore, love. You've got to have it every couple of hours."

Arlene pushed her buttocks against the counter. "You scare me, you really do. Someone's going to squeal about the surprise you've got us offering clients. You end your dependence on Lady C and maybe we'll talk raise." She dipped her head and patted the little blossom. "I'd give this to you if you'd let me, you know."

"Knock it off, Arlene." Fritz blocked a yawn with his fist.

"And you?" Raven blurted. "You seem to like the Lady well enough. Anyway, who's going to sing, the way you and Fritz have got this setup figured."

Arlene carried her mug past the facilitator to a spot on the banco furthest from her husband.

"As far as the coke goes, I'm strictly recreational, believe it," Raven said.

"I don't."

"Me, neither, Rave."

"Your choice. But one thing, Arlene, you gotta stop telling guests I'm into sports. My old lady forever messed up her knee bowling and my old man broke his leg playing softball for the bricklayers' local. I hate all sports—except what we do here, okay?"

"Whatever, love. Is last night's footage hot?"

"Hey, it's seven in the morning! I haven't looked. At least I know we got footage—no thunderstorms last night." Raven grabbed another tissue.

"Give her a break, babe."

"And you can shut up."

Fritz's teeth clenched. It struck him that his wife was a knock-off of his mother: cold and obsessed by baubles, like those slabs of fool's gold looped this morning over her cotton-propped boobs. Even the purple aster jutting from her hair, plucked early from the balcony outside their bedroom, seemed plastic. How he looked forward to weekends, two nights of freedom from spending fifteen minutes tonguing her clit until she came.

He masked his sigh with a bite of toast.

"Just past dawn and I'm already exhausted," Raven said, "and only half as old as you two. Three hundred days of Santa Fe sun is all that keeps me here, folksies."

Light shot through the crook of the birch, igniting the still leaves. For today the weather bureau had forecast a climb to eighty-three degrees. Raven tilted her chin, craving the yet-to-come heat.

"You and I need to do something fun together," Arlene said to her. "You both keep telling me we're all business."

"I'm talking shopping."

"Sure."

"I want to buy you a new outfit, an expensive one."

"Yeah?"

"I do, Raven."

Besides Arlene's certainty that without this well-made young woman, Beautiful Tomorrows was a toppled house of cards, she also longed for Raven's devotion. At age seven, Arlene's sister had tumbled into an abandoned well. Often at night she reheard the screams, a splash, her own futile dash to ask the aunt who was raising them to phone the fire department. Later, with Fritz, she'd wanted, and not wanted, children, but soon ended the fruitless struggle to conceive.

"How'd it go with *your* pigeon, babe?" Fritz asked.

"I showed him how to bring himself and yours-truly off at the same time."

"No fooling."

"I've been experimenting anally with that dildo you bought me — wanted to surprise you when the weekend's over.

"Great," Fritz lied.

Raven kept silent.

"Afterward, Jimmy started wheezing," Arlene said. "But he's a good lay and I wish I had him this afternoon. Pete's a crybaby."

"You're right there," Raven said.

"What about the editor?" Arlene asked.

"Tough case," Fritz said. "I gave her the longest head I've ever —"

"Raven'll break her."

"Yeah, sure, me, slaving for crumbs."

Arlene leaned sideways to place her hand on Raven's thigh. "I'm going to get you into a twelve-step program."

Raven moved her leg away from Fritz's. "Nope. You're not."

"Look," he interrupted. "Rave's got to prepare three guest breakfasts before eight. I want to talk about who we're going after next week."

"All three, as usual, what do you mean?" Arlene asked.

"I realize I have no vote but I say leave Germaine alone, though I bet she's the gold mine."

"You can't tell by a client's clothes," Fritz said.

"The thing is, Boss, she's the one who really might blab, or even write about us."

"If you can get an orgasm out of her, she'll agree to anything," Arlene said.

"I wonder."

"We probably have damning footage of her doing coke awaiting your look-see in the den. Bring her off this afternoon twice and I tell you what— Fritz and I'll discuss bringing you into the partnership."

"You're kidding!" Raven jumped from her chair, stepped toward where the sun emblazoned the TV, and kissed Arlene's cheek. "I can keep my supplier?"

"We'll discuss it. Who is your supplier, by the way? Where do you two do your connection?"

"I can't tell you that."

"Let's at least agree we don't need cocaine to accomplish what we're here for, okay?" Fritz said. "Whether we go after all three, or forget the editor, I'd like to increase our donation to Kat."

"Why's that, husband mine?"

"The Coalition for the Homeless receives lots of city and state funds. Saint E's has a million-dollar budget and half that comes from the city, state, and feds. Salvation Army gets public funds for winter overflow. But Kat's a maverick—the Harbor's not even 501(c)(3). She pretty much depends on us. The cops are on her side. And she's made a deal with the School of the Deaf not to have the refuge patrolled. She'd like to bring in another intern besides Vonnie, shore up the garage, slip a couple of bunks inside. She'd like—"

"Hold it!" Arlene slapped the chair's arms. "I'm going to talk fast because I just heard a door shut in the hall. Beautiful Tomorrows has been giving Kat money for nearly a year. In that time I've bought one measly new outfit and this necklace, period. Our BMWs are three years old. Homelessness is increasing—"

"Just my point," Fritz said.

"Shut up a minute! At least fifteen-thousand homeless in New Mexico and from what I've read, most of those who rehabilitate go back out."

"Not true!" Raven cried.

"How would you know?"

"Kat's told me story after story of chicks who kick booze or meth or smack, hole up in a halfway house until they find work, then move into a subsidized apartment."

"Exceptions," Arlene said. "What *I've* read is that substance abuse is a problem most homeless won't address. They stop taking their meds. And because mental illness is so prevalent, they can't follow *any* program for long that helps them rejoin the human race."

"I suppose we could talk about changing who we give the funds to," Fritz said.

"No!" Raven blurted.

"Why do you care?" Arlene asked. "Oh, sure, your supplier must be homeless."

"It's not that. Dealers are—"

"Good morning, all."

Though sunlight flooded past the sashed curtains, the bags under Germaine's eyes matched Raven's. She'd hung her mother's pearls over a silk top printed with purple ivy.

"Hi, there, sexy," Fritz said to Germaine in monotone.

"Don't give me that. I'm famished. Coffee? There it is."

"Sit, please, I'm way behind." Raven left her chair. "Orange or tomato juice?"

"Orange."

"Huevos rancheros and scones coming up."

"Raven?"

"Yep." She set a steaming mug in front of Germaine, opened the refrigerator, and began to remove eggs, tortillas, and a jar of salsa.

"I want those photos deleted."

Raven waited to speak until she returned to the counter, hoping to maintain her cool. "How come?"

"I talked with my boyfriend this morning. He insists."

"Not a problem, hon. I'll go fetch the camera in a sec."

— — —

Raven idled the van three hours later near the southeast corner of the Plaza, opposite the La Fonda Hotel. She lowered her window so that Germaine and Jimmy could hear the violins and trumpets of the mariachi gathered under the bandstand's copper roof. Nearby, vendors had set up booths and covered tables with oilcloths. Across the street, Native Americans sold silver, coral, and turquoise under the portico of the Palace of the Governors.

Merrymakers swarmed the Plaza or sat squashed together on iron benches beneath ponderosas and the yellowing leaves of cottonwoods. A couple of mustachioed *trompos* players, cell phones buckled to their chinos, flung swirling tops off their strings onto the red concrete surrounding the war-memorial obelisk. A small crowd—Hispanic and Anglo teenagers in chinos and shorts, and a tourist wearing a pullover imprinted *Old Glory* that billowed over his belly—cheered the players on.

"I'll pick you up in front of the entrance there on Old Santa Fe Trail," Raven said, flipping a thumb ringed in turquoise past her shoulder. "The hotel's Plazuela restaurant is fab."

She'd renewed her persona, after a hit of coke at nine, by trading her robe for a yellow knit and cutoffs that accentuated her breasts' curves and shapeliness of her legs. "Think I'll march Pete to the public rose garden and see if I can't goose him up for this afternoon with Arlene. Now Jimmy Jammy, don't you go playing footsie with some plainclothes cop in the La Fonda's little boys' room. Remember you're not Idaho's Senator Craig. We don't want you resigning before you see what Fritz has to offer you. Germaine, I'm—"

A low-slung Oldsmobile that had circled behind them blasted its horn, enameled flames streaking over its hood toward a darkened windshield.

"I'd better scram. You two have a good time."

Germaine opened the passenger-side door as Jimmy slid back his. From the brick sidewalk they watched the van's bumper sticker, *Slow Down for Beautiful Tomorrows*, recede north toward Palace Avenue.

The buttery scent of hot burritos spread from a crockery pot. A fat woman, black hair peeping from a scarf, grilled cobs of corn under the cart's striped canvas. The noise of mariachis, now including guitars and bass, mingled with *Olas!* and the siren of an ambulance that screeched right and sped along the facade of the Museum of Fine Arts.

"God, Jimmy, it's ten times the frenzy of Washington Square. Let's rest a moment."

They found a bench under a pine. A man pushing a stroller thrust his middle finger at three teenage boys who swerved past on skateboards. Germaine clutched the silk top's tulip that covered her heart, and sucked in breath. "Before we go, I'd like to buy a ring for my boyfriend."

"Are you two pretty serious?" Jimmy lifted his hip to pull a handkerchief from his shorts. He wiped his forehead.

"He may be, but I don't mean that kind of ring. We've only been together five months."

"Within five months after my wife passed, I'd married and divorced my CPA. She couldn't stop having affairs with her clients."

Germaine laughed and cupped Jimmy's knee. She released it when he frowned at her. "Look there, Jim. Beneath that cottonwood with Christmas lights still on it. How lucky you and I are."

Flasher had embraced the ancient tree's trunk to keep from falling, as if leaning on a lover. He wore fatigues, combat boots, red beret, and a camouflage shirt rolled to his biceps. His chest spasmed as he coughed against the back of his hand. Black bristles shadowed his cheeks. Tish, an inch taller in a copycat shirt, stood smoothing tufts of red that sprang from underneath her rolled sombrero. She pulled a cigarette from her lips and stamped it under a boot.

Byron squatted on a blanket nearby, a hole ripped in the thigh of his khakis. Quentin sat next to him, scribbling musical fragments in a notebook. A ponytail longer and whiter than Byron's fell to Quentin's shoulders. Grizzled hairs masked his face.

"Dirty bastards," Jimmy said, pink jowls shaking as he wagged his head.

"They look like they may be homeless."

"Damn panhandlers."

A Hispanic policeman, cap low over his eyes, cruised by on a mountain bike.

"Do they frighten you, Jimmy?"

"My sister went homeless in Fort Lauderdale after she backed over her three-year-old. I'm the one who kept her fed—met her Sundays in an alley. She died on me four years ago, wouldn't keep up her meds."

"Oh, Jim." Germaine set her hand on his knee.

"I wouldn't do that. Unless you'd like to start something up."

"No, no, I'm sorry."

He mopped the back of his neck.

The band began Moreno Velosa's bossa-nova hit, "Deusa do Amor." Couples started to weave, swinging their elbows.

"Are you ready to walk around?" Jimmy asked.

"I think I'd rather talk. Do you know my father was probably sitting right here two weeks ago? He'd written a piece for Santa Fe's classical-music festival. The last I saw him I was *thirteen*, Jimmy. He kept his goatee and sideburns perfectly trimmed but Mother was always ragging him to cut his fingernails. Can you believe I still hear them clicking against the piano keys?"

"Don't know why not. So how was it for you with Fritz last night?"

"That organ of his is like a peeled zucchini, except—"

"It squirmed?"

Germaine began to giggle. "I couldn't cum."

"No wonder!"

"How about Arlene?" Germaine asked.

"Clinical. Like she was giving my pecker and balls a physical."

"She made you cough?"

"No, *handled* them a while. Before climbing on top. After I came and started wheezing she rolled off and just lay there staring at the ceiling."

The crowd on the concrete slab began to clap as a woman in a long skirt ran up the bandstand's steps, clicking castanets.

"Oh, Jimmy, you hombres with your easy orgasms. I'm so sick of my frigidity."

He squeezed her waist. "Trust Raven. She and I gabbed a little while you were walking after breakfast. I watched her delete the images she shot of you and Fritz."

"That's reassuring. Do you have a partner, Jimmy?"

"Chin Lo, my Pekinese."

They laughed, then sat in silence staring at couples dancing below the bandstand.

Meanwhile, over by the cottonwood, Flasher announced to his cohorts, "Listen up, people. There'll be cops swarmin' aroun' here by noon. Buzzy Wuzzy, you go say now what me an' Tish trained you to. See if you can soften the hearts of those Anglos there on the bench." His three gemstone rings sparkled as he karate-chopped the air.

"Shit-and-a-half, Flasher, it's Q likes this life so much. He's the one should practice."

"I'm willing," Quentin offered, reaching past the blanket's edge to pluck up a fallen twig. He placed it beside a branch.

"Nope. We got to get us some grub until we can scarf a hot lunch at Kat's tomorrow." Well said, Flasher thought. Keep 'em thinkin' Tish an' I are strapped. "Buzzy's the cleanest lookin' an' the youngest," he finished up aloud.

"Wish I *were* a kid again," Byron muttered.

"Tomorrow lunch shouns fine." Tish snuffled. The single red hair sprouting from the mole beside her lips twitched like an antenna.

"Clam it—you're spacier than a rocket."

"Far'face." Her thumb flicked a nostril as if to nag a match into flame.

Byron falsely limped across the grass in the stained, pink polo that he'd worn the day he'd left Kullman College.

"C'mon," Germaine said, grabbing Jimmy's hand. "Let's go try to have some fun. Maybe I'll find jewelry for Jock *and* me."

Jimmy pushed a porkpie hat onto his thinning hair and rose. "It's yourself you need to be good to."

Byron stopped just beyond the water fountain and faced them. He clamped a palm to his chest and cleared his throat twice, as instructed. "Hello," he rasped. Classy woman! Ashamed, he dropped his head as if she'd poured it full of lead.

Her stomach knotted and she pressed her shoulder bag to her ribs.

"You're blocking our way," Jimmy said. "You don't smell so good, you know that?"

Byron raised his eyes. Why was she with this pudgy nothing? He'd love to undress her. "I have an advanced degree," he said. Well, that sounded stupid.

A lone woman in an ankle-length skirt and embroidered top belted out from the bandstand the song, "Vámonos, Cara Mia."

"Advanced degree in phony baloney," Jimmy said. Germaine took his hand; this time he let her keep it.

"I've lost my job at the college."

"College of Easy Living?"

"I wrenched my knee in a culvert last night," Byron lied. He swung his hand back toward his companions. "We have nothing to eat."

"Oh, dear!" Germaine exclaimed.

"Beat it, goddamn it," Jimmy said.

"Please." Byron stretched his fingers, nails mottled with grime.

A foursome of Anglos—the women in sunglasses, one of the men in blue-striped shorts and loafers—plus some of the teenagers who had been watching the two Hispanic gamesters, now circled Byron, Germaine, and Jimmy.

"I'm begging you. Anything. My wife has three children with a fourth on the way."

"Get lost!" Jimmy threw his palms against Byron's shoulders.

Germaine plucked the side of Jimmy's shirt and whispered, "Walk around him."

Tish's sombrero flew off as she pushed through the onlookers, her hair a conflagration.

"Bow wow wow," she barked, nose dripping. Stolen Chanel No. 5, which she'd sprayed on her neck for this morning's foray, plus the smell she'd be showering off at Kat's tomorrow, created the aroma of a freshly skinned cottontail. She clenched her fists at Jimmy and Germaine and pumped her forearms up and down. The cuffs of her camouflage shirt flapped.

Byron hurried back between the Anglo couples to join Quentin under the cottonwood. Flasher strode past him and vised Tish's left wrist. She struggled a moment, then cocked her right elbow and landed a slap.

He drove his rings into her cheekbone.

Germaine reached out but Tish was staggering toward a bench. She clutched the nearer of its filigreed arms.

Flasher came close, unzipped his fly, wrenched his balls and erection into the open, gripped a tuft of Tish's hair, and yanked her face down until it was inches away. "You know what happens when these act up. You come on quietly now."

She shook her hair as if to fling off something wet. "I'm sorry, Papa. Don't! I'm with you, darn tootin' I am, you betcha."

Flasher, pausing to retrieve the sombrero, propelled her through the crowd to where Quentin and Byron sat.

Germaine and Jimmy goggled dumbfounded at them.

The policeman seen earlier came pedaling fast down one of the seven esplanades that converged on the war obelisk. Germaine watched a blonde, swaying against a Native American, stash a six-pack of beer beneath her skirt.

The cop's brake pads squealed as the rubberneckers parted. "What's the trouble here?" he asked.

Germaine moistened her lips, unable to speak. Jimmy pointed to the cottonwood. Tish had wrapped both arms around Flasher. He was coughing against her neck, shoulders heaving.

"Soliciting?" The cop's high voice seemed wrong for his bulk.

"Soliciting, yes, sir," Jimmy said.

"I know a couple of them." A holster bobbed against his hip as he walked his bike to the blanket.

"Take off, Flasher, you and Tish and your two pals there or I haul the bunch of you to headquarters."

"Could use a square an' a cot for the night, Frank."

"Darn tootin' we could, Frankie." Tish's tongue started darting out and in.

He reached in his back pocket for a billfold and gave Flasher ten dollars. "This says don't let me see you again until Fiesta's over."

Germaine watched Quentin gather up the cottonwood twig and branch, and stoop for others that lay on the grass. How strange! Early on Sundays her father used to lop off dead limbs and sweep twigs and leaves from the sidewalk fronting their two-story brick home in Brooklyn.

Quentin grabbed the blanket by a corner that looked chewed and tucked it under his elbow.

The policeman waited until everyone rose. Byron maintained his false limp as the quartet began the mile-and-a-half walk back to the refuge.

Three trumpets blared from the bandstand. Germaine slumped to a bench beside a buck-toothed girl talking to her doll and clamped her ears.

Jimmy pried one of her palms away. "Are you all right?"

She wagged her curls no, shook her captured hand free, propped both on her knees as if in prayer, and stared at her silver flats.

The two *trompos* players had resumed hurling their tops onto the concrete apron.

"What about Indian jewelry?" Jimmy asked.

"I can't."

A woman with a birthmark below her eye appeared. The little girl next to Germaine stood, dangling the doll by one foot. They walked off together.

"Let's go have some tea at the restaurant Raven talked about."

Germaine nodded.

Jimmy started toward the signal, stopped, patted his forehead with the handkerchief, and looked around. "Are you coming?" A damp triangle darkened his armpit.

Germaine was gazing after the homeless foursome, who had reached the lamppost bearing glass globes half a century old, at the Plaza's southwest corner. Her brain registered the pigtailed man dumping branches into a green receptacle. But all she could see was her father standing above her bed two decades ago, fingernails clicking on his belt buckle.

Jimmy returned, circled her waist to help her rise, led her to the corner, and into the La Fonda.

— — —

By one-thirty, Arlene, Germaine, Pete, and Jimmy had gathered on the sofa in the Hacienda's living room with the day's start-off, chilled margaritas. Half-straws lay beside the grooves whitened once more with snow. The vase sprouting six-inch-wide orange and yellow cactus dahlias, two blooms drooping, rested on floor tiles near the table. Raven stood lowering Roman shades on the windows.

"I'll be sending a formal complaint to the police about this morning's unpleasantness," Fritz began, arms wrapped around his ribs. He turned to the stack of electronic equipment that rose to the ceiling, and dimmed the lights surrounding the room's single spy cam/smoke alarm. Cold air blew through the ceiling vents. Nabiha Yazbeck sang a lover's complaint from the *Sahara Lounge* CD that Fritz had set spinning, accompanied by Spanish guitar, accordion, and techno.

Raven knelt on the Zuni throw that reached under the table. Still braless in her yellow knit, she'd traded cutoffs for a denim mini, her flip-flops for two-inch heels. She'd sunk the pink teeth of a comb into the renewed bun at the back of her head. Coral pendants swung from her ears.

"Arlene and I feel just sick about the incident," Fritz continued. He threw out his left hand and with the other pinched a point of the silk hankie that flared from his shirt. "Luckily we've still got two hours before Raven hustles you back to Albuquerque. Pete's ready right now to roll with my wife. True, Peter?"

"Here's hoping." Pete snapped a strap of his suspenders.

"This time I'm betting you don't fall asleep," Fritz said.

"Thanks for nothing, Boss." Raven wiped her nose.

"Last night? Not *your* fault," Pete said to her.

"Want me to shoot a few photos?"

"Sneak a peek in half an hour and we'll see."

"C'mon, stud," Arlene said, sliding her hand under Pete's butt and rising. "Drink up and snort your line and I'll snort mine—whadduhya know, that rhymes. Start of a beautiful poem." She knelt beside Raven, kissed the facilitator's cheek, did her own one-n-one, stood, and shut her eyes. She'd shadowed their lids green to match her skirt and sweater.

When Pete had snuffed his quarter gram, they headed toward the hall, passed the wire unicorn and its monkey opposite the stairs that led up to the Josephs' master suite, and entered the room nearest the bath. Raven had dropped the shade and folded the scarlet bedspread against the footboard. Chris Martin was crooning in falsetto from speakers in all three bedrooms, "Look how the stars shine for you, they're all yellow," from Coldplay's *Parachute*.

"Go on and get naked," Arlene said, unhooking the butterfly buckle of her belt. "You'd like to start with fellatio, I expect?" She relished the cocaine's rush and sweetness dripping down her throat.

Pete stripped off his suspenders, kicked his sandals away, and lowered his shorts.

Arlene moved to the dresser. She opened the top drawer, removed a foil packet, a tube of K-Y Jelly, a kneeling pad—and started to close the drawer. "Fucking splinter!" She gazed at the forefinger. "Raven can pull it out later. Pete, friend, I'll be working a nerve that few men know about. To make up for last night. It's a fuse compared to the famous one that runs up that shaft. No fair coming fast."

"So where do you want me?" He hauled off his shirt.

"On the edge of that caned chair."

She reached into the half-opened drawer for a box of ClingWrap and brought her implements to the rug in front of where Pete was perching, more hair on the folds of his belly than on his chest. "Enjoy my alpaca, señor." She stripped everything off except the sweater and, for a moment, massaged what breasts she had underneath it.

"What's the plastic for?"

"Never seen it used like this?" She unwound a foot of saran and ripped it free along the yellow box's row of teeth. Into its middle she squeezed a glob of K-Y and smeared it to form a circle. "Dental dam, Pete. You'll love how it slips and slides." She shoved the square's jelly-free side into her mouth, kneaded his balls, flicked his erection until it twitched without coaxing, then buried it between her lips. He jerked as her forefinger began to stroke the nerve beneath his balls.

At the same time Fritz waited on the edge of the mattress in the room at the hall's far end, shorts, socks, and flowered black shirt draped over a chair. "How long since you've been with a man, Jimmy?" He reached to the side to caress his client's inner thigh.

Jimmy's clothes and coin bracelet lay heaped near his feet, seemingly far too small to support his paunch. "Couple of years; three." Jimmy wiggled his toes. "Ummm."

"Enjoy." Fritz gave his own eight-inch erection a couple of strokes, then wet two fingers and moved them along the underside of Jimmy's organ, which listed to the right.

"The motorcycle mechanic I was with smelled like engine oil," Jimmy said. "I couldn't get a hard-on."

"Doing just fine this afternoon."

"Half the length of yours."

"I was genetically blessed. Let's dry you off."

Fritz, dong bouncing, walked through the dimness to a stenciled dresser and extracted a foil packet and towel. He carried them into the closet where last night, on tiptoes, Raven had pushed up a switch in the farthest corner. Fritz stood flat-footed to do the same.

"What's going on in there?" Jimmy asked, maintaining his frown as Fritz emerged.

"Needed to make sure the air-conditioner works," Fritz lied.

"I've been hearing it humming."

"It does that. Towel under those arms, would you?"

Through the speaker Chris Martin wailed over the techno beat, "My heart is young, I won't let you down."

Jimmy's double chin jiggled as he blotted perspiration. "Now what?"

"Between your legs, too."

Jimmy complied.

"I'm going to show you a position you may not have thought of. I used to do a bit of fishing with some investment-banker buddies around Princeton across the Hudson. We were single or married, though all of us were horny. At night in camp, after a few beers, we'd hold contests to see who could bring off the next guy quickest. Some of us learned to like male-to-male better, some of us stayed bi. But we all discovered what heaven's hidden in the prostate. Weekdays, when we could break from the phones for a sandwich, we'd bat around new-position ideas the way the other guys talked sports. C'mon, pal, scoot closer. Revive that toy soldier for me."

Jimmy moved off the folded quilt and began to massage his organ.

Fritz lay back on the sheet and settled the pillow under hair cropped all over and squared at the neck. Once more he wet two fingers and stroked his lengthwise nerve.

"Go ahead now and straddle my hips, facing me, knees raised." Fritz ripped open the foil packet, pinched out a pre-lubed condom, and rolled it down his erection. "While you ride me, Jimmy, I'll be working you." He pumped his fist slowly up and down.

Jimmy crawled forward, sucking his lips between his teeth. He rested a moment beside the older man, then lifted a leg across Fritz's thighs.

In the living room Raven knelt at the table after raising the shades.

Germaine sat rigid on one of the sofa's cushions. She stared above the facilitator's head out the corner windows where the lobed leaves of a New Mexican locust fluttered. How Germaine repented not staying put at the Hacienda this morning. Or, better, staying home in New York! Her left temple throbbed.

"A fourth gram is the right dose to loosen you up, hon, especially after what came down at the Plaza." Raven reached to push her pink comb deeper.

"No cocaine, not this afternoon."

"Why?"

"I'm afraid."

"Of what?"

"A bad trip."

"That's what acid does, dopey."

"My boyfriend's brother is a cokehead. Living hand-to-mouth in Jersey somewhere."

"Can't happen with this little bit of snow," Raven said.

"Last night was plenty."

"You don't mind if I indulge, right?"

"But you're driving us to the airport."

"Only half a line then." She pulled a Kleenex from the pocket of her mini, blew, and shoved the tissue past her knit's V-neck into her cleavage.

"I'd as soon you didn't," Germaine said.

"Ah, Jesus, okay, let's go make whoopee without it."

"No photos."

"I deleted last night's—Jimmy saw me." Raven rose and bent for her camera.

"No more photos!"

"Go easy, I heard you. Pete said he might want them." As Raven stomped around the table's corner, her calf caught the square vase holding dahlias on the tiles. It fell forward, pitching out stems and a pint of brown water, darkening the throw. "The hell with it!"

"Shouldn't we at least mop up?"

"No!" She grabbed Germaine's glass and tossed the last half of the margarita down her throat.

Germaine hoisted her bag from a cushion. She followed the twenty-four-year-old into the hall and through the doorway of the second bedroom opposite the locked door to the den.

"Can't do much with our clothes on," Raven said, laying the camera on a side table, yanking the comb from her hair and fingering black waves down her shoulders. She removed her glasses, plopped onto the sheet, and peered up at Germaine.

"Can you turn that music off?"

"Nope." Raven began snapping her finger and thumb to the beat.

Electronica hounded Coldplay's guitar and bass as Chris Martin belted out, "You want me to change? Well, I'll change for you."

"At least it's cool in here," Germaine said.

"There's a vent beside every smoke alarm."

"Isn't the afternoon light delicious, filtering through that shade's honeycombs?" Germaine asked.

"So what are we waiting for?"

"I'm not going to have sex with you, Raven."

The facilitator stiffened, controlling the urge to scream, Boss's wife says I've got to make you come *twice*. "Why not?" she managed aloud. The muscles in her neck tightened.

"Can't we just talk?"

"But I can solve your problem, Germaine. We've got to try." Raven hoisted the hem of her yellow knit, exposing a tattoo reading *First Burn* above her navel as well as the nipple rings.

"Please, don't undress." Germaine backed against the door.

"What's the matter? You'll have wasted the seven-hundred-fifty bucks these weekends cost. You want to lose your boyfriend, too? You know he'll find *someone* who can reach multiple orgasms just fine."

Germaine moved to a wicker armchair and for a moment chewed her lip. "That man—"

"What man?"

"On the Plaza. He forced a woman's face inches from his crotch. 'Don't make me, Papa,' she pleaded."

"You told us that earlier."

"He didn't look *old* enough to be her father. But his words were almost what I said to mine." Germaine clapped a palm to the side of her head. "The truth is I *wanted* my dad to take me, Raven. I wanted his erection in me. I worshipped him! My boyfriend at the time only had the courage to ask if he could press my chest. I had hardly anything there yet. But my father… I swallowed his semen and a week later, when he laid me on my back, I realized we were caught up in something terrible—I twisted down off the bed. What we both wanted we never got. Wouldn't surprise me if I'm still saving myself for him." Germaine pressed the pearl into her earlobe, filling her lungs until she thought she'd explode.

"Maybe that's what turned him gay, hon. But *I'm* not your father. Not even a man. C'mon over here."

That the editor obeyed astonished her. Germaine pried off her flats, padded across the carpet, and lowered herself to the mattress's edge.

The facilitator reached to cup the tulip draping Germaine's left breast. The turquoise on her thumb flashed. "I love that blouse, is it silk?"

Germaine nodded.

"Where'd you find it?"

"Saks."

"I can feel your heart. Can I unbutton you? "

But Germaine took Raven's hand and inserted it between the facilitator's thighs. "I think I must hate sex, what it does, you know?"

"Like what?" Raven asked.

"Changes intimacy into dependence. Deep down, do I hate my boyfriend? Probably. At least I don't hate you so far."

Germaine pulled Raven's head against hers. "Such low-rent work you do, yet such gorgeous hair." She pushed her lips to Raven's ear, kissed the lobe, and faced forward, gazing at the painted carving of St. Francis that hung beside the door. "I guess whom I hate most is me."

"But why?"

"For not kneeing my father in the testicles, for not running away like you."

"You were thirteen."

"And you?"

"Thirteen—okay. This cruddy nose. Coke burns away the cilia." Raven pressed one nostril closed, inhaled through the left one, then shut the right nostril and inhaled. Her cheeks dimpled. "Low-rent? Perfect! Only work I know. And the Lady's all that keeps me from firing the silver bullet." Raven jabbed her temple with her forefinger. "Bam!" She grabbed her camera and stood. "Past time for me to go see what Pete Sweet's up to."

The door clicked shut. Germaine clutched her temples, then leaned toward the bag she'd left at the bed's foot and removed her cell phone.

"So is it working?" were Jock's first words.

"I'm using it to call you."

"Not your cell."

" Oh. I can't wait to make love with you."

"That's great news, princess!"

"Have you seen Judy?"

"Why would I do that?"

"To go over your new contract."

"It's the weekend, remember? I've been installing your bookshelves. Judy's probably in the country fucking her heart out with her boyfriend."

That's what happens, all right, Germaine thought. We fuck our hearts to death. "Dinner at Ye Waverly tomorrow night?" she asked.

"You bet!"

She tucked her cell into her bag, fell sideways, drew her knees up, and yanked a pillow over her head to muffle the electronic *de boom, de boom boom* that pulsed out from high on the wall. She'd told one lie to Jock. How many had he told, she wondered?

WHO'S BOSS HERE?

Monday 3 September 2007

By noon on Labor Day the temperature had reached eighty-four degrees. Fifteen women and men waited on the covered porch of the old adobe that Katrina Ulibarri had refurbished three years ago and dubbed Kat's Harbor for the Homeless. Most shouldered sleeping bags, backpacks, and bedrolls. They waited for Veronica Trumble, Kat's six-month intern, to check off the first dozen who were clean-and-sober for the hot lunch Kat served twice a week. The odor of lamb stew drifted past the shelter's front door, on which Kat had tacked the following:

> *No Loitering. We want to be good neighbors*
> *and keep the peace.*
> *No Estar. Tenemos que mantener*
> *la paz en la vecinidad.*

Next door to the north, two cars missing tires perched on railroad ties alongside another adobe. Santa Fe Public Schools' Computer Annex and a vast, barbed-wired parking lot filled the block across the street. The homeless refuge began south of the creek bed bordering the Public Service Company of New Mexico's substation and a couple of acres of undeveloped land.

Vonnie, a freckled twenty-seven, sat in a rickety chair in a sundress, holding a clipboard. The intern was in Santa Fe to collect oral histories for her PhD thesis at the Columbia School of Journalism.

"Welcome, Mr. Cobb." A smile dimpled her cheeks. "Hello there, Miss Tish Earp—except, jango! You're having trouble standing—and I don't like the blood in those eyes. Mr. Cobb, that's not cologne, is it?"

"Celebratin' this great country's nobody-works-today, Von Bon," Flasher said. "Say, I 'preciate the effort you put into that upswept hairdo. Lookin' good."

"You going to do a Breathalyzer for me?"

"No fuckin' way, girlie!"

She twirled a loose, auburn sheaf around her left forefinger. Her voice kept its customary lilt, as if Flasher had not flamed her. "Tish, I'll need a urinary analysis before I can sign you in."

"Bow wow wow." Mucus ran from Tish's nose. She thrust her head forward and pumped a forearm up and down.

"C'mon, c'mon, move it," someone shouted near the queue's end off the porch, beside a table piled high with secondhand clothes.

"Touch my lady," Flasher squeaked to Vonnie, "an' we'll be pluggin' the culvert with ya."

"It's not to your advantage to threaten me, Mr. Cobb." Vonnie tensed her lips, trying to calm her stomach.

"¿Qué pasa?"

Kat, who'd been watching, hoping Vonnie could control this pair, burst through the doorway and placed her bulk between Flasher and Tish. Her long, jet-black braid whipped as she threw her head left, then right. "You two know Kat's rules. Try us Thursday. ¡Vámonos!"

Flasher started to unzip.

"Lock that pecker up or I call the cops."

"No way you're gonna do that."

Kat stepped forward in scuffed combat boots and gripped his shoulders. "Don't push me too far, oddball. The folks behind you are starving. Go plant yourselves under the apricot and Vonnie or Clara or I'll bring out a couple of plates after Vonnie registers everyone. Hey, I like you better rakish." She pulled his red beret over an eye. "Give us ten minutes."

Flasher grabbed Tish's hand, lifted his cleft chin high, and held the eyes of all of those waiting as he passed. He led Tish off the bricks toward the tree near Kat's tumbledown garage. Her pickup stood nearby.

"Take charge," Kat told Vonnie and marched back inside.

Quentin and Dirk, in line in front of Byron, cradled gunnysacks that bulged with dirty clothes.

"Welcome, you two." Vonnie lifted a freckled arm. "I'll need that knife, Mr. Pellington."

"Oh, yeah, forgot about Mahdi."

She slipped the poppy-handled blade under her clipboard. "Anyone else got a weapon?"

A hand gripping a switchblade near the end of the queue shot up.

"Bring it to me, please."

The bare-chested organizer of the culvert's anger-management class sauntered forward. He placed two polyethylene, fruit-shake bottles that held purple asters and rabbitbrush's pale blossoms on the table beside her, relinquished the knife, and doffed his cap that shaded sunken eyes. He'd knotted the arms of a shirt bare of buttons across his belly.

"We love the bouquets, Mr. Weathers, but you'll need to put that shirt on." Vonnie scribbled *Stormy Weathers* onto the sheet the clipboard held. "Stand aside, sir, until it's your turn to go in. Oh, and I'll need to keep that Bacardi safe for you."

"Haven't had a pop since breakfast."

"I believe that but you know the rules."

"Damn." Stormy lay the half pint from his hip pocket next to the flowers, and stepped to the porch's end railing.

"This is my buddy, Buzzy," Quentin said, moving up.

"Hello, sir. Welcome." Her upper gum glistened above perfect-seeming teeth—brows knitting against the roar as the next-door neighbor gunned his Harley out of the drive and leaned into a left turn.

Byron glanced at the cleavage beginning at Vonnie's square neckline. He noticed a reddish splotch above her collarbone. Birthmark? Boyfriend? He raised his eyes to her green ones.

"Full name, please?"

"Can't you just write Buzzy?"

"I guess so. Listen, I'm gathering data on what it feels like to be homeless. May I get your story sometime? Yours, too, Mr. Q," she added quickly, breaking her gaze, "and Mr. Pellington's. I've recorded most of the others here. I assume you gentlemen have registered to use the washer?"

"You got it, sis," Dirk said.

He limped inside ahead of Quentin and Byron as Vonnie wrote down the names of the Native American couple waiting behind them, their toddler, and the wheelchair-bound Hisi.

Mostly the adobe's largest space served as a great room, with two sofas and three easy chairs scattered throughout, and a TV in the southwest corner. On Mondays and Thursdays it served as a lunchroom. The two doors set on sawhorses, separated by walking space, had become dining tables. One faced the kitchen and laundry to the west, the other an upright piano near the front door facing east. Kat and Vonnie had pushed the sofas and chairs against the wall opposite the dining tables. Others, laden with a cooler of soft drinks, salad, corn bread, and a chafing dish of beans, sat under windows looking out on Kat's gravel apron and the old apricot—against whose trunk Flasher now rested, Tish's red hair fanning across his lap.

Along the Harbor's north wall stretched women's and men's bedrooms that held a two-tiered bunk each, the unisex bathroom, Kat's bathroom, and the master bedroom where she and her granddaughter slept.

Right now the eleven-year-old was forming triangles of paper napkins and laying them at eleven places (the toddler made twelve).

Clara, the bristle-headed woman who had bicycled out of the refuge Friday to sleep here—waiting for her daughter to call her down to Las Cruces—was readying posole in the kitchen. Kat had rejoined her.

While Quentin and Dirk veered toward the laundry, Byron stopped beneath the kitchen's lintel. "Hot chow!" he exclaimed to Kat over the noise of the fan. "Can you hear my stomach growling? How'd you get into this game, anyway?"

"Game? You're new at this life, ain't cha?" To Clara, Kat said, "Get that burner off and the posole and a big spoon into that bowl." She wiped her hands down the sides of a paint-splotched smock and drew her wrist along her brow. "Best game in town, saving other folks' lives when the daughter you had at fifteen gets raped by a homeless mutant, and the child she died from turns out to be a black-haired angel." She pointed a fleshy forefinger. "That's her out there, setting table. We're homeschooling her. Beatriz. What name do you go by?" She scratched a spider bite on her neck so hard that Byron could hear her nails abrading the skin.

"Buzzy."

"Well, Buzzy, welcome to the world of the down-and-out. I'm strict but do my damndest to level the playing field. Take that bowl and have my granddaughter tell our bozos to come and get it."

Byron watched Beatriz in her Mary Janes and pinafore shake a cut-glass bell. He blinked away tears, seeing his own three children, and set the posole next to the mixed greens near the TV. Kat came out swinging the pot of stew, steam rising as if from a hot spring. The chow line began to form.

The nearly bald Clara had disappeared into the women's bedroom. Now she carried a sleeveless knit top, bath towel, and Levis with rolled cuffs into the bath.

Quentin had been scribbling a couple of musical phrases in the laundry. He stashed the notebook between his chest and a plaid shirt torn at one shoulder, while Dirk emptied his gunnysack on the lid of the drier. Quentin grabbed the septuagenarian's arm. "Wait a minute. I'm first. You're after lunch."

Dirk wrested himself free. "Hands off, sport. I'm ready to rock 'n' roll and you're not." He clutched the box of soap and shoved the composer aside. "And dirtier than you are. With a failing prostate."

The front door slammed and they turned to watch Vonnie, on her way back to the kitchen, intercept Kat. "All accounted for," they heard her say.

Kat patted the intern's cheek, aware she'd grown too fond of this Anglo in her frolicking-rocking-horses dress. It had been three years since Kat's partner left. Since then she'd kept her vow to stay celebate. That's what, she suspected, had caused the weight gain. How she ached to cajole Vonnie into her and Beatriz's bedroom, sit her in front of the oval mirror, brush out the long hair.

Quentin faced Dirk again. "I'm supposed to feel sorry for you? Maybe I do. Doesn't mean you can muscle in. Go look at the list. I signed up Friday. Buzzy and I are leaving here together."

Dirk lifted the washer's lid.

When Quentin slapped it down, Dirk launched his elbow into the other's ribs. "Strappado next time. I'm serious."

Vonnie rushed close. "You two tomcats want lunch or not?"

"He can't go first." Quentin jerked his always-on rain hat so far down it bent his ears.

"Let me see what sort of loads you've got."

Quentin raised his sack.

"Mr. Pellington?"

The old man opened the washer.

"They'll both fit, gentlemen."

"You think I'm going to mix my garments with this vagrant's?"

"Mr. Q," Vonnie sighed. "Don't make me bring Kat over."

"I'm already in their faces," Kat said, smelling of lamb and potatoes. She gripped her hips. "Quit the squabbling, you two cookies, or you're out." She hunched her shoulders and threw her hands at the two men, fingers spread. "In or out?"

"In," Quentin said. "I'm hungry."

"In," Dirk growled. He twisted a knob on his Songbird hearing aid. "God-blasted squealing."

"C'mon, Vonnie." Kat pinched her intern's earlobe and as quickly, face flushing, let go. "I don't like abandoning the unwashed masses too long."

When the men left the laundry moments later, Kat was kicking open the kitchen door that led down to the gravel apron and apricot tree. She vanished balancing two plates heaped with beans, corn bread, and stew.

By now everyone had found a chair in the great room. Quentin noticed that Byron had taken a seat catercorner to Vonnie. But he also saw that the young man had canted the back of a chair for him against the table's edge.

The room buzzed with talk. Dirk, his plate loaded, limped to the table facing west to join Reuben, Hisi at an end, Beatriz, Clara, and a toothless African-American from New Orleans named Chiffon. A white mouse peeped from the pocket of Chiffon's blouse. She'd begged five dollars in front of Wild Oats this morning to rescue the pet from the animal shelter.

Stormy Weathers, a veteran of the 2003 invasion of Iraq, placed one of his Odwalla vases in front of the wheelchaired Hisi. He took the other fruit-shake bottle to the napkin Beatriz had folded nearest the piano, and left to get food.

Back two minutes later, he stopped lifting the first spoonful of kidney beans toward his mouth and leaned toward Quentin, who was jotting down groups of notes. "Say, pardner, you planning to squeal on us or what? Looks an awful lot like code, those notes you're writing out there."

"Looks like but isn't, well—I suppose—sort-of is," Quentin said without looking up.

"He's a composer, well known," Byron said. "You should hear—"

"Bag it, Buzzy." Quentin shifted to remove a long brown hair that dangled from Byron's sleeve. At the same moment, Vonnie placed her hand on Byron's forearm.

He felt his penis stir as she said:

"I've got to get your stories. No real names, okay?"

"Better ask him," Byron mumbled. Her palm lingered, warming his flesh.

To buy time, Quentin took a swallow from his can of cola. "You'll need to interview us together," he said at last.

At the other table, Dirk turned to Chiffon, who had drifted to Santa Fe in July from El Paso and now slept in the women's lower bunk. "What we need to do," Dirk said, stroking his short, white whiskers, "is take that rodent to the Plaza this afternoon. You start diddling its chin for sympathy and I'll ask for money."

"Ummm, just had myself a thought," Chiffon said. "How you going to get to the Plaza with that bad hip? Mighty Mouse can't carry you!" She tickled its ear with her left hand because her right had become a claw. A wrangler in El Paso had thrown her against a rail and stomped on the fist she'd roundhoused him with.

Reuben grinned across from Dirk, teeth shining where tobacco hadn't stained them. "We could leave Hisi at the lean-to with Wilda and the dog and fit you into her wheelchair. I'm a helluva pusher, guy, and that's a pun." He hoisted his arms so that the brown biceps nudged up the sleeves of his T-shirt.

"You think I can't negotiate a mile and a half on my own?" Dirk asked. "How do you suppose I made it up the hundred and seventy miles from Socorro? Walking, mostly. Who invited you to our picnic, anyway?"

"I invited me. You want to be rude twice? After we shared that chicken and let you spend the night? After I just offered you a ride? Motherfucking Anglo. Don't you know your history? The Palace of the Governors started out a pueblo." An artery in his temple swelled as he and Dirk, each planning to outstare the other, rose.

"Daddy, Daddy, no!" Hisi wailed under her pink stocking cap. "Kat won't let us back in." She clutched her bear and scooped up posole as if it were a last bite.

The back door slammed and heads turned to the clomp of Kat's boots. "Ingrates!" she shouted. "Watch me truck this food over to Saint E's. Mother of Jesus, can't stop bickering when I'm gone? Vonnie, you got to put your foot down. You bozos paying attention? This sweetheart's my straw boss. Wait a minute, Miz Beatriz, what are you doing there with that mouse?"

The chubby little girl had toppled her chair to run past Hisi, take Mighty Mouse from Chiffon, and cup him in her palms. Black hair straggled down her face. "He's scared, Abuelita. Look at his whiskers go."

"You know Grandma says no pets inside."

"Please?"

"Can I hold him now?" Hisi asked.

Beatriz glanced at Chiffon. The black woman nodded.

"Abuelita, please? Today is a holy day."

"Holiday. Not holy."

"I know that." Beatriz offered the mouse to the crippled nine-year-old. Wincing, Hisi stashed the teddy bear between her thighs, reached for Mighty, and pressed his ribs to her cheek. The white tail drooped. Beatriz pushed her lips to Hisi's other cheek, righted her chair, and studied the nails she'd painted violet this morning.

"All right, you knuckleheads," Kat called out. "Eat! Show me hands who wants coffee."

Seven went up as Clara stepped out of the bathroom fresh from her shower. Three days' worth of golden bristles shone on her scalp. She finished drying, tossed the terry cloth on an empty chair, and strode toward the side tables.

"I need volunteers to make this room a lounge again!" Kat bellowed. "You've got thirty seconds or names *will* be named. I do remember who helped out Thursday."

Clara raised her hand.

Fifteen seconds passed.

"Two more. *Double*-time."

Quentin grasped Byron's wrist, lifted it, and raised his own free hand. Dirk raised his at the same time.

"Way to go, amigos!"

Vonnie left the table to help Kat clear space for the spouted coffeemaker and Styrofoam cups.

"Shit-and-a-half, Q, why'd you do that?" Byron asked. "I'm not ready to get involved here."

"You need to hang around anyway. That old eccentric and I have laundry to dry."

"You and I have to leave at the same time?"

Quentin did not respond.

Byron, Stormy, and he wolfed down their stew and beans while Wilda opened her shirt to the toddler. Quentin sponged up the leftover lamb stock with a slice of bread. He reached to the tiles to unzip the backpack. His irritation grew amid the sounds of nursing and Stormy's slurping.

"Whacha got there?" Stormy asked. "Lemme see that." His two prominent teeth made him seem a gopher.

"This congregation needs music." Quentin opened the blue pouch and unrolled his keyboard.

"Lemme try that. I play piano pretty good." Stormy flung out an arm, sending his bouquet and the bottle he'd filled with water skittering. Vonnie ran close and grabbed Clara's towel.

"Hands off, nitwit." Quentin jerked the keyboard from Stormy's grasp.

"Down on the floor and give me fifty push-ups, pervert," the former marine replied.

Kat watched in front of the coffeemaker and cups that she'd lined up while Vonnie—looking neither at Quentin nor Stormy—mopped the table, emptied her water glass into the Odwalla bottle, and returned the flowers to it.

Stormy pushed back his chair, seized each end of the piano bench, lowered his butt, and began to bang out "Show Me the Way to Go Home." "Played it for the sand niggers in Baghdad. Talk about anger management— you shoulda seen those horned toads grin. Sing along, everbody!" Bouncing, he began to roll his shoulders. "Show-me-the-way-to-go-home—oh! I'm-tired-an-I-wanna-go-to-bed—ooh! Done-had-a-little-drink-about-an..."

"Alcoholic," Quentin muttered.

Dirk left the table nearer the kitchen and started to come over.

Quentin rose, too, after stuffing keyboard and pouch into his pack. He squeezed between his table's end and the window that looked out at pots of geraniums Kat's granddaughter was in charge of keeping watered.

"You're leaving?" Byron asked.

Quentin wagged his ponytail no. "But who can digest lunch with that noise?" He reached the piano ahead of Dirk and clutched the buttonless gingham that draped Stormy's arm. "Hey, there, it's my turn."

"Who you, daddy? I'm stationmaster here."

"Hell's broth..."

"No more fighting!" Hisi shrieked, hoisting her bear at the end of the further table.

"Time to break it up," Dirk said, cocking his forefinger at each man.

Quentin stepped away but Stormy, squinching deep-set eyes, curled his fingers into fists, thrust one arm high, and jerked his elbow back.

"Vonnie!" Kat called. "Get a handle on this."

Wilda, the Native American, had pulled a green shawl from her basket and covered the toddler's and her head. Vonnie stood up at the near table's end, catercorner to them. "Mr. Weathers! Mr. Q! The Harbor is a *sanctuary*. We need you to help keep the peace."

"You're learning," Kat said, more to herself than the intern.

Byron had circled behind Vonnie—how fresh she smelled, even in the room's heat—and came close to Quentin. He arced an arm around his friend's shoulder. "Let's go get us a coffee, Q. C'mon."

Quentin blinked at him a moment, then shifted his eyes to Stormy's. "Look, I'm sorry. Keep playing."

The veteran of Operation Iraqi Freedom shook his head and slumped on the bench, staring at the fingers he'd pressed between his knees.

Dirk followed Quentin and Byron toward the coffeemaker while Vonnie, who had heard the washer's grinding stop, headed to transfer the men's clothes to the drier. On the way, as she and Byron exchanged glances, she brushed back hair the barrette had failed to keep off her forehead.

Half an hour later, Clara, Dirk, Quentin, and Byron had folded the legs of the three serving tables, stored them, the doors, and the four sawhorses in the laundry, and moved sofas and easy chairs to their accustomed places. Quentin shouldered his backpack and, cradling the gunnysack stuffed with clean underwear and shirts, walked out onto the porch. Byron eased the screen door shut. Above them, the American flag drooped along its pole beside the TV's satellite receiver.

They stepped down to the drive and in a moment were walking side by side along the street's asphalt toward the steel mesh that fenced off the refuge's fire-blackened elms. A pocked sign read, *No Trespassing.*

Byron sprang the chain-link gate free. A spotted yellow butterfly darted among beer cans thrown into the thrusting blossoms of sweet clover lining the path. A grasshopper leapt from the shade of a clump of ragweed. "Here," he said, "let me carry those clothes."

Quentin stopped and handed the bundle to him, pulled a clean handkerchief from his ducks, and, before replying, mopped his forehead. "A few days ago I said I'd take care of you. Now you're taking care of me. At the piano and… you and Vonnie."

"Vonnie?" Byron frowned.

"Toweling up the mess that idiot caused grabbing for my keyboard. And before, in the laundry, pulling Dirk and me out of a totally stupid dustup that, okay, I started." He paused. "She's a good-looking thing, isn't she?"

"Thing?"

Quentin brushed away the gnats dancing near his face. "Buzzy?"

"What?"

"I need to tell you something."

"What's that?"

"I've fallen in love with you." He leaned forward, trying to reach Byron's neck, but the other pulled away.

"Don't do that, Q."

"Love you?"

"Love me if you like but no moves, understand?"

Quentin placed his fingers on Byron's wrist.

The younger man's muscles tightened. "Take your hand away."

Quentin did so.

"I told you last night that as long as I have to hide out, I'll be your friend and play your music. But as the Gershwin song implies, don't ask for anything more. I'm not bi."

THE PLOT THICKENS

Tuesday 4 September 2007

The perspiration finally dried on Germaine's neck as she lay naked beside Jock in her apartment in Greenwich Village a little past noon. He'd draped the top sheet, blanket, and forget-me-nots coverlet over the footboard while she'd lifted the telephone from her mother's antimacassar and closed it in the antique table's drawer. The air conditioner in the window overlooking West 8th alternately hummed and whined, competing with Dave Brubeck's solo CD, *Just You, Just Me,* on the dresser near her monitor.

"Did I do a good job?" Germaine asked, staring at a bit of plaster curling off the ceiling. She inhaled the scent of freesias she'd bought before Jock and she had snatched a cab to drive them here from her office.

"Not bad, princess." Jock scratched the down-the-middle part that divided his lush hair.

She twisted to kiss the stubble on his cheek. "Your semen always tastes sweet, crème fraîche with bite. Today I had no trouble swallowing you. No cramps. So the weekend in Santa Fe did *some* good."

"Yeah?" Jock reached down to squeeze a last drop from his penis.

"What's the matter?" Germaine asked. Hate, like a blade unsheathed, ripped through the closeness she'd been feeling toward him.

"You know damn well what's the matter."

"C'mon, darling!" She elbowed herself upright and scooted backward until her buttocks caved the pillow lying against the headboard. She crossed her ankles. "I had such a good time with you yesterday at Cirque de Soleil—cotton candy, the ferry ride, our restaurant. But it was my first day home, Jock. I was exhausted, especially after that incident in Santa Fe on the Plaza. I just wanted you to hold me."

"I did that. When you phoned on Sunday, you claimed you couldn't wait to make love."

"I couldn't, then."

"Couldn't wait because the Hacienda's owner had just showed you how to cum."

"If I said that, I lied."

"Huh?" He gripped one of her ankles and pushed himself to his knees.

She pressed her breastbone to calm down. "Maybe I didn't lie. The cocaine turned everything to *Alice in Wonderland*."

"I'm not into illegal drugs."

"I know about your brother. I just got curious to see what would happen."

"So seven-hundred-and-fifty bucks for nothing except a coke high, jamming a stranger's cock down your throat, and this?" He leaned over the mattress's edge to grab a bolo tie by its turquoise clasp. It lay atop the shirt and khakis he'd flung across the back of the armchair. "I never wear neckties."

"I wanted to bring you a souvenir."

"There's only one thing I wanted."

"Me, too!" She rocked forward to clutch his face but he dodged her fingers, lost his balance, and toppled to his side.

She started to laugh.

"Cool it."

"But you look so helpless."

"So maybe I'm the problem. You said his cock's a donkey's."

"Peeled zucchini is what I said."

"Huge, anyway."

"So? Size makes no difference. It wasn't yours."

"We should have taken that cab to *my* apartment. This place reeks of your mother." He wriggled forward as if dodging a sniper, reached out to grab the antimacassar, crumpled it, and tossed it at her.

She draped it over her crotch. "Sexy?"

"No."

"Give me a few days to decompress, darling. Then I'll come to your place and stay overnight, maybe two. After hot-tubbing. No more trying to make love at noon. It's too bright. I get embarrassed."

"Oh, come off it, Germaine."

"That's the phone."

"Don't even consider opening that drawer." He pinned her wrist to the mattress.

She shook her arm free but kept her voice even. "Maybe we should eat those sandwiches I fixed before walking to work this morning. And a nip of scotch."

"Good thinking." He rolled to his back and began to massage his balls as the phone's muffled ringing stopped. "Wouldn't surprise me if that was your mother calling to pick a lunch date with your dad. How cozy. Makes me thank You again, Lord, for killing off my parents with an eighteen-wheeler while they were heading into town. Smackeroony; gone. So grateful my uncle persuaded Mom and Dad to let him keep Lincoln and me home to grill us on what he told them would be the multiplication tables. Stud poker's what my uncle had in mind. I'll tell you what the real problem is with you and me."

"I already know that, Jock."

"Not only what your father did to you. I mean your mother's denial. She could have brought him to trial, opened the closet, have him locked in prison where he belongs. Or you could have. Still can, I'll bet."

She wagged her black curls no.

"Why not?"

"He never penetrated me and he did some lovely things before breaking off contact."

"Like what?"

She shook her head again and pressed her eyeballs with the heels of her hands.

"Daddy, Mummy, Germaine, intruder," he said.

"Intruder?"

He formed a fist as if hitchhiking and thumbed his chest. "Who wants to love you fully."

"You've said you do." How did we get pulled into this dead end again, she wondered?

"Impossible without—"

"Mutual orgasm. Oh, my God, the male's need: orgasm, orgasm, orgasm, orgasm."

"Simultaneous," he whispered to the wall below the corner windows.

"Everybody's got to cum at the same split second once a day, twice, three times. Women and men, men and men, men and sheep, men and you-name-it. Makes me puke." She leaned on an elbow to reach Jock's level. "Terrifies me, too, okay? The Hacienda's sex facilitator says you'll soon find someone who can explode with you on demand. Maybe you have. Judy, maybe?"

"Oh, boy." He swung his legs off the sheet. "I'm going to max the air conditioner, it's getting too hot in here."

She clamped his jaw between her palms, her right temple pounding. "Then you *have* slept with her. I knew it!"

"Let go, for Christ's sake." He jerked his head free, padded to the window, and twisted a knob, increasing the *whoosh* pushing through the conditioner's fins. His breath whooshed out as well. "It doesn't really matter if I haven't bedded her. You've somehow got to blame me for your inadequacy."

"You're the asshole who makes me feel inadequate! Oh, Jock, first the glare and now I'm embarrassed twice." Her breasts bobbled as she hid her face in her hands. "Oh, oh, oh, oh, fuck it!"

He moved close and bent to wrap her shoulders. "I apologize, princess. What are we doing? I love you and I haven't slept with your assistant."

She wiped her eyes and looked up at him. "You've never said that unless you're about to cum, do you know that?"

"Said what?"

"I love you."

"Well, hooray for me, a miracle." He lay a forearm across his hips, the other across his back, and bowed.

"Shall I make you hard again? At least I get wet before you go into me. Would you rather use my breasts? You still like them, don't you?"

"You know the answer to that."

She brought her ear to his belly. "Your stomach's rumbling." She pulled away and glanced at the old wind-up clock capped by a bell, her mother's. "Look at the time! I'm staying with you tonight. I'll pick up a vibrator from that video place on Tenth on the way over. We're going to make what you want to work, *work*, damn it."

She took his half-hard penis in her mouth, pursed her lips around the strawberry, then, swinging her torso, jumped off the bed. She pulled bra and bikini off her skirt and lavender blouse, and lifted a foot. "Lovely things my father did… when I was about to turn ten, I had a crush on a Jewish boy. My father hated Jewish, maybe jealousy that so many Jewish composers are famous, Philip Glass, Aaron Copeland, Meyerbeer, Mendelssohn, who else? Anyway, he told Mother I should invite whomever I wished to the party and that he'd provide the music. He followed through! Rounded up the drummer and bass and an alto sax he did gigs with. They jammed on a Sunday afternoon with no break for over two hours. Easy rock, some jazz. Daddy played piano. I think I'm going to cry again, Jock."

— — —

Two hours had passed. Germaine sat in her office at Bennett Books on the top floor of a gray-brick building on Fifth Avenue near West 17th. The *Times* lay unfolded between her monitor and the framed photo of herself perched in a high chair between her mother—hair bobbed, lips compressed—and her father waving a baton.

"Look at this, Judy!" she called out.

Her assistant, a year out of Yale, loped through the open doorway tucking strands of chestnut hair behind a close-set ear. She wore no lipstick.

Germaine caught herself wondering if Judy managed mutual orgasms. She read aloud, "'Not only have congressional auditors found *progress lacking in Iraq'*—note the tetrameter, my dear, and internal rhyme. 'Researchers also have discovered that bipolar disorder in children jumped fortyfold in ten years from twenty-thousand cases in 1994 to eight-hundred-thousand cases nine years later. No surprise. You have no kids yet, I'm guessing?"

What was that scent her assistant wore? Sandalwood? How Germaine despised her own jealousy. But at the moment she discovered herself wishing that, instead of hiring Judy, she'd promoted the office's older receptionist.

"No children, Miss Edwards." Judy faced her, tilting forward in a black dress hemmed above beautifully-dimpled knees. She'd clasped her Botticelli hands behind her buttocks.

"You know," Germaine said, "you can call me by my first name if you like. Your three-months' probation ended Friday. Do you *want* children?"

Judy shrugged shoulders much too bony, lifted a perfectly-plucked eyebrow, and smiled.

"Are you dating someone who does?"

"Mike's got three kids already—Germaine. I doubt he's interested."

Quit quizzing the girl! sped through her mind. Trust Jock, will you?

"Anything else, Miss Ed—Germaine? Oh! Jock called..."

The bitch easily calls *him* by his first name, Germaine thought.

"...to say he's coming in to sign the amended contract. Do you want a peek first?"

A peek? How'd that mosquito get in here? Germaine lifted the first dozen sheets of a novel that topped a pile of manuscripts. She folded the sheets in half and whopped the makeshift swatter against her copy of the 2007 edition of *Novel & Short Story Writers Market*.

Judy jumped, then smoothed her sheath over her hips as Germaine stared at the reddened ooze of the smashed mosquito smearing the annual's title.

She yanked a tissue from the box sitting beside a yogurt carton bristling with ballpoints and pencils, wiped the annual's cover clean, and pinched up the mosquito's corpse. "Here's hoping I didn't jinx this rather-famous author's first try at a novel. Her agent plans to send out multiple submissions if we don't want it. Why don't you give me your opinion? Just scan these few pages."

"Sure."

Judy swallowed—what do you know, she's got an Adam's apple, Germaine thought.

Judy grasped the sheets the editor held out.

"What about Jock's contract?" Judy asked. "You want to see it?"

"Well, I do have to sign it."

"I'll bring it in. By the way, my counterpart in San Francisco tells me on the q.t. that our west coast editor may move to Harper's, and that your name has come up. Any interest?"

What first flashed in Germaine's head was Jock's insistence that the caca in *their* punchbowl was her mother and father living so close by. She felt her forehead flush with ambition. Did it show? West coast editor! "That might mean a step up—"

"It definitely would," Judy interrupted.

Oh, she wants me out of the way, is that the agenda here? "I like New York," Germaine said. "And I have big hopes for you. I'm assuming you don't want to relocate?"

"Not so long as I stay with Mike. But three kids, especially his fourteen-year-old daughter..."

Germaine's private line suddenly rang and the red button began to flash. Jock? Her mother? Her father by some far-out chance? "You'd better shut the door, Judy."

"I understand."

Germaine waited until Judy had left before picking up the receiver. "Hello?"

"Germaine?"

The harmonics sounded familiar, a sort of growl. "This is she, yes."

"Arlene Joseph in Santa Fe."

The usual hum of traffic passing the trio of ginkgo trees fronting the building seemed to become a flash-flood's roar.

"Have you a moment?"

"Hold the line. I'll have our receptionist take my calls."

Germaine set down the receiver and moved around the desk, passing the conference table and four chairs. Her furled umbrella swung on its hook as she opened the door. "Felice?"

The older woman twisted around.

"Take messages, will you?"

Felice nodded.

"I'm back," Germaine said into the receiver.

"This won't take long."

"If you're calling to see if I'm planning a follow-up trip, I can't really say right now. I'd like to bring my boyfriend if I do."

"He's welcome, surely, though we'll need his SxCheck results. Actually I'm phoning about another matter."

"Oh?" Germaine pulled out a tissue and blotted her neck, though the vents in Bennett's suite of offices were emitting maximum cold air.

"As Fritz explained a few days ago, we donate most of the profits from Beautiful Tomorrows to charity, the majority to those who serve New Mexico's fifteen-thousand homeless."

"I remember." Was the woman summoning the nerve to ask for more money?

"To advance those contributions, but mostly to give our clients another opportunity to order visual mementoes—"

"Raven assured me that she deleted all photos involving myself," Germaine broke in.

"And I'm sure she did. Because clients tell us later, over and over, that they wish they could change their minds about photos, Germaine, we employ a back-up system at the Hacienda. Video cameras are installed unobtrusively in the living- and private-room ceilings."

"What?" Germaine slid her forearm up the *Times*'s front page.

"Killer-quality equipment, I'm proud to say."

"These cameras were running?"

"They were. We have some particularly arresting footage of you and my husband. As well as takes of your learning to snort Lady C."

"Oh, my God!"

"We're happy to send the tapes to you. UPS Next Day Air has proven the most reliable."

Germaine shut her eyes and emptied air into the receiver. "Destroy them."

"Well, no."

"I don't want them, am I clear?"

"Your boyfriend may be curious."

"He isn't!"

"Perhaps your employer?"

"My employer?"

"I'm hoping while we're talking that we can arrange a payment schedule."

"For what?"

A sigh sounded at the line's other end. "Germaine, I'm gathering you'd just as soon we didn't send the footage along. For you to buy that kind of insurance may seem costly. But, in addition to Good Samaritans like Fritz and myself, New Mexico's homeless have few charities to depend on for staying alive. Also, to remain current with top-of-the-line recorders requires a bit of loose change. Let's say—"

"Stop a minute!" Germaine clamped her palm on the receiver and massaged her left temple with the heel of her other hand. She stared at the orange umbrella. How jaunty—and protective—it looked hanging there by its bone handle. She took three quick breaths. "Let's say what?"

"Two-thousand dollars a month for twelve months and we next-day-air the tapes to your home. The end. Unless you'd like to make separate donations resulting from an upcoming visit with your boyfriend."

"Are you kidding?"

"Not at all. We have several clients—"

"This is blackmail!"

"You know, Germaine, that hurts. You're welcome here anytime. Raven especially would enjoy—"

A knock caused the umbrella to quiver.

"Yes?" Germaine shouted, not hearing the rest of Arlene's words. All she could think was, Are Jimmy and Pete getting calls, too? She had no idea what the men's last names were, only where they lived. Why hadn't she paid attention to the full name on Pete's library card? She couldn't recall if she'd told Jimmy whom she worked for.

Judy's hand, clutching a sheaf of papers, materialized past the door she'd pushed ajar. The obsidian lozenges of the bracelet she wore gleamed under the ceiling's fluorescent panel. "Jock wants to wait while you read this over and hopefully sign it."

"Hold on," Germaine said into the mouthpiece, scooted her chair back, and hurried over to grasp the contract. "Tell him fifteen minutes and I'll be out."

"How long have I to decide about this?" she asked Arlene, standing beside her chair a moment later.

"Does Sunday next seem reasonable?"

"Have I a choice?"

Silence at the line's other end.

"You're talking with Jimmy and Pete?"

"I'm sorry, I'm not free to discuss that. Have you got a pen?"

"I'm an editor, remember?"

"The number I'm going to give you reaches my office upstairs. I know we can work out something that we can all be comfortable with."

CRAVIN' RAVEN

Sunday 9 September 2007

"**W**ho you?" Dirk asked five days later, shirtless in white overalls, standing beside the threadbare sofa at the entrance to the refuge. He pulled his knife, Mahdi, from its scabbard and with the heel of his left hand smashed a gnat on his forehead.

Raven had returned from dropping three clients at Albuquerque's Sunport and, minutes ago, parked the van out of sight around the corner. She'd hurried past Kat's while finishing the burrito she'd picked up after exiting I-25 at Cerrillos.

Now, in Levis belted in pink to match her glasses' frames, she faced Dirk. Her halter revealed *Sixty-Nine & Counting* tattooed high on the shoulder that supported a burlap satchel. "Stow the cat-gutter," she said. "I'm a friend."

"A what?" Dirk cuffed his ear twice and twisted the stem of his Songbird hearing aid.

"Friend, friend!" Through a break in the thunderheads, the six o'clock sun glared past the flag fluttering above Kat's. Raven pushed her clip-on sunshades against her lenses. Who was this old coot with the flying hair? She badly needed a hit.

"Staying here?" he asked, holstering Mahdi. "Don't like the purple under those shining eyes. *Do* like the outfit."

That's for Boss to strip me out of—not you, turkey wrinkles. If I can stay awake. "Visiting," she said aloud, jumping at the buzz of a grasshopper that leapt from a bunch of buffalo grass. "Foreflasher's my pharmacist." She raised an espadrille-clad foot and brushed off a couple of red ants.

Two men holding a third by the armpits hobbled down the path leading from the camp where Dirk and the Native American family slept. Noise like drumsticks trying to batter a violin playing out of tune drifted from farther away. The tallest of the men, wearing a muscle shirt and cap worn backwards, bent aside the branch of a locust until the two other men squirmed past. Green and yellow gobbets that smelled like vomit hung on the T-shirt of the one being helped. So did what looked like clots of blood.

"Ho, Dirky," the plumpest one said. "Ovy here took his anticonvulsant with a half pint of mescal. Gotta get him to La Fam's fast, around the corner from Saint E's, see if Saint E's can put us up."

Dirk slipped a watch from his bib. "La Familia Health Center's probably shut for the night."

"Don't matter, Juan sleeps under the floor, he's found access."

The three skirted the substation's barbed-wire fence toward the Santa Fe Southern Railway's abandoned right-of-way. A gust blew Ovy's shirttail off a white fish belly ballooning above his low-riding jeans.

"Near closing time," Dirk told Raven and looked up through the limbs. "Want to be under my tarp before the downpour begins. Getting chilly." He rubbed bare nipples from which gray hairs waved.

"Flasher said be here by six-fifteen. Is that some kind of music I'm hearing?"

"Our resident composer and his Robin."

"Weird."

"Not staying overnight, then? Pass-name?"

"Cravin' Raven."

"Okay, he told me. Headquarters. You know the way?"

She nodded and proceeded along the path to Dirk's right—ducking under a branch, brushing rabbitbrush fuzz from her halter. By the time she emerged into the clearing she was panting. Her big toe smarted, having stubbed a boulder, and her chest ached. No comfort from Lady C since three this afternoon. She patted the wad of bills wedged between her breasts.

Flasher squatted over a grill in a black fur coat—fake or real she couldn't tell—though her van's thermometer had showed an outside temperature of seventy-six degrees. A circlet of rocks enclosed flames that licked the bottom of a kettle. The triangular-faced little man stirred with an aluminum spoon. A French Legionnaire's beret slanted over an eyebrow.

Hubcaps he'd lifted off parked cars garnished the edge of his and Tish's lean-to. He'd hung them so that, like now, they clanked when the wind blew. Tish's feeders lined the lean-to's open sides. Two black-chinned hummers flittered nearby. Tish filled the see-through cylinders with water sweetened by honey that Flasher stole from Wild Oats.

"Me, Foreflasher," Raven announced, retucking her hair into a French roll. The aroma of buffalo stew made her suck in breath.

"Welcome." He flipped his wrist to see his watch. "Right on time."

"Aren't you boiling in that coat?"

"Kat's shower wouldn't heat up, don't need me no head cold. Moseyed over to watch a docudrama on murderabilia. Ever heard a that?"

She wagged her head no.

A mottled mongrel, patches of skin shining near its hindquarters, wandered out between clumps of elm suckers. Flasher grabbed a rock and hurled it. The dog fled.

Raven walked close to the fire and hugged herself. "Those dweebs we service weekends do me in. They can't cum fast enough, or they cum too fast, or only want the boss, or Boss's wife because she has no tits, or me because I do. No one's asked to hump a dog yet. I'm crazy needing a touch, Flasher."

"Figured that, bubblehead. An' more for the Beautiful Tomorrows' gang-o?"

"I brought ten C-notes. Move it, will you?"

"Hey! You innerrupted me!"

"I did?"

"Oh, yes. My sis an' I—"

"You have a sister? Here I've been thinking you and I were lone wolves. Unlike you, your sister lives in a renovated apartment overlooking the Hudson, her hubby curates the sculpture collection at MOMA, their two chickies are enrolled at Brearley, and their rooftop's ablaze with pansies and petunias. Am I close?"

"What's that crap? My sister's none a your beeswax. Innerrupted me again!" He shuffled out of the coat and tossed it under the lean-to. She noticed some tattered armed-service bars pinned to his camouflage shirt. He'd rolled its sleeves to his biceps. A pack of Chesterfields stretched the cotton taut.

"Long time ago, Sis an' my mom was hearin' about the sixth-grade friend I'd made, a blond kid with a little gold ring right here." Flasher pinched an earlobe. "His folks had just moved from Detroit to the Duke City an' he'd asked me to spend overnight. Mom's sayin', 'How nice,

Nathaniel, I'll phone his mother,' when Dad, the Grand Pooh-Bah, butts in. 'All steamed up to play footsie with a faggot, are you, Nate?'"

"Jesus, Flasher, why telling me all this? I'm about to fold." She hoisted the hundred-dollar bills from her halter. "Where's the stuff?"

"I empty the pepper shaker into Pooh-Bah's coffee can an' later slash two tires of his truck, the ass humper. That's what these awards are for," he said, slapping the service bars on his shirt. "You know what those C-notes of yours invest in?" He rimmed his lips with his tongue.

Raven threw her palms up.

"A Duke City mansion I bought Mom after Sis an' me figured how to put the Pooh-Bah underground. Mom's also got herself a gardener an' a maid. You don't mess with Flasher."

"I'm dying here, Flasher."

"Patience, bimbo." He sauntered to the double-wide sleeping bag, extracted a lunch sack, and waved it at her. "As I was sayin' 'bout murderabilia, turns out the belongins of serial killers make hot sellers on the Web. Like the startin' bid for a hubcap from Ted Bundy's Beetle that the FBI had impounded, thirty-five hundred clams. He was fried eighteen years ago for stranglin' sumpin' like fourteen girlies, one, then another, then another."

Flasher pretended to choke himself, at the same time tightening his hold on the lunch sack.

Raven sank to one of four directors' chairs as the Ford and Chevy hubcaps hanging near her banged. Flasher dragged close a crate topped by a broken windowpane. A dozen finches, crowns glimmering red in a moment of sun, flared up from their rabbitbrush hideaway.

"How much for the gorgeous hooker?" he asked, sitting.

"Me?"

He looked around. "Don't see nobody else, do you?"

"Quarter gram."

"I'm feelin' generous." He dumped the contents of two bindles onto the broken pane, pulled a paring knife from his shirt's inside pocket, and began to chop. He covered the cocaine with his hand as wind whistled through the clearing, sending the *Courier*'s business section, which he read daily, into a patch of ricegrass.

Raven let out a long sigh.

"Do it up, girl." He fished out his own Franklin, rolled it tight, and gave her the makeshift straw.

She leapt at the glass and knelt, wincing at a pebble's sharp pain. Her black hair tumbled down as she thumbed a nostril closed, clamped her lids shut, and inhaled. Her heart started to race. She changed nostrils and leaned in to snort the rest.

"Lord, thank You, oh yes." She keeled over onto her satchel, shifted, and stretched out on her back, staring at the leaves that seemed to have changed into gargantuan lily pads, rising and falling on pond water. She threw her legs wide and cupped her vulva. "Someone's playing a lullaby."

"Happy, bitch?"

Raven smiled, relishing her bed of goatheads and shards of quartz.

"You want a cock in that cunt and I'd say let's do it 'ceptin' my antidepressant mostly keeps me limp. Besides, I don't like to cheat on Tish."

"I'm a sucker for lullabies," Raven murmured, visualizing Fritz's tongue stretching to lap up the sweetness on her palate. The heel of one hand pressed her jeans' zipper while the other roved from nipple to nipple.

"Get the hell up, let's do business an' I'll escort you over to meet Q, our composer. 'Bout time anyways for Tish to take the sofa from Dirky. Gonna dump big-time. You can smell the rain. C'mon!"

She let him tug her elbow before rising, sure the hand was Boss's. Flasher picked burrs off her sweater and slapped the dust from her butt.

"Hunnerd bucks a gram. You said ten? Make that fourteen, you buy regular—twelve cuz I've weighed an' wrapped the blow into quarter-grams—'an I'll throw in the double hit for you. Better go steady yourself against that tree trunk, though, 'fore we move on."

She complied, crotch buzzing, brain scheming how to get Arlene to leave the Hacienda tonight. She wanted Fritz for herself. Arlene, go buy me some Extra Strength Tylenol, I passed a head-on above Cochiti. Arlene, go buy us a fudge cake from Wild Oats, I witnessed a decapitation.

Flasher shook his lunch sack onto the jagged pane and counted out forty-eight bindles. He was coaxing a Chesterfield from the pack when Raven came close again and stuffed the little packages into her satchel. He squeezed the hot match out between thumb and finger without wincing.

"Foreflasher, listen, I gotta get back." She handed him the C-notes. "Boss's wife leaves me the dishes."

He stuffed bills into his back pocket. "Fuck her, Cravin'."

"That's what she's hoping."

"Hey!" He jabbed a nostril closed and, snuffling, shot snot a foot in front of his boot, then did the same from the other nostril. "You want Flasher's prices, you 'cept his invitations." He pulled his coat off the sleeping bag, slipped into it, stepped to the grate, lifted off the kettle, and threw handfuls of dirt on the flames.

She followed him along the path, grinding her teeth, swinging her elbows, kicking at bottles he stepped across, blinking away gnats that swirled in the smoke his cigarette left behind. He gave her no warning of the badger's den that angled down from the right, almost trapping her foot.

She recognized only Tish in this second clearing, which was far neater than Headquarters. Quentin had lopped off some of the Siberian elms' low branches and found quilts from the giveaway tables at St. Elizabeth's to spread on the ground. Raven brushed a beginning few raindrops from her cheek and stopped fifteen feet from the lean-to on the far side. Two ponytailed men, one with gray whiskers, sat cross-legged on a tarp. The younger one balanced a keyboard on his thighs.

A third, tanned and bare-chested, perched in a beach chair. His two front teeth made him seem a gopher. A single desert sunflower drooped from an Odwalla fruit-shake bottle filled with cloudy water. It sat snug in a holder fashioned at the end of his chair's arm. From the dirt he lifted a pint of Bacardi Gold, put it to his mouth, tilted his chin, and swallowed.

A crack of thunder made Raven jump.

Flasher hugged himself in his fur. "You met Stormy Weathers, Cravin', our war hero? Back last January from dodgin' car bombs in Iraq. Stormy done missed the burnin' of Old Man Gloom at the ballpark Thursday, an' the kiddies marchin' their doggies yesterday, but balls if he didn't see the whole Hysterical Parade this afternoon. What float you like best, Storm Born? Tell the girlie."

Stormy hung his head and wagged it from side to side.

"What you done now, Tish, scared Stormy stupid after him an' Q went through all that heartache to make up?"

Tish perched on an overturned U.S. Postal Service bin in a flounced red skirt and pullover she'd fashioned from a sack of beans. "Beat it, fartface," she told Flasher, "and haul that rag doll out with you. We was having a good ole time stompin' to this boy's music."

Flasher shook his finger and guffawed. "You tryin' to upset me, Tisher? Can't be done, right, Cravin'?"

Tish yanked a short length of vinyl clothesline looped and tied at each end from under her pullover. She gave Flasher a grimace and, gripping each loop, snapped the line taut.

He jerked out his paring knife and pointed its tip at her. "Manners there! You an' me needs to keep our secrets *secret*."

She wedged the clothesline back between her skirt band and tummy and pulled the sackcloth over it, then pumped her forearms at him like a drum majorette.

He turned, squeaking loudly, "Everbody, this here's Cravin' Raven, a businesswoman. Buzzy Wuz? Play her somethin' of Q's that's screechy, she's kinda been Miss Pushy." His ruby, opal, and white-sapphire-ringed fingers vised Raven's upper arm.

"Screechy, Flasher?" Byron asked.

"*You* figure it out."

Dirk limped into view. "Tish's shift," he said, approaching. "What's going on here, Flasher?"

"Not your concern, Dirky. Buzzy, play, like I asked you nicely."

Lightning zigging through the darkening branches silenced their talk. Raven wrenched her arm free and stepped back as Byron pressed a couple of buttons at one end of the roll-up keyboard. He flipped pages in Q's notebook, then leaned it against a stump. His head wagged like a metronome as organ tones, honking like geese, raced up the scale. He stabbed a button to produce twittering and stabbed two more to create a dissonant basso continuo. The noise brought to Raven's mind the locomotive slowing for the station near her childhood home.

"Whew!" Dirk exclaimed.

"Darn tootin'! Double time." Tish pursed her lips and started nodding to the fractured rhythm.

"It's going to pour, Flasher," Raven said. "I gotta go."

"Hey!" He threw his thumb over his shoulder. "We copped us a porta toilet down in the willows by the creek bed for that."

"Stop bugging me! If you had to put up with the kooks we scam, you'd show a little compassion. The Josephs pay me peanuts." Now she discovered she did need to pee and began shifting from foot to foot. She noticed gopher mouth staring at her.

"Look at this mane of mine!" she blurted to Flasher. "It used to glow. Take a look at this skin." She pulled some flesh from the side of her elbow. "Hippopotamus hide. I want to go home!" With her wrist she swiped away tears welling from frustration.

Stormy clamped his lips across his teeth and, walking over, hauled a gingham handkerchief from his pocket. He extended it to her but yanked his hand back. "Wait. This other's cleaner."

She took the other, smiling.

Now Dirk came close. "What kind of scam were you talking about?" he asked her quietly.

"Is this dude safe?"

"Long as I'm superintendin' this snake pit," Flasher said.

"Okay, then. We bring in the haves from around the country for a weekend of sex, margaritas, and cocaine. Then we blackmail them. Our ceilings hide spy cams."

"Who's 'we'?"

"My boss and his wife, though we're all involved."

"And they get richer while you get nothing."

"They claim our proceeds go mostly to charities for the homeless. Like Kat's."

"No kidding!" Byron exclaimed.

"But you don't know that's true," Dirk said.

"Nope, I don't." She handed Stormy his handkerchief.

"I spent years uncovering scams in the Middle East for the New York Times," Dirk asserted. "Would you like to make sure that the homeless get taken care of and that you get a decent slice of the pie?"

"Huh?"

"Blackmail them."

"The homeless?"

"Your employers. Legally, you're prostitutes. That's a misdemeanor. So is possession of cocaine—a felony if you cross state lines to sell it."

"Ruff ruff," Tish barked.

"Blackmail them how?" Raven asked, then gasped as she understood. The only back-up videotape she lacked was of Boss doing lines.

"Dirky, you got yourself an idea there," Flasher said. "Turn the spy cams on them."

"Oh, gee, oh, gee, go do it, Pushy," Tish added.

Flasher shoved his fur cuff up and consulted his watch. He pulled a vial from his pants, shook out a pink tablet, and stepped over to curl Tish's fingers around it. "You got some water there, Storm Born? Time for my sweetheart's anti-freak-out med."

The Iraqi-Freedom veteran handed Tish his canteen. "The idea's not complicated enough," Stormy told Dirk. "You shoulda heard the schemes we cooked up to talk Syrians into sneaking us out of Baghdad."

Flasher rubbed his chin. "Cravin', girl, you're gonna need protectin'. For a cutta the proceeds, natch. Go ahead an' accompany Tish to the sofa. First ten minutes with alprazolam, she's dingheaded. Hand her the pistol, Dirky, and gimme your knife."

Thunder boomed and with it came the first regular pattering of drops. Wind rolled an empty can of stout along one of Quentin's quilts. The mutt Flasher had scared off came bounding across the camp, upsetting the chair Quentin had relinquished to take his roll-up keyboard from Byron and slip it into its nylon pouch. The dog vanished along the path leading toward the Native Americans' camp. Their part-husky began to howl.

"Anyone got an extra umbrella for Tish?" Flasher asked.

"I found a couple on Saint E's table yesterday," Byron said. He walked toward the lean-to, its corners braced by an aluminum strut and single elm branch.

Dirk pulled the snub-nosed .38 from his overalls, handed it to Tish, and released Mahdi for Flasher.

Now the rain pounded down, jerking leaves on the ground as if they'd been shot. Raven nudged her satchel's strap close to her neck, opened Byron's umbrella, and clasped Tish's hand. They began to run. The heels of the Raven's espadrilles slapped the new mud.

———

The van's bumper sticker, *Slow Down for Beautiful Tomorrows*, had no effect on its driver—Raven careened south from Alta Vista onto Luisa, then west onto Columbia as if the storm were an oncoming tornado. Her glasses were fogging up. She timed her blinks to the wipers' swings. The tips of the Hacienda's cedars swayed like giant antennae as she passed the coyote fencing. The tempest had turned the hollyhocks black.

Flasher had given Raven a brainstorm. So far Arlene had not attended a single Fiesta event. Tonight's candlelight march from the Cathedral, she recalled reading in the *Courier*, ended Santa Fe's weeklong gala. Well, yes, it was raining but evening storms usually didn't last here long. How persuade Fritz's wife to take off?

Raven wrenched the wheel again under the cobra-headed streetlamp at the corner of Ybarra Lane, and stomped on the brakes. The van skidded sidewise behind a pickup parked at the opposite curb. Lucky break—Raven watched Arlene, a quarter block away, gunning her BMW backward out of the drive. Its rear tires spit gravel as the garage door ground its way down.

Raven switched off the van's engine. In a moment the headlights darkened and she rested her forehead on the wheel, chest heaving. Arlene going where? And for how long? Fritz, too? Raven had seen only her. She doubted Arlene had spotted the van. The BMW's taillights receded. Raven turned her engine back on, angled down the street, and slowed onto the drive.

She stepped out to the rattle of raindrops on the garage's tar-and-gravel roof, leaving Byron's umbrella in the van. Was that the stereo playing? The living-room's Roman shades glowed as she marched over the fragments of slate set into the path, and unlocked the front door.

To her left, Fritz looked up from the wraparound sofa. She wiggled her fingers at him and approached under the arch. Fritz wore his usual khaki shorts and moccasins, though tonight's flowered black silk dangled unbuttoned all the way. A rectangular bottle of José Cuervo Black Medallion Añejo and a blue tumbler sat on the coffee table. Electronically enhanced violin and oud—one of Fritz's favorite tracks from *Sahara Lounge*—shook the loudspeakers.

Raven walked over to lower the volume, looped her satchel over the neck of the wire nude riding the unicorn opposite the stairs, and returned to slouch in the chair beside the grooved table. She kicked off her soaked espadrilles. "What's up with you, Boss?" She plucked out the comb and shook her hair. Drops of water darkened her halter.

He emptied his tumbler and refilled it halfway. "We fought."

"Oh?" Raven felt glee inflame her face and hoped he didn't notice.

"She wants a 135i sports coupe. She wants a weekend to shop in Albuquerque—"

"With me?"

He shrugged. "She wants to buy a hidey-hole in Belize."

"My, my."

"Where have *you* been?"

"Buying backups of Lady C. When's the wife heading home, you think?"

Fritz stuck out his lower lip. "An hour. Two? Never? Thinks she's going to march with hoards of merrymakers up to the Cross of the Martyrs."

"Seems appropriate. But the idea's all wet."

Fritz didn't return her grin.

Raven combed fingers through her long, black waves. "What do you know, we're alone."

"While you were gone," he answered in monotone, "that editor, Germaine?"

"Yeah?"

"Phoned Arlene. Wants to fly out next weekend with her boyfriend. Says they'll bring along the first two grand."

"Watch out, Boss."

"I thought you liked her."

"She may be a little too smart for us. What about the dweebs, Pete and Jimmy?"

"Payments arrived Friday."

"Sufficient?"

"What is this, a quiz?"

"Now we have *this* weekend's three pigeons to go after."

"We? Not we yet."

You bastard, Raven thought. "I could use some of that good stuff!"

she exclaimed, jumped up, skipped over, took the tumbler from his hand, bent over to thrust her tongue into his mouth, tasted onion behind the amber-colored, forty-dollars-a-bottle añejo tequila.

"Dangerous, Rave." He licked his lips, then rubbed the skin where the barber two days ago had shaved away in a ramrod-straight line the gray fuzz at the back of his neck.

"Dangerous, yep." She drank. So much richer than the tequila plata they served guests.

"Arlene ran out because I wouldn't watch a replay of some Belgian broad win her second US open and become—ho hum—the greatest woman tennis player in history."

"First come, first serve, Boss. You stay right there." She freed her satchel, walked across to the slider masked by a pleated shade, pulled it open, stepped into the downpour, and smacked the slider shut.

When she emerged from the casita, she had changed into fuzzy slippers and pajama separates, pink-striped bottoms and a sleeveless knit top. The rain thudded onto a black umbrella adorned with sparklers, stars, and rockets. Her right hand fisted two bindles and half-straws and the necklace she'd been saving to make Fritz hers, though not—until tonight— to betray him.

Lightning above the Hacienda's parapet made her hunch her shoulders. A thunderclap followed. She hurried along an iris bed to the farthest bedroom, pushed in the door, and dropped her umbrella on the rug. She ran to the closet and reached on tiptoes to nudge up the spy cams' master switch. From the dresser she added a condom to the bindles and a twisted-hemp string of amethyst beads, large as grapes, that she'd picked up in Istanbul on a tour touting her prize-winning porno film.

The shade trembled as she heaved the slider open, wedged the umbrella through, and stepped back inside the living room.

Fritz remained staring at the Zuni throw, chin propped in his palm.

She set her treasures on the grooved table and walked over to turn the CD's volume up. She placed her glasses beside the necklace and, to Zeid Hamden's Lebanese reggae/trip-hop mix, brought the hem of her top above her head and tossed it onto the chair.

Her slippers were icing her toes. The rain had bunched the nylon fuzz into tiny pink spears. She yanked the slippers off.

"Wanna dance, sailor?" She hoisted her breasts and sashayed left and right to where Fritz waited, lowering her chin to plant a kiss.

"You're crazy."

Like a fox, she thought, took his wrists, placed his palms on her boobs, and squashed them with her own hands. "Crazy for you," she said aloud. "Gimme that bottle."

He handed her José Cuervo's best and, tilting it, she gulped a couple of slugs.

"Rave, I'm pretty darn sure she'll be back."

"It's time our feeling for each other came to a head, Boss. If worse comes to worst, I've got the ultimate out."

"What's that?"

"PBC."

"What's that?"

"Boss, your needle's stuck. Hold on, I'll show you."

She jammed on her glasses, heaved the slider wide, and ran barefoot to the casita. He watched the rain slick her black waves.

When she returned, she was grasping a small, brown bottle.

"*Hola, mi amigo.* PBC." She shut the door behind her. Water dripped from her chin. Grinning, she held the bottle high and shook her hair.

"What is it?"

"Phenobiconal. Barbiturate—goofballs! Bluebirds! Thirty years under glass. An old john gave them to me five years ago in the Big Apple. Unused. His doctor switched him to a benzodiazepine because, guess what? Barbiturates like PBC bring a too-easy death, euphoric, one, two, three, ten and you're out. The lungs say that's it, bye-bye." Raven snapped her fingers. "If Arlene nails what we're about to do, and you're game, we split these babies up and hey, Romeo and Juliet. I keep them safe in my fridge.

"Aren't you tired?"

"Nothing the Lady can't fix."

"You're sopping!" Fritz grabbed a throw from the Saltillos.

"Leave me alone—no. Stand up. I want to meet Junior.

Sighing, he rose and she reached to knead his crotch. "Apologies. I meant Senior."

He laughed before saying, "Everything's gone rotten, Rave."

"Not us."

"I'm sick of Beautiful Tomorrows. You gorgeous whore."

"I'd rather…" She reached for his zipper and jerked it down while grasping his khakis' clasp. "Pull that monster out."

He grappled with his briefs until the hard-on and its wrinkled attendants sprang free.

"What's that tattoo mean?" he asked, pointing to the words, *First Burn*, above her navel.

"Abortion. When I was sixteen. Boss? You've been such a good boy all these weekends. I'm going to show you why bad's better. Come with me."

Still dripping rain, she led him by his erection to the low table. She pushed at his shoulders and knelt herself, unfolded the bindles, reached for the paring knife hammocked in a hankie strung Friday to the table's underside, and began to chop the cocaine. She shuddered happily to feel his fingers worm between her pink-striped thighs. Be my friend, she prayed to the spy cam above, and, using the knife, maneuvered the white grains into two grooves.

"You've watched Arlene and me do it. The slant end's for the Lady. Fear not, it's cut with talcum." She handed him a half-straw.

"That necklace looks expensive. What's it for?"

"You."

"Me? How come?"

"Uh oh!" She sniffled hard.

"Now what?" He raised his head, the cut straw swinging from a nostril.

"Think we've got a leak."

"Shit!"

"Hear it? On the tiles below the TV."

"I'd better go grab a bucket." The straw dropped from his nose to the tiles.

"No, no." She pressed his neck down. "Half a line each nostril, like this." She snorted the groove empty, licked her pinky, drew it along the groove, and rubbed her upper gum. "Now you do it."

Suddenly, with a muffled boom of thunder, the lights winked out.

Zeid Hamden's Soap Kills band went silent, as if thrown from a cliff. The refrigerator stopped humming. Son of a fucking bitch, Raven thought, the spy cams have died on me, and I don't care. She grabbed for her glasses. "Sniff it up!" she commanded.

"I can't see."

"You don't have to see. Why does this keep happening here? You and Arlene paid big bucks for this shack. A backup generator should have come with it free."

"Hasn't happened for a month."

"I'll get the candles."

"Only need one."

"I know that!" She got off her knees. Lightning zigzagging between the spruce and cottonwood lit the room and she scurried to the glass-doored cabinet holding Arlene's grandmother's dishes. She yanked open its lower doors. The coke had dilated her pupils, but she spotted candles and matches standing in their incised bowl.

"You remember how I told you?" she asked, returning and holding a lighted taper near his face.

"This is stupid, Rave."

You aren't kidding, she thought. "Pick up that straw and do the deed before I ram this torch up your rear end," she said aloud.

"Ouch!"

They broke into giggles as drops continued to dribble off a ceiling latilla.

"Soon you're gonna be one happy dude."

"Yeah?" He bent his head, snorted his line, and sniffled. "Zowie."

"Told you. Motherfucker!" She threw down the candle and snuffed it with her hand.

"Now what?"

"Hot wax hurts. Get out of those clothes—no, I'm gonna do it. But me first." She stood in the new dark, untied her pajama strings and, gripping the edge of the armchair's seat, freed one leg, the other. She drew her bikini over knees, ankles, and heels, kicked it off, sidestepped to the sofa, felt for the bottle of añejo tequila, clutched its neck, and swallowed.

"That hooch's making me dizzy, whoo," Fritz said.

She stepped close to haul him up by his armpits, rubbed her nipples against his chest and her nest against his dong. His chin dropped to her shoulder. No way—she needed her areolas licked! She backed him to the table, peeled off the shirt strewn with red hibiscus, and undid the longhorn buckle. Though his zipper was down, two buttons still held the ends of his waistband. She yanked them apart. A button tinkled into the vase on the floor holding gladiolas; the other bounced off her thigh.

His khaki shorts fell to his ankles.

"Stand up!" She pushed at his briefs.

"You'll break it!"

"Sorry." She pressed the fleshy, eight-inch bowsprit to his belly, stretched his briefs' elastic over it and down. "I've been waiting nine months for this." She cupped a breast and thrust it at his face.

"Umph."

"Lick."

As he did, she began to squirm.

"That nipple ring's cold!" He backed away. The clothes that had bunched around his ankles nearly toppled him. "What time is it? We'd better dress, Rave. I'm dizzy."

"Lick this one."

He managed to obey.

She kicked the sealed PBC aside. "Do you have to go potty?"

"Potty?"

"Potty, potty. Defecation."

"Why?"

"Not telling."

"Don't think I do."

"Then get free of that junk."

"Junk?"

"What's left of your clothes."

He stooped to shove moccasins, shorts, and briefs from his feet.

"Down on your fists and knees and keep that trophy dick frantic." She pinched the necklace's silver clasp. "Last year my boyfriend and I did this to win Best Interracial. Spread your cheeks, Fritzy Witz."

He lifted his fists from the Zuni throw and, balancing on his knees, inserted his pinkies at the corners of his lips, pulling them into a grin.

"Not *those* cheeks, dum-dum." She moved behind him and patted his ass.

He reached to stretch his buttocks apart.

"Trust me and relax." She bent to twist the necklace's beads into his rectum.

"Oh, jeez!" He began to pant.

She left the clasp and last amethyst showing and stepped around to face him.

"Prostate heaven," he wheezed.

"Purgatory, Boss. You'll see." She felt her juices flow, further wetting her thighs. Massaging one areola, she knelt in front of him. They gazed at each other, coke-and-booze-entranced. Neither blinked.

"Straighten your spine," she murmured, lowered her face, and thrust it forward until her lips had engulfed his strawberry and two-thirds of the veined shaft. As she started sucking, she snaked a hand around and slowly drew out the beads.

His chin hit his chest as if praying with angels but he groaned like a man seared by flame.

She stopped a moment and backed off. "Good?"

He answered by squeezing his eyes shut and wrenching his lips into a grimace.

She had pulled the sopping necklace almost out.

"Soon?"

He managed to nod.

She speeded up her milking until he gushed. Rearing, she pumped his shaft with her hand and let the rest of his spunk ooze through her fingers. She took his temples between her palms and, tonguing his lips apart, spit the warm mix into his mouth.

They tumbled sideways together onto the Saltillos.

Within half an hour he lay supine, his condomed erection inside her. She rode him slowly while he licked whichever breast she told him to, the ends of her hair grazing his chin and collarbone. They paid no attention to the rainwater dripping through the plastered ceiling, splashing the puddle that grew.

Nor did they hear Arlene pull into the drive next to the van. The BMW's headlights, igniting what had finally turned to drizzle, made the garage door's white slats glitter.

Arlene thumbed the remote. Nothing. The sedan's exhaust started seeping through the floorboard. She coughed and punched the remote — uselessly. Dead battery? She thrust the car door wide, unfurled her umbrella, and slammed the door shut.

She realized when she turned the key that Fritz, or Raven, had left the front door unlocked. Electricity flooded the circuits just then, and she heard recorded voices sing out among a flurry of drumbeats and the thump of an electric bass.

Lights had sprung on in the living room. She passed under the arch to see a candle abandoned beside her wide-eyed husband, who lay under the still-humping facilitator. The tip of Raven's tongue dozed on her lower lip while she attempted to grind out yet another orgasm, goggling at the gladiolas upright in their vase.

Fritz had thrown his legs apart and arms akimbo past his head. His white-gold wedding ring glimmered; his hairless chest barely moved. Water had spread from near the glass-doored cabinet and passed Raven's umbrella to where it bathed his buttocks, calves, and heels. It drifted toward the bottle of Phenobiconal.

Arlene watched a couple more raindrops add to the puddle before letting fly her first shriek.

GREEN-EYED MONSTER

Monday 10 September 2007

"**Y**o, bub," Kat called to Byron the next morning, emerging from her bedroom to find him and Vonnie laughing together in the great room. They sat cross-legged on one of the two doors that would soon serve as dining tables. "You really want to help out here? Leave off the chitchat. Vonnie's got her job-and-housing-possibility chores, there's a lunch to set up, and I've got to make nice in an hour to nail down new funding."

Kat finished tying a scarlet bow that matched her shawl to the end of her braid. She threw it back over her shoulder. The day's blouse, embroidered with bougainvillea, had been a gift from her partner before leaving Kat's bed three years ago, unwilling to help transform the home they'd bought into a shelter for street people. At least she'd agreed to keep paying her half of the mortgage, though today at noon would be the first time since then that they'd meet.

"Clara!" Kat shouted, advancing past photos in the short hall of Kat's daughter, murdered in her early twenties. "Haul your ass into the kitchen. I can't smell potatoes frying and I can't smell no eggs. You work out 'Bonnie Lies Over the Ocean' on that piano later."

Kat stopped and scratched her neck hard where a spider had bit during the night, watching her intern and Byron lift a third door. Universal Cosmic Divinity, a new guest whom the other homeless had dubbed Uni, preceded Dirk from their room. Earlier, Dirk had accepted Kat's invitation to take the other of the two bunk beds vacated by a father and son. The men's guest room, aglow under twin skylights, had been Kat's partner's painting studio. In those days Kat's granddaughter had slept in what was now the women's guest room.

Uni wore a sheet like a poncho. He hefted a sawhorse while Dirk, clad in his white overalls and a yellow T-shirt, hefted another. They followed Byron and Vonnie onto the roofed front porch, half lit by the morning sun.

Kat cupped her hands around lips painted pink for today's lunch with the Josephs at her former partner's café. "Bub, don't you stay out there with her."

Byron returned to the great room past the screen door. He wore a scavenged shirt and Levis cut off ragged at the knees.

Kat reached for his bare elbow. "I'm thinking of bringing a second bunk in. I'd like to give you and Q a shot at saying yes at sleeping here. But you have to show me you can handle chores."

"Sure we can!" 'Byron exclaimed, eyebrows rearing. "I'll go talk to him."

Quentin had propped his shoulders in scattered shade against the apricot that loomed halfway between Kat's garage and the giveaway table piled with hangers, clothes, and shoes. He sat on a folded bedroll. His pack and tied-up sleeping bag rested next to Byron's roll and bag. Through the leaves, the sun's rays dappled his blue corduroys, threadbare at the knees. The brim of his rain hat kept his nose and eyes in full shadow.

As Byron crunched along the drive, Quentin's left fingers drummed staccato on his hip. He moved his head as if dodging bullets, humming in jerks while his right hand scribbled along the staves of his notebook. Byron noticed a tome he'd never seen spread open beside Quentin's leg. Sweat dampened Byron's armpits as he came close and squatted to have a look.

"What've you got there, Q?"

"Herr Alfred Blatter's *Instrumentation and Orchestration*. You know it? My whores have decided they want a piece titled *Sonata for Cello, That Sexy Chanteuse*. Like it?" A wrapper from a mocha-chip energy bar blew against Quentin's ankle and, bending, he grabbed it and crumpled it into his shirt pocket.

"Good title, yeah. But how come you've been hiding Blatter from me?"

Quentin pursed his lips and pressed his forefinger against them. He clenched his eyes, nodded, opened them, and wrote down a succession of chords.

"Fucking tritones," he said. "After lunch you've got to show me how they sound." He dropped his ballpoint and clamped his ears. "Hell's broth—that's enough! You bitches quiet down."

"I've never talked about my wife much to you," Byron said.

Quentin blinked at him. "What's that have to do with anything?"

"Wait—we met at the San Francisco Conservatory of Music where Val and I took a semester in Blatter. She kept shouting 'Right on!' in class and the director urged her to apply for a Fulbright. Pissed me off so I got her pregnant late one morning after we'd smoked some weed. Married a few months later in a park at the end of Golden Gate Bridge. Impregnated her again after I started teaching in Santa Fe at Prep. Our third, Michael, appeared two years later. I wanted to exhaust her with kids—and *me* to be the musician. Nothing I'm proud of. But I couldn't stand the bedlam of three children screaming and I hated Blatter by then. Shit-and-a-half gnats!" He swished his hand back and forth across his face.

"You came outside for a reason?"

Byron kicked out from his squat and sat hugging his knees. "Vonnie wants to record our stories this afternoon."

"Hmmm."

"She says an hour and a half max for the two of us."

"It's too hot to sit still that long, Buzzy."

"Look, you want feedback on your music from me and *I* want to help her complete her research for the thesis."

"First you play this."

"Of course I will."

"So what else?"

"Something big."

"Go ahead."

"Kat hopes to get another double-decker bunk inside. She's inviting you and me to use it."

Quentin gazed at his companion and sucked his lips between his teeth. "You just have a hard-on for her."

"Are you crazy?"

"I don't mean Kat."

"Oh. Vonnie has her own apartment. Near Wild Oats."

"She's invited you there?"

"No, no."

Quentin pulled his rain hat down till it bent his ears. "I love our life outdoors, making faces at the moon when I can't sleep."

"Dirk's inside now."

"So?"

"You guys seem to be hitting it off."

"That old dude's a pain in the ass. Unhealthy and has a bad temper." Quentin's graying ponytail swished as he clapped his hands to his ears. Byron swiveled his gaze south to the vacant land bearing the Public-Service-Company-of-New-Mexico substation. A bulldozer had just gunned its engine and was burrowing a blade through the cheat grass. The truck that had carried it in waited beside a dump truck. Two motorcycles suddenly roared from Kat's neighbor's drive and looped around the street's dead end before accelerating north.

"You want to move closer to all that? Besides, Buzzy, we've lucked out as fugitives for three weeks now. Especially you. Your wife's suing for alimony, the college lawyers want you, your landlady…well, mine, too. But New York's history and three thousand miles away. Though I suppose by now we both have bill collectors. Why haven't they found us? Because we're in the urban wilds is why. We'd be a lot more exposed in Kat's Harbor. You want to go to jail?"

"You haven't told me where you've been hiding Blatter's book," Byron responded.

"Wrapped in foil in a hole I dug beside my sleeping bag."

"I might have enjoyed looking through it, you know."

"You said you hated the damn thing."

"That's a few years ago." Byron rose and brushed off his cutoffs. "I really want to move inside, Q. Doubt Kat'll talk. I'll ask. Gotta go help her now with pre-lunch chores."

But he did not cross the gravel apron to the sweet clover that flowered against the kitchen stoop. Instead, he retraced his steps along the drive past the warped table where two men and a woman pawed through hand-me-downs.

Beatriz was watering geraniums on the porch, an iPod clamped to her ear. Vonnie sat with her laptop at a door supported by sawhorses in a dark-and-light-green-striped tank top and sweatpants rolled to her calves. Pamphlets lay scattered to her right. Universal Cosmic Divinity leaned toward her from a folding chair as Byron passed the next in line, a scowling Stormy Weathers.

"I'm wondering if you and the head lady might spring for a rower or spin bike," Uni said to Vonnie, flapping his sheet to stay cool. "I need to keep in shape for when the call comes." He sprang up and somersaulted between the table and the porch's white end railing. His black nylon briefs and black canvas high-tops glimmered in the sun. On landing, he pulled three tennis balls from a pocket in his sheet and began to juggle them, keeping two in the air while batting the third with his cropped head.

He stowed the balls, sat again, and grinned at Vonnie. "Didn't know your houseguest was so talented, didja? How 'bout this?" He ducked to reveal on his scalp a purple tattoo of a sword piercing a heart and the words God Slept Here. "When I'm drinking I have no money, when I'm not drinking I have no money, when I'm…but cash is on its way. Only need to stay fit, only need—"

"Mr. Divinity," Vonnie broke in. The forced smile caused her upper gum to shine. "I understand from Mr. Flasher and Reuben Lightningfeather that you've left a dog in the refuge that's running loose and causing a bit of anxiety. If you'll tie it up or build an enclosure, I'll talk to Kat about obtaining an exerciser for you and our other guests."

"Why can't I bring—"

"Rules, sir, I'm sorry, pets aren't allowed indoors." Vonnie twisted a sheaf of hair around her forefinger.

Uni flipped his thumb back at the New Orleans refugee, Chiffon, the African-American who waited at Stormy's left. The white mouse she'd bought for five dollars peeped from the pocket of her faded blue dress. "She has a pet!"

"And until Friday to give up her bunk or find the animal another home. You're here now to look for interim work. Let's see what we can find online."

"I'm a street artist, I just demonstrated!"

"Perhaps you can also type?"

He wagged his head as if shaking off water. "Can cook some, can plant flowers."

"Well, there you go." Vonnie glanced at Byron, then rubbed her eyelids. "First, Mr. Divinity, I note we're keeping some medications for you. It's time to take your milligram of Haldol."

"It's the dose before bedtime that Mixmasters my mind. Nightmares about my two kids. Horns blaze. Headlights blare."

"I'll call La Familia Health Center and see if we can't cut that dose in half.

"I'd be much obliged, dear."

As Uni washed the pink tablet down with lemonade, Byron stepped around the table. "Did you bring your tape recorder?"

Vonnie nodded.

"Q has agreed to give his story after lunch. I'll shower meantime and then let's tackle mine."

"I'm surprised you could persuade him. I think he's gotten jealous."

"You're right."

"Because we're both freckled? Because you taught math and I was an undergraduate math major? Probably because we both love to watch Formula One smashups. Like Robert Kubica's in the Canadian Grand Prix last June? Wasn't that right out of *Clockwork Orange*?"

Byron laughed. "Q's jealous because you and I are clicking." He grasped the handle of the screen door and disappeared. Chiffon, barefoot, followed him inside.

"All gone!" Uni cried, clapping his nearly empty glass onto the plywood. "Let's get me a job somewhere."

"I been homeless longer than this flapping teepee," Stormy Weathers blurted. "I need my meds, too. Especially with that rain. I had to sit most of last night in the portable crapper Flasher copped for us from somewhere, holding my bag and bedroll like the six-year-old cripple I held once in Kirkuk."

Uni squinted behind him at the mustachioed man wearing a long-sleeved shirt, its buttons gone, and a sombrero over a Capital Motors cap. "Your turn's coming up," he said to Stormy. "The Lord provides."

"Listen, cupcake," Stormy persisted, "soon as a bed opens up, I want it and *deserve* it. Fair?"

"Jango, Mr. Weathers, stop shoving," Vonnie said. "The bunks are full up for a while. Two weeks ago you said clonazepam made your left arm shake. You went a couple of days without it and then tried to tear off Clara's ear after she'd been shaved for chemo. You told us women with no hair were witches, you remember? Mr. Divinity and I need to finish up our business here."

Inside, Chiffon and the chubby Beatriz had started to fold napkins on the first door Byron and Dirk had set on sawhorses. Beatriz still wore her iPod. From the kitchen came the whir of the fan and the scent of potatoes frying.

The two men had already carried three easy chairs and one of the sofas to the wall between the guest bedrooms. "You and Q," Byron said to Dirk, waiting for the septuagenarian to limp to the second sofa's end, "seemed to get along pretty well yesterday."

"Your pal isn't much of a conversationalist. Spends most of his time courting whores nobody else can see. Unh!" He pressed the small of his back. "Though I don't like to talk much myself these days. Most of it seems like prattle. To fend off isolation? Don't like to drink much anymore, either. My woman south of Socorro swilled herself into a mortuary oven after an eagle snatched up her Pekingese down at the Bosque del Apache."

"A lot of information from a man of few words," Byron commented.

Suddenly, Beatriz screamed.

"Pissant, that crazy broad from New Orleans is at it again!" Dirk exclaimed.

Chiffon, toothless, grinned over at him and knelt. Beatriz grabbed a fork and scampered after Mighty Mouse, who was streaking toward the second sofa. He disappeared under it.

"Here, Mighty, honey; here, Mighty." Chiffon extended her clawlike right hand. "Does need his exercise, Dirky."

"Quit calling me Dirky."

"Flasher does it."

"Flasher's different."

"Honeybunch, then. Gentleman. Here, Mighty."

Beatriz shrieked again as the mouse skittered past her. Chiffon cupped her hands and began to coo but Mighty veered under a sawhorse, white tail stiff as a spike, and rushed into the kitchen, triggering a yelp from Uni.

Clara came running out—golden bristles wrapped in an orange scarf, face gleaming in sweat—and Beatriz smacked into her. The blow wrenched the iPod from the eleven-year-old's ear. Chiffon bent to help her up and pressed the child to her potbelly. Beatriz was shaking with sobs. They shuddered together as Clara slammed herself inside the women's guest room.

"I gonna go grab him," Chiffon announced. She had spied her pet quivering among salt-and-pepper shakers gathered in a corner of the kitchen counter. Mighty, however, black eyes as shiny as the bob Kat had given Beatriz before breakfast, watched the African-American release the girl. The instant Chiffon lunged, the rodent leapt to the counter's edge and scampered down a cupboard door onto the worn linoleum and out.

Chiffon and Beatriz emerged from the kitchen to see the fold of a blanket emerge under the guest room door—Clara was taking no chances.

At Beatriz's first shout, Kat had delayed dashing from their bedroom in hopes that Vonnie would take the lead to defuse whatever the new crisis was. But the intern had heard nothing. She and Uni had moved down to the table of cast-offs to choose a looking-for-work outfit less astonishing than his sheet.

At Beatriz's second cry, Kat was applying mascara to her lashes. She feared being late for her meeting with the Josephs if she smeared and had to start fresh. So, cursing Vonnie, she finished putting on her face.

"¿Qué pasa?" she bellowed now, swinging her purse and briefcase, marching into the great room in patent-leather flats with black bows. The tightness of her best skirt's hem forced her to take short steps.

Byron and Dirk had squatted to pick up the napkins Mighty had upset, but they rocked back, stood, and tiptoed away when the mouse decided to use napkins as his next hideout. Only the pet's twitching tail showed as Dirk arced his forefinger to beckon Chiffon and Beatriz near.

Kat, huffing, got there first, and seeing the tail protruding, yanked her braid around to her bosom. At the same time Vonnie opened the screen door and gestured for Uni—who cradled slacks, a shirt, two pair of underpants, and a handkerchief—to precede her. Stormy came in close behind them. All formed a rough circle around Mighty's retreat. The napkins trembled each time the winded mouse breathed.

"Chiffon," Beatriz whispered, "I'll go get the big strainer for a net."

She had half turned toward the kitchen when she stammered, "Abuelita, no, what are you doing?"

Kat had set her purse and briefcase on the varnished planks and taken a step forward. She had lifted her left foot, raised fleshy arms like a dancer, and was pile-driving her heel onto Mighty's cover.

A single squeak—more a whimper—followed the crunch of bones cracking. The straight tail whipped into a circle as blood and brown mush and a loop of intestine squirted out. The napkins nearest the floor turned red.

"No pets," Kat growled, shaking. "Vonnie, go get me a rag."

The homeless crowd scattered. Byron tripped on a sawhorse but managed to lurch upright.

Uni dropped the clothes he was carrying, tilted his chin up, crossed his thumbs against his forehead, and prayed to the ceiling's latillas, "Bless this mouse heart that has stopped pumping in Your service, necessary sacrifice to bring peace in Your name, Lord of all and probable Creator—"

"Oh, shut up," Kat barked. "Vonnie, move it, I'm late."

The intern sucked in her breath and hurried with her laptop into the kitchen. "Eggs are turning dark, Kat!" she yelled. "The skillet's smoking."

"Clara's problem—where the hell is she? This mess *here* stinks, too. Get that pan off the burner and turn on the vent—stop it, child!"

Beatriz had started pummeling Kat's hip. Chiffon had sunk into one of the armchairs pushed against the northern wall and spread her legs. Her tongue wet her lips clockwise, counterclockwise, clockwise, counterclockwise.

"I said stop! Kat exclaimed. "It was *necessary*." She vised Beatriz's wrists and flung the small hands with their violet nails outward.

"I hate you, Abuelita!" Beatriz shook free and ran to the slouched Chiffon, who hoisted her to her lap and pulled her to her chest.

Byron and Dirk were lifting a door onto their sawhorses when Vonnie returned with a dishcloth. Kat grabbed it, slipped off her shoe, and wiped it as clean as she could. A bit of the mush stayed caught in the bow. She re-shod herself, picked up her purse and briefcase, grasped Vonnie's elbow, and guided her to the front porch. "I'm sorry about the mouse. Sweetheart."

"Don't say sweetheart—it's inappropriate. And *I* just told Buzzy I love smash-ups. Oh, jango!" Vonnie started to weep. She covered her bowed face with her hands.

How Kat yearned to hug her close. "Spend an hour with Beatriz on those polynomial or whatever-they-are equations, will you? Please? I mean it, I'm sorry. We need more help here or I'm gonna have to throw my granddaughter into public school. I'll be back by two, unless she throws a fit, then call my cell and I'll cut lunch short. Look, there's Flasher and his girlfriend. Let's hope they're clean-and-sober for lunch. Or give them something to eat under the apricot, will you? Without that bozo keeping order in the refuge, we'd have a lot more trouble at the Harbor."

— — —

Fritz and Arlene Joseph arrived early at the Patio Café—near what locals called the Roundhouse, New Mexico's capitol—for their quarterly meeting with Kat. They had not spoken during the short drive over. Arlene's tunic of appliquéd bachelor buttons scattered among red and yellow stripes, plus rainbow-striped capris, hid her fury at discovering that Fritz and Raven had fucked each other last night. The facilitator was *hers*.

Arlene opened the picket gate to the Plazuela de Compasión fronting the café. In two rows, pansies and violas paraded their brilliance near a coiled hose. Filigree-iron tables and chairs surrounded a massive maple planted a century ago in the property's four-hundred-year-old well. A tin pennant, *¡Bienvenidos, Gastrónomas et Gastrónomos!*, swayed like a weather vane from a low branch. Above, juncos and finches tried to out-sing each other.

Arlene clicked the latch shut before Fritz could follow, and was feeding quarters to the *Courier*'s vending machine when Fritz reached her.

"I'll see if Kat's inside." He slogged in moccasins, khaki shorts, short sleeves, and silver chain toward the adobe's arched entrance. His outfit included a white handkerchief whose points sprouted from the shirt's pocket. Everything seemed so happy-go-lucky except for the collar that he'd buttoned down.

Arlene was staring at the sports-section's headline, *Red-hot Woods Birdies to BMW Win*, when Fritz emerged. He passed a man and woman in matching boaters leaning forward from their chair-backs to kiss. The brim of the woman's hat knocked his to the table. Her eye muscles crinkled plum-colored liner as they laughed together.

"Zeet! Kew-kew," sang the black-headed junko atop a trumpet vine in the mini-plaza's far corner. Fritz sat opposite Arlene and cleared his throat.

She did not look up.

"Kat's not here yet."

"Get out of my hair," Arlene replied, plucked a purple aster from one of her streaked ducktails, and threw it to the bricks.

She yanked at her emerald-encrusted ring. "I'm recalling when you gave me this. Goddamn horror won't pull off." Her eyebrows sprang up. "'Open marriage?' I asked you. 'Not unless we figure how to profit by it,' you laughed. 'We both grew up poor,' you said. 'Our parents cheated on each other and split, but we're smarter than that.' Oh, you bet! 'Stay monogamous, stay in love, and investment banking'll make us rich.' Robin Hood and Maid Marian, you said we'd be. What beautiful hair you had then, and you were such a liar, and I the fool to suffer through two face-lifts."

A lanky, flat-chested woman in a barber-pole-striped apron strode out. Below her slacks, her thick-soled sneakers squeaked. A brightly enameled pendant swung from only one ear. "*¡Bienvenidoth!*" She then asked if they'd like something cool to start, after handing them plasticized menus. Arlene ordered hot coffee, Fritz a gin fizz.

Sedans marked *State of New Mexico* and pickups plied the dirt alley running past the café. The noise of motors mixed with birdsong to envelope the silent Josephs, plus chatter from a family who'd appeared. The man, head shaved except for a black crown, opened the gate for two children and a woman using a cane.

Fritz sighed. "Arlene…"

"You think I want to hear anything you have to say? Unless you want to share when you plan to have our roof and ceiling fixed and the tiles underneath regrouted. Or know where Raven's gone to."

"Her note said she'll bring the van back tonight." He stuck out his lower lip.

"Means nothing."

He stared up into the leaves, grasped the rolled brim of his new Stetson, removed it, palmed his graying crew cut, gripped the back of his neck, and pinched his lips vertically between thumb and forefinger.

The aproned woman in the squeaking sneakers returned with their drinks. "*¡Buen gutho!* Are you ready to ohdah?"

"We're waiting for a third party," Fritz said and gulped down half his highball.

"Would that be Katrina?"

"You know Kat Ulibarri?"

"Used to very well. Last saw her three years ago. She called this morning."

"This is our first time here," Fritz said.

"I'm the ownah."

The aproned woman left to ask the family of four, "Inthide or out?"

Arlene sipped her coffee. "Bitter," she muttered. "I may head back to Lansing, pull Mother out of that nursing home."

"Don't know if I'd go that far," Fritz quipped in monotone. "Do know I'll understand if you decide to."

"And wouldn't you like that, you and Raven? Though deep down I've decided you're probably a fag."

"Bisexual's closer." He found himself focusing on the coral-and-silver pendant dangling between Arlene's almost-nonexistent breasts, the half-dozen strands of turquoise surrounding the pendant, the gold bracelet he'd given her studded with coral, turquoise, and malachite. She looked like one of those mannequins at Sanbusco Center. Yet making her nipples swell used to inflame him. He swallowed at realizing how he'd hurt her feelings last night.

"Our coke whore wouldn't stay with you long, anyway," Arlene said. "If *I* decide to stay, I want one of those new 135i sports coupes shipped over from Leipzig."

"You said that at breakfast."

"And you've done nothing about it."

"Give me a chance, Arlene!"

"I want a metallic silver 135i upholstered in red leather and four outfits to go with it. I want a cabaña in Belize. And now that you've discovered what Lady C can do, I want you to get Raven so wired—assuming she does come back—that you can persuade her to spend the night with me."

He started to nudge his Stetson around the tabletop. "Spend the night where?"

"Upstairs."

"While I—"

"Check into a motel. Solo."

A lowrider, its muffler removed, accelerated past.

"A cabaña," he repeated, "and a 135i and—"

"Raven," she said.

"We'll have to scale down our charities. I'm not sure I'm willing...."

"Then I leave you and hire a barracuda. I know a couple in New York who'll strip your bones so bare you'll be rapping on Kat's door by Thursday begging hot lunch and a bunk."

"Raven has backup videos of you snorting snow," he said, kneading his eyes.

"I have plans for her, too."

"Which are?"

"Wouldn't you love to know. There she is."

"Raven?" His knee knocked the underside of the filigree-iron top.

Arlene guffawed and fluttered her fingers toward the gate.

Kat swayed toward them. The end of her braid reached her waistband as it swung back and forth. "Hi, there!" she called in a false-hearty voice, glad she'd found tissues in her purse to scrub her flat's bow clean.

Arlene grinned as Fritz stood and shook Kat's hand, tiny for her girth. He pulled a chair from the table and she sat, rising halfway when the screen door slapped behind the café's owner—who carried cloth napkins, menus, and glasses of water for the family of four.

"Hey, you," the aproned woman called to Kat then, striding over and placing a menu down. "Long time. Doing well? I read in the *Courier* once in a while about goingth-on at the Harbor."

"I'm struggling." Kat flicked olive eyes at hers and lowered them. "But doing heart's desire. Painting still?"

"Mornings when I can."

"Always did have more talent than time. Have you introduced yourself?"

The woman shook her ponytail.

"Marta Fitzheimer, meet Arlene and Fritz Joseph. These good people help fund the Harbor."

"Hello!" Marta extended her arm. "How about refillth?"

"Yes," Fritz said.

Arlene waved her head no.

"Katrina, for you?"

"Iced chai."

"That hasn't changed."

Kat pulled the sides of her blouse out from her waist. "I've put on weight."

"You look fine to me." Marta shrugged and left.

"First time here for us," Fritz said again, feeling constrained as a trussed holiday turkey.

"The same." Kat leaned over to lay her briefcase on the bricks, unsnapped its catches, and took out a folder and legal pad.

"I decided it was time to bury the hatchet," she said. "Marta and I were lovers for years. She still pays half my mortgage. We met as nurses in the psychiatric unit at St. Vincent. But outside the hospital she wanted nothing to do with the poor. She grew up in a three-story house, not in a van like me. Her folks owned three cars. She inherited a wad when they passed on."

"Let's have a look at this menu," Arlene said. So Kat was gay. And Marta had money.

Marta returned with another gin fizz and Kat's tea. Fritz ordered homemade tamales with *calabacitas*, Arlene a burger made of Pecos Valley beef, and Kat a farmers' market salad.

A couple of finches hopped near. Kat bent down and made kissing sounds at them, hoping to relieve her guilt at crushing the mouse. Relax, she told herself. If Beatriz throws a tantrum, Vonnie will call.

A gust swirled leaves past them.

"So how is everything going?" Fritz asked.

"I brought the six months' interim with me."

"Got a copy for us to take home?" Arlene asked.

"I try to remember always to bring you a copy." Kat displayed it.

"At our June get-together," Fritz said, "you talked about wanting to expand, hire another intern, shore up the garage, add a toilet and sink, move the men out there."

"Maybe it's these mideastern wars our country's started," Kat responded after thinking a moment. "Or maybe losing so many jobs to South Korea and China and India. Whatever's causing the anxiety, I've got too many squabbles breaking out at the Harbor. Could use three interns for discipline and chores and case management. We need a dress code and mandatory showers. Food in the bedrooms disallowed. More emphasis on finding jobs."

"I've kept my trap shut until now," Arlene blurted, "but adding plumbing to a rebuilt garage as well as personnel won't come cheap. We don't have unlimited funds. In fact—"

"Simpler if I do the talking, Arlene."

Arlene shoved fingers through one of her gelled ducktails and glared across at her husband.

Kat summoned her best baritone. "We can cut costs by admitting only the homeless with skills—carpentry, plumbing, wiring, tile work. Flavio up in Española says that his shelter's getting ten percent more applicants this year than last. So are we, at least that."

"Fuck Flavio," Arlene said, "and I'm going to talk my little head off, Doctor. We check everyone out, Kat. Nine years ago Flavio was jailed after trading heroin for sex with a sixteen-year-old female. Even Lydia Myers at Battered Families down in Albuquerque was skimming money to play the horses in Ruidoso before her cook turned her in. The gal who runs La Communidad up at Taos did three years at the women's facility in Grants. She'd been laundering building-permit kickbacks at the blackjack tables in Pojoaque. Received them as mayor. Play ten thousand, lose six thousand, clear four thousand. We fund only you, Saint E's, the Salvation Army, and the Coalition. Finis."

Arlene swept her palm low over the table, retrieving it in time to miss toppling her tea.

Before Kat could decide how to answer, Marta appeared with a tray holding their lunches.

"All Patio Café specialtieth," she announced, setting platters embossed with red and green chiles in front of the trio.

"You with anyone these days?" Kat asked, scratching the spider bite on her neck.

Marta shook her head. "You?"

"I'm raising Beatriz."

"How old now?"

"Eleven. Would be starting sixth grade but I'm still homeschooling her. She don't need the drug culture, the filthy language and violence. Though her fits have gotten worse."

"I'd like to thee her, Katrina."

"I'd like you to. Maybe all of us need to catch up."

"Call me, will you?"

"There may be someone," Kat decided to say, wondering if she could stop Vonnie from returning to New York.

"Thomeone?"

"I'll explain later."

"Be a good idea. Enjoy your meal, folkth." Marta squeaked back over the bricks.

"I guess it really hadn't sunk in that you're lesbian, Kat."

"Arlene," Fritz exclaimed, "what the hell! Maybe she's AC/DC. Like, as a matter of fact, a man and wife sitting right here we know pretty darn well."

Kat managed to keep her voice even as she asked, "Is learning that I'm a gay woman going to be a problem?"

"I'm not sure," Arlene said.

"Here's the report." Kat handed it to her instead of Fritz. "And here's an as-is balance sheet, and a second one reflecting the hoped-for increase. As best I can calculate, by boosting our interns to three and using homeless labor on the garage, what we need before January is thirty thousand dollars. That's in addition to what you're so generously sending every month."

No need to share that, beside sending money from coke sales to his mother, Flasher gave Kat a thousand a month to keep cops out of the refuge and to let Tish believe she was helping Kat and Vonnie homeschool Beatriz.

"Jesus H. Christ, lady!" Arlene exploded. "You think we're the Gates Foundation?"

Fritz felt sweat build in his armpits and the near corners of his eyes. "I'm not sure we can do that, Kat."

"Goddamn right we can't!"

"Give us a few days," he said. "I've got some ideas my wife doesn't know about."

"What do you mean 'my wife doesn't know about'?"

"We'll e-mail you before Friday, all right?" Fritz said. "Hey, I bet that salad's warming up." He smiled as best he could, stabbed a slice of zucchini capped by two cowboy beans, and, raising them halfway to his lips, noticed Arlene's stare. "That burger of yours is starting to rot," he added.

THREE'S A CROWD

Tuesday 11 September 2007

Cold air purred through the vent above Fritz and Arlene, who sat slouched the next morning at nine before emptied plates in the nook of the Hacienda's kitchen. White cloudlets, like inflated balloons, hung in the sky outside.

Still in her satin robe, Arlene had not bothered to gel her ducktails, even to wash her face. She stared out at the neighbor's honeysuckled fence and sprawling Russian olive across Ybarra Lane, cheekbones pressed into her palms. Fritz sat catercorner at the table's end in work boots, a shirt stained with motor oil, and Levis ripped on one thigh.

"At least our slut brought the van back," Arlene muttered as if speaking to no one. She looked down at the day's *Courier* scattered between them. "More cover-up by General Petraeus—six hours of feeding Congress lies. Nothing about how fast Iraqis are abandoning their homes. As I may mine, after the 135i you finally ordered arrives from San Diego. At least the sports world has good news. Can you imagine? Tiger winning sixty trophies in—"

"Arlene," Fritz interrupted, and said nothing more.

She had flipped up the sports section in front of her swollen eyes. "Sixty trophies in just eleven years? And look at this. Roger Federer collected his twelfth Grand Slam at Sunday's US Open."

"What are you doing, please? We've got decisions to make before Raven shows her face and I get up on the roof. Phone calls ruin the rest of my morning. And that letter I promised Kat."

"Another thunderstorm expected this afternoon..."

"Stop it!" Fritz slapped his palm on the table.

Eyebrows soaring, she turned and squinted at him as if sighting along the barrel of the derringer she kept upstairs.

"I've got some ideas," he said.

"Do you." She twisted her pinky in her ear.

"Everything was too raw yesterday. We can start fresh now."

"The hell we can, buddy boy."

"Our broker says your new car's not a problem."

"And?"

"Nor the outfits. Add a couple for Rave."

"Wouldn't you two love that."

"I heard you promise her a week ago."

"Umm hmm. Before you and she—"

"Right." He bunched his jaw.

"I wonder where she drove off to yesterday," Arlene said. "*You* seem to have bounced back nicely from your Sunday revel. I think I'll have you rent yourself a motel room two or three nights a week—our gorgeous slut needs my care. If I stick around."

Fritz snuffed phlegm into his throat and swallowed. "Starting now, Raven and I make the decisions," Arlene said. "You're the handyman. Who this afternoon needs to rip out those tiles in the living room."

"You just whisked yourself to Oz, babe."

"Oh? I may decide to rescue Mother from the nursing home and break your financial legs. Male prostitution is a crime. We've got backups of all the videos locked in the den."

"I know that! You're on tape for *everything*. I've never done cocaine," he lied.

"Those half-straws on the floor Sunday were for root beer? Didn't want to record your coming-out party? And what was the brown bottle I noticed lying on the floor? The label said pheno something."

"I guess sedatives she takes."

"With booze? Sounds dangerous."

"Helps with sleep," Fritz said. Not a total lie.

"She's never told me about them. Gotta ask—so what are your big ideas? Not that they're worth much more than Enron common."

Mind whirring, Fritz waited while his heart slowed. Next time Raven took off somewhere, he'd go with her—he wanted those amethyst beads! He'd do more lines of coke with her, you betcha. But they needed to figure out, after fleeing, how safely to frame Arlene. "Here's what I'm proposing, babe," he said in monotone.

"I'm not your 'babe,' Fritz. Arlene'll do fine."

"Arlene, I'm proposing this." He shut his eyes to regain control. "Beautiful Tomorrows pulls back to giving half of what we've been donating monthly to the Salvation Army, Coalition for the Homeless, and Saint Elizabeth's. That way we can afford Kat's request for the extra thirty grand."

"Who's our resident nutcase now?"

"I assume we're agreed Rave's got to hang around to keep Beautiful Tomorrows viable," Fritz said.

"We could find someone else."

"But you don't want to."

"I want bed time with her!"

"She's still what you called her yesterday, a coke whore, right?"

"Something like that."

"You'll never get her into a twelve-step program, Arlene. You heard her the other day."

"So?"

"I think she's buying her snow from someone Kat helps out."

"What makes you sure?"

"I'm not sure! What I said was *I think*."

"So maybe the best way to keep Raven from ratting on us is to keep Kat happy?" Arlene asked.

"Yes."

"Flimsy figuring, donghead."

"Kat's ambitious for her street people," Fritz said. "And she's buttoned-down financially."

"Buttoned-down?"

"Responsible. Look at those reports she gave us yesterday."

"Handing her thirty grand is your best shot at a good idea?"

"For now, anyway." Until Rave and I can figure how to slog out of this mess, he thought.

"*Bad* idea. Raven will think so, too."

Fritz clamped his teeth.

"You want to know why bad?"

He shrugged.

"Throwing thirty grand away does nothing to make this world a better place. And I miss New York. If I have to choose between Belize and the City, I choose a little place off Washington Square."

"Plus parking for the silver streak."

"Naturally."

"Our Santa Fe haven for the sexually challenged is starting to seem like a dungeon for the Marquis de Sade," he said. Hoo, that's good, he thought. I'll tell Rave.

"It may become a dungeon if she doesn't clean her act up. You can't trust addicts."

"Which you aren't," Fritz said.

"Damn right which I aren't."

"Whaddya know, we're agreeing. How about this, then? We stop serving cocaine Saturdays and Sundays."

"I kinda like the Lady," Arlene said. "And when I phone guests to arrange payments, it doesn't hurt adding that of course the videos show them snorting snow. Besides, even if I leave you, wouldn't you rather do this kind of work than go back to Wall Street? Just think, you and the cokehead partnering, no me."

Two raps sounded against the door, though it already stood ajar. Raven filled the opening, holding a videotape against her thigh. She'd gotten herself together in the fuzzy pink slippers of Sunday night, plus an old blouse hanging over short-shorts. No amount of self-abuse could change the shapeliness of those legs. Behind her glasses, though, the bags cradling her eyes were as black as her penciled brows. Her shoulder-length waves of hair fell tangled.

She brought the back of a hand to her nose and snuffled. "I ended up in Taos yesterday for some blackjack at the pueblo's casino. Peanuts. Hung out at the Apple Tree for dinner, watched a street performer's white mouse ride a cat riding a dog, did a lot of thinking, got home late." She took a breath. "Arlene, I betrayed you Sunday."

"Not late-breaking news, love."

"I feel pretty awful about it."

"Because of that or too much coke?"

"That. I also meant to betray you, Boss. A bunch of guys in the refuge—"

"Didn't I tell you?" Fritz blurted to Arlene.

"Told her what?" Raven licked her upper lip.

"A private matter," Arlene said.

"I have a friend who's hurting," Raven lied. "She lives with the refuge guys. I bring them leftover food from our weekends." She hung her head, then raised it. "That's not what I came to confess."

"More?" Arlene's plucked brows lifted.

"Sunday, I was upset. About my salary. My friend in the refuge said to blackmail *you* two. We've got backups of Arlene doing lines but nothing with Fritz. So Sunday night I turned on the cameras. But lightning blew everything out. So this is blank." She held the tape aloft. "There, I've said it. What are you going to do, can me?" She scrubbed her lips with the turquoise ring on her thumb.

Fritz worked his jaw muscles as Arlene attempted a guffaw that sounded more like a nicotine fit, though she didn't smoke.

"I'll be in the casita until you decide on a course of action." Raven turned and disappeared, barely lifting her feet.

"Well, husband-in-name-only?"

His elbows knocked the tabletop and he braced his temples with his fingertips. "I have no idea."

"Spilled them all? I've got an obvious one."

"What's that?"

"Get rid of her."

"Rid of her…"

"Shut her up permanently, but not before I get my night. Have you ever knocked anyone off?"

"No! My God!"

"Ever hired it done?"

"What do you think?" Fritz asked, incredulous.

"Not a clue."

"Of course I haven't hired anyone!"

"Might be an interesting exercise."

"Why not just smother her after you've both cum?"

"She's stronger than I am, Doctor. Kat must know someone in the refuge we can pay. Or to show us a nifty way to do it. Maybe use that sedative Raven keeps."

Fritz pushed his hands along the edges of the *Courier*. Had Rave truly meant to blackmail Arlene and him? She might try again—they were definitely worth the risk. Their 2006 Federal Return had showed something like an adjusted gross income of a million bucks. Add a million five for the Hacienda.

His mind suddenly did a double take. "Show *us* a way to do it?" he asked Arlene.

"Us, yes. So that neither can set the other up for life and forget parole."

"Therefore, Kat gets her thirty grand."

"Ummm, don't know yet. Right now we go tell our dear Raven how much we appreciate her honesty and that we accept her apology, that we don't want to lose her. Then you take me shopping and then you buy me lunch at, let's see—El Chamiso."

"El Chamiso's ten miles out! Plus being outrageously overpriced."

"Indeed."

— — —

That same Tuesday morning in New York at Bennett Books, rain attacked windows that looked from the top floor across Fifth Avenue at a newly scrubbed high-rise. Jock faced Germaine at her desk where a bouquet of dahlias that he'd brought in sat. Germaine's assistant, Judy, had carried the vase from the kitchen and placed the vase between two stacks of manuscripts.

Jock presented himself in a short-sleeved, blue-striped, oxford button-down and khakis; Germaine wore her black skirt and ruffled white blouse, and, as usual, had kicked her flats off under the desk. Jock's umbrella angled open on the carpeting while her orange one, dry—she'd arrived at seven before the storm began—hung on the shut office door.

She pursed her lips. "I take it we're in sync, then? You'll add interviews with two or three radical Muslims, including the Shiite head, Mustapha al-Uraibi in Florida, to counterbalance what the moderates have told you? Jock, the manuscript also needs, up front, an expert's guess of what percent of Muslims the radicals comprise in America."

"More work for me."

"And I've signed off adding ten thousand to your advance and extended your deadline to April."

"Okay, princess, okay, fret not."

Acid spurted up Germaine's throat. She shook out a couple of Tums, downed them with the last of her third cup of coffee, and reached into a drawer. "Take a look at this clipping Mother sent me from the Friday *Times*'s 'Weekend Arts.'"

Composer Disappears
Quentin Edwards did not show up last Monday for his first semester of teaching at the Third Street Music School Settlement. Well known for his leadership in adding aleatoric elements to traditional rhythms and harmonies, Edwards was last seen mid-August in Santa Fe, where his To My Daughter *premiered at the High Mesa Music Festival. Citing his despondence at losing a chance for tenure at the Mannes School of Music, Edwards' ex-wife fears the worst. Santa Fe police have been alerted.*

Germaine retrieved the clipping, careful to avoid the dahlias. "Mother phoned Rudi Shasky, the Festival's director, who said he'd written Dad a check for two hundred dollars. A man Dad had picked up stole his wallet."

"Surprise, surprise, as Bennett Books' most tyrannical editor loves to put it."

"People walked out of the concert, Jock. The director claimed Dad had raved about needing to find freedom for his whores."

"Huh? He's been pimping?"

"Mother says he calls his muses whores. She thought she might hire a private detective but I'm going to ask her not to. Let's see if we can change flights to go a couple of days early to look for him ourselves, okay? Even if he's, you know, dead. He's got to have left some kind of trail. We'll start with Shasky. I want to reconcile with my father! It may prove the key to opening me up sexually. For you, darling. I wonder if he's still got a goatee and those fingernails."

She watched her boyfriend fidget. "What's the matter?" Her right temple continued to throb.

"Maybe the third largest art market in the country has a mosque, Santa Fe style. I've yet to interview any Muslim painters. While *you* go search for your father. I have no friendly feelings toward him. I'm afraid how I might respond if we met. Just you and me trying to persuade the Beautiful Tomorrow owners not to nail you seems like plenty for a weekend. You're bringing the two grand?"

"Yes."

"Cash?"

She nodded. "Oh, my head." She massaged the back of her neck, disheveling her curls.

The doorknob turned, smacking the wall before Judy burst in. "Matt rang! He wants to see you."

Germaine winced. "You don't knock?"

"Apologies. Hi, Jock."

He twisted his torso to face her. "Hi, good-looking. Where you been? Love that necklace."

Today Judy displayed, in addition to the all-black lava-glass bracelet, a necklace of the same obsidian flecked in white. She wore a creamy sheath belted with a chain, as if dressed early for a gallery reception. A silver comb secured her updo.

"I'm sorry, Germaine. I just got excited for you."

The editor's cheeks heated and she discovered herself grinding her teeth. "What's Matt want, anyway? All he has to do is walk across the hall."

"C'mon, he wants to formalize the offer in private. I'm not positive but Shirley in San Francisco gave me a heads-up earlier and made me promise to keep my trap shut."

"About a move," Germaine said softly.

"Move? Promotion! Bennett Books' West Coast Editor!" Judy set her hands on bony hips.

"I'm feeling bushwhacked, people. There's too much going on. When does he want to see me?"

"ASAP but for sure before lunch."

"Tell him I'll be over in an hour."

"Will do!"

To Germaine, Judy's fluttering her fingers before closing the door seemed a gesture for Jock.

"What's this mean?" Germaine held her hands up and flapped them.

"Huh?" he asked.

"Two huhs in five minutes? Judy, waving tah-tah to you."

"Being friendly, I suppose."

"You stay away from her!"

As if he hadn't heard, Jock made a fist and hoisted his thumb. "Congratulations, kiddo."

"Don't know if I want to move. I need to find out the terms."

"Damn right you want to move, princess."

'So you and Judy can—"

"Oh, come off it! For Christ's sake, she's dating someone."

"With a fourteen-year-old daughter who Judy tells me is a hellion."

"I wouldn't know."

"And I don't believe you. Wonder when Matt wants me to start."

"Don't look at me."

"Does San Francisco appeal to you?"

"Everyone loves the city by the Golden Gate."

"You'd come out with me?"

"New York's home base, princess. Resettling three-thousand miles away might take some pondering."

"Pondering? Pandering, you mean?" She shoved her empty mug aside and bent forward. "The panderer in this relationship is *me*."

Jock rose and wandered to the windows, which rain continued to splatter. He looked toward the ceiling, turned, and pointed up behind him. "You've got a leak there where the aluminum casing reaches the corner. See the streak where water's trickling down? Better tell Felice."

He walked back to his chair. "Another reason we're heading out west in four days is to see if your Raven or Fritz or Arlene can come up with a last-ditch suggestion for ending your coldness."

"Cold? I'm not cold toward you!"

"You know what I mean."

"Go, Jock—fuck!" Pain shot through her foot; she jerked her baby toe against the leg of her desk. She rolled her chair away and stood. "Beat it!"

Three fast knocks came, the door pushed open, and Judy appeared again. "Germaine?" She looked from her to Jock.

The editor threw her hands toward her assistant. Judy eased backward and out again, and closed the door to its jamb.

"I mean it, Jock, no way you're flying to Santa Fe with me. Go cancel your ticket. I'll have to add Monday and Tuesday to mine if I want to look for Dad. Day after tomorrow I've got a lunch with Barbara Kingsolver. We want her at Bennett—what are you sitting there for, with your jaw hanging?"

He stood and watched the drops coalesce and dribble down the outside of the double-pane glass. "Your father really messed you up, you know that?"

"Go mumble Muslim prayers on your cell with Mustapha al-Uraibi."

Sighing, he picked up his umbrella.

Germaine's intercom sounded as he left.

"What?" she shouted.

"There's some guy calling says he met you at that New Mexico dude ranch."

Dude ranch, she laughed silently. "Did he give his name?"

"Jimmy. Says you'll know the rest."

Germaine brought her hand to her breast. "Where's he now?"

"Miami."

"What line?"

"Two."

"Put him through—and Judy? Change my ticket to fly me home Wednesday instead of Sunday. And book that tribal hotel your boyfriend told you about. Get me a queen if you can. For three nights."

She kept her palm pressed to her blouse until she hit the button. "Jimmy?"

"Hi, there."

"How'd you find me?"

"You mentioned your company when we were at the Plaza a week and a half ago."

"It seems a year. Have you talked with Pete in Maine?"

"Never got his last name."

"Me neither. I'm so glad to hear from you, Jimmy! And you're not wheezing."

"Miami's smog-free. It was Santa Fe's seven thousand feet that got to me, I guess. You heard from Arlene?"

"Did I ever. Last Tuesday. Have you sent money?"

"First payment."

"Jimmy, listen. I'm flying out early Saturday with two-thousand dollars to try to persuade Arlene and her husband not to continue this. Or I think I'm going to inform the Santa Fe police. Even though it could screw up a promotion I may be offered soon—offered in an hour, matter of fact."

"Talking to the cops could land you in a lot of trouble."

"What's the law say about coke and paid-for sex, do you know?"

"No."

"Meet me in Santa Fe, Jimmy! We can boost each other's courage."

"Germaine, I…" He went silent a moment. "I can't. This weekend I'm hosting an opening on Key Largo's south shore for an upscale development I helped finance. Single homes, condos, country club, tennis, golf, the works."

"Damn it. I can just see you in your silk shirt and high-end slacks and that jingly coin bracelet of yours. Mopping those freckles, bustling around with your little Pekingese—making people glad they showed up."

"You forgot the yachting cap and deck shoes," he laughed.

She could envision his pink jowls shaking.

"Did you solve the impasse with your boyfriend?" he asked.

"You mean…"

"Yes, that."

"The weekend didn't help, Jim. I was hoping he'd be patient. But just before you called, we fought—major, I'm afraid."

"Boyfriend's loss."

"How about you? Have you met anyone?"

"No, but my little doggie, Chin Lo, got a female companion Sunday. I'm changing his name to Chin Hi."

Germaine started to giggle. She wiped her eyes with a knuckle. "I love you, Jimmy."

"Call with news when you get back, will you? Here's my cell."

FOOLS

Friday 14 September 2007

Universal Cosmic Divinity stopped washing breakfast dishes to untie a suds-soaked apron. He and Vonnie had shaped it from the sheet she'd persuaded Uni—street-artist-turned-would-be-sous-chef—to stop wearing.

Two fans, one on the counter and one atop the refrigerator, whirred at top speed, though it was only eight-thirty in the morning. Sweat slicked the tattoo, *God Slept Here*, peeking through Uni's cropped, blond hair.

He sniffed an armpit and muttered, "New friends deserve better." He hauled off the apron and then the sweatshirt he'd insisted on sleeping in all week. He'd promised his bunk mate, old Dirk, to wash the shirt this afternoon.

One of Uni's threadbare tennis balls had slipped out of the apron's pocket. Bare-chested and cooler, he retrieved the ball from under the sink before tying the apron back on. "Oh, this is the life," he sang, the five notes skipping upward. He circled steel wool around the skillet he'd fried sausages in for Friday's regulars, plus Quentin and Byron. Vonnie, as usual, had breakfasted in her apartment near Wild Oats.

Right now Byron was pushing a wet mop under the piano near the great room's front door, propped open by Kat at dawn. Vonnie sat tutoring Kat's granddaughter at one of the makeshift tables. The intern wore leather sandals, knee-length denim skirt, and a yellow blouse highlighted by scarlet leaves.

Dirk and Quentin sipped coffee among emptied dishes at the table closer to the piano. A couple of green garbage bags stuffed with laundry that Quentin and Byron had brought in for their weekly wash leaned against the composer's boots. Quentin wore his rain hat, though the weather bureau had predicted today's temperature hitting a sunny ninety.

Chiffon, the African-American refugee from New Orleans, and chemo-bald Clara, had already started walking the half mile to St. Elizabeth Shelter, where a representative from New Mexico's Department of Labor was holding a workshop before St. E's usual Friday lunch.

Uni entered the great room in canvas high tops, carrying an empty tray and whistling.

"Mr. Divinity?" Vonnie asked.

He stood grinning, rocking the tray as if it were his baby.

"Would you mind? Beatriz and I need to finish her history lesson so that Kat can return the book to the school library."

"Sure, sure. Music verboten."

"You've got five minutes to write out," Vonnie instructed the little girl, "how you think Joan of Arc wielded such power over soldiers twice her age. Pretend you're she."

"Me?" Beatriz asked.

"Who else, pumpkin?"

"Excuse me, gentlemen," Uni said, setting down his tray.

"Don't take my cup," Dirk told him. "I need to talk the improbable Q into coming to his senses. Take the plates or I'll do them later."

"No, sir, part of my training." Uni swung one arm across his waist and the other across his back, bowed, swept the plates onto the tray, and headed for the side table.

"Give up camping, Q, you've got yourself another cold," Dirk urged.

Byron plopped the mop's head into a half-full bucket holding a wringer and gripped its wooden handle with both hands. "The pighead won't listen. Thinks his whores enjoy the woolly wilds. My dad made my mother join us weekends tramping around the Sierras till she contracted pleurisy. Coped with oxygen until she caved in. Left Dad to nurse his grudges alone, twenty-one years now."

"*Boring*, Buzzy." Quentin's cold had turned his voice husky. He blotted his eyes with his paper napkin and honked into it.

Vonnie used one freckled hand to keep her place in the Webster's left behind by Kat's former bedmate, Marta. "Mr. Q, why not stay inside here the month you're allowed? Build up your strength—then fly back home or apply for a job in the College of Santa Fe's New-Music Department. Or teach jazz at the community college."

Outside, a siren began to wind up and down as a clattering of pans issued from the kitchen.

"All you buttinskies? Butt out!" Q snuffled hard, sucking phlegm down his throat. He snatched up his and Byron's dirty-clothes bags and his backpack, and marched past Beatriz and Vonnie into the laundry. "We don't even know if Kat's found a second bunk," he shouted over his shoulder. He dropped his cargo and swung his elbow up to muffle a burst of coughing.

"Don't bother washing mine," Byron called.

Quentin pitched his friend's bag of clothes into the great room as Kat's baritone echoed in the short hall.

"¿Qué pasa?"

She'd dressed as she had early in the week for meeting the Josephs at Marta's café: blouse embroidered with bougainvilleas and much-too-tight black skirt. Though this morning she'd not tied a bow at the end of her braid.

"Vonnie?" she said, leaning on the painted table outside the guest bath. "I need you."

"We're only a page from the end of the book," Beatrice protested.

"Plenty of time before I go, mija. Vonnie?"

The intern bit her lip, wrapped a wisp of hair around her forefinger, rose, and looked down on her scowling pupil. "We'll go over your answer in a bit, Bea. Then one more question and we're through. This afternoon: math."

Vonnie followed Kat toward the hall. "We'll get you and Mr. Q inside eventually," she whispered to Byron.

In the master bedroom, Kat pointed to a green-painted chair whose back and seat were wickerworks of patinaed copper. She and Marta had braided each other's hair in this chair. Their last kiss had occurred here. It faced Kat's makeup table and mirror framed in hammered tin.

Kat took the swivel chair at her desk. Above, a window looked out at sun-drenched hollyhocks that Marta had planted four years ago, enclosing them with river rocks.

The Harbor's director picked up a letter from the blotter and rolled close to Vonnie, who wrinkled her nose at the perfume. Violets? Gardenias? Too damn strong.

"Where am I going to get the funds?" Kat passed the sheet to Vonnie, aching to caress those fresh, freckled cheeks.

The intern glanced at the *Beautiful Tomorrows* letterhead, read the three short paragraphs and Fritz Joseph's signature.

"He's cutting our monthly four thousand in half and snubbing my request for funds to refurbish the garage," Kat said.

"I can see that."

"So put your thinking cap on."

"The Frost Foundation? McCune?"

"I could try. But who's getting the extra two grand we're not going to get now?" Kat asked.

"Beats me." Vonnie wished Kat would roll away.

"Some of that money goes to Frank Montoya to keep the cops at bay, and some to the School for the Deaf to keep snoopers out of the refuge."

"I don't want to hear about it right now," Vonnie said.

"I used to live with a woman who inherited major *dinero*," Kat said.

"Then call her."

"She grew up with a lawn surrounding the house. Me? On the highway. That mirror's my mother's. Hung in our van for years."

"You've told me how poor you were, Kat."

"Half starved...Marta's hair was darker than yours. Curlier. Not so pretty."

Vonnie squinted through the glare. At least the heavier woman had stopped saying 'sweetheart.'

"Your hair looks tangled this morning."

Vonnie glanced backward to make sure she'd left the bedroom door open. She watched sunlight pour down the hall through the great-room's screen door, watched Uni swing it wide and disappear.

"Hand me that brush," Kat said.

"The brush? Why?" Vonnie felt the perspiration build, though she rubbed on deodorant every morning after her shower.

"It's a sin not to take better care of yourself." Kat extended her arm.

Vonnie saw threads waving off the blouse's frilled cuff before she jumped sideways off her chair. "You've got to stop it, Kat! And I've got to finish up taping stories. My advisor wants me back no later than October first."

"You contacted your university?"

"Yesterday after lunch."

"But I need your help here. Can't you hang on?"

"You advertised this as a summer position and I've already overstayed—my lease ended last month. I'm paying by the week."

"But Beatriz has bonded with you. And what about this letter?"

"What about it? I've a PhD to complete."

"What's the good?"

"Jango, Kat! Move out of the way."

Vonnie kept close to the queen-size bed, as if she might need to snatch up the scarlet coverlet and throw it like a matador's cape. She sidled past Beatriz's single bed and vanished into the hall.

Kat flipped her braid over her bosom and opened the address book to where Monday after lunch she'd written down the number of Marta's café.

In the great room, rock gospel roared from the radio that Uni—back from his breath of fresh air—had turned on in the kitchen.

"Too much racket, Mr. Divinity," Vonnie called out, then asked Beatriz, "Did you answer the question about Joan of Arc?"

Beatrix nodded.

"Here's the other one. Ready?"

The chubby preteen stared at her.

"What do you think Saint Michael, Saint Catherine, and Saint Margaret said to Joan that helped her lead the French to victory at Orléans?"

No reply.

"An okay question?"

"What are *you* going to do?"

"I need to consult these gentlemen about something."

Beatriz looked askance at Byron, Dirk, and Quentin, who had gathered at the table by the piano. She picked up her pencil.

Vonnie headed toward the men. "What's the matter?" she asked Dirk, seated, who had leaned forward in his white overalls and was pushing four fingers between his buttocks. He smells clean, like baking soda, she thought.

"My prostate's stinging."

"You going to be all right, Mr. P?"

"Don't know."

"If it keeps up, Kat or I'll get you over to the Health Center. At the moment, I could use your advice." Vonnie smoothed her skirt under her thighs and sat. "Kat's pretty disconsolate, fellas. She's just shared a letter with me from our major benefactor, Beautiful Tomorrows. They're cutting our funds in half. No reason given. Any thoughts for raising some cash?"

Byron posed a non sequitur: "You like how I scrubbed the floor?"

Smiling, she rose halfway to kiss his cheek.

Quentin swept crumbs into his palm, dumped them into a fresh napkin, folded it, and shoved it into his pocket.

Dirk, sensing Quentin's hurt, decided to stun the young woman. "I guess you don't know that Beautiful Tomorrows fronts a sex and blackmail ring."

"Who told you that?" Jango, she thought, what a book this could make! Her mother and retired-surgeon father, both learning to live with titanium knees in Syracuse, would collapse off their walkers.

Kat emerged from the hallway in time to hear what Dirk had blurted. Her face felt feverish, though a white fan on the piano pushed air at it. She had meant to sneak away for her ten o'clock with the sixth-grade teacher at Alvord Middle School but remembered the library book. She set her purse and briefcase beside the screen door. Her skirt's elastic felt like a steel band. "¡Pendejo!" she bellowed, jamming hands to her hips. "What's this garbage about sex?"

"You give me a big headache, you know that, Abuelita?" Beatriz clutched her temples. "I hate it here." She thrust back her chair and jumped up. "Other kids go to public school—why can't I?"

Uni danced out of the kitchen juggling tennis balls as Kat hurried past the dining tables and reached for her granddaughter. "I don't like to see you hurt, mijita. Public schools are full of violence, kids using terrible language—malísimo."

"No different from home!" Beatriz wailed.

Uni kept the balls rising and falling to the beat of an electric bass. "Our Lord of all there is," he chanted over the kitchen radio's chorus, "loves little girls as much as slugs and worms and ladybugs and puppy-dog tails. Our Lord of all there was and all there will be throws candy kisses when his creatures—"

"Can't someone shut that clown up?" Beatriz cried.

"Come to me," Kat said, stooping.

The director's teeth clacked shut as the little girl let out a shriek. Beatriz shoved the plywood door off its sawhorses, sending the book, a half glass of milk, her pencil, and the yellow pad to the floor. "No, I won't. Go to hell!" She rushed into the hall; the slam of the master bedroom's door followed.

Quentin sucked in air, rose, walked toward Kat, and took a wrinkled elbow to help her settle into the chair Beatriz had left. Kat reached down for *Joan of Arc: Sainted Child* and started drumming her knuckles against the cover.

Uni had dashed into the kitchen and come back, crouching to towel up the milk. "Reuben Lightningfeather says a successful sous-chef deals with every detail."

Kat, her neck shiny, continued her rat-a-tat-tatting, staring out the window at her truck and the old apricot beyond. Her blouse billowed and collapsed with her breathing.

Byron came close. "Kat? I'm aware it's a bad time, but what do you do about bill collectors and police looking for guests? I'm thinking ahead, if you do get another bunk, and Q and I move in."

"I've got to pee something awful," Dirk said.

"That's crude," Kat snapped over at him. "Do I talk about guests to the law?" she answered Byron. "Never. And the cops know it."

"You truly want to be part of this madhouse?" Quentin muttered to his camp-mate.

Kat jerked her double chin up to address Dirk. "Have you gone loco about Beautiful Tomorrows? Blackmail? Sex? I don't believe you. How do you know the Josephs?"

"Can't talk now." Dirk pushed himself upright, and, squeezing his crotch, hobbled toward the guest bathroom.

"Vonnie, bring over that handbag and case, will you? I'm late."

When Vonnie returned, the director said, "Look, I'm really sorry. About what happened between us in the bedroom. Go see if you can calm my granddaughter down. Will you? Please?"

Vonnie scrutinized her a moment before responding. "Sure."

Kat smoothed the blouse's cotton over her breasts, pushed herself up, and lumbered into the kitchen. Uni was arranging pans in preparation for Reuben Lightningfeather's private cooking class in an hour. Kat left by the back door.

"Mr. Q," Vonnie said before heading for the hallway, "Can't we three be friends? Mr. Buzzy's *your* companion, you should know that."

"He's wearing *your* shirt."

"No. I rescued it to cheer him up, from the box a woman in a Land Rover left yesterday on the clothing table. Don't you like it? I'm out of here forever in a couple of weeks, Mr. Q."

"Green and yellow checks are old fogy."

"But colorful!"

Byron bit the end of his pinky and counted the seams between the planks that separated the intern from himself.

Uni trotted into view. "Mr. Divinity," a relieved Vonnie asked, "what are you doing about that dog of yours running around the refuge?"

"Stormy Weathers and I are working on a solution."

"Which is?"

"He'll be here any minute. Mr. Lightningfeather has offered to hammer in stakes if Mr. Weathers can find them somewhere."

"You mean steal?"

"Mr. Weathers has promised to ask our Lord's will."

Vonnie rolled her eyes. "I'll need to see that dog constrained before I ask Kat about an exerciser for you. You've got maybe twelve days."

"Not a bunch of time."

"I'm going back east to finish my education."

"Aren't you learning enough here?"

"Gotcha," she laughed.

Through the window screen they listened to Kat rev the pickup's engine, then churn gravel. The tires squealed in a left-hand turn.

Dirk opened the bathroom door, limped toward the men's bedroom, and shut himself in.

"Buzzy," Quentin said, breaking the silence, "my muses want to hear you play out the cello's early melody. It has a lot of shifts. First come help me sort out our coloreds and whites."

He stood and grabbed Byron's elbow but the younger man shook free. "I'm doing my own laundry, Q, I told you!"

"You two fools." Vonnie placed her hand against the seated Byron's chest and raised the other hand toward Quentin's. "Friends?" she asked him.

"You're gone in two weeks?" The composer's ponytail flicked as he averted his face to snuffle.

"At the max."

"But you can't!" Amazed at his own outburst, Byron clapped a palm to his lips and glanced up at Quentin.

"Hiya there, Uni. I brought planning tools for the cur." Stormy Weathers stood inside the doorway in pointed boots, blue jeans, and a T-shirt blotched with sweat. He waved a pen in one hand and some paper rolled up in the other. "Wait a minute, what are you two jerk-offs doing here?" he asked Quentin and Byron, pulling at his mustache.

"Pardon me, Mr. Weathers," Vonnie said. "Everyone removes their hat indoors, and you've got two."

"Done, cupcake." He held the billed cap and sombrero that had covered it beside his knee. "Hey, what about Q? He's always got that headgear on."

"We give him special permission—he suffers migraines when it's off." Maybe he really does, Vonnie thought.

"So do I. Bad." Stormy jammed the cap backwards onto his black crown, topped it with the sombrero, and pushed the creased straw down.

The last thing Vonnie wanted was a fight. "Okay, for this morning, I guess. I need to go see what state Bea's in."

Quentin followed her.

"You're the bodyguard?" Stormy asked.

The composer stopped in the laundry's doorway. "I'm a washerwoman."

"Yeah?"

"Stormy, listen, maybe we can try some four-handed improvisation, like yesterday, soon as I start my clothes."

"Maybe, maybe not." The Iraqi-Freedom veteran straight-armed the bass piano keys with the heel of his hand, causing a low-pitched crash. "So why'd the cupcake hightail it away from me, you think?"

"Kat's granddaughter threw a tantrum," Quentin said.

"How come?"

"It's a long story, Stormy."

"Yeah? Thought I could maybe get me an extra hit of clonazepam. Feeling l'il shaky this morning." He started for the hallway.

"Rum on your cereal again?" Quentin asked and immediately bit down on an imagined bar of soap.

"Better leave Vonnie alone for a while," Byron said, unable to believe Quentin had made the crack.

"Ho, Stormy, hop on over to the table and let's think the canine problem out," Uni added.

"*Now* I've figured out why you two chuckleheads are here," Stormy said to Quentin and Byron. "Our flapping teepee turned cook and bottle washer is helping you move in."

"There's no bunk for us, Stormy," Quentin replied and leaned into a fit of coughing. He started throwing underpants into a pile.

"There'll be another bunk here soon, I heard the cupcake say so on the porch a few days ago—right, Uni?"

"Don't recall, Stormy."

"The hell you don't!" He lurched forward, stopped at the end of the nearer table, and punched his own jaw. "Sure! I get it. Kat loves the fairy's piano playing. She wants *him* to stay. But *I'm* the one deserves a mattress and inside plumbing. So what if my technique's all thumbs?"

"Who says that?" Byron asked.

"Didn't you just hear me, fag-o?"

Quentin left his knees and marched into the great room until he stood three feet from the taller man. "You foulmouthed alcoholic. Breathe on me, I dare you. Ah, forget it—scram!"

Instead, Stormy shot a foot forward, thrust his tongue between his lips, and buzzed a raspberry at the composer.

At the same time he yanked his knife from a back pocket and thumbed the button. The blade sprung free. He lunged at Quentin but, throwing out his arms like wings, Quentin sidestepped the attack.

Stormy crashed to the floor, flinging the fist gripping the switchblade's ivory handle away from his ribs.

Byron leapt up. "Give me the knife!" He lifted his boot to pin Stormy's wrist.

The former marine rolled to his left, pushed to his feet, ducked, and spun. "All yours, boy toy." The steel, ripping through Byron's tattersall, sank into his left triceps just under the bone, and emerged on the other side, its tip gleaming in a ray of sun.

Stormy retreated between the two dining tables, jammed his sombrero to his ears by its rim, raised his elbows, and cocked his fists, one in front of the other.

"Shit-and-a-half," Byron groaned, collapsing. His face whitened and he started breathing fast. He curled his knees toward his belly. Blood pulsed from the muscle, up close to the shoulder, turning the floor black and his shirt and cutoffs scarlet.

Uni ran into the kitchen.

"You gopher-faced, sociopathic sot," Quentin shouted but Stormy stood defiant, chest heaving, teeth thrust out to clamp his lower lip.

Uni reappeared, apron crumpled in one hand, the tennis balls gone from its pocket. He crouched to stanch Byron's wound around the blade .

The doorknob smacked the master-bedroom's plaster as Vonnie ran out, Kat's granddaughter close behind. The cuffs of the pink sweater that Beatriz had wrapped around her dress flapped below her waist.

"Buzzy, darling!" Vonnie cried. "Don't touch the weapon, Mr. Divinity—you'll do more damage by trying to pull it free." She nudged him aside and pressed her palms against the sopping apron. "Get more dish towels and a glass of water. Bea, grab a cushion from the sofa. Mr. Weathers, *sit down.*"

"Oh, yuck," Byron moaned. The stench of feces rose as brown fluid dribbled from his shorts.

"Call nine-one-one, Mr. Q. Do it!"

"No," Byron pleaded, "wait for Kat. The law wants me—"

"Buzzy, you stink." Beatriz had perched on an arm of a sofa and was pinching her nose.

"Yes, and he could bleed to death," the intern said. "Bring me that cushion."

Beatriz approached and raised her elbow. The cushion dropped into Vonnie's lap.

"Mr. Divinity," she called, "where are you?"

"Right there." He hurried out past Quentin, who was holding the phone's receiver to his ear, and squatted beside Byron.

"We need to stretch you out, Buzzy," Vonnie said, feeling his forehead—cold and damp.

His eyelids closed.

"No! You've got to drink some water. Bea, press those towels to his wound. Don't touch the blade."

Vonnie rolled Byron from his hip and other shoulder to his back, clenching her eyes a moment to the smell as he straightened his legs. She raised his head, kissed the lips drained of blood, and nodded to Uni. He lifted to Byron's mouth the rim of the glass he'd brought in.

"You seem to know everything to do," Uni said.

"My father was an orthopedic surgeon."

"Was? Dead?"

She wagged her head no. "But old when I came into the world."

Byron opened his eyes, sipped and swallowed, sipped again as Vonnie watched his Adam's apple bob.

"Paramedics will be here in fifteen minutes," Quentin said. "Where do you think *you're* going?"

"Thought a little music might be welcome." Stormy had left his chair and reached the scarred piano, but did not lower himself to its black bench.

"Bea," Vonnie said, "slip that cushion under Buzzy's heels. "Mr. Divinity, go get a blanket, he's starting to shiver." She raised her eyes. "Mr. Weathers!" Her chest and neck muscles locked.

Stormy had run forward, shoved Bea away, and jerked the switchblade free. Blood spurted from between two towels before Vonnie could squash them together.

"Business elsewhere, cupcake," Stormy announced.

The jamb knocked his sombrero to the aluminum threshold as he shoved past her onto the porch. The screen door slapped behind him like a shot.

DESPERATION

Saturday 15 September 2007

"We'll have a second double-decker in the men's guest room by Wednesday, bub," Kat told Byron the next evening. "Flavio from the Española shelter is trucking it down."

Kat and Byron sat in armchairs facing each other in the Harbor's great room, she in a paint-splotched smock that Marta had left behind, he in the yellow-and-green tattersall that Vonnie had brought him from the clothing table outside. A white-strapped, blue-twill sling secured Byron's left arm.

Yesterday the paramedics had rushed him off to the ER just before Kat returned from her ten o'clock with the principal of Alvord Middle School. She and Vonnie had picked Byron up an hour later—irrigated, sutured, gauzed, and slung. Stormy Weathers had already cleared his belongings from the Lightningfeathers' camp, telling Reuben, Wilda, and Hisi that he needed to lay low.

A fan on top of the corner TV fluttered Vonnie's auburn hair, plus Beatriz's black hair and Tish's wanton red. They sat bent at a card table over a geology text Kat had brought her granddaughter from the school library.

"How," the eleven-year-old read aloud, "has the movement of tec, tec..."

"Tectonic," Vonnie said, wiping perspiration from her palm on her shorts and exhaling upward to cool her forehead.

"...tectonic plates helped form the land-scah-peh..."

"Landscape."

"...landscape of New Mexico?"

"Bow wow wow, you got it, kitty." Tish rared back in a T-shirt reading, *Careful or you'll end up in my novel,* and jeans she'd sheared at the knees. She'd dabbed her brow and the insides of her wrists with stolen Chanel No. 5 for tonight's dinner Kat had offered her in thanks for helping Beatriz learn to read.

"How can I answer about tec plates when I can't even pronounce the word?" Beatriz asked Vonnie.

"Look them up in the index," Vonnie said.

"Could be saucers," Tish added, flicking the single hair sprouting from a mole.

"Saucers?" Beatriz bunched her eyebrows.

"Saucers, glasses, forks, knives, or teacups."

"It's the alprazolam I just gave her," Vonnie said. "Makes her loopy at first."

"Darn tootin'." Tish grinned.

"Oh, don't go back to New York!" Beatriz cried. "I'll only learn nonsense from this *idiota*. Abuelita, keep Vonnie here, can't you? I'll forgive you for wiping out Mighty Mouse. Or let me go to school. Please? If Vonnie leaves? There's band, there's cheerleading, there's soccer, there's a science lab where we dissect rats. Marcelina down the street told me."

"I can teach you swell, bitch kitty." Tish patted the knee of Beatriz's pink capris. "Only wish my brother'd quit dealing and figure another way to support Mama. He scares me."

"Where does your brother live, Miss Earp?" Vonnie leaned down to bring the laptop she'd placed under the table to her thighs. She flipped up its lid and typed in *columbia.edu/cu/jobs*.

Flasher's companion frowned. "Long, long, *long* ways away."

"Vonnie," Beatriz asked, "when are you going to show me how to work Facebook? Marcelina doesn't have a computer but says we can sign for one at the library."

"Vonnie's trying to homeschool you, not play games," Kat commented, looking over.

"Facebook's not games!"

"After dinner," Vonnie assured Bea. *Homepage for Job Opportunities at Columbia* filled the screen and she double-clicked on *Recruitment of Academic Personnel System*. "If your brother's so far distant," she asked Tish, "why are you afraid?"

Tish stared at her. "Sometimes he comes too close. I don't want his baby."

"Can't Flasher protect you?"

"You betcha he can, Flasher can, sure he can, *double*-time. I'm his tiny bear and mama bear and Goldilocks, even with this frizz." She yanked a red coil straight. "But he—"

"Vonnie," Beatriz blurted, "she talks crazy!"

"Hey! You 'n me do fine." Tish swung her shoulders and pumped her fists at the would-be sixth grader.

Vonnie threw up her hands. "Give me a moment, Bea. We're going to look up 'tectonic' and 'plates' in the index. Then we're going to Google 'tectonic plates in New Mexico.' Then you can answer the book's question. First I need—"

Beatriz jumped up. "What? What? Why can't I see?"

"You can." Vonnie lifted her ThinkPad to the table and clicked on *Search Positions*. When the page appeared, she typed in *Department* following *Any*. "I want to find out about job openings after Christmas."

She raised her voice. "Those *calabacita* quesadillas smell awfully good, Uni."

"Fifteen minutes," he replied from the kitchen.

"If Chiffon and Clara miss dinner again," Kat said to Byron, "they're toast, and we cart their bunk into the men's room tonight." She spread her knees and gripped them. "You've no business sleeping in the weeds with that wound, bub."

"Where were Chiffon and Clara last night?" Byron asked. The hammocked arm moved and he winced.

"Hustling loose change, probably," Kat said. "You think Q will come in with you?"

"Ahhh!" The former professor clutched his shoulder. "Stings when I suck in breath. Q come in? Doubtful."

"Who the hell is that?" Kat rose to peer out one of the side windows.

"Two positions open!" Vonnie exclaimed.

"Yeah? Lucky you," Byron said.

"Adjunct Associate in the School of Social Work and Assistant Professor in Classics."

"You know anything about Greek or Latin?"

"No, but a new friend of mine does." She smiled at him.

"That's a cop pulling in behind my pickup," Kat said.

"Shit-and-a-half!" Byron sprung up.

The car's door slammed.

"What's Frank Montoya want?" Kat wondered aloud.

"Wants me! Had to give all my personal data to the registration nurse yesterday. Be my cover, Kat." Byron ran toward the guest bathroom, clamping his left forearm to his chest with his other hand.

The uniformed policeman who rode a mountain bike on the Plaza two weeks ago stood on the porch round-shouldered and capless. A revolver hung on his hip, and his black T-shirt hugged the bull neck. His badge sparkled in the porch light that Kat now turned on, though sunset wouldn't bloom for an hour.

"Hello there, Frank. Come on in." Kat pulled open the screen door. "You know Vonnie and Bea. I s'pose you know the redhead helping Vonnie with Bea's schooling?"

"Know Tish well." Frank smelled salty as he approached.

"Hi, Frankie, got another handout for Flasher and ole me?"

"Where is the man?"

"At the refuge, prolly, while I and Von Bon help the Bebop with homework. Whatcha up to, Frankie?"

"Come in and sit, Frank," Kat said.

"Got to get me on back and a shower." He leaned against the door. "Chief sent me along. Any chance you've come across a Byron Hurd? Checked into the ER yesterday morning with a knife wound. Described the attacker as black and obese. Nurse tells us Hurd is freckled with a ponytail — slim, balding, your height. Says he speaks careful, like he'd written the words down first. Our records show his wife's suing for alimony and child support. He blew off his court date. Former landlady says he owes for two months. Deb Tang at Saint E's don't know him so thought I'd try you next."

Black and fat? So Buzzy hadn't sold the brown, scrawny Stormy down the river. Kat's braid swished as she smiled and shook her head. "Can't help you, Frank. *Can* bring you a cup of Guatamala's finest."

"I better go try Salvation Army before heading home. Okay me using your restroom?"

"Never no need to ask, Frank. Use mine, though, at the end of the hall. Had an overflow in the guest bath."

"Sorry 'bout that."

As the policeman passed the bathroom Byron hid in, Uni danced into view, wearing his white apron and a floppy chef's hat. Reuben

Lightningfeather had swiped the headgear from a bin following a failed job interview at La Fonda. "Is our visitor staying for quesadillas?" Uni asked.

"No, and you keep your mouth shut," Beatriz piped.

Minutes later Frank clomped back into the great room, hunching and straightening as if each step hurt. He clutched a scrap of paper. "Forgot. There's also a person missing from New York I'm told to ask about. Quentin Edmunds, some kind of composer, gay man in his sixties." Frank consulted his notes. "Ex wife reports he says, 'hell's broth' a lot."

Kat shook her head no.

"Coming up with zip—as usual, aren't I." Frank waved to the others near the kitchen. Beatriz waved back, wildly.

When Kat heard the car's engine rev, she walked to the first bathroom's door and banged on it. "All clear, bub."

The door swung inward. Byron leapt forward and embraced the Harbor's startled director with his free arm, clamping his teeth at the pain that shot through his left, though pressing her massive breasts calmed him. "They're gonna get me sooner or later, Kat."

"You and the composer are safe with me. You're leaving?"

"Gotta find Q." Byron hauled open the screen, stepped onto the porch, and pushed the door closed. The taillights of the cop's black Chevy shrank in the direction of Camino Sierra Vista. A gaggle of moths and beetles swirled around the porch light and snapped against the yellow bulb.

"Serving up," Byron heard Uni call, then:

"Buzzy, wait!"

"You're going, too?" Kat asked.

"I'll fix my own dinner," Vonnie said.

"It's not safe to walk home now."

"I don't care!"

"Get in the truck, I'll drive you."

"Vonnie, you promised to Google the tec plates!" Beatriz yelped.

"I'm sorry, pumpkin."

"You're handing me a tantrum, you know that, don't you?"

"Let me *loose*, Kat." Vonnie tried to wrench her shoulders from the larger woman's grip.

Kat gazed into Vonnie's green eyes a moment, then let her own arms drop.

— — —

Close of this day brought a rare serenity to the refuge. No wind shook the shadows of the elms and New Mexican locusts. Scarflike clouds of magenta and salmon colored the western sky. Though the sweet clover had lost most of its blossoms, purple asters and cowpen daisies spread theirs. Even the grasshoppers seemed to have fallen asleep early. Seed heads on the wild rye and hairy-leafed kochia sparkled along the path to the sofa where Reuben stood guard.

Byron and Vonnie had not yet showed up. At Headquarters, a black-chinned and two broad-tailed hummers drank the honey-flavored water Tish refilled their feeders with every other morning.

Quentin, Dirk, and Flasher stood talking with Raven near the fire circle where Flasher warmed two cans of chile, supposing that Tish would join him before the seven-pm curfew he'd imposed on the refuge last spring, after they'd moved down from Truchas.

Quentin waved away a squadron of heat-seeking gnats and stooped to set the business section of Flasher's *Courier* in some buffalo grass further distant from the burning logs. Raven finished her story:

"I kid you hombres not, Boss wants to run away with me, I don't know where, and use our backup videos to put his wife behind bars. He hasn't a clue how he and I are to stay out of the slammer. Dirk, I tried your idea of spy-camming Boss snorting coke but lightning queered it—sorry, Q. Boss tells me his wife wants to fuck me and then off me somehow or hire someone in the refuge to do it. Am I frazzled? Oh, yes. Foreflasher, I need one-hundred-percent blow just for me, and no funny business, because tonight I've got to look happy humping an editor from New York whose boyfriend wimped out from flying west with her. Tomorrow Boss wants to do group grope. So hurry up with the Lady but tell me first what those green stakes and chicken wire mean so I don't totally freak."

Raven plopped her butt, wrapped in a denim mini, on a stump and spread her espadrilles on the dirt. The pink hair-comb jiggled as flickers from the cooking-fire made the tattoo on her shoulder, *Sixty-Nine and Counting*, seem to sweat. She frowned up at Flasher, one hand on her tummy purse.

"Settle your bones, girlie. Those stakes are for Uni's mongrel prowlin' aroun' here somewheres. Reuben an' Stormy were buildin' a run but now *Stormy's* run off. We're waitin' on his haulin' his ass home. I'll go weigh out that bindle."

Home? Raven wondered. This place? These elm suckers' bite-and-worm-riddled leaves? The empty bottles? But Dirk smells fresh, like the baking soda my father brushed his teeth with. Raven listened to the chile bubbling. Okay. This home hiding a composer honking into his handkerchief.

"I need a gram, don't dilute it, I'll pay extra," she called to Flasher. When I can, she thought, and wiped her nose with her wrist. "Q? What music you working on?"

"Cello sonata." He looked down, nonplussed to see her nipples and their ripe-plum slices under her yellow halter. He dried his palms on the seat of his corduroys and stepped toward Dirk.

"How do you go about making music out here?" C'mon, Flasher, c'mon. Raven imaged her fingers goosing him.

"You really interested?"

"Wouldn't have asked."

"No doubt you'll think me wacko."

"Aren't we all?"

Dirk guffawed and punched Quentin's shoulder.

"That hurt!"

"Sorry, old buddy." Dirk placed his palm on his rain-hatted friend's back. "Sensitive spirit," he said to Raven.

"This goddamn cold." Quentin hauled out his handkerchief, blew, and wiped. "Headache, too."

"So how *do* you compose?" Raven persisted.

Before he could respond, Flasher came striding from the lean-to in fatigues and black muscle shirt that showed off his thin upper arms. The red beret now almost covered his left eye. "Hunnerd bucks," he said, slipping between Dirk and Quentin, pinching the oversize bindle by its corners. "No charge for no talcum."

"Flasher, listen, I gotta ask for credit."

The hatchet face flushed as if sprouting a rash. "So long, bimbo."

"Till I get paid."

"Soundin' to me like mebbe you never will."

"Say, Flasher?"

"What?" he snarled at Dirk.

"I keep fifties on me in case I need to hit the ER. Give the coke to her, the prostate pain's eased some." The cracked-lipped old man reached to unbutton his overalls' back-pocket flap and eased out two Ulysses S. Grants.

"Huh?" Flasher traded the bindle for the bills, then—mistrusting their worth—flipped them to each side and crinkled them.

"Why're you paying?" Raven asked Dirk. "Looking for my services?"

"Doubt I can get it up any more."

"Sure you can, sniff a little nose candy."

Dirk gave her the bindle. "You've got great ankles and all the way to the top, but no. Q and I want to help you try again taping your boss doing lines. Secure your salary—raise it! And keep the jack flowing to the Harbor."

"What are you saying?" Quentin blurted. "I want to help her—"

"Try taping—"

"That's what I thought I heard. No way I'm getting involved in this, Dirk. Let Flasher help. Or Buzzy! Wait, his wound. But his mind's wily. Mine's crammed with muses wishing they were virgins, I've told you."

A dog started barking.

"Guys? Help me or whatever later. I need a hit." Raven grabbed the broken windowpane that was leaning against a locust, set it on the crate marked *Artichokes*, lay the bindle down, and unfolded the corners, noting how sticky her palms had grown in the evening's heat. "Foreflasher? Go first, will you? I'm paranoid."

"You think I've cut it with laxative, mebbe, or warfarin rat poison to speed the rush?"

"Just do me the favor."

"No bitch talks to Flasher that way. Take the cash back, Dirky."

But as Flasher slid fingers into his pocket to return the money, the noises of crunched stones and a branch breaking came from the path that connected Quentin's and Byron's camp to Headquarters. Flasher yanked off his beret to hide the white pile of cocaine.

Byron hurried into view, pushing the sling against his ribs to keep the shoulder still. Burrs clung to his gray slacks. Vonnie stumbled after him. He stopped beside Flasher's real or faux black-fur coat draped over a candy-cane-striped pole. Recently Tish and her companion had lugged it from fronting the barbershop on Early Street.

Byron and Vonnie waited for their breathing to slow. She brushed part of a tent caterpillar's web from her hair, then ran her fist down Byron's ponytail to clean it.

"Thank God the Lightningfeathers' half-breed's leashed to the sofa," Byron said to Flasher. "I thought he must be the one-headed son of Cerberus with all that barking!"

"Huh?"

"Forget it—Q, we better talk."

"What's she doing here?" Quentin stared at Vonnie, who herself was staring down at Raven. The Beautiful Tomorrows' facilitator had taken one of the director's chairs and tucked each foot under a cellulite-free thigh.

"Vonnie's told me something I need to share," Byron said. "Ouch! Monday I gotta get someone at La Fam to change this dressing."

"Share what?" Quentin asked.

"Later—hello, Raven. You know Vonnie?"

Raven shook her head, straightened her legs, and bent to retrieve the comb that had fallen to the dirt. She blew on it and jammed it into her waves of hair.

"I'll meet you at our digs in a few minutes," Quentin said. "And take the intern with you. We have a score to settle here first."

Byron grasped Vonnie's hand. They disappeared beneath the overarching limbs.

Raven snuffled, pulled a tissue from her purse, and wiped the perspiration from her forehead. "Don't abandon me, Foreflasher. Keep Dirk's money, I'm begging you."

"Ask nice, Flasher's no total asshole." He set the beret back on his head, scooped the long nail of his pinkie into the edge of the powder, pressed the left side of his nose closed, and drew the Lady into the open nostril. He shuddered and sniffed, stamped a boot, lowered his lids, and raised them. "No talcum, no laxative, no fuckin', speed-it-up warfarin."

Raven left the chair, took a wallet from her purse, and pinched out a MasterCard. "You got a straw handy?"

Flasher slid one of the fifties from his pocket and rolled it into a tube.

She plucked it from his tobacco-stained fingers and knelt, shifted, and carded a line along the glass. She jabbed a nostril tight, pushed the bill into the other, snuffed up the grains, and sighed, breathing heavily through rouged lips before standing. She blinked at Dirk while handing the bill back to Flasher. "You don't want any?"

Dirk wagged his head.

"You?" she asked Quentin.

"My whores stay clean-and-sober."

"Whores?"

"Muses. This rain hat shades them. They sing me songs or scream out demands and I write them down. In a notebook. In that backpack near the lean-to. Then Buzzy plays the music on a roll-up keyboard. Then I revise in the notebook and Buzzy plays it out again."

Dirk limped toward the fire, turned to Raven, and twisted the knob of his hearing aid. He kept his bass voice soft. "What time's your orgy starting up tomorrow?"

"One-thirty—oh, jeez, this stuff's good, Flasher." Her eyes had wet and their pupils had started dilating."Gotta scram, guys, lickety-split."

"There's shrubbery growing around the windows where this free-for-all's taking place?" Dirk asked her.

"Along the front windows. Thorns and red berries."

Pyracantha, sounds like. My neighbor grew it south of Socorro." Dirk limped to where Quentin stood and arced an arm around his shoulder. Quentin jerked but stayed within the former newspaperman's grip.

"This gent and I'll find us a couple of throwaway cameras over at Walgreens. You pick us up at one o'clock at the sofa back here. Pretty sure your boss'll be snorting a line?"

"He sure liked what I did for him as a result last time."

"Keep those spy cams rolling and Q and I'll shoot stills. Just like one of the stealth assignments I took on for the *New York Times*."

Quentin swung Dirk's hand away. "I told you I'm not getting involved."

"I'll have *someone* with me," Dirk said, "if this bird's too chicken."

"Chicken is right." Quentin hitched up the beltless gabardines he'd found at St. Elizabeth's. He strode over to retrieve his tattered pack, and, hunching into its straps, kicked up more dust as he started along the path Byron and Vonnie had come and gone on. Ahead, a cottontail hopped over dead leaves into the underbrush.

Forty yards away, obscured by suckers and thistles, Byron had laid out the mat and sleeping bag that sat rolled beside the composer's. He and Vonnie had lowered themselves to the quilted blue cotton, and now sat with hips touching. Behind them, the aluminum strut and the branch Quentin had stripped with his loppers continued to prop up the lean-to.

The soaring, high-pressure sodium lamp marking the refuge's southwest corner clicked on. A yellow radiance suffused the clearing, turning the nylon of the lean-to gray. The scents of piñon burning and a chicken roasting reached them from the Native Americans' camp, as did the renewed bark of Hisi's black-and-white dog. Or was that Uni's mongrel wanting a fight?

Vonnie tugged Byron's hand from his knees and swung his good arm around her shoulder. "I'm so glad I found a transitional-living place that accepts pets for Mr. Lightningfeather's family to move into soon." She fingered the top button of her blouse free and, without looking at Byron, guided his hand under her bra, smiling to feel him tremble.

"Q's on his way here," he murmured, but began to rub his palm over her hardening nipple. He moved gingerly not to crimp the bandage on his left arm.

"Ummm. My ex never learned how to touch me, Buzzy. I think you and he would like each other, though. He decided to remarry his first wife and she gave him two kids. Now he heads up the philosophy department at Barnard."

"You've told me that." Byron's hand stopped moving.

"Have I said he loves tennis? Maybe you two—"

"You're going to beguile me back there somehow, aren't you?"

"But you're perfect for the assistant professorship in Classics! You must know that Columbia has a Great Books curriculum, like the University of Chicago and Kullman. If the Classics position's filled, there're scads of—"

Byron pulled his hand free of her bra. "You've taped my story—I probably have a pregnant ex-girlfriend in Rhode Island."

Vonnie shifted on the sleeping bag. "Look at me."

He swung toward her.

"I can help you find a steady job. I know lots of people in the City. And my advisor has said she has two editors she wants *me* to interview, probably in February. Until we find our own apartment, we can live with my aunt in Brooklyn. You can start paying child support again, and you said your ex is going to ask for alimony, too."

"Well, she doesn't get alimony. Daddy Leroy's living with her. I told you she's already pregnant by him."

For the first time tonight, a gust bent the green tips of suckers toward the chair Byron had hauled from the culvert. A grasshopper buzzed. They watched it leap out of buffalo grass into the streetlamp-yellowed air, and settle on a thistle.

"If your ex-girlfriend has a kid, you'll be close by for visiting rights."

He laughed, crossed his ankles, pressed his sling, and managed to lean forward far enough to reach her lips, then swung his right arm to clasp the back of her head. They French-kisssed long and hard while another burst of wind flapped the lean-to's nylon.

"You're so naïve!" he gasped. "Shit-and-a-half, Vonnie. You think her folks are going to let me visit? A paternity suit's more likely. She was only a freshman."

Vonnie waited until her own breath quieted, braced herself on one hand and a knee, and pushed Byron over, even though, or more likely because, she heard footsteps.

"Hey!" Byron gazed at the gang of house finches that rose squealing into the darkening sky.

"I don't care," Vonnie said, climbed on top of him, felt his erection pressing her vulva, and wet his cheeks, ears, forehead, neck, and lips with kisses.

"Not on *my* bag. *If* you please." Quentin had appeared between two slim, blackened trunks and paused on the carpet of wild barley that Stormy had flattened when Quentin encountered him snoring two weeks ago. Two weeks? They seemed months—how defeated the composer felt. He leaned back until his pack hit one of the trunks, and let his arms dangle.

Vonnie rolled off Byron. "It's not your bag, Q, it's Buzzy's. See the pruners or whatever they're called near yours?"

"Loppers. I've been keeping the site tidy for us." Quentin trudged toward a chair, pulled free of his load, and lowered himself. His head jerked down in a series of coughs he didn't bother to cover. He stared at the two lovers.

Byron licked Vonnie's saliva from his lips and sat up.

Quentin brushed his palm over his thinning hair.

"You wanted to tell me something?"

"I have to beat it, Q. The law's about to catch up with me. The hospital has a record now. A cop was asking questions at Kat's an hour ago. I was hiding in the bathroom. I don't know if he asked about you."

"He did," Vonnie said.

Quentin kept quiet as Byron took her hand. "I came to tell you that for a while I'll be sleeping at the Harbor in a bunk or on one of the sofas," he said.

"Or at my place. Until we fly back to New York." Vonnie squeezed his hand, let go, and hugged her bare knees as a gust blew hair across her eyes.

"At least you won't have to hear me snoring any more," Byron said. "Or pester you where you've hidden *Instrumentation and Orchestration*."

"I've already explained where it is," Quentin whispered. "Go." He clutched his head. His ladies had begun thumping spoons against their thighs.

"I can't hear you."

"He said—" Vonnie offered.

"Go! Away! Get out!" Quentin half rose from the wooden seat and waved his hand as if swatting gnats.

All three of them stood.

Quentin leapt for the long-handled loppers and disappeared behind a clump of rabbitbrush. "Shut up," he told his whores, but they were singing scat to the clack-clack-clack of spoons.

Byron hoisted his own tattered, black pack with one hand. Vonnie adjusted it to his shoulders, then scurried to roll up his bag and secure it on top with an S-shape of rope lying close by. She rolled up his mat and tied it underneath the pack.

"Any of this soup yours?" she asked.

Byron shook his head, gazing at the dirt.

"Darling," she said to cheer him, threading her hand through his good arm. "Tomorrow, think! On the speed channel, the Belgian Grand Prix. That La Source hairpin's the tightest first corner in all motorsport. Maybe next June we can get to Indianapolis to watch the race live."

She paused. "Stay with me tonight?"

He said nothing. They started along the path that skirted the Native Americans' site and from there to the refuge's entrance at the sofa.

"You're not answering me," she said.

Byron stopped and looked back. "Q!" he called out. "Goodbye, Q." The elm leaves rustled. Hisi's half-husky had long ago stopped barking. Byron could hear the faint squeak of Flasher's voice from Headquarters and "Woman, move!" from Reuben thirty yards to the southwest.

"Okay," Byron said as he and Vonnie resumed their departure. "Your place." His wound hurt bad.

Quentin, meanwhile, had started pruning the New Mexican locusts as if amputation would stop the pain that seared his chest like water slung from a kettle. He whacked away or waved the lopper's blades at insects. His fists grew numb and his wrists and upper arms ached. The fallen limbs surrounding the lean-to began to form a thorned barrier. Soon he was wheezing as if attempting a four-hundred-yard dash.

His whores had abandoned their nonsense songs, thrown down their spoons, and fallen to their knees, flinging notes at him like rocks.

"I'm not through," he cried to them, and when all the limbs he could reach had dropped, he started cropping tangles from rabbitbrush, slicing the heads off stands of rye and barley, shearing sprays of sweet clover, and now even buffalo grass, thistles, and foxtails lay scattered about, until his back spasmed each time he straightened.

"Enough!" the ladies chorused in an uproar like cars slamming head-on.

He flung his loppers, their short blades grown hot, onto his sleeping bag, clutched the lean-to's aluminum pole, and managed to yank it out of the hole he'd dug. The nylon flapped and collapsed as, pressing his palm to his spine, he scuttled like Quasimodo to the branch holding up the lean-to's other corner.

"All right, Dirk," he spat, and began to cough, hoisting the branch from its mooring. "I'll sleep inside. And all right, I'm crazy, but not so crazy as you and that tattooed female, Raven."

He sank to the crumpled nylon, wormed his pack from underneath by a strap, freed his pen, and began to ink in the notebook's staves with a roller coaster of thirty-second notes.

EDEN IN HELL

Sunday 16 September 2007

About ten the next morning, Dirk and Quentin waited for Walgreens's door to slide back, then walked inside and turned left between the two cash registers. The old men had dressed up as best they could for the heist, Dirk in trousers and a buttoned-collar shirt that Vonnie had seen on Kat's giveaway table, Quentin in a white beret, not worn since the music festival.

"Let's stop here, *compose* ourselves," Dirk whispered, his breath sweet from a double brushing. He picked up a set of stereo headphones sealed in polyethylene and pretended to scrutinize the backing's text. "Roomie," he said, "I'm proud of you—all that's needed now is to cover me from behind. Bravo that Buzzy walked over from Vonnie's after breakfast so you two could reason things out."

"She's mortally wounded him," Quentin said. "So I decided, why not give Dirk a hand—those fluorescents are hurting my eyes. Let's get on with it."

He followed Dirk to the end-aisle display—*Single-Use 35mm Cameras with Flash*—catercorner to the hour-photo counter. Kodak and Walgreens brands filled the two racks, flanked by batteries and albums. Underneath sat a shelf of assorted sweets. "Swipe a box of Aplets and Coplets while you're at it," Quentin said.

"Now," Dirk commanded from one side of his mouth. His breath fluttered the white hairs of his mustache.

"Ready, set…"

"May I help you gentlemen?"

A squat clerk, black hair coiled atop her head, raised beautifully thick brows as Quentin's heels left the vinyl tiles and clopped down. The jolt shot pain into his neck. He stooped to pick a gum wrapper off the floor and looked around. "We…"

"Need a couple of these," Dirk finished up, sliding his fingers from the higher-priced Kodaks to grasp a couple of Walgreen throwaways. "Do we pay at hour photo or in front?"

––– –––

Meanwhile, half a mile to the southeast, the Josephs were sipping coffee with Germaine in Fritz's iris garden, between the living room and Raven's casita. The sex facilitator, as she did every Sunday morning, was driving clients to the Plaza in the Hacienda's van. The forty-five-thousand-dollar 135i BMW sports coupe that Fritz had brought home from the dealer three days ago—0 to 60 in 5.1 seconds—waited in the garage beside the Josephs' older BMW. The cars' twin grilles faced the door and the gravel drive beyond. Arlene had slapped a sticker the dealer had given her—*Is There Life After Death? Touch My 135i and Find Out*—to the new BMW's rear end.

"So lovely here," Germaine said, wondering how best to bring up a major reason she'd booked this weekend. "Those clouds, like foam. Cottonwood leaves rattling like, what, gourds? That spruce a mast over the garage. That rock wall and…"

"Coyote fencing, oh, shit!" Arlene's tunic trembled. Her elbow had sent the half-full mug inscribed *City Different* to the flagstones, snapping the handle off.

"I'll go get you another, hot," Fritz said in a careful monotone, and rose in his moccasins and shorts. The points of an orange-colored handkerchief sprouted from the pocket of a stiff-collared, scarlet shirt.

"Sit down," Arlene told him.

Fritz stuck out his lower lip and descended to the chair's cushioned slats.

"The Doctor always wants to make things right, though as our beautiful coke whore puts it, wrong's easier. You didn't partake of the Lady last night, Germaine."

"No." She drew a palm over her mother's pearl necklace.

"You and Raven were okay together last night?" Fritz asked.

"Fabulous." In fact, Germaine had faked her display of multiple orgasms.

"In a few hours we hope to give you—"

"What do you mean, hope?" Arlene asked.

"You don't know what I was about to say."

"Of course I do."

"Chances are," Fritz continued, massaging the back of his neck, "that the group session we have planned for this afternoon will provide a lifetime of therapeutic memories."

A spurt of stomach acid burned Germaine's throat. She thumbed the pearl in her earlobe until the pressure stung, and threw her hand toward the long bed of iris ending at the oven-shaped outdoor fireplace. "We sometimes get to see iris in Greenwich Village."

"So that's where you hang out." Arlene's tongue circled thin, heavily-rouged lips.

"In rent-controlled bliss for eleven years." The editor shut her eyes and breathed in the morning's already-hot air.

"Most of my collection of iris is dormant," Fritz said. "Those unusual few with leaves will have lavender-blue flowers in November. The two orange-and-yellow beauties you see are bearded, reblooming now. For the rest I've got to start lifting and dividing the bulbs and rhizomes."

"Doctor?"

"What?"

"Enough." Arlene sealed her lips and ran her forefinger across them. "You into sports?" she asked Germaine.

"Not really, no."

"You're aware of Tiger Woods?"

"Who isn't?"

"The FedEx cup is probably his; we'll know this evening. The cup and ten million smackeroos."

"Smackeroos, Arlene?" Fritz asked.

"You don't know the word? Ten million big ones."

"Look," Germaine said, leaning forward. "Before Raven gets back, I want to share something."

"Please," Fritz said.

"Mostly I came out this weekend to find my father."

"Oh? We assumed—"

"Let her talk," Arlene snapped.

"A month ago, this city's High Mesa Music Festival premiered a piece of my dad's dedicated to me. It wasn't well received. Later my mother and I learned that the festival up at Red River wants to offer him a composer-in-residency and to commission a sonata for piano and cello. But he's disappeared. His wallet was stolen. We think he may be homeless in Santa Fe."

"Oh?" Fritz said again, his voice dull. "Perhaps we can help." He glanced at Arlene.

"I'll do the talking," she said.

Fritz clamped his teeth.

Why are they so nervous, Germaine wondered? I paid my first installment last night.

"We know several heads of agencies in Northern New Mexico," Arlene said. "And shelter directors, because of our charity work. We know few of the homeless themselves. Mostly they're shiftless, addictive, or mentally ill. Not a lot of gumption or smarts."

"Arlene."

"Yes, Fritz?"

"I doubt Germaine's father—"

"Dad's bright, or was," Germaine said. "And loving. We used to build sand castles on the beach at Coney Island. Sets from *Das Rheingold*—Valhalla, and Nibelheim, the dwarves' home." Her vision blurred with the memory. Across the glass-topped table, the Josephs—his scarlet shirt, her rainbow capris—seemed multicolored ripples in a pond.

"*Das* what?"

"The opera, Arlene. Wagner's *Ring*."

She swallowed the last of the coffee from her husband's mug. "What's your father's name?"

"Quentin Edwards."

"Description?"

"I haven't seen him for nineteen years."

"Long time!" Arlene twisted her head. "I hope she hasn't taken off in the van again."

"Raven?" Fritz asked.

"Who do you think? I need her help for this afternoon."

After a drawn-out silence, "My wife and I are glad to see you," was all Fritz could come up with.

"You may not be so glad when I tell you the other reason I flew out."

The blue-and-yellow striped umbrella rising from the table's center did not yet shade them from the sun. Arlene plucked a linen napkin off her thigh, flipped it over, and patted her cheeks and forehead.

"I hope to talk you out of requiring the rest of the two-thousand-a-month payments."

"We feel somewhat like Maid Marian and Robin Hood," Arlene said. "The payments go mostly to charity."

"I'm not rich."

"No one else has objected."

"They're probably afraid."

Arlene narrowed her green eyes and started shoving the turquoise-and-silver bracelets around on her wrist. "You wouldn't be thinking...."

Don't show your hand yet, Germaine told herself. "Thinking?" she asked aloud.

"Of telling someone about your experiences here. About my phone call afterward."

"My boyfriend knows."

"Of course. Your mother?"

"No."

"Certainly not your employer."

Germaine wagged her curls.

"The installments must be made, Germaine, dear. We consider them a moral obligation. That's got to be the van." As Arlene rose, the bottom of a brocaded slipper soaked up coffee that hadn't yet seeped between the flagstones. She kicked the broken mug against a table leg.

Raven stopped on the other side of the river-rock wall. Calm down, she told herself, dropping her hands and shaking the tension out. Braless in yellow halter, cutoffs, and rope-soled sandals, she marched past the thorned pyracantha that shielded the front windows from the street. Her watch read eleven. Three hours more and Dirk and whoever he brings will have nailed Boss on film, the person I loved—chill, Raven.

She paused, pressed her hand to a breast, and headed for the front door. Would she have to encounter Fritz alone?

The living room looked empty. There they were, in the patio, all three. Raven paused beside the wire unicorn. Using her pinkies, she stretched her lips to practice a smile, then skirted the dozen loose tiles and slid open the glass door.

"Hello, everyone. Isn't this a day?" The tone seemed right. "Isadella and Jonah were on cloud nine to have a couple of hours on the Plaza by themselves. Wouldn't surprise me for them to ask to pair off after group. Wowee, fun." She smiled as wide as she could, reaching behind her storm of black hair to adjust the pink bow.

"We'll be inside," Fritz said to Germaine—glumly, it seemed to Raven.

"You stay put." Arlene turned to gaze down at him. "Maybe we *should* let the editor off the hook a bit. Talk it out and come up with a new plan for Raven and me to review. Right now we've got work to do. Tequila sunrises, you're thinking? C'mon, love." She stepped forward and took the sex facilitator's elbow.

As Arlene hauled the glass door shut, Germaine sat perplexed. Was Raven now a partner in this enterprise? She'd said nothing about it in bed last night.

"I needed to get you alone," Arlene told the facilitator after sliding the door shut. "Let's go grab some blankets out of the bedrooms. Careful of those tiles. His nibs swears a mason and the roofer will be here tomorrow."

She preceded the twenty-four-year-old past the stairs into the hall, stopped beside the locked door to the den, wheeled, pressed Raven's cheeks, and kissed her lips. Her fingers dislodged an earpiece of the pink-framed glasses. "You didn't take a hit last night. Why not? I did notice, you know." Arlene backed away.

"I've decided to clean up my act."

"For me?"

Raven nodded.

"Cold turkey? We had such a good time together with the Lady upstairs Thursday after I sent Fritz to the Desert Inn for his overnight."

The sex facilitator shrugged, wrinkling the tattoo on her shoulder.

"Think you can get clean on your own?"

"Gonna try, Arlene."

"You're a good-looking specimen right now. Stopping coke'll make you drop-dead gorgeous, erase those wrinkles from your eyes."

She took Raven's shoulders. "Listen up, love. I located that taped bottle of barbiturates in your refrigerator and—"

"You what?" Raven's knees weakened. She wiped her nose with the back of her hand.

"Went ahead and powdered three tabs, enough for a line. Just like you dreamed up Thursday when we woke for a midnight snack. Bitter, like your john said. And strong! A hundred fifty milligrams each? Let's hope he was also right about them acting fast."

"That was five years ago!" Raven tried to swallow, failed, and squeezed her eyes shut. She reached back to feel for the wall.

"I returned the bottle taped so you wouldn't notice and refilled one of the bindles under your doormat. All you need do is persuade my husband to snort it. Same as you did the last night of Fiesta. Only this time we want witnesses to testify, as will we"—Arlene extended her arms, palms up— "that my husband, an exhibitionist and long despondent, decided to snuff himself out in front of us all."

Raven sensed her legs could no longer hold her without support. Fritz had confessed two days ago that he had been unable to stop himself from falling in love with her!

She managed to reach the door of the bedroom opposite the den and half sat on the table in the hall. "Fritz said *you* wanted to off *me*, that he and I would run Beautiful Tomorrows after he'd figured how best to off *you*. But *you're* going to off *him*? Everything's too complex! I'd better not switch on the spy cams."

What should she, Raven, tell Dirk when she drove to the refuge in a couple of hours to bring him here? Mommie, I want to come home, be your baby girl, watch you bake sugar cookies, clap my hands when you bash Dad's head with a can of Crisco. Mommie, live again, I'm begging you.

Arlene walked over and pulled the young woman to her. "Do you know how I crave kissing your nipples?"

All Raven longed to do was stumble into the bedroom and bury herself under the spread.

"We need the spy cams on," Arlene murmured. "Of course we do." She reached down to massage Raven's crotch. "Sweet girl, we're in this together, so that later, neither can blame the other. You and I are taking over this gold mine. Let's go find those extra blankets. And don't quit Lady C yet. I'm crazy to undress you in the casita before our afternoon's free-for-all."

— — —

At one-fifteen Germaine sat in the first bedroom with one shoeless foot tucked under her thigh on the mattress's edge. She gazed at the light that filtered through the shade's honeycombs as she talked into her cell. Her suitcase lay on a wicker chair. Cold air pushed through the vent next to the ceiling's smoke alarm.

Unknown to her, Raven had switched on the spy cams after secretly bringing Dirk and Quentin here from the refuge a few minutes earlier.

"Yes, yes," Germaine was saying. She clutched a breast under her silk top to quiet her heart. "Tomorrow around noon in Albuquerque—perfect, Jimmy. Take the shuttle to the Hotel Santa Fe. My assistant booked me a deluxe double for three nights. Two queens because I didn't want to feel nostalgic. I sleep in a king at home."

From the speaker above the stenciled dresser sounded Ali Bahia El Idrissi's "Arhil," guitar and Moroccan frame drum digitally mixed on Fritz's CD, *Sahara Lounge*.

"Yes, I want you with me when I see the police. Yes, I'm resolved, whether I find my father or not." She smoothed her palm across the scarlet spread's tufts. "Fritz made me a deal of fifteen hundred a month and I bet you can get that, too. But I can't live like this, Jim. Maybe you won't even get asthma if we're able to give each other courage."

She paused. "Right, I told my supposed boyfriend not to come. Why does he have to know about you? Phone me your flight number when you can."

She shut her eyes and gathered breath for the imminent orgy before slipping her cell into her purse and standing. She passed the painted retablo of St. Francis near the door and turned right in the hall toward the unicorn opposite the stairs.

Outside, Quentin and Dirk sat cross-legged on leaves blown from the cottonwood, their hair hidden from possible viewers indoors by the stuccoed half wall below the windows. Red-berried pyracantha masked the men from the street. A throwaway camera in its cardboard case, plus a gingham handkerchief to mop perspiration, lay on Dirk's lap—a camera and white handkerchief lay on Quentin's. The composer startled at the thorn that bit through the back of his guayabera, and scooted forward an inch toward the house. Raven had told them to start shooting, no flash, when she tapped on the double-pane glass.

"Any prostate trouble?" Quentin asked.

"Not so far," the former *Times* reporter whispered back.

The living room looked different than it had on Germaine's first visit. Arlene and Raven had covered the Native American throws and dozen loose tiles with cushions and blankets. On each cushion rested pink and blue vibrators, IUDs, foil-wrapped condoms, ben wa balls, dildos with flared bases, and harnesses for strapping them on. After arranging the room, the two women had slapped together salmon-salad sandwiches for themselves, Germaine, and Fritz.

White powder now lined a couple of the coffee table's grooves. Bindles with their folded-in corners rested alongside, as did a couple of sunrises in highball glasses, grenadine on the bottom paling to orange juice mixed with tequila covering the ice.

There on the wraparound sofa, near the TV, sat Isadella Duncan and Jonah Knudsen, backs straight, hands nestling between their thighs, tequila sunrises waiting on the coffee table. She, chunky, cheeks scarred by acne and wearing rimless glasses, worked—Germaine had learned at breakfast—as marketing director for Genesure Biotech south of San Francisco. He, lanky, married twenty-seven years, three children in college and a tremor in his right arm, lived in Omaha and traveled for a chain of printing franchises, Gunga Graphics, about to expand into the southwest.

Ali Bahia El Idrissi's techno pulsed through the speakers flanking Fritz and Raven, who faced the others in front of the electronics gear that towered toward the vigas. Raven had exchanged her sandals for two-inch spikes and released her black waves to cascade over bare shoulders, obscuring her tattoo. Thank God she'd prepped herself in the kitchen with straight José Cuervo. She picked up her cocktail here and swallowed half, keeping the ice at bay by pursing her lips.

Germaine stepped gingerly across the blankets and lowered herself to the sofa beside Arlene—who turned from talking with Isadella, and slid her palm along the editor's thigh.

"We've tried," said Fritz, throwing out his hands, "to provide you with everything you'll need to practice joyfully a supervised togetherness designed to help you embrace the glories of the human body. The mechanical aids you see are handily available from the Internet. We'll give each of you a list of Web sites before Raven drives you back to the Sunport.

"As promised last night, again we're offering a medicinal quarter-gram of cocaine, which we prefer calling Lady C. And again, there's nothing to pay. After those of you partake who wish to, Raven will demonstrate with my wife and myself several ways we might all want to proceed."

His bare forearm touched Raven's, and a shiver rippled between her shoulder blades. I can't watch you murdered, Boss, I can't do it. Can have you taped and filmed, can decide with Arlene what's next. I'm so muddled, oh, Jesus, show me how to get that bindle she marked off the table.

Raven pressed against Fritz.

But he moved away and spoke to Isadella and Jonah. "Drink up, you two. I see my wife forgot to pull the front shades. There's no need when we use the bedrooms, but this afternoon . . . Excuse me."

Raven opened her mouth, could think of nothing to say. She downed the rest of her sunrise, grateful for its eighty-proof fire. Heart, cool it! She felt her throat go dry and sniffled hard.

Ali Bahia El Idrissi's drums gave way to Justin Adams's blend of electric guitar and North African flute. Fritz moved past the glass-doored cabinet holding candles and Arlene's grandmother's dishes.

"Say, Fritz," Isadella called out, twisting in a jacketed white blouse and black trousers on the sofa's cushion. "Can't you leave those shades alone? I'm claustrophobic. My meds help and those bushes seem to work fine. But would you mind raising the side shades? I'd like the chance to glance out at your garden while we're about our business here."

Raven's head went light. Was the spy cam's tape rolling? She advanced a couple of steps to sink onto a cushion free of sex aids near the grooved table, and stretched out the long legs she'd shaved this morning. The cushion's corduroy woke nerves in the backs of her thighs. She reached for Fritz's cocktail, gulped a couple of mouthfuls, and set the glass back.

Isadella turned toward Jonah. "Okay by you, Jone? I mean the shades." She took a sip and smacked her lips. "Delish."

"You and the rest decide on shades," Jonah rasped and drank. "I'm way nervous enough. Not being allowed to smoke's no help, trust me on that one."

"Raise 'em, Doctor!" Arlene snapped at Fritz. "These people aren't paying for wibble-wobbling." Even when she squinted, Arlene's two face-lifts kept the corners of her green-mascaraed eyes wrinkle-free.

Fritz strode to the glass slider leading to the patio and and hauled on the cord. The pleats bunched to the left. The brown heads of hollyhocks lining the high fence-and-rock-wall appeared in the breeze to nod assent.

"Who's for asking the Lady to grace us before we start?"

"*Grace* us, Fritz?" Arlene guffawed. "Nice."

"Not me," Isadella said.

"Me, neither," Germaine agreed.

"Last night no need, thanks to her," Jonah said. He stared at Arlene and grinned. "But I'd better take some today or I'll never perform in group the way I want to. Chance of a lifetime."

Raven recalled she was to signal the two photographers outside by tapping the window. As she rose, dizzy, she made a decision—pretend to snort the marked bindle herself if she couldn't pocket it without Arlene noticing. She felt unfit to watch Fritz die, gentle though her john had sworn the process to be. But the tablets of barbiturate, given their bitterness by what her benefactor had dubbed an 'onset accelerator,' were thirty years old. Who knew how they'd act now?

An idea for an out hit her. "I'd like to be sure this batch is pure," she blurted. "It should taste sweet."

"Didn't you test it?" Fritz asked.

Arlene's forehead crumpled as she eyed the younger woman. "Love," she said calmly, "this morning you told me your dealer had added a touch of warfarin to speed the buzz, as a personal favor. A *soupçon* of bitterness improves the taste, *n'est-ce pas*? We want Jonah to know that, at Beautiful Tomorrows, we save the best for last."

"Right," Raven managed. Perhaps if she herself snorted half the line, or faked sneezing the whole mess out of its groove, she could save Fritz's life. She moved toward the front windows.

"Isadella has requested the shades stay up," Fritz reminded her, staring at the drink beside him she'd half-emptied, then wrapping his arms around his chest.

"I know that. Just double-checking no one can see through those bushes." Raven peered down at the heads of the two old gents huddling on the dirt and realized that Dirk was not wearing his knife. She turned to face Fritz then and, like him, wrapped her chest.

"Doctor?" Arlene said. "Open the bindle with the green X. Let's all three snort a little to reassure our guest it's primo."

Why all this back-and-forth? Germaine felt her stomach roil. Were Arlene, Fritz, and Raven planning more than a debauch, some kind of hidden agenda? She thumbed the pearl hard against her earlobe and dropped her palm to a knee.

"Good idea, Arlene." Fritz moved to the table, spread open the corners of the marked packet, and grasped his wrist to steady it as he shook the crushed Phenobiconal into a third groove. "There we are. Go ahead, Rave."

"You and me together," she countered.

"Together, bright eyes? A bit awkward."

"Not if we start at each end and meet in the middle." Did he suspect the double cross Arlene had planned? Two days ago he'd rambled on to Raven about how sick he was of his wife, the over-the-top jewelry, her rudeness, her streaked ducktails. Of all the time he spent wondering— cramps in the belly—which pigeon would snitch first.

Forget Arlene's slogan about the Josephs being Robin Hood and Maid Marian, Raven thought. Fritz and I are about to do the Sex Pistols, Sid and Nancy fast-forwarded to now. She reached behind her to rap her knuckles twice on the window, and zigzagged through the cushions on the floor to the table. "C'mon, Boss, come in close."

"Purgatory," he whispered, kneeling beside her.

Nope, she said silently. This time we're heading down.

She handed him a red-and-white half-straw. "Watch how it's done, Jonah. Both of us, Boss!" Amplified keyboards drove guitar and flute into a whirlwind of sound.

Raven's black hair fell over her halter as she grabbed her own straw, plugged a nostril, bent, and started drawing in the white powder. It stung, making her eyes water, and the bitterness dug like claws into the back of her tongue. But this was not what made her reel. Instead of plunging his straw into the PBC, Fritz was snorting the line next to it, the cocaine cut with talcum with which she and Arlene had filled the grooves after lunch.

"You said you'd fallen in love with me!" Raven cried out. She wanted to die. She threw her elbow against Fritz's jaw, toppling him to his side—changed nostrils, and quickly inhaled the rest of the ancient barbiturate.

A sense of euphoria mixed with dizziness. Her pupils started to roam the latillas, tiles, unicorn, the blurring outlines of the guests. She thrust fingertips against a blanket, pushed down on her right foot, stood—reeled, and collapsed. Her body trembled with cold.

She heard a smash and the tinkling of glass—another, louder tinkling—and watched a pair of moccasins and Arlene's slippers streak past.

The living room became a tureen of vegetable soup. A great dollop of it in her gut wanted out. From the base of the stairs she heard Fritz yell, "Our precious has been talking suicide for a long time!"

"Help," she bleated. She seesawed her wrist across her nose, clutched her tummy, and flung out her legs. One jerked to the side. She gripped her elbow to stop the right arm's shaking but her fingers wouldn't hold. Flowers from childhood filled her mind, the Queen Anne's lace she'd picked in armfuls from the vacant lot next door, the sweet peas her mother had tried to grow.

She started choking.

Hands gripped her shoulder, forcing her onto her back.

When Dirk, pocketing the cameras outside, had lifted a flagstone and hurled it through one of the twin windows, Isadella, Jonah, and Germaine had leapt up as if zapped by the techno pounding from the speakers.

Isadella now stood where she'd risen, vising her temples between her palms. Jonah had run to the front door and through a gate that led to the sidewalk. He sat slumped in full sun on the curb at the corner, blowing out smoke from the cigarillo he held, attempting to reason what to do. Sweat darkened the pink Ralph Lauren knit above his belt and under his arms.

The hands pushing Raven to her back had been Germaine's. She'd started slapping the facilitator's cheeks to keep her awake. But why was Raven's forehead turning blue?

Raven gasped and tried to swallow. Every few seconds her head jerked. Had the Josephs run upstairs for car keys, she wondered? Her fingertips had numbed. All she yearned to do was fade out. Fritz had lied.

Minutes ago, upstairs, Arlene had yanked open a dresser drawer to grab the tortoise-shell-handled derringer she kept under her bras and hankies. Now she and Fritz sat bickering about whether or not to call 911 to report a break-in. Fritz wanted to phone, then flee in the 135i, but Arlene countered—cocking the hammer—was he nuts? If he lifted the receiver she promised to send a bullet through his elbow.

In the living room, Germaine heard a gruff "Move away." In a half crouch she crab-stepped to the grooved table and settled. The hem of her skirt slipped up toward her tummy as she raised her knees.

The older of the two strangers, a hearing aid stuck in one jug ear, shoved Raven onto her hip and arm and thrust his fingers into her mouth. "Throw it up, sis. Do it!"

He slugged her in the belly.

Raven's lids shot open and then like a dog she growled. Gobbets of snow peas and strands of salmon speckled the slurry she spewed over a cushion.

Dirk turned his face away.

Quentin stared at Germaine, feeling his brow heat. Couldn't be, could it? Hell's broth! But the woman pressed her earlobe, as Germaine used to as a girl. He turned and wiped his lips with his fist. His daughter? In this bordello? Was it possible?

Germaine glanced at the shattered window, at the sunlit halo of shards sparking the gold-plated ben wa balls perched on a cushion.

"We're friends of hers," Dirk muttered to the editor. "Don't let those two up there get her into their car. Who's got wheels here?" He slapped Raven into wakefulness.

Genetech's marketing director stopped palming her spikes of hair and started toward the unicorn, puffing but keeping her gaze level. She vanished into the hall.

"Take the van." Raven managed, then gurgled, tongue clogging her throat. She coughed it free.

"What?" Dirk twisted the stem on his hearing aid. He had pillowed her cheek on his lap.

"Key, right fender. The van."

"Do you know what they poisoned you with?" Dirk asked.

"Bottle. My fridge."

"*Your* fridge?" Germaine asked. She stooped to clean Raven's lips with a tissue pulled from a pocket while Dirk lifted Raven's head.

"In my casita. Sick, can't see right." She shivered. "So cold."

"Get that bottle fast," Dirk told Germaine.

Raven's left foot kicked, sending the sandal flying against the vase Fritz had filled that morning with gladiolas. The ceramic teetered but stood. The foot kicked again, though Raven's body—yellow halter speckled with vomit—slumped across Dirk's thigh.

Germaine dashed to the slider, hauled it wide, and hurried along the bed of iris. The fresh air seemed shots of oxygen. She yanked open the casita's glass door crisscrossed by iron bars.

"Q, c'mere," Dirk commanded. "Pull her so her head's pillowed."

Quentin tugged at Raven's ankles, bluing like her forehead, until her neck pressed Dirk's thigh. The black hair, still shiny, had tangled into knots. Quentin rescued her glasses from the tiles and set them on her nose. Her jaw hung slack. He stared at the gold capping two molars.

Her chest heaved and she began to choke. "The tongue's slipped back," Dirk said. He thrust her upright and started slapping her spine.

Germaine, clutching the refrigerated barbiturate, re-entered the hacienda through the third bedroom's outside door. She ran past Isadella who was sitting on the edge of the mattress as if stoned, brushing imagined dust off the back of each finger. Isadella did not look up.

The editor reached the hall.

In the first bedroom, she stashed the brown bottle into her shoulder bag, snapped her suitcase shut, and raced into the living room.

Dirk and Quentin had draped Raven's arms over their shoulders, Dirk grimacing at the pain with which the weight tortured his bad leg. Vising her wrists, they dragged her among the sex-aid-bejeweled cushions to the vestibule. Germaine hurried past to open the mahogany door. The men followed along the flagstones until reaching the van.

She touched a key under the dented blue fender and peeled back what felt like electrical tape. Futz! She'd forgotten to snatch the purse she'd seen perched on Raven's dresser.

"You guys come with us, huh?" Germaine said. "I have no idea where the hospital is."

"No, sorry, no, can't do that. Can't." Quentin pulled open the passenger-side door. His heart lumbered as he and Dirk eased the comatose Raven onto the seat. Beads of sweat glistened on her bluing forehead.

The woman behind the wheel had to be his daughter—*had* to. Those eyes, those cadences, though their tone had deepened from—truly? Nineteen years ago? All Quentin could see suddenly was himself entering her bedroom, spotting her at the study table he'd bought, watching her press her earring while chewing on a pencil, illogically stating that he wanted her to lie down because he had a secret to share, and after she did so, standing at the bed's edge and unbuckling.

"Why can't you come with us?"

"I can't help with this anymore," Quentin said.

Dirk squinted over at his friend, then from Raven to Germaine, who had started the van's engine. He twisted down the volume of his Songbird. "See that fellow smoking on the corner? Turn right there until you reach Galisteo. Right again until Hospital Drive on your left."

"How do you know where to go?" Quentin asked.

"Vonnie drove me in for a rectal exam. Gotta go back next Friday."

Hadn't Germaine seen these two guys sitting under a cottonwood at the Plaza a couple of weeks ago? Wait! Could the one with the ponytail be her father? Those long fingers, the five furrows like crinkled parchment when he frowned, the sharp nose.

Where could she find him again?

She bit her lip, aching to ask. But the young woman sagging against the door looked dead. Germaine jerked the shift into reverse, backed out, wrenched the steering wheel to the left, and stomped on the accelerator.

Fritz and Arlene came running out, off the front stoop, and along the path. Finding the van gone, they veered across the gravel into the street in time to watch *Slow Down for Beautiful Tomorrows* disappear onto Columbia.

Dirk and Quentin lay low behind the neighbor's hedge until they saw the Josephs rush back to the drive. The two bunk mates, corners of the throwaway cameras biting their thighs, edged between coyote fencing and shrubbery toward Lucia, and St. Francis Drive beyond.

Behind them they heard the Hacienda's garage door grinding.

HUGS

"**R**aven swore to me three mornings ago," Arlene said, "after us getting it on the night before, that crushing three high-octane tablets of her Phenobiconal or whatever should easily do you in. This while you were shagging some floozy at the Desert Inn."

"Nope, babe; wasn't."

"Don't call me that, I told you."

"Cream puff?"

"No!"

"So what are we going to do?" Fritz asked.

The Josephs sat in their upstairs bedroom about ten, Arlene hunched on the edge of the spread, Fritz facing her in a leather bucket chair. Cold air pulsed through the vent tucked between ceiling latillas, though the sky would stay cloudy all day and the outside temperature reach only seventy-eight degrees.

A breeze rattled dry leaves in the cottonwood's canopy spreading near the spruce in the patio. Arlene gazed over rooftops to Tetilla Peak thirty miles to the southwest. She'd lit a stick of sandalwood incense to calm herself. A wisp of white smoke snaked up from the table.

"Yesterday afternoon," Fritz said—wearing long pants for a change and a khaki-colored shirt—"we should have followed the van all the way to the hospital. One of us should have driven it home."

"You're the van driver." Even in the conditioned air Arlene felt hot. She jiggled her blouse away from her chest.

"No one drives the 135i except you, I understand that, unless you let me," Fritz said.

"Why'd you tell me to turn around?"

He swiped at his crew cut. "Panicked that our pigeons would coo and the cops would greet us."

"Dead wrong, weren't you?"

"Didn't I just say that?"

"And Jonah on the curb smoking, and Isadella or -bella or who-the-hell pouring herself a third mugful of our best shade-grown. Did she look beached or what? I thought she'd come down with Parkinson's."

Fritz's dry laugh turned into coughing. He squinched his eyes and grabbed the silver chain looping his neck.

"Not funny. At least we unnerved our guests enough riding in the 135i down to the Sunport to stop them from squealing. You think?"

"You actually want my opinion?" Fritz asked.

"Ummm, no."

"I'm going to close the Web site."

"Today?"

"Not sure."

"Doctor Wishy-Wash? One thing we've got to do fast is figure out how to finish off our coke slut and the editor. Maybe they're still at Saint Vincent. And who were those two senior citizens who smashed the window in?"

"Rave's dealer and his pal?"

"But why here?"

"Witnesses? Maybe she'd told them you planned to poison me. That incense of yours'll do the job quicker."

Arlene jumped up. A ducktail flew out above her right ear. "Let's go check the hospital."

"Then the Harbor. We need Kat's advice, where to find—"

"A hit man."

Fritz tapped his temple with two fingers. "Wife's brain's still working. Pay one of those geezers who broke in? Homeless, probably; needs the bread."

"Go get the checkbook, yeah."

Fritz strode to the dresser under the view window and zipped open Arlene's sequined purse. He threw the keys at her and clamped the purse to his ribs.

"Goddamn it," she muttered, stooping for the keys, then yanking the purse from him. She jammed the hot end of the incense into its sandbox before leading him down the stairs.

The living room still looked trashed. Earlier, Fritz had hauled two carved doors from the garage and stashed them against what remained of the front window. He and Arlene had wedged the doors against its frame by lugging the wraparound sofa close. The glass-fronted cabinet now stood hiding the slider's lock and much of its see-through glass. Fritz had also slanted a broom handle between the slider's aluminum casing and the threshold, and pulled the pleated shade across.

"We paid a million five for this dump?" Fritz commented, careful to step around the tiles tilting up from their mortar as he headed for the vestibule.

"And the rotten eggs you scrambled for breakfast still reek."

— — —

Six hours later, Raven lay propped by pillows printed with eagle feathers in one of the queen-size beds in the deluxe double that Judy had booked for Germaine at the Hotel Santa Fe, owned fifty-one percent by the Picuris Pueblo.

A white terry-cloth robe wrapped Raven's shoulders. Germaine had found it in the closet opposite the bath that separated bedroom and sitting room. Thanks to yesterday's stomach pumping, followed by doses of activated carbon and an adrenal stimulant—plus today's light lunch at the cafeteria before Germaine drove her here—the sex facilitator looked pretty good, though wan. The blue discolorations on her forehead and temples were gone. The editor had tied back Raven's black waves with ribbon she'd picked out at the hotel's gift shop.

But Raven's chin seemed palsied—and, without pencil, her eyebrows seemed plucked in the wrong places. She licked dried lips. "I've never been clean this long," she complained, wiping the drip from her nose with the back of her hand, then knuckling moisture from the corners of her eyes. "We've got to get to the refuge! All my stash is at the casita under the mat."

Germaine had pulled a chair close to the bed. She'd been skimming a manuscript that Judy thought merited the editor's eye. "What you need is bed rest, Raven." She kicked off her flats without looking up. "I've hidden the van, by the way."

"Fuck that. I need blow. You don't know addiction. What am I going to do? The Josephs want me dead. Bet they want you long gone, too. Have you got a Kleenex?"

"On the bed table."

"Oh, yeah." Raven yanked out a tissue, dabbed her eyes, and snorted.

"Today you and I do nothing. You're recovering from a rough night and I'm to make sure you take your Vitamin D and the stomach stabilizer. Jimmy had a five-hour delay in Dallas but he's on his way. Tomorrow when you've got more strength, we go see the police. I kept your bottle of Phenobiconal."

"What about the photos from Dirk and the guy you think's your father."

"Tomorrow."

"Hey, I can't go back to the Hacienda for the video!"

"Don't need to, Raven."

"Where's Jimmy Jammy gonna sleep?"

"The couch in the sitting room has a pull-out mattress."

"Put me in there and close that accordion door, goddamn it. Give yourselves some privacy."

"Calm down, huh?" Germaine squared the pages of the manuscript and laid the pile on the carpeting. "I already have one boyfriend."

"Some boyfriend. He wouldn't even fly out with you."

"Because I told him not to."

"I've got to connect with Foreflasher!"

"Who?"

"My dealer. He and his girlfriend camp out near the composer. Don't you want to see him?"

"I saw him yesterday."

"But how can you be sure he's your father? Okay, calling himself Q seems a giveaway but you two hardly talked." Raven whooshed out her breath and swiped black strands from a forehead shiny with sweat—though the central conditioner was humming. She thumbed up the pink frames that kept sliding down her nose. "I feel ants crawling all over me. Let's beat it."

"Time enough tomorrow, if he is my dad, to tell him about the Red River Music Festival and get the photos developed. Today we're staying put."

"You're staying put. I'm heading out." Raven hurled off the blanket and black-and-white spread, and swung her feet to the carpet.

"You don't have your purse."

"So what?"

"Your license."

"Then you drive."

"Stop it, Raven!" Germaine stood and bent to grip the other's ankles. "After the blood test, you told the hospital psychiatrist that no way had you meant to kill yourself. I told the crisis counselor, before I left, the same. Were they lies?" She hoisted the sex facilitator's ankles onto the sheet. "I'll go buy you your Lady C—alone."

"Nope, you'll never get into that refuge on your own. Flasher'll think you're a narc."

"Raven…"

"Shut the fuck up!"

They stared at each other as Raven arced her bare feet to the carpet.

"All right. I washed the puke from your halter. Go shower while I order us something from room service. And shove those two vials of pills into a pocket."

— — —

An hour before dark, Germaine parked the van on Sierra Vista around the corner from Kat's Harbor. Raven led the way. She felt woozy but the dark clip-ons for her glasses lay in her purse at the casita.

She opened the chain-link gate at the end of Felipe and wobbled in her two-inch spikes from yesterday along the path toward the sofa.

Tish raised the broken-handled .38 and tipped back her rolled sombrero.

Germaine realized she'd seen this red-headed specter at the Plaza two weeks ago.

"Put the fucking heater down. I'm Cravin' Raven—Foreflasher's my street pharmacist. Where is he?"

"Bow wow wow." The hair on Tish's mole twitched. "Harbor? Headquarters, maybe? You been crying?"

"No hit for over twenty-four hours. Where's Q?"

"Can't you hear him? His new playmate don't know squat about working a roll-up keyboard. Though he claims once he played the organ for some church choir. Hoo boy."

A waterfall of tones, which sounded to Raven as if produced by a honky-tonk piano left out in the rain, came from the direction of Quentin's former campsite. Raven pushed at her updo of hair, secured by a ballpoint from the hotel. "Yeah, I hear it." Her arms started shaking. She jerked her head toward the editor. "Kleenex?"

Germaine produced a tissue and Raven blew.

"And who's this?" Tish asked.

"Maybe Q's daughter."

"Maybe? She okay?" Tish pumped her hand holding the snub-nosed revolver up and down.

"Of course she is. Bringing good news. Festival up north wants to pay to play Q's music, if you call it that."

"So hot diggety! Permission to pass granted." Tish swept her free hand toward the path leading to the Lightningfeathers' camp, and the camp beyond that Stormy was using, now that Quentin bunked inside with Dirk.

"That high voice from Headquarters sounds like Flasher's," Raven said. "Gotta go see him first."

"So do it." In her camouflage shirt, Tish curtsied before Germaine, spreading a flounced red skirt between thumbs and forefingers.

Gnats danced around the editor's face as she followed Raven under the elm and locust branches.

At Headquarters, what turned out to be five voices grew louder. As Raven veered toward the lean-to, Germaine spotted two women and three men, all talking at once, gathered around a circle of rocks topped by a grate. Beyond, green steel stakes secured a chicken-wire fence enclosing a mottled dog—its forelegs bones, barely furred. Patches of skin gleamed on its hindquarters.

A grasshopper whirred up, making Germaine gasp. She ducked into the clearing.

"Flasher, listen," Stormy was saying, sombrero set over his Capital Motors cap. He stroked the ends of his mustache. "Only reason I came back was to help you and Uni pen in the bowwow, so Cupcake can ask Kat to get Uni his exerciser."

"Okeydokey, but," the refuge's self-appointed overseer began.

"Lemme finish up here."

"Mind the attitude, Storm Born, you're on probation." Flasher now addressed Raven. "Be with you shortly, gorgeous, even though you look sleep deprived. Who's your lookin'-like-no-prob-sleepin' friend? Girlie who drove you to the hospital? Don't talk—Q an' Dirky's tole us everthin'."

Flasher turned his hatchet face to Germaine, who stood straight-arming the top of a charred stump, gawking. "Sit, please," he squeaked. She lowered herself into a director's chair and set her shoulder bag in a clump of buffalo grass.

Raven bit her upper lip, snuffled, and sank into a chair under Tish's hummingbird feeders. Her tummy hurt. She extracted the vial of promethazine from a side pocket and gulped down a capsule dry.

Flasher pulled the Chesterfields from the camouflage T-shirt's sleeve rolled above his biceps, brought a small box of matches from the pocket sewn to a thigh of his fatigues, and lit up.

"Here's the deal, Flasher," Stormy said. "And I betcha Clara, and Chiffon herself, will back me. I want to relocate from Q's to Reuben's camp, get closer to Clara's setup. Then Chiffon can escape the crowd by moving her ass out to where I'm holed up now. Clara doll, you dig it?"

The chemotherapy-bald former blonde glanced at her toothless African-American friend, who pushed out her lips in a pout. "Well, Lord, it's a possibility," Chiffon offered.

"No, it ain't," Reuben said. "Kat threw you two girls out of the Harbor and my wife and Hisi said well, sure, come on, sleep with us till you get to your feet." He grunted, doubled his tattooed forearm, and clamped the bicep with his right hand. "That in no circumstances means we want the knifer with us. I'll sic Hisi's mutt on him."

"No fair, Reuben." Clara said and clutched the orange scarf crossing her neck. "Stormy's good company when he's not drinking."

"And not gonna, Reuben. Keep the faith."

The big Native American grunted.

"Foreflasher," Raven bleated, "I'm dying here."

"Seems to me you've been saved."

"I need—"

"I'm aware of that item an' gonna supply you. Just hold on a moment, you an' your chaperone there."

He faced Germaine. She caught a whiff of cologne.

"Guessin' you're our composer's daughter. Guessin' right?"

"Probably," the editor whispered and smoothed a palm down her skirt.

"And I'm off the bottle forever," Stormy blurted to no one.

Uni's brown-and-white mongrel, quiet until now, had begun to moan. Because in Quentin's former camp, Dirk playing the roll-up had switched piano tones to a high-pitched line on the cello? The mutt paced the wire, back and forth, watery eyes gazing at the crowd of seven, hind legs as fleshless as those in front. Like Dirk it limped a bit, and one ear hung loosely.

"I'm purposing to ask Kat if she'll let us flop inside again," Chiffon said. "Those bunks are still empty."

"No! Clara and I're getting tight, aren't we, doll?" Stormy raised a forefinger to diddle the fold under Clara's chin. She stepped away.

"She drinking, too?" Reuben asked.

"She's not and me neither. Give it a rest, will you?"

"Hold on!" Flasher scraped his three rings with his thumbnail. "How 'bout we try you promisin' no more rum an' I take that blade of yours for safekeepin'?"

"Do that," Chiffon said, "and if Kat don't relent, I'm willing to go it alone at Q's camp, long as there's no more him and Dirk sneaking back to play his damn noises."

Stormy mouthed his lower lip. "Flasher, dude? Days, the switchblade stays put." He patted a rear pocket of his jeans. "To protect my sweetie."

"Don't believe I'm pregnant," Chiffon said in an apparent non sequitur. She rubbed her potbelly. The right hand that the cowboy had stomped into a claw dangled beside the faded dress.

"You better not be," Clara said.

"Don't mean by that one." The African-American swung her claw toward Stormy.

"Look," Reuben said to him, "I gotta go fix dinner. Understand me carefully. A man who stabs an unarmed man like you stabbed Buzzy does not sleep where my family sleeps." He started toward the path leading to the sofa.

"Go to hell," the Iraq war veteran muttered. His lip lifted to display four oversized incisors.

Flasher took a drag from his cigarette. His guts growled as he bent to cough. "Storm Born, you want to camp with Clara Bare, you clear out the rabbitbrush an' thistles next to the mutt. Otherwise, you keep hangin' at Q's. Or you're history here."

Raven jumped up. The ballpoint holding the black waves clinked a hubcap swaying from the lean-to. "Let's go find your father." She hauled Germaine from her chair, wincing at the cramp in her belly. "Buzzy with him?" she asked Flasher.

"Buzzy Wuz has pretty much moved in with Von Bon."

"That's Vonnie, Kat's helper," Chiffon started to explain to Germaine. "The Flasher's chippie and her teach—"

"Shut your mouth, you black slut," Flasher snapped. "Tish's my sister."

"Sister!" Clara burst out. "Huh?"

"Ever since she left the womb."

"Give him his fun," Stormy sneered.

"You implyin' just what there, Storm Born?"

"Implying nothing, Flasher, 'cept you and she make ends meet with one sleeping bag."

"Yep, we do. Bein' dead sure our mother's properly looked after pretty much drains our funds." Flasher sucked air through his Chesterfield until the tip became a coal. "You aimin' to argue that?"

The sombrero tumbled off the billed cap as Stormy wagged his head no. He bent to pick it up.

"All I planned to mean, Mr. Foul Mouth, sir, is Tish assists Vonnie to homeschool Kat's granddaughter." Chiffon turned to Germaine. "But Vonnie's leaving soon and Buzzy's traveling with her. Q's gonna miss Buzzy more than all of us missing the both of—"

"Girlie, clam it, can't you manage?"

"—them!" Chiffon spit at Flasher. She knuckled her lips dry. "Clammed."

A black-headed grosbeak began a series of whistles from the thorned branch of a locust.

"I'll return pronto," Raven said.

"You got funds?"

"She doesn't but I do," Germaine said.

"Nah. Tonight's on the house."

Free blow from Flasher? He must have decided to cheat on Tish. Raven snuffled hard and kicked an empty pint of bourbon off the path— avoiding the badger's den she'd almost stumbled into a week ago. But her joints ached and her head felt as if swelling with helium.

She brushed away a clump of rabbitbrush and saw Quentin in his rain hat and flowered guayabera sunk into a beach chair beside a juniper. No wind fluttered its needles. The overarching sodium lamp at the refuge's southwest corner clicked on, yellowing the evening's clouded light. Stormy's sleeping bag lay open nearby. A disheveled, thorny fence of the branches Quentin had felled encircled the composer, Stormy's bag, and the heap of nylon that had served as Quentin's lean-to. As Germaine came up beside Raven, they heard what sounded like a street sweeper grinding the end of its brush against a curb near the Harbor.

When Quentin saw Germaine, he jerked as if gripping a live wire. He stared at her and Raven on the far side of the clearing, where he'd first encountered Stormy two weeks ago drunk and snoring. His forehead became wrinkled parchment.

"Hello, Dad," Germaine risked. Acid coursed into her throat. She pushed the pearl into her earlobe.

Quentin thumbed an imaginary earring into his own lobe and stretched one side of his lips into a shy smile. "Hello."

"I'll be back at sundown," Raven said. She wheeled and hurried toward Headquarters.

As Germaine advanced, she pressed the blouse covering her heart, letting gnats flit freely around her face. "So you knew yesterday. Is that why—"

"I wouldn't get into the van?" Quentin looked down, sucking his lips between his teeth, and scraped a dab of dried mud off one knee of his gabardines. "Yes," he said, lifting his eyes. "Hell's broth, I was ashamed." He rose. The keyboard flapped to the dirt, covering his spiral notebook and pen.

"Oh, Daddy!" She broke into a run and, before hugging him, simply let him enfold her.

She kissed his neck and stepped away. "Daddy—but this is a miracle. No more goatee. A ponytail! Face hair, scraggly…show me your hands."

He extended them, palms down, then straight-armed the juniper. His Adam's apple clogged his throat.

"No long fingernails to click on the keys? Even after all these years with no wife to nag you about them, Dad?"

They laughed and clutched each other.

"Aren't you going to have to pay an awful lot on your credit cards? Your back rent in New York?"

"I guess so. Germaine? It's *you*, isn't it?"

"You're crying." She dropped her hand past her shoulder bag to find a tissue in her skirt, and reached to blot the near corners of his eyes. "You actually keep composing in this strange place?"

"Will you sit by me?"

They stepped toward the second beach chair.

"Daddy? Rudi Shasky called Mother. The director of the Red River Music Festival—it's somewhere north of Taos—was in the audience here in Santa Fe when you premiered the piece you wrote for me. The woman loved it! She wants you for composer-in-residence up there in a couple of summers. And she wants to commission a new work."

Germaine let Quentin be the one to bring the extra chair close, smoothed her skirt under her thighs, and sat. When he had sat, too, she placed her hand on his.

He sighed and dropped his chin.

"Aren't you happy, Dad?"

"About the call from Shasky?"

"Yes!"

"Happier having you close by."

"Daddy, Daddy, these rags you're wearing, that beautiful Mexican shirt, torn. You're coming home with me. Day after tomorrow. I forgive us both for, you know, so many years ago, getting enmeshed."

Quentin blinked but could not stop more tears. "I need that Kleenex," he murmured.

"Let me do it, Dad." She found another tissue in her pocket, and dried his eyes.

"Raven seems to have recovered awfully fast," he said.

"She's as unbelievable as everything else that's been happening."

"How were you mixed up with that gang at the hacienda yesterday?"

She felt her face heat. "I'm embarrassed."

"You don't have to tell me."

"But I want to. I've never held onto a boyfriend for more than a year, Daddy. Never been able to give myself wholly to anyone—" except to you, my soul, she thought, gazing at the weatherbeaten lines in his cheeks.

"What do you mean, wholly?"

"I'm embarrassed.

"Let's leave it, Germaine."

"The trouble happens mostly in bed. Men like to feel they can help you, okay, climax at the same time they do. I've never been able to cum at all, even on my own."

"Oh."

They stayed silent, watching a butterfly lower and raise its mottled wings. At last it flew off the ragweed pod and zigzagged upward, disappearing toward the Lightningfeathers' campsite.

"That house where you found me," Germaine said, "I discovered on the Web: Beautiful Tomorrows. All those sex toys you saw on the cushions? The idea is to spend a weekend learning, well, techniques. But it's a blackmail ring."

"I know all that. Beautiful Tomorrows has been a big contributor to our homeless shelter nearby, but the owners have pulled back funding. Dirk, my sidekick yesterday, who made Raven throw up, thought we could do our own blackmailing."

"Raven explained some things this morning. But where's the young man with you at the Plaza two weeks ago?"

"You saw us?" Quentin asked.

"Sitting beside a cottonwood. I didn't recognize you then."

"His nickname's Buzzy. I don't know his real name. He'd play out my scores on that keyboard." Quentin leaned over to retrieve it and shook the dust off. "I can't talk about him, I choke up. He's decided to head east with a girl."

"So Dirk's your partner now?"

"Friend, like Buzzy, who didn't want to—"

"Don't say any more. But aren't you lonely? Why aren't you—"

"Living at the shelter? I am, for now—free meals. But I miss the outdoors. As do my ladies."

"Ladies, Dad?"

Quentin explained.

"But, Daddy, you can't keep living like this! You've got no home."

"This refuge feels more like home than my row house in Queens. Breathe this air, look how the elm branches embrace in that grove, those three ravens sailing over the street lamp. At night, the owls and coyotes sing. I have no responsibilities except to eat, shower once in a while, and make music. There, in those weeds, see how that black beetle rears, settles, and rears again? What's he hearing? Us? What he's showing me is how to end the second movement of my sonata."

Quentin bent to grab his notebook and ballpoint off the dirt, opened to a blank page, and began to ink in quarter notes staggering up the scale. They plunged to the bottom line to become eighth notes, then soared through two octaves in couplets and triplets.

He closed the pen in the notebook, stashed it between his thighs, filled his lungs, let the breath go, and grinned across at his daughter.

She extended her arms.

Like angels' wings, he thought.

"You can do ladies and beetles in New York, Daddy. Please! Winter's two months away. I don't want to worry about you. And if my promotion goes through, maybe you'll move to San Francisco with me."

"I don't know, darling."

Darling! What she called Jock. The word warmed her like a comforter and made her stiffen, equally. Was she inviting a bizarre reprise of the two years in her early teens that this parent had been her lover? "All right," she said, trying to smooth her curls with one hand and brush away gnats with the other. "Not day after tomorrow—take a week to think. Then I'm flying out here."

"Germaine?"

"Yes?"

"Your mother's said how well you've been doing at Bennett. But what's she been up to since I've stayed in Santa Fe—a month now? A year?"

Germaine gave him news.

Soon Raven shambled into view, face sweaty, pupils swollen to the edges of her irises, hair fallen to one side.

"Doan wan' you miss Jimmy Jammy." She leaned against the trunk of a locust, mouth slack.

Germaine hoisted her shoulder bag and stood. "Jimmy's a friend I'm meeting, Dad—oh. The throwaway cameras. Have you got them?"

"Dirk does."

"I'll pick 'em up affer I drah you off," Raven told Germaine.

"What do you mean, drop me off?"

"Flasher says s'mores tonigh'. Says Dirky's goan for Hersheys an' grahams an' marshmells. Maybe your father'll play lullaby 'e wro you."

"A lullaby, Dad?" Germaine's emotions began to muddle. "Wait a minute, you can't drive!"

Raven laughed and clutched her tummy. "Doesn' have a car."

"I mean you!"

"Learn a' swee' sixteen, hon."

"Your wallet's at the Hacienda. Daddy, I want to hear my lullaby."

"Now?"

"Yes—no! Jimmy's due at the hotel."

"I'll be here tomorrow."

"Oh, Daddy." She rushed over and bent to pull his head to her breasts.

She released him. "Why don't you just stay at the refuge?" she called to Raven. "You brought the stomach stabilizers and the vitamin D?"

Raven exaggerated a nod and slapped the left pocket of her shorts.

"I'll pick you up after Jimmy and I talk."

"Tha's all you're gonna do?"

"Unless he hasn't had dinner."

"All?"

"Oh, shut up, Raven. Last night you were almost done for and look at yourself now. Stoned."

"Aftercare."

"I'll be back for you."

But the sex facilitator pushed off the tree, wobbled past Quentin in her heels, and followed the editor.

The Lightningfeathers' part-husky started barking.

Germaine stopped, spun, and cocked her forefinger at Raven. "You stay put!"

"Noo, noo, noo."

"Why?"

"You my gooh-luh charm."

"Well, you're not coming back here tonight."

"Okay," Raven lied, determined to give Germaine and Jimmy time to tumble in the hay. She felt warm and fuzzy toward the pudgy dweeb.

— — —

Five minutes from Kat's Harbor, Germaine swung the van off Cerrillos into the front lot of the Hotel Santa Fe. She spotted an empty slot below the bronze Picuris chief on his knees, praying. Shuttles to the Sunport and the hotel's purple minibuses waited beyond the sculpture. But tube lights at the entrance scared her off—what if the Josephs, or police, were hunting the van? She wrenched the wheels right and parked around the building's corner.

She turned off the engine and stole a look at Raven. Her black waves spread across the yellow halter. She seemed to be sleeping, mouth wide, breasts rising and sagging. Germaine couldn't believe Raven still carried the faint scent of the hotel's soap she'd showered with, what, two hours ago?

As the editor pulled the key from the ignition and gripped the door handle, Raven jerked into action. She grabbed the key from Germaine's right hand, thrust down the handle on her own side, elbowed the door wide, and hopped out, snuffling hard.

"Raven!"

"Cash me!" She slammed the door shut.

Germaine leapt to the asphalt and ran around the van's grille while Raven skirted the rear bumper, climbed into the driver's seat, and thumb-locked the doors.

Germaine began beating the window, her forehead pleating like one of the Hacienda's Roman shades.

Raven grinned at her, then thrust the key into the ignition, twisted it, and stomped the pedal to the mat. At the roar, the editor pressed against the hotel wall, goggling as the van backed away.

The facilitator threw the shift into Drive and rolled her window partway down. The turquoise ring on her thumb glowed in the yellow light that fanned over the asphalt. "You two have a time. See you with the cam'ras roun' mihnigh,' affer I turn into a pum'kin."

Germaine clapped her palms to her ears as the van raced around the corner and squealed out of the lot.

She hoisted her shoulder bag and trudged toward two huge pots, each holding a spruce. She passed under the lintel painted with the Picuris's *mah-waan, mah-waan* welcome into the air-conditioned lobby.

Jimmy faced her at the oaken table that held magazines and guides, plus menus in a green binder. A nylon duffle waited beside him. He wore the bracelet of coins and red silk shirt rolled to the elbows that Germaine remembered from their weekend at the Hacienda early in the month. He seemed to have shed some pounds—his cheeks, though just as pink as then, did not jiggle when he looked up.

"Hello, Jimmy." She smiled, blew out air, and pressed a pearl to her earlobe. "I'm so glad you're here. You should have used my name, gone on up."

"They wouldn't give me a key card."

"Oh, dear, I forgot to tell the front desk." She took a tentative step. Before she could take another, he had jumped up, rounded the table's end, and was holding out his hands.

He *had* lost weight; no spare tire spread out against her as they embraced.

A family of Anglos—the man in jeans and a Stetson, the woman in thigh-length skirt and salmon-colored boa, the boy wearing a Santa Fe Rodeo cap, the little girl displaying a shirt imprinted with hobbyhorses—followed a Native American bellhop pushing a cartful of luggage through the glass door. Germaine and Jimmy moved toward the table's end to let the family pass.

"Did you buy today's *Times*?" Jimmy asked.

She shook her head.

"Our new defense secretary says he's going to recommend that Bush veto the Senate's bill to give troops more rest, before resuming their acts of mayhem in the Middle East. And the Iraqi government has taken away Blackwater Security's right to fight there."

"Jim. Jim." She took his elbow. "No more."

"You like my new shoes?"

She glanced down at the white tasseled loafers. "I'm not sure, Jimmy."

"No need. My doggie and I and my doggie's new friend had such a hoot Sunday a week ago shepherding the hoards to our south-shore, Key Largo sales office that I wore the same shoes today to bring you and me luck. Have you searched for your father?"

"I found him, Jim. What a story to tell you."

"Can we do it in the restaurant? I'm famished."

"You didn't eat at the airport?"

"I was too eager to see you." His cheeks' pink deepened and his freckled forehead dipped. A shock of blond hair fell over a brow. He brushed it away and raised his eyes. "We go to the police tomorrow?"

"I think. So much has happened since yesterday when I phoned you. Poor Raven! I'll try to explain…. Just wait till you taste the food here. She and I dined on elk and wild mushrooms in our room."

"She's here?"

"Not right now."

Germaine led him between the bar and kiva fireplace to the stand where the Native American hostess waited, a white tummy apron spread across her black slacks.

By eight-thirty Germaine and Jimmy stood in the elevator, rising to the second floor. Germaine could hear a wheeze coursing up his throat, though his lips stayed closed.

The door slid aside and she took him along the diamond-patterned carpet to her room, inserted the card, twisted the knob, and—entering—switched on the floor lamp in the sitting room. "Voilà. Let's see if the sleeper couch works."

"This is first class!" He plopped his duffle next to the dresser.

Germaine had tossed her shoulder bag to the pine chair and began to drag the coffee table aside. She and Jimmy tumbled pillows and three cushions to the carpet and hauled on the aluminum bar that brought the mattress up and out, then stepped back to stretch it full length.

"Jimmy, dear, I'm drained. Okay if we just go to sleep? I'm sorry." She placed her hand on his forearm. "We'll be together tomorrow night. Meantime, think how we're going to approach the cops."

"I may read a little to wind down."

"Do you need to use the bathroom first?"

He shook his head and attempted a smile, dimpling his cheeks. "At least so far my asthma's just a purr."

"Hooray!" She raised her fists. "Open the cabinet and you'll find a minibar. If you hear a knock later, go ahead and let our addict in."

In less than an hour Germaine had showered, shampooed, brushed, turned out the light over the fireplace, and slipped under the covers nude, as she always slept. She lay on her back, hands cradling her head, breathing in the sweetness of the hothouse mums set next to the telephone between Raven's and her beds. The hum of traffic below the balcony leaked through wooden blinds she'd shut on the French doors. Cool air rushed intermittently through a vent in the ceiling.

She discovered herself recalling a Sunday afternoon with her mother and father, years before he'd asked her to lie on her bed and started unbuckling his belt. They were playing Monopoly cross-legged in the living room, sipping the cider he'd mulled. She had been winning; she won all the hotels and her father was in jail. "Have you no mercy?" he'd asked, and her mother and she had had a grand time laughing, and he'd joined in and crawled over to give both a hug.

She rolled to her hip facing the door she'd decided not to close to the bath that separated Jimmy's and her room. "Are you awake?" she called. Light filled the doorway on his side that he'd left open, too.

"Yes."

"I hope someone at the refuge found a sleeping bag for Raven. She shouldn't be driving."

Germaine heard something in his room clang. Springs? Okay, she admitted to wishing he'd come in. She tucked her knees toward her tummy, closed her eyes, and sighed.

She heard what sounded like slippers shuffling across the bathroom tiles, and his faint wheeze.

She smelled salt before she felt his shoulder, covered in fabric smoother than the hotel robe's terry cloth, nudge her toward the center of the bed.

In the false dusk she opened her eyes and discerned his own staring. "You're wearing pajamas," she whispered.

He stroked her exposed cheek, then pressed his lips to hers. As their tongues caressed, a buzzing began in her vagina. She straightened out her legs. His erection, smaller than Jock's, certainly smaller than Fritz's zucchini, flattened the veins on the back of her hand.

"I thought what if we don't get a chance tomorrow?" he murmured.

"Are you wearing silk?" She fumbled for and untied the string of his bottoms.

"Korean."

"It feels so slithery, Jimmy. But this half goes." She pushed the waistband to his ankles and he shrugged his feet free.

"Are you safe?" he asked.

"Safe?"

"I brought a condom."

"I'm on the pill but maybe you should use it."

"I've been dreaming of this since you called." He kissed her again and asked her to roll to her back.

She scrunched her breasts together. "Let's not talk."

She felt a sensation she'd never known, a whirlpool beginning.

"Open your legs, will you, Germaine?" He eased the condom on.

But instead of mounting her, he threw the covers back, turned, and settled a knee on each side of her waist. She gasped and clasped his head with her thighs. The whirlpool inside gained speed and began to heat.

She trembled and drew air between her teeth. "Would you like me to...?"

He lifted his face. "I don't want to cum yet. I want to be the one to give you—"

"Then keep going, Jimmy!"

He buried his head again.

"Yes, Jim, oh, yes." Her hands massaged his shoulders. "Ohhh." She lifted her buttocks from the sheet and moved them in small circles.

He quickened his pace and she longed for the whirlpool to never stop spinning.

"Jimmy, I..." Her whole body shuddered with an orgasm, not transforming, just a for-instance of joy, like leaping nude out of frigid air into a steam-plumed spring. She arched her back and flung her forearms around his neck.

A minute passed before either moved. He raised his head smiling and said, "Yes!"

"It's never happened, Jimmy!"

"I know that."

"Get inside me, I want you inside me, Jimmy darling."

"It's just lovely," he murmured and after a few moments of pumping, gasped, "I'm cumming, I'm cumming, I'm..."

He fell on her, staying inside, and kissed her lips, her cheeks, her neck, and her black curls.

"I loved that pajama top flapping around while you were screwing me, Jim. And I came, I really came!"

"We both did."

He slid off and she reached to pull the blanket and sheet to their chins, then turned to face the balcony and doubled her legs—and he cuddled against her, throwing his left arm over her shoulder to enclose a breast.

THE NOOSE TIGHTENS

Tuesday 18 September 2007

Germaine woke at eight the next morning to Jimmy's snores in the sitting room. Why had he left her bed?

The air-conditioning had not yet clicked on nor had the sound of traffic below the balcony built past an occasional roar.

The editor turned from the sunlit blinds and tucked her hands between the back of her head and the pillow. She closed her eyes to replay reconciling with her father, feeling safe in his embrace, listening to his talk about his ladies and the beetle, watching him compose, breathing the scent of dry grass on his neck and forearms.

Then lovemaking with Jimmy, his tongue! She inserted her right hand under the covers, surprised by her sudden yearning to be in bed with Jock, caress the black strands curling from his chest, discover if…Jimmy! Why did you leave? Jock has never done that. But neither does he snore.

Her saliva tasted sour. She pushed upright against the pillow and yanked the sheet over her breasts. "Jimmy!" she shouted. "I want to go home!"

No reply. She mussed her curls, wiggled her feet into fuzzy slippers, rose, and grabbed the hotel's robe she'd draped across a chair arm. She slipped the terry cloth around her, tied the sash, and walked over to open the blinds darkening the balcony's French doors. Over the hotel's ponderosas and still-leafy wisteria she gazed across Cerrillos at the sun-bleached umbrellas of the Sage Bakehouse adobe.

"Germaine?"

She turned.

Jimmy appeared barefoot in the bathroom that separated the two rooms, clad in the red silk pajamas she'd not really seen until now. One hand held the *New Mexican Courier*, the other swept a shock of blond hair from his forehead. "Did I hear you call?" He squeezed his eyes shut and opened them.

"I wanted you to wake beside me."

"My wife used to say I make noises when I sleep. And I thought maybe I'd been too pushy."

"Dear Jimmy, you pushed beautifully."

His lips spread in a grin. "You see the paper? No, of course not—I hopped downstairs to buy one. Thirty-eight hundred of our soldiers as of yesterday have died in Iraq."

"I want to go home early, Jimmy. Not tomorrow—today."

"It occurred to me you might."

"We don't even have the negatives that my father and his friend took Sunday. To develop and show the cops. That damn Raven."

"Dealing with her demons somewhere." He tossed the paper on the spread, skirted the chair, and threw out his arms. "Morning hug?"

Germaine tilted her face. "Of course."

They held each other.

"I haven't even washed," she said.

"And I'm trusting you not to smell my breath."

She laughed as cold air started blowing from the ceiling vent and she stepped out of its flow. "I'll call my assistant to change my ticket. Then let's head down for the buffet."

"The desk clerk said all rooms have high-speed wireless. I'll change both our tickets—I brought my laptop. Maybe we can at least take the same plane to Dallas."

"Oh, Jimmy, you pink-cheeked lug. I wish...." His scent seemed a warm muffin's. "I'd better phone the police and tell them to call off the hunt for my father."

"I'll do it if you like. But what about exposing the Josephs?"

"I'll be in far better emotional shape to hand over photos—and videos if Raven can retrieve them—when I get back in a week."

— — —

Clean-ups at the Harbor took place on Tuesday afternoons but so far Kat had failed at roping in volunteers. She'd not yet settled on who should get Clara's and Chiffon's bunks: Uni was helping Stormy clear a campsite and dog run; Dirk had begged off as a favor to Quentin to attend a seminar at St. Elizabeth's on winter survival tactics, and then to glean tips from Quentin and Byron for playing a roll-up keyboard.

After three years away, Marta *would* have to choose today to visit—sometime before five, she'd said. Kat had donned her work boots and Marta's paint-spattered apron, and tied a dish towel over her looped braid. She stood in the kitchen doorway holding a faux-feather duster.

Vonnie sat in cutoffs and red T-shirt blazing with yellow flames at a door-on-sawhorses dining table near the TV. Kat's granddaughter gripped the table's edge with a chubby hand as she read aloud for clarity—and, hopefully, comprehension—the first three pages of Jimmy Santiago Baca's story, "Matilda's Garden."

"Louder, pumpkin, I can't hear you over the fan," Vonnie said.

Kat looked past her shoulder at the clock. She was about to lasso Bea and Vonnie for work detail when she startled at four rapid-fire knocks on the screen door.

"Marta!" Beatriz yelped.

"Your *abuela* asthed me to surprithe you, little one."

It was only two-thirty—*damn* it. Kat had meant to bring in some of the blossoms from her former lover's hollyhocks. She'd meant to climb to the roof to wash off the two skylights above Marta's old studio become the men's guest room. She'd meant.... But she clomped forward with a "Welcome, stranger," and let Beatriz receive the first embrace.

Kat heard her own teeth click as Marta's arms encircled her. Just as they used to hug before meals instead of saying grace. The remembered cool of the café owner's lone, hand-enameled pendant, swinging from her left ear to settle against Kat's temple. She closed her eyes, relishing the delicious flatness of Marta's chest, draped in a white blouse and embroidered vest.

"The young woman is Vonnie, my intern," Kat said, releasing her lanky former lover.

"My teacher!" Beatriz exclaimed. "But she's leaving in a week with her boyfriend to go finish college."

"Tish will be able to help you, *mijita*." The flesh under Kat's arm wobbled as she circled her granddaughter's shoulder.

Beatriz ducked and stamped her shoe on the floor. "She sets me back a grade! Half the time she's high."

"I let no one in who's high, you know that."

"She coaxes me outside, where she leaves her stash."

Kat shook her head at Marta and turned up her hands. "I'm trying."

"You're not!"

"Stop now, Bea. Just stop. You promised no more if I let you start going to Alvord with Marcelina in January." And where would the Harbor find the thousand dollars Flasher paid Kat monthly to let Tish call herself Bea's teacher? And to buy Kat's help to keep cops out of the refuge?

"Maybe you'll homeschool me when Vonnie leaves?" Beatriz asked Marta. "I thought you and Abuelita were mad at each other. Did she invite you here?"

"To thee you, Bea." Pink sneakers squeaking, Marta walked to the sofa near the southern windows.

Beatriz followed in a flowered skirt. Dimpled at the elbows, her arms encircled the belt of Marta's slacks.

"Marta has no time to school you, Bea. She—"

"How do you know?"

"That's rude," the Harbor's director said.

"Kat?" Vonnie called from across the room. "There're people on the porch. They were here yesterday—I forgot to tell you."

At the single, hard knock Kat turned to recognize the unsmiling Josephs, their sunroofed, metallic-silver 135i glittering at the curb. No hat protected Fritz's cropped hair. He hadn't shaved for a day.

Arlene carried a sequined purse.

The director covered her mouth—no time to have done her face or dabbed on Sweet Violet. "Hello!" she managed and turned again. "Bea, take Marta out to see how her garden's thriving. We'll talk later about your attitude. Vonnie, have her recite for Marta under the apricot, where it's shady. These folks on the porch are our major benefactors."

Maybe they've relented over slashing their commitment, Kat thought, opening the screen door. "I was just starting to clean. Please. Come in." She remembered the dish towel wrapping her hair, and blushed. "Excuse me." She uncovered her braid and smoothed it down, then threw the towel onto an armchair. "Here, by the wall, on the sofa. Please. Coffee? Some wine?"

Neither Joseph replied. Fritz's loafers slapped the planked floor as Arlene, bereft of jewelry, followed in a pleated skirt and limp blouse. Kat lugged a chair close from beside the piano.

"Who are those people you sent away?" Arlene asked, lowering herself beside Fritz.

"You probably remember Marta. She owns the café where we had our quarterly last week. Vonnie's my intern. She homeschools my granddaughter. You were here yesterday? Why didn't you call? What's going on?"

"We need to know who's been selling Raven cocaine, Kat, and fast," Fritz said in monotone. "For the favor there may be a financial windfall for the Harbor."

She tidied her hair. "You'll restore your donation to three thousand a month?"

"I didn't say that."

No way Kat intended to squeal on the man who gave her a monthly thousand, who hadn't missed since appearing with Tish down from Rio Arriba County in May. "Raven?" she asked. "Who's Raven?"

"Our housekeeper. Don't play stupid," Arlene said.

"I'm not playing at all."

"We need to find out now," Fritz said. "Also, where our van is."

"How should I know where your van is?"

He jumped up, turned right, yanked open the door to the men's guest room, peered in, took three steps to the guest bathroom, peered in, and then into the woman's guest room.

"Wait a minute, you!"

Kat felt fingers clamp her forearm." You do the right thing, nobody's hurt."

"Huh?" She jerked her arm from Arlene's grasp and stood.

Fritz had disappeared into her bedroom.

"Empty," he announced, striding back.

"The garage," Arlene said.

He moved toward the front door.

Kat was debating if grabbing his leather belt made long-term sense or not. "Who do you think you are, some lay cop? This housekeeper you're after—couldn't be connected with what I've been hearing. That you and Arlene are running some kind of sex and blackmail ring?"

"Fritz?"

He returned.

Arlene zipped open her purse, pulled out the derringer, slanted its barrel up toward the director's jaw, and cocked the hammer.

Kat had planned to run into the kitchen and down the back steps, but stopped, goggling sidewise at the tortoiseshell-handled weapon.

The next moment Fritz, shorter by an inch, grabbed her collar and began to twist. "We need to know where she and the van are, and we need to know who she's buying her blow from."

"You must be fond of your granddaughter," Arlene said. "Are you fond of the little girl?"

"I'll do the talking, Arlene. Are you fond of her, Kat?"

The director's face was purpling. "Thah hurts!" She could barely wrestle the words out. "Leh me loose!"

"Certainly," Fritz dropped his hand. "Who is Raven's dealer?"

"Vonnie!" Kat yelled. "Marta!"

Fritz smacked her once then backhanded the other cheek. Arlene rose and jammed the pistol's sightless, two-inch barrel into one of Kat's nostrils.

"That cute little butterball granddaughter's done for, you realize," Fritz hissed.

Kat snuffled. "He's called Flasher. In the refuge. At dusk."

"Short and sweet—now what about Raven and the van."

The outside kitchen door slapped shut.

Arlene released the hammer, pulled the derringer's barrel free, snatched the dish towel to wipe its end, and zipped it into her purse.

Beatriz, Vonnie, and Marta rushed into the great room.

"What's the matter, Abuelita? Your nose!"

"Exhaustion," Kat muttered and pulled a tissue from her pocket to staunch the blood.

"A few questions for your grandmother," Fritz said. "We're hoping to increase our usefulness to the Harbor."

— — —

Hours later, Tish and Flasher faced each other in the blue chairs across the circle of rocks that held the cooking fire. Hummingbirds flitted about, dipping into the feeders that, with the hubcaps, fringed the lean-to's brow. Tish stirred potatoes, carrots, and chunks of bottom round she'd set stewing on the grate. Today's temperature had not reached eighty and the breeze that had just sprung up— waving the stands of hairy-leafed kochia and remaining leaves on the elms—had caused Flasher to wrap himself in the black, faux-fur coat.

"Listen to this," he said, reading from the *Courier*'s business section. "'No reason for risky loans. Realtors claim they can still get one hundred percent financin' for first-time home buyers with credit scores as low as six hundred.' Whatever 'credit scores' means. Think a tramp an' his sister can qualify? Hell, in six months we'll be showin' cash."

"You mean it, Papa?"

"Why not? Though mebbe we ought to refinance Mom's place first."

Tish fingered the red frizz bulging below the brim of her rolled sombrero. "I'm gonna get me a fuzzy wuz like that spaniel Mom and I found before Pop drowned it. Oh, boy, oh, boy, didn't we give Pop his reward."

"What'd you go change your name from Cobb to Earp for last year, anyways?" Flasher asked. "Could make it harder for us to buy somethin'. Do know needin' only one signature saves me big headaches with Mom's house."

Tish knocked her chest with her fist. "I already explained it, simp. When you decided you'd rather be big cheese in these camps than get us indoors, that dealing was safer with no permanent address, I decided this tootsie needed a boost in self-esteem, a new name and go make it official."

"Name like Earp brings you self-esteem?"

"Cuz no one else would ever think of it and fuck you, Nate. Us being intimates ain't no secret I treasure."

She jumped up in fatigues and matching shirt and pumped her fists. "And now you go and cheat on me again!"

"How do you know that?" He picked an aluminum shaker from two on the stump and peppered the stew.

"By your stink when you came back to the lean-to. I'll kill that tattooed floozy!"

"No, you won't. Or this goes up without a rubber." He stood, coat flapping at his ankles, and started to unzip. "You lookin' to bein' a homeless mother?"

"Then tell Miss Raven Cokehead to go back where she came from. Or I'll strangle her, Nate. You recall how I followed through with that toots in Truchas, before we drifted down here?"

"She caught me nekked in the river, Tish."

"An' that's where she stayed, ain't it. Zzzzzk." Tish tightened an imaginary clothesline around her sunburned neck.

"Let Raven heal one more night down in the willows. I hid her van on Cortez. Nobody can spot it behind all that rabbitbrush."

"How could you dupe me after the s'mores and all our laughing last night, trying to sing Q's cuckoo music?" Tish screwed up one side of her lips to snuffle hard.

"The girlie came on pretty strong, Tish." Flasher sat back down.

"You think I care?"

"Look, what we two did means nothin'. I shouldn't have drunk Stormy's rum is all."

"You shouldn't of is right." Tish began to cry. She smeared the tears with the heels of her hands.

"I'm sorry, okay? My gut hurts pretty bad aroun' it—that's what guilt does to a man." The squeak of his voice softened. "Or mebbe I'm just hungry."

"I don't care about your gut, I care about your loyalty. You swore the first time you sweet-talked me into peeling off my panties that from then on, no strange pussy for you. What if she's venereal, Brother?"

"I know it, I know it. Gonna go buy you a coral necklace, how zat? From one of those Zunis squattin' on the Plaza."

"Hey, man, give a couple of comedians a hand for a minute, will ya?" came a shout from twenty yards away.

Stormy Weathers and Universal Cosmic Divinity had been spading kochia, ragweed, and shoots of elm from a plot between Headquarters and the railroad's abandoned right-of-way. They planned to clear a campsite for Stormy and Clara abutting the wire enclosure for Uni's piebald mongrel. She curled up now tied to her metal stake, a bowl of water near her nuzzle. Stormy stood double-hatted, resting his elbow on the end of a shovel.

Uni—wearing the now-dusty chef's hat Reuben Lightningfeather had presented him—sat clutching his tanned knees.

"Gimme that bottle," Stormy said.

Uni handed up the pint of spring water. The Iraq-war veteran chugged what was left and wiped his long mustache with a gingham sleeve.

"Flasher? Hey? Uni and I're gonna croak before I can get Clara over here. She and that toothless nigra are driving Reuben crazy with their squabbling, and his crippled kid threw up two nights ago on her teddy bear. I've suggested all three attend tonight's Anger Management in the culvert."

The refuge's hatchet-faced leader threw his coat across the edge of the windowpane he and Tish used for carding cocaine, and started for the clearing.

But he stopped short and turned toward the path that led to the sofa. "Listen. Dirky's let someone in," he told Tish. "Can't be Raven; wrong direction. New referral?"

Fritz Joseph marched into view, now dressed perkily: white sombrero, hibiscus shirt showing the points of a white handkerchief, Texas-longhorn silver buckle, shorts, long black stockings, and loafers. Arlene, even more decked out, followed in a tunic striped red and yellow that half hid her blue capris. Golden sneakers, golden ear hoops, and a necklace of fool's gold. She pushed aside the head of a thistle—startling at the bee that flew up.

"Freaks or narcs," Flasher whispered to his sister. "Go pocket the thirty-eight."

Tish headed for the lean-to.

"Your sentry didn't want to let us pass," Fritz said. "He pulled a knife and we pulled a gun. That geriatric trashed our home yesterday, he and his ponytailed pal."

"Heard somethin' 'bout that. Then you gotta be the Josephs."

"So you're Flasher."

The dealer nodded and crooked his fingers at Tish, who'd been waiting cross-legged on her sleeping bag under a feeder.

She rose and moved closer.

"My girlfriend."

Fritz arched his back to seem taller. "We're looking for a woman named Raven."

Behind him, Arlene twisted a pinky in her ear below one of the gelled ducktails.

"That a fact?" Flasher tugged down a side of his Foreign Legionlike beret until it tickled.

"She works for us and buys from you."

"Who says?"

"She stole our van, Flasher. We think you may know her location."

Flasher reached through the flaps of his shirt to unwrap a pack of Chesterfields plucked from the sleeve of his black tee. He tapped the pack upside down on his thumb, grabbed the first cigarette to appear, refolded the sleeve over the rest, teased a small box of matches from his fatigues, and lit up. He inhaled and blew the smoke just to the left of Fritz's face. "Haven't a clue where she might be, friend."

"Isn't smoking a little risky out here?" Fritz asked.

"Not when I'm doin' it, Fairy Canary."

Fritz clamped his jaw. Then: "We need to buy some of your Lady C for personal use and we need a recommendation."

"For what?"

"Someone to teach our flyaway housekeeper a lesson."

"Bow wow wow," Tish exclaimed.

"You fellas there," Flasher called to Uni and Stormy, who were tossing brush to the fattening pile where they'd doubled back a section of chicken wire. "Knock off. We're lookin' for a little privacy. I'll pitch in with you two tomorrow."

Uni hesitated a moment, turned to free his dog, and clutched her rope collar. Mongrel and the men sidled between trash and a fence stake and headed for the Santa Fe Southern's old roadbed.

"What kind of lesson?" Flasher asked Fritz, after inhaling and blowing out smoke.

"Raven's in a position to do our clients and ourselves a lot of damage," Arlene explained behind her husband.

"What my wife is trying to say is that we want to be able to continue financing Kat's good work—the Harbor is one of our major charities."

Flasher shrugged.

"Are you perhaps acquainted with someone who can teach our precious an indelible lesson?"

"Meanin'?"

"Oh, c'mon, Fritz, say it—someone to put the bitch underground."

"I can do that!" Tish's mass of red bobbled beneath her sombrero. She raised her shirt to reveal the gray length of vinyl held by her waistband, looped and knotted at each end. She yanked it free, approached the back of her brother's coat, threw the garrote over his beret, and crossed the ends behind his neck until the line dug into his Adam's apple. "See? No noise, you betcher buttons."

"Hey! Get that off!" Flasher managed between coughs. He reached to grab a handful of his sister's skirt.

"Derringer," Fritz snapped to Arlene.

She set her purse on a stump, unzipped it, cocked the hammer back, and pointed the diminutive pistol at Tish.

"Boogie-woogie, only a demo. I scared you all good, huh?" Tish loosened the noose, dropped an end, and pulled the clothesline to her. "Wrap a hankie on it, no mark." She stuffed it in two coils between her waistband and tummy.

Flasher was breathing hard. He cocked the forefinger not holding his cigarette at her. "Tonight you and I make babies."

"I was just fooling, Papa!"

He directed his pale eyes at Fritz. "Tell your squaw to zip up the heater."

Had the grandpa with the poppy-handled blade sneaked in from the sofa, Fritz wondered? He noticed what could be a gun in the pocket of Tish's fatigues. The lump going down his throat felt like a wad of tinfoil. "Do it," he said to Arlene.

She released the hammer and placed the derringer in her purse.

No one spoke.

"We'll pay you well," Arlene said at last.

Flasher took another drag, pulled the cigarette free, and circled his lips with his tongue. "How well?"

"Enough," Arlene said, "so you can leave this outback and find yourselves a real home."

"Nate?" Tish asked.

"You shut up."

"We'll pay you double," Fritz said. "Say forty thousand if you'll teach the same lesson to a woman named Germaine. She was our guest this past weekend, though last night or today we think she flew back to New York."

"Turn that plane around!" Tish started thumbing the hair sprouting from her mole.

"We may know your girlie," Flasher said. "Black curls?"

"Yes."

"Could belong to one of our residents. Tole me an' Tish in a week she's plannin' to be out here again, to take this resident I just mentioned home."

"This is the guy who broke through the window in our place with your sentry?"

"Too many questions, señor."

"One more," Fritz said. "Might you be able to locate Raven?"

"Might."

"Sure as shooting we can!" Tish blurted.

"Clam it! We keep our secrets secret."

"You didn't keep your word."

Flasher swiveled to face Fritz. "We'll need ten grand down for Raven an' ten down for the curls."

"Done. Once you find her—"

"Her?" Flasher asked.

"Raven. You have to convince her she's what keeps our business thriving. You know about our business?"

"Heard somethin' about a sex scam."

"A bit harsh. You tell her we'll make her a partner." He glanced at Arlene who had stepped forward. "Right?"

She nodded.

To Flasher Arlene smelled like a campfire's drenched coals. "I thought you wanted the girlie removed."

"Just tell her what I told you. My wife and I will then arrange to—"

"Gotta be cash," Flasher said. "In twenties."

"Whatever. First we have to know you can deliver."

"Have you got a few bindles you can sell us now?" Arlene asked. "I need to leave the world myself for a while."

NEVER SAY DIE

Friday 21 September 2007

Three days later in Greenwich Village, Germaine and Jock paused in the five-o'clock heat to catch their breath after climbing to her third-floor landing. She handed him the bouquet of alstroemeria she'd bought on the walk from her office, their stems rubber-banded in waxed paper, then extracted keys from her shoulder bag, turned one in the double lock, and pushed in the door.

"Ugh, musty." Jock coughed and followed her in. He pulled the collar of his checked button-down—sleeves rolled to his elbows—away from his neck. "Why didn't you leave the air conditioner on?"

"Too expensive!" She paused in the short hall that connected bathroom to bedroom. "Put those blossoms in water and fix us a scotch-and-soda while I jump in the shower, will you?"

"Complain, complain, don't I, princess? Are you glad to see me? First time we've been alone since you flew back to the news of your promotion."

"Yeah, meetings every night after Wednesday's party. It was hard, you being so close and us not able to make love."

"I'm way hornier now."

"Get those drinks fixed but stay out of sight till I've got my new outfit on."

"Kinky?"

"Costly."

Jock swept a hand over his brown hair parted in the center and strode into her railroad kitchen.

She threw her bag on the white spread, moved to the window, and turned the conditioner's knob all the way to the right. A rasp, then a hum preceded the whoosh of air. She stooped to let it chill her face and blow her curls, straightened, and gazed down onto West 8th. Three African-American girls in blue NYU T-shirts skipped arm-in-arm down the middle of the street, stopped, pivoted, and mounted the curb to gaze through the window beneath the *Yo Mama* flashing above the shoe store. Next door, a man whose graying hair curtained his eyes hawked bagels from a wooden tray strapped around his neck.

Germaine hurried into the bathroom to shed blouse, skirt, shoes, nylons, bra, and bikini. She pulled her earring loops free, adjusted the shower's temperature, and drew vinyl imprinted with sandpipers across the tub.

She had shampooed and was scrubbing under an arm when fingers curled around the edge of the curtain. Jock, buck-naked, stepped in. He brought her to him, his penis a rod and his chest hairs scratchy, and pressed his mouth to hers while the water shot around them.

"I couldn't wait. Scrub my back, will you?" he asked.

"Me first— you owe me fright money. When I saw those fingernails, all I could think was *Psycho*."

She carried her clothes, wearing a hand towel like a turban, to the bedroom's walk-in closet, and pushed them onto one of the bookshelves Jock had installed while she was at Beautiful Tomorrows early in the month. After giving her hair a final fluffing, she eased from the hanger a dress the color of raspberry sherbet that seemed the weight of a spiderweb. She'd found the knee-length wonder yesterday at Bergdorf Goodman.

At the hem and above the neckline, the voile underlay gave way to see-through crepe de chine. She slipped it on near the bed and ran her palms over breasts and tummy—smiling to discover that, though she'd dried her thighs, her bush had dampened. She buttoned up the dress's front.

Jock came in carrying two scotches-and-sodas. His erection had turned the terry-cloth wrapping his waist into a tent. He set the glasses on the antimacassar on Germaine's dresser, locked his hands to his hips, and stared.

"You like?" she asked, and twirled.

"Lovely. Take it off."

"Not yet—I want you to ache."

Before he'd appeared, she had switched on her monitor and now stepped to the keyboard and double-clicked on Internet Explorer. "I haven't had time to think what to do about the Josephs except phone Jimmy Holstein, a guy also being blackmailed I met my first time in Santa Fe. He urges me to talk to the cops after I fly back in two days to pick up Dad."

"Assuming your dad'll come." Jock pressed his hard-on to his belly and moved close. "You smell like peppermint, princess."

She peeled his palm from her neck. "Back off, sonny. I'm in training as a tease."

"And I feel like a heel not being with you last weekend."

"Good!"

"I want to go along this time."

"Guess what. Judy has already booked two tickets flying out and three for returning Tuesday."

"Brilliant!" He embraced her before she could push him away.

His bare skin, and oh, that erection, could it do what she hoped? "Jimmy said to write out everything that appears on the Hacienda's home page, that the police will want to know." She freed herself and walked to the dresser.

"Nice ass—no panties. Write it out? Doesn't that seem superfluous? The cops can log in as well as you."

She exaggerated a wiggle, gulped her drink, took an extra swallow, and brought him his glass. "Suppose the Josephs shut the site down?"

"Nah. You're all too scared of the publicity for them to worry."

"They'd better worry about me."

Bush Threatens Veto of Child Health Bill, the headline on the monitor read. When she sat, her five-wheeled chair's cushion tickled the backs of her knees. She scooted forward, blued out *nytimes* and typed in *beautifultomorrowsinstitute.org*. A sign popped into the screen's upper left corner: *The page you are seeking cannot be found.*

"Jock!"

"Maybe your server's screwy. Try craigslist."

Craigslist's home page took but a couple of seconds to appear. She couldn't find *beautifultomorrows*.

"They've cut and run, Jock."

"Try again."

Same result.

"No way we let the Josephs ruin tonight," Jock said. "In business less than a year? If they've already fled the coop, your worries may be over."

"True."

"So shut the damn thing down."

She clicked on the boxed *X* and *Turn Off Computer*, then drained her glass. "Pour me another, Jeeves. I may have a different kind of surprise for you."

Lord, may it happen, she prayed after he'd gone. She pulled the blinds, closed the white phone in a drawer beside her bed, turned away the face of her mother's bell-capped clock, and started to undo her frock's top button. Stop—Jock's job. She hauled her blanket and spread to the bed's foot, folded over a corner of the sheet, and sat waiting.

He returned with ice cubes clinking, hard-on gone.

"Looks like I'm needed," she laughed and smoothed a palm down his penis. She reached for the glass, drank down half, and set it on the table. "Undo me, will you?"

"A pleasure."

She shrugged the dress off and lay on her side. "Come here, Jock."

He stretched beside her. She took his head and French-kissed him while her fingers reached between their bellies, rummaging among his balls and her bush and his swelling organ.

In a few moments she squirmed down toward the footboard until his erection nestled between her breasts. She squeezed them together. "Pump."

"My God, Germaine, I can't hold."

She scrambled back up to face him. His usual two-day growth and that nose as narrow as her father's blurred. "You and I have never done a sixty-nine." She whipped around before he could respond and pressed her vulva to his lips.

"You're sopping," he mumbled.

"So pitch in." When she felt his tongue probing, she cupped his balls and mouthed his shaft, careful not to bob too fast. Her groan was louder than she'd meant it to be as she circled her hips—pressing against the flexed tip of his tongue—and snaked two fingers past her belly and his chin to speed the whirlpool beginning.

She pulled her lips free. "Let's get head-to-head, darling, and try not to cum, please?"

Still facing the ceiling, he used his feet and elbows to turn. He felt his big toe bump a glass, heard a clink but no crash. His shoulder touched hers.

He arced his hand to her curls and sunk his tongue between her lips, then lay back panting.

She mounted him and inserted his erection. A drop of perspiration fell from her eyebrow. He startled at the cooled splash and gripped her buttocks, then massaged the small of her back while—moaning— she fucked him.

He clutched his balls as heat spread like shrapnel through his groin, thighs, and belly. The muscles in his neck tightened and he clenched his jaw to fend off orgasm.

"Who are you?" he whispered.

She was fucking him as he loved to fuck her, plunging, straight-arming the mattress, heaving up. Her breasts pitched up toward her collarbone, down toward her navel. "Thank you," she whimpered. "Oh, yes!"

With the second "ohhhh" sounding like the keening of a Muslim mourner, she collapsed. Her breath spurted out, steaming his shoulder.

He flipped her over, pumped, and came.

When his own breathing had quieted, he licked the rim of her ear and said, "I've told you never to fake it with me."

"No fake, Jock. It happened again."

His butt squirmed into the softness of her cast-off dress as he struggled out from under. "Again? What in hell. You've *never* cum."

She raised herself on a forearm. "I've something to tell you that you won't like but I had to find out if the logjam had broken."

"Huh?"

Germaine explained about Jimmy.

She fingered Jock's forehead but he pulled her hand away, swung his feet to the carpet, and sat up, presenting the tufts of dark hair that flanked his spine down low.

"If you decided to use someone else to test your theory that forgiving your father would free you to have an orgasm, where does that put yours truly?"

"With *me*, Jock, like this."

"After the year you and I went through agony to find a cure for your coldness, you were unable to wait a few days?"

"I can't hear you."

He twisted around. "You couldn't wait a few days?"

Germaine sucked in her lips. "I just couldn't face failing with you again."

He said nothing.

"I want you to come to the Bay Area, Jock. My salary doubles next month. We'll find an apartment."

"You may change your mind on that."

She shook her curls no, dropped down against the sheet's dampness, and nestled against his bare back.

The only sound was the air conditioner's hum until:

"Why might I change my mind?"

He pulled his legs onto the mattress and lay, knees up, to stare at a strip of plaster he'd never noticed curling out above the mirror. "I have my own confession."

"Judy," she said softly. "That bitch!"

"She's a terrible lover, Germaine—like a dead sheep. I had to get even when you said you didn't want me in Santa Fe. We made love Sunday and Tues—"

Germaine curved a hand up to stop his mouth, then rolled over, rose, and took two gulps of scotch. "You want some?"

Silence.

"We're even-steven," she said. "Well, no."

"No?"

"Me once, you twice."

"You got more from it."

"You don't know that."

"Are you asking Judy to relocate?" he asked.

"What do you think, after what you just told me?"

"Anyway," he said, "Mike's asked her to marry him."

"Poor fool."

"You still want me to come out with you?"

"Make a guess."

"What I guess is we should celebrate with dinner at Ye Waverly tonight, take a soak at Hot Tub Dreams, and hurry back here to..." He leaned on his elbow to kiss the flesh above her left nipple.

"Guessing right." She relished the glow spreading in her chest, clutched the pillow, and thrust it between her spine and the headboard. "Call the Josephs, Jock. Will you? Hang up if someone answers."

"Now?"

"Scared? Like me?"

"I just hate to break the mood, princess."

"Before we leave for our evening?"

"Okay."

She stretched down to kiss the organ lazing on his pelvis, threw her feet to the braided throw, and padded to the dresser. She took an address book from her purse and inserted a finger at *B* for Beautiful Tomorrows.

Clasping a bra and bikini in her other hand, she spread the book over Jock's appendectomy scar, grabbed up her dress, and headed for the bathroom.

Twenty minutes later she emerged. Jock was sitting naked on the mattress's edge, facing the white phone, its heft pinning the address book open. She stood in the doorway gazing at the mussed hair, muscles bulging under his arms like budding wings, two moles below his collarbone. He glanced back at her, lifted the receiver, and punched in the numbers.

He set the receiver down.

"What?"

"Gone."

"How do you know?"

"Don't know. Only that a voice says the line's disconnected."

— — —

In Santa Fe two hours earlier—mountain time—Raven and Flasher huddled in the lean-to at the refuge's Headquarters. Her hair, shampooed at the Harbor after lunch, hung in waves that reached the scarlet, V-necked tee Vonnie had picked off the giveaway table for her, along with a pair of denim bell-bottoms.

A thunderclap followed the zigzag of lightning that sent Universal Cosmic Divinity's mongrel racing around her pen. Rain streamed off the hubcaps hung from the lean-to's brow and streaked the candy-cane swirls on the old barber pole Flasher and Tish had stolen days earlier. Winds bent a nearby stand of rye grass. Sections of the *Courier* lay scattered on the tarp.

"Beside all the prunings there, that mud hole filling up in Stormy's and Clara's clearing, what's it for?" Raven jiggled her glasses' pink frames. "Creeps me out—too shallow for a grave."

"Clara Bare's 'fraid of storms, girlie. When it's deeper, Storm Born's gonna line it in plastic, roof it in plastic an' plywood. Throw a mattress in."

In the lean-to, his camp stool sat on plywood capping a smaller hole that concealed his safe. It now held the rocks of cocaine his connection had sold him midweek, his grinder and scale, plus ten-thousand dollars in twenties, rubber-banded in sets of five hundred. The Josephs had brought Flasher the money early this morning while Raven dozed near the outhouse down in the willows.

"You're lookin' not so bad, bubblehead. Puffs under those gorgeous eyes have disappeared. How's your insides?"

"Working okay again."

"Flasher knows his nursin'."

How she wished the afternoon's rain would stop. The damp and Flasher's cigarettes—or was it simply that he needed to wash?—made the lean-to's nylon smell moldy. "Thanks for the nose candy," she said, "and the milk and soup. Spending the last three days high is what I needed. I'm gonna pay you back, you know, Foreflasher, if *your* promise holds."

He yanked his beret toward an ear. "Flasher's word's always good. Question is right now, do you feel up for the visit?"

A gust blew in rain and elm leaves, spotting his and Tish's double sleeping bag.

He stood and wrapped his faux fur around him. "Josephs're sayin' they're hatin' themselves for the double cross Sunday. Say they need you back there pretty bad. Plannin' on makin' you a partner, as I mentioned. If they fink out, trust me, Storm Born an' Dirky an' Tish an' I'll ensure they never cook up another falsehood."

"You keep saying that and don't tell me how."

"We have our little plan."

"Which is?"

"Not a great idea to share it."

"Why?"

"Too many questions, girlie!" He bent double to cough.

"I'm frightened, Foreflasher." She pressed the tips of her middle fingers along her lids as if to smooth on mascara.

"Supposedly Dirky's pickin' up his an' Q's photos at Walgreens as we speak. You need to swipe or duplicate a few videos showin' Fritz an' his ball-an'-chain snortin' snow. Your insurance policy. Tell 'em, sure, you'll spend the weekend. They've said you can use the van, pick up guests, whatever. Find out what partnership would mean to you in cash. If you don't like what you hear, hustle on back tonight with your clothes an' shit."

"They're not going to let me."

"Course they are. Tell 'em your street pharmacist just received a delivery of primo blow that he's promised special customers, such as youself, not to cut. I'm tellin' you those two do seem regretful, Cravin'. An' you heard Kat say if you pass the Breathalyzer, an' give a clean UA, you've got a bunk an' grub at the Harbor for thirty days—Kat's max."

"But look how I'm shaking."

He swept the coat from his shoulders and draped her in it. "We'll go tell Tish that I'm showin' you where the van's hid."

"How's she feel about us screwing, anyway, Flasher?"

"She knows what rum can do."

"She doesn't have it in for me?"

"Tish? No way. Blown over."

"You'd better give me a touch of the Lady before I leave."

"Ummm, best to stay clear-minded for the powwow."

He fumbled in a wooden chest for umbrellas and unfurled them.

She trailed him toward the sofa.

— — —

Rain pounded the roof of the breakfast nook where Fritz and Arlene waited under the lit fluorescent for Raven's arrival. Rivulets down the east window obscured the veil of a birch's battered leaves. In the wall frieze, jackrabbits chased cottontails, round and round.

"Hadn't you ought to lay off the hooch?" Fritz asked.

Arlene raised penciled brows at him, drained her glass, poured another to spite him, and set the José Cuervo next to a white envelope packed with ten fifty-dollar bills.

Fritz had dressed somberly to build Raven's trust during the upcoming rendezvous: black slacks, long-sleeved black shirt, silver chain.

Yesterday he'd had his brush cut trimmed and squared. Arlene, meaning to demonstrate wealth yet openness, had slung over her black capris a tunic picturing planets and red moons. Three loops of gold and coral hung past a boatneck that displayed her long collarbones. Golden ear hoops completed the array. She'd gelled her ducktails half an hour ago.

"Late," she muttered, flipping her wrist. "Ten-thousand smackeroos to someone we hardly know? Did anyone see you passing the box of bills to that stained-tooth fugitive from the Foreign Legion?"

"Only his weirdo girlfriend. The three of us met at that ripped-up sofa."

"He better get our coke whore here."

"He does his part, we do ours, then he and his girlfriend do theirs, and all's well."

"The editor's still free-range, Fritz." Arlene upended her glass. "So are those two seniors."

"First things first." He scooted around the table, snatched her bottle of tequila, and poured the four fingers remaining into the sink.

"Our van just turned the corner," he announced, staring out at Ybarra Lane.

Arlene stood, smoothed her tunic, and followed him to the vestibule, where the sound of drops splashing into pails in the living room grew.

The chimes tinkled. Filling and emptying his lungs, Fritz stepped forward to open the door. "Hello, Rave!" He swept his arm back toward Arlene and pivoted out of the way.

Raven walked in.

"Oh, God," Arlene gushed, "you're back! Are you all right? Did those people feed you? You're drenched!" She slapped her fingers to her lips and dropped them. "What's that pelt you're wearing?" She helped the twenty-four-year-old out of Flasher's coat. "Let me run you a hot bath."

"We feel awful about this, Rave, the misunderstandings," Fritz said.

Though no air conditioners purred, Raven began to shiver, wishing she'd insisted to Flasher on a hit. "Misunderstandings my ass."

"Tomorrow morning when we're fresh," Fritz said, arms dangling, "I'll explain. Go bring one of her sweaters, Arlene, after you've started her tub."

"No, I showered at the shelter. A sweater, though? Could use one."

"How about this throw we leave here?" Fritz unfolded a blue-and-gray plaid from the top of a ladder-back chair and covered Raven's shoulders. "That should put a stop to the trembles."

"Mostly I'm nervous."

"No wonder, love," Arlene said. "Thank the Lord the editor got the van rolling, and thank the Lord the doctors knew what to do. Stomach pump, I suppose? Did it hurt?"

What is all this, Raven wondered? "Can we sit down?" she asked.

"Of course!" Arlene strode to the unicorn and hung the wet faux fur on the monkey's head.

"My dealer tells me you've an offer to make." Raven turned toward the living room but Arlene grasped her elbow.

"Doctor Fritz assures me that Monday early the tile man, the roofers, and the Anderson-windows guy will all assemble here. Meanwhile, you see? The floor's a mess and the roof leaks worse and the window's boarded up and we've got clients arriving at the Sunport tomorrow. No living-room orgy this weekend, I'll tell you."

Arlene's laugh sounded to Raven as if she were gagging on a bone.

"How 'bout we use the dining table," Fritz said.

Arlene hurried past it into the breakfast nook to retrieve the white envelope.

Returning, she took a chair beside Raven, who had sat facing Fritz. "By any chance you see today's big sports lead, love? The oh-six Tour de France champ got his title stripped. Doped himself up with testosterone. Now the PGA's pitching in—going to start testing golfers. It's an epidemic. And I need a drink."

"No, you don't," Fritz said.

Raven half rose. "If you two are going to start in again, I'm leaving."

"Really? On foot? The van stays."

"Arlene, goddamnit it," Fritz said.

"Sorry." The beads on her necklace rattled as she dropped her chin.

"Rave, the brutal truth is, to keep this enterprise going, we need you with us," Fritz said.

"We're prepared to make you a partner, Raven."

"Meaning what?"

"Meaning equalizing profits all round. Starting tomorrow. If you'll stay," said Arlene.

"About how much jack is that a month?"

"I'll show you the books tonight, if you like," Fritz said.

"And the real estate?"

"Real…"

"A third ownership in this place, what's it worth?"

"You're kidding!"

"Arlene, please. We hadn't talked about the Hacienda, Rave."

"Tomorrow's fine." But increasingly sure all this palaver about partnership was pure crapola, Raven already was figuring how to escape. Even beg Kat to help her sign into rehab. Not being high was the pits. She felt sick, dizzy. "Folksies? Gotta lie down. I'm whacked."

"Of course—love? Afterward? Forget what I said about wheels. Stupid. Willing to return to the refuge for a few bindles? I'm afraid most have vanished from under your mat. We've put some money in the envelope."

"We'd appreciate it, Rave."

"No problem," Raven exulted, sure she could carry her belongings to the van undetected by using the path along the far side of the garage. But how lift backup videos from the den, even though her purse contained a key? "Maybe I should check the spy-cam console to make sure everything's hunky-dory for tomorrow night?" she asked. "Especially since the roof's leaking."

"We'll eyeball the equipment for you." Fritz glanced at Arlene. "Take a break, Rave, you deserve it."

"Your purse is on your dresser, love. We're so relieved to see you're on the mend."

— — —

"But Dirk's learned to play the roll-up fast, Q. He says it's not much different from playing the organ. Shit-and-a-half, he can render your scores as well as I did."

"Wrong."

"Well, this sling makes the subject moot. One more week and it's gone."

A mile from the refuge, Byron and Quentin waited for Dirk in aluminum chairs at one of the tables under the portico fronting Wild Oats Market, between the public phone and man-high dispenser signed *Refreshing Beverages*. They watched the traffic surge and halt along St. Francis Drive.

By five o'clock the rain had shrunk to drizzle. Drops fell from corbels topping the portico's pillars and hit the terrazzo below. A couple of Subaru Outbacks, a battered Chevy with a low front tire, and assorted pickups awaited their owners behind a line of empty shopping carts. Homeless youths lounged about, thumbs in pockets, or sat drinking free coffee the market handed out.

"Buzzy, don't go, please. Tell her." Quentin placed a sunburned hand on Byron's forearm.

"Last Sunday you swore not to beat a dead horse, Q."

"But it's only three days until you and that intern fly two-thousand miles east."

"Her name's Vonnie."

"Believe me, she'll never be one of this composer's whores."

"Look, your daughter and her boyfriend will be here in a couple of days to fly you back to the City," Byron said. "You and I can easily visit each other."

"Knowing you and she are sleeping in the same bed?"

"What's the big deal? Where's Dirk, anyway? I'm hungry—yo! Here he comes."

The septuagenarian had left Walgreens and was limping toward them in his overalls. He waved the yellow-banded packet of photos that he and Quentin had snapped through the Hacienda's window almost a week ago. Plus the sack holding gauze and disinfectant Byron had paid him to buy. The holstered Mahdi hung from a hip.

"Take a look at the pics, they're damning—vivid and clear." Dirk sat and slid the photos across. "When's your daughter arriving?"

"Sunday." Quentin rested a cheekbone on his knuckles.

"Having second thoughts about deserting us?" Dirk asked.

"I've told you how I feel."

"Talk's cheap." Dirk scratched his scalp through ricegrass hair. "Hey, old buddy, I never thanked you for coming with me to the hospital this morning. Prostate cancer's in remission? Looks like it! Buzzy, tell that woman of yours how much I appreciate her driving. Still glum, Q? So play the fool and stay in Santa Fe. Myself, frankly, hopes you do."

"He's pouting because Vonnie and I are leaving town."

"Is that it?"

Quentin rose. "Let's head on home."

"You damn stupe." Dirk wiped the drizzle from his forehead. "I don't know if you and Buzzy ever got it on and I don't want to. Do know that sharing a cup of French roast with a pal beats sex anytime. No postpartum wondering How'd I perform? No false dreams or memories of better foreplay, no angst over now what, no testicular agony, no accusals during the next morning's leave-taking. Pals after a second cup just toss their Styrofoams in the trash. And Q? I've been a privileged man. Learning to make music again, seeing how an old fart conjures up work so powerful that if this burg doesn't like it, Red River or *somewhere* will. Enough said?" Dirk hung his thumbs above the buckles of his straps.

"That's some friend," Byron said.

"Go to hell, both of you." But Quentin reached out and clasped their hands.

"Let's toddle in to have us a double toffeenut latte with whipped cream sprinkled with cinnamon," Dirk said, clapping Quentin's shoulder.

He stood and moved toward the sliding doors. A young man and woman in knit caps rolled above their ears— his jaw stubbled, hers jutting— moved closer to the bedrolls and tattered backpacks they'd left beside the phone, to let Dirk pass.

"Goodbye, Q," he heard Byron say to Quentin. "Till New York; we're staying with Vonnie's aunt."

"Lucky you."

Before Dirk could enter the market, a broad-shouldered redhead cradling two paper bags stepped out. The composer found himself staring into the bloodshot eyes of Milt, the bent-nosed boy toy who'd stolen his CD player, billfold, and laptop more than a month ago, following the disastrous premiere of *To My Daughter*. He was wearing one of Quentin's pink-and-white dress shirts.

"You owe me, auntie!" Quentin shouted. His ponytail flopped as he snatched away one of the paper bags.

The redhead launched a boot toe against the composer's shin, losing his grip on the other bag. Inside it, a bottle smashed and a dark green liquid seeped onto a square of terrazzo.

Milt turned but Quentin grabbed his belt with his free hand.

Two of the homeless young men edged close, one yanking sunshades down from his hair. The remaining three stayed where they were. The knit-capped couple had scurried into the market.

"Police!" Quentin yelled.

"Q, are you bonkers? I'm still wanted." Byron wrenched the groceries from the crook of Quentin's arm.

Milt swung but Dirk blocked the blow with his forearm.

"Scram while you can," Byron warned.

The redhead darted among the tables, fled past the bulletin board, and lurched around the corner out of sight.

"Shit-and-a-half, Q."

"He owes me a hundred bucks and two credit cards!"

"So what?"

Dirk flung his arm around the composer. "Listen, sport, it's our lucky day. Two bags of food, no charge, minus whatever that green slop is. Let's go have us that java."

"Mucho thanks, Dirk," Byron said, handed him the bags of groceries, and grabbed up the sack from Walgreens Dirk had brought him. Without looking back, the former professor hurried toward the signal at Cordova, to head for Vonnie's apartment three blocks distant.

— — —

By six thirty, mud and dead leaves floored the campsite Quentin and Dirk had reoccupied after vacating the men's guest room at the Harbor. Kat had promised to keep serving them breakfast and dinner until her bunks filled again. Stormy Weathers continued sleeping near them, after Reuben Lightningfeather's angry refusal four evenings ago to let Stormy move in with Reuben's family.

Quentin and Dirk sat under their lean-to in folding beach chairs, discussing with Stormy the chances of more rain. The Iraqi Freedom veteran had earlier discovered a packing crate with one side gone, large enough for two to lie in, against the chain-link fence of the School for the Deaf. He and Uni had tin-snipped the wire—refastening it afterward with doubled Twist-n-Ties—lugged the crate here, and draped its top in a weathered polyethylene sheet they had discovered rolled up near the PNM substation. Soon they planned to relocate the crate next to the 'storm cellar' dug at the site they were clearing for Stormy and Clara near Headquarters, so that the couple could begin housekeeping.

Now Stormy faced Dirk and Quentin in an armchair whose stuffing curled from the cushion like smoke. Leftover rain dripped from the edge of the crate's ersatz roof onto a clump of elm leaves, causing a tapping as regular as that of a metronome. Through disappearing clouds, the evening sun thrust past the American flag rising from Kat's Harbor into Stormy's eyes. He swung his cap around, upended a half pint of Bacardi, and tossed it against the loose fence of locust branches Quentin had amputated a week ago—after Byron announced he was flying east with Vonnie.

The composer rose, slopped through wet buffalo grass, and stooped for the bottle.

Stormy lifted a buttock to draw his switchblade from his back pocket.

"At ease, Stormy," Dirk called out. "Q means you no harm. He's simply anal retentive."

"Huh?"

"A neatnik." But Dirk flicked his thumb to unsnap the strap holding Mahdi.

"Don't like litter, Stormy, that's all," Quentin said. "Nothing personal."

"Stow the blade, buddy."

"In Baghdad we broke off their necks to use bottles as weapons for solving personal issues," the former marine said. "Beg pardon. Gut reaction." He shoved the knife into his pocket. "Yeah, Q and me have a deal cooking. Calling ourselves The Dynamic Duo—my idea." He stroked the hairs of his bare chest. "Four-handed jazz piano for parties, hotel lobbies, meetings when the Convention Center's got itself built. You still with me there, Q?"

Quentin had pulled a handkerchief from his gabardines and was cleaning off the heel of a boot.

Dirk elbowed his ribs.

"What's the matter?"

"Planning to play piano with Stormy?" Dirk asked.

"We talked about it yesterday."

"Sure did. Hey, want to show you bozos before dark where Clara and me's setting up shop. C'mon."

"I gotta get the snub nose from Tish, anyhow," Dirk said, standing. "My turn tonight on the sofa. You know, Q, if I didn't think you had a shot at fame, there's no way you'd have talked me back outside here. Who's gonna pop off first when winter comes?"

"Age before beauty," Stormy said, holding aside a branch. He brought up the rear as they headed along the path.

At its far end, to the left, Uni's mongrel snored, curled around her dish in the mud, an ear lolling on her neck. A crushed beer can lay in the quarter-inch of water lying at the bottom of the 'storm cellar' that Flasher had helped Uni and Stormy deepen. The rain had sweetened air already pungent with cut ragweed and kochia piled near the gate of the mongrel's pen.

Flasher had produced two sheets of plywood from the pile he kept camouflaged with suckers and cheatgrass behind the lean-to, and had laid them in front, where Raven now filled a director's chair, drumming fingers on her knee. She'd given Flasher three of the Josephs' five-hundred dollars. Tish lounged against the trunk of an elm in sheared-off denims and her *Careful or You'll End Up in My Novel* T-shirt. No sombrero covered her red frizz.

"I'm not going back to the Hacienda!" Raven shouted to the hunched-over figure inside the lean-to, weighing out bindles. "You and Tish, you've been super to me." Raven smiled over her shoulder, puzzled at seeing Tish's hand dart from her waistband.

The sex facilitator faced the hubcaps and feeders again. "Oh, aren't we going to put the Josephs away! Even though I couldn't figure how to snatch the backup tapes. I'm sick of playing coke whore, Foreflasher, you know? Hurry up, can't you?"

The dealer emerged in his beret, brandishing a Baggie holding a dozen, quarter-gram packets. One of the sheets of plywood squished as he clomped across it. Far away a siren started up and from the tunnel of trees leading to the sofa came a dark-eyed junco's trills. Flasher glanced at his sister, who was drawing the clothesline and a dishrag from her denims.

"We'll get that windowpane set up on the stump, girlie. Gotta a local library card, mebbe, to chop the coke?"

"You putting me on?" Raven asked.

Chesterfields had browned the grin he gave her.

"Isn't there a knife under one of these chairs?" Raven started to reach down, heard a branch snap, twisted her head, and spotted the white vinyl strung between Tish's hands as if she intended to start a game of cat's cradle—except that a rag draped the cord.

Raven gasped and tried to rise. But Flasher, having stuffed the Baggie into his shirt, raised his knee to stomp on the toes peeking from Raven's espadrille. He raised his other knee to stomp on the toes of her right foot, and forced her wrists against the chair's splintery arms.

The pain felt like he'd butterflied both feet. "Someone help!" she cried, gagging at the stink of his sweat. She jerked her head forward to strain free.

No use.

The cord whooshed over her head; at first the dishrag cooled her throat. But it heated as Tish, behind her, pulled the makeshift handles back, crossed them, and tightened the noose until the only sound Raven could make was the "arghhh" of strangulation. Her tongue snaked between her lips.

"Be over quick, bimbo," Flasher said. "A lot of money's comin' our way for this. Who zat?"

Dirk emerged past the clump of rabbitbrush. He had unsnapped Mahdi—now aimed beside his hip at Raven, Tish, and Flasher—and loped forward. Quentin threw his fist to his mouth and, at Stormy's shout behind him, moved aside. The gopher-faced veteran reached the trio before Dirk did and thrust his blade's tip into the hollow under Flasher's jaw.

Dirk did the same under Tish's.

"That hurts, fartface!"

"Let her loose," Dirk commanded.

Tish relaxed the line and the rag descended across Raven's tee.

Flasher kept Raven's feet and wrists pinned. "Fuck off," he told Stormy in the high voice that seemed more whine than snarl.

Dirk addressed Stormy. "Don't cut him unless you have to. We don't want hospital records." He shifted his knifepoint to dimple Tish's cheek, and threw his free hand toward the stump. "Move."

"Let the girl go, dickhole," Stormy said to Flasher.

The refuge's self-appointed leader stepped back and roundhoused the fist knuckled in gemstones at Stormy. The taller man crouched, swinging his shoulder forward to dull the blow. "Go get next to her," Stormy said. "On the ground."

"Ground? Goop," Flasher said.

"Forward, march!" Stormy prodded the dealer's buttock with the tip of his switchblade.

Raven sat staring above the pink frames that had slid down her nose. Both hands clutched her throat. She sounded as if gargling. The rag drooping from the clothesline seemed a bib.

"Too close," Stormy snapped at Flasher and his sister. "Leave a space between you clear. Getting those bee-hinds mudded up good, ain't you?"

Quentin had been stepping from rabbitbrush to thistles to patches of ragweed to backing against the mongrel's chicken-wire gate. Through it all the dog had kept on snoring, a natural basso continuo.

The prone Flasher planted his fingertips past a circlet of daisies. His beret toppled into the mud as he scooted sideways from Tish, squashing the white blossoms. He let the beret lie.

Dirk limped over to Raven. He pulled the dishrag and garrote from her chest and stuffed them into his bib overalls. "Can you walk?"

"How optimistic," Raven said. "But Flasher's got my nose candy and cash."

"Where?"

"On him. I need a touch bad."

"Cough up," Dirk told Flasher.

Stormy grabbed the fallen beret and held it like a begging bowl until Flasher had emptied his shirt pocket.

Stormy passed the filled hat to Dirk.

"Q, you help me get her to Kat's," Dirk said.

"My CD player and all my clothes are in the van."

"Later, Raven." Dirk turned to Stormy. "Use your knife if those two move—wait a minute. Where's that heater, Tish?"

"Lost it, bowwow," she replied without looking up.

"Stormy?"

The mustachioed veteran advanced. His blade prodded Tish's upper lip from her gum. "You planning to try smiling with a harelip?"

"Peek under my bedding," she managed.

"Sleeping bag?"

"Wow bow, booby."

At that, for some reason, Uni's bitch yawned, wobbled onto furless legs, lapped a bit of water, stretched her muzzle toward the evening star, and began to howl.

COMING CLEAN

Saturday 22 September 2007

"**H**igher," Vonnie commanded the next morning in her pre-furnished apartment near Wild Oats. She enfolded the soap in a washcloth, standing barefoot outside the tub in bra and panties.

The water poured over Byron's blond hair, free from the band that usually gathered it. His blue sling, and the gauze and hydrogen peroxide Dirk had brought him yesterday from Walgreens, sat on the toilet seat. Byron raised his right arm and—gingerly—the wounded one, and sucked in breath. "Easy! It hurts."

"I'll be through in a sec. You're going bald, you know that?"

"Surprised I'm not a billiard ball."

She soaped and scrubbed under each arm and along his ribs. "It's too hot in here, Buzzy. Crank the window open."

He unstuck the handle. Through the now-slanted glass he gazed at the top of the Afghan pine and the flaking white houses across the street.

The mirror over the sink cleared.

"Turn around." Vonnie soaped his belly and balls and between his thighs as he cradled his left forearm in his palm. She gave his penis a couple of strokes. It flopped back down.

"It refused last night, too, Buzzy."

He stepped from the blast of water and swiped soap from his eyes. "I don't want to call, is all."

"She and your kids should hear from you before we fly out."

"Let's change our tickets from Monday to Tuesday or Wednesday, what about it?"

"Jango! You don't want to call, you don't want to leave." She diddled his penis.

"Stop that."

"You're already tired of me, aren't you?" She reached to his side to turn off the water and palmed a wisp of hair back from the birthmark on her neck.

"You and I are just getting started."

"It's Q you want, isn't it? Are you a homosexual, Buzzy?"

"Oh, bag it!"

"Bi, then. What kind of physical stuff did you and Q get involved in, anyway? C'mon out so I can dry."

She took his elbow to help him onto the mat. "Well?"

"Well what?"

"Bend down." She started fluffing his hair. "What kind of physical stuff?"

"He kissed me a couple of times—that's it." Byron bit the end of his pinky.

"We're leaving today! Raise your arms a little."

"You told me the landlord's given you till Thursday."

"I'm tired of your impotence, Buzzy. We haven't made love since last week."

"Can't you understand? I'm scared."

She lifted the sling, hydrogen peroxide, and gauze, and lay them on the hamper with his clothes. "Sit."

She began to towel the rest of him, kneeling to dry his feet and calves. "So, you're scared," she said.

"Scared for us. I'm afraid it won't work, and I'm afraid it will."

She fetched his jockeys and cargo shorts. "Stand. Afraid it *will* work? Lift your foot."

He gripped the edge of the shower door, causing it to rattle. "First off, I'll be two-thousand miles from my kids."

She rolled her eyes. "You haven't called them since you went homeless."

"How do you know?"

"Intuition. Lift the other foot."

He helped her tug his shorts up. "I didn't want the cops to find out where I was phoning from."

"Oh, bullshit." Dimples bracketed her lips. "I'll tell you why you're afraid that you and I will click. Because you'd rather be with Q, helping him make his music, doing at night whatever you used to do."

"We slept. All right, maybe I miss him. I don't want to *be* with him. I want to be with you."

"Hold still." She unscrewed the top from the peroxide, wet a wad of tissue, and dabbed the opposite lines of stitches where Stormy's blade had pierced through his triceps. "You're going to have those two scars a long time." From the roll of gauze she wrapped his upper arm, ripped the strip free with her teeth, and fastened it with adhesive tape she'd laid on the counter. "Let's get your shirt on—lift."

She and he managed to ease it over his head and slip his hands through the sleeves. She fit the strap's perforated pad to his shoulder, lifted the blue cradle to cover his forearm, and sealed its Velcro lips. "Kiss me, okay?" she asked.

He stared at her, then pecked her cheek.

"Not like that!"

He grasped the back of her head and pulled her mouth to his, keeping his lips closed.

"Better. Now go call. You remember what we rehearsed?"

He nodded.

"I'm going to get on the laptop to Southwest Air."

"The reason I want to wait at least until Tuesday, Vonnie, is to find out if Q's daughter talks him into returning to New York. She's not flying into Albuquerque until tomorrow night."

"Why?"

"Why what?"

"Why do you care?" She twisted an auburn sheaf around her forefinger.

"He was my friend."

"Was. Good."

"Is."

"And that's why we're going to try to fly out this afternoon."

Byron knotted his jaw and, hair bobbing, followed her into the bedroom.

The whir of the evaporative cooler grew. Instead of moving to the small desk where her laptop waited, she plopped into a barrel chair and folded her arms. He sat on the mattress's edge and lifted the receiver.

"I've forgotten her number."

"Four-one-one, Buzzy. Always works. Unless you've forgotten her last name, too."

An automated operator put him through.

"Yeah?" a man's voice answered.

"Leroy?"

"Yeah?"

"This is Buzzy. Is Val there?"

"You're still kicking? She might be here. You're calling why?"

"I want to say goodbye."

"She's been trying to run you down for weeks. We thought you'd conked."

Byron felt the sweat drop from his armpits. He held the receiver from his ear as Vonnie whispered, "Taste the huevos rancheros I'm fixing after you're done. Visualize a week from now, watching the Japanese Grand Prix on the widescreen at the student center, sipping lattes."

"You're kidding!" Valentine's voice burst through the earpiece.

His hand jerked away. He brought it closer.

"No funds for a month, you hairy-assed coward, you caricature, you son-of-a-bitch sleazoid, where are you?"

"Heading down to the Sunport. I'm moving to New York."

"Oh, no, you're not."

Vonnie watched Byron's face crumple. She left her chair and plopped beside him, pressing her thigh to his.

"Let me finish, Val. I've probably got a job teaching at Columbia. I'll be sending child-support payments along soon. It won't—"

"We've got a court case to settle."

"I know that. We can do it long distance."

"The hell we can!"

Byron gathered breath. "Val, I'd like to say goodbye to the children. I'll be making regular visits out."

"Is that so?"

"And I'll need to ask you to ship my cello east when we—I—find a permanent address."

"I heard the 'we,' shitheel. Guess what—Leroy shoves your cello backside between his legs so Michael and Pooh can pound on it. While Rachel dances. They'd never let you have it now.

"Hey, Leroy? How do I trace this call?"

At eight-thirty that same morning, the roar of a motorcycle leaving Kat's neighbor's driveway woke Raven up. She snuffled back phlegm and rubbed her eyes—massaged her larynx where the garrote's rag had pressed it, and tried to swallow the wet sawdust that filled her mouth.

She knocked her skull on the iron frame of the upper bunk, trying to sit up. Groaning, she leaned forward, having noticed that Dirk or Quentin or somebody had left her tummy purse on the bed table alongside a glass of water. She reached for it, gulped half down, hauled a couple of vials from her purse and a bindle of cocaine, and gulped the vitamin D and last tablet of stomach stabilizer. Her two suitcases sat on the old pine floor under the Harbor's north window. In the easy chair nearby lay sweaters, dresses, and skirts. Her red, winter coat stretched across them.

She cleared the bed table of all but the bindle, spread its corners, and—using her thumbnail to close one nostril, then the other—ducked her face, snorted the white powder as best she could, and closed her eyes. How she loved that sweetness, the wait for the brain to clear, make room for euphoria. She pressed her breast under the pajama top and smiled at her pounding heart.

But she was resolved.

Last night while Raven slept, Kat had agreed to let Quentin and Dirk stay inside and to consider bringing Clara and Chiffon back in. Dirk had sneaked Tish's .38 out to Stormy Weathers, asking him to guard the two women by sleeping in the Lightingfeathers' camp after Stormy had secured Reuben's reluctant okay.

Already through the curtains and twin skylights the sun was warming the women's guest room. Raven walked over to the chair by the window, slippered her feet, knelt, unzipped the smaller suitcase, and extracted underwear, her toiletry bag, and an outfit for the day.

She emerged from the bathroom in sleeveless knit top and striped bottoms, brows penciled, hair tied behind her neck with the orange ribbon Germaine had bought her five days ago in the hotel's gift shop. She held a tissue wadded in her fist to staunch the dribble from her nose.

Though dilating behind her glasses, her pupils were able to make out Kat sitting in combat boots and paint-splotched smock at a door laid on sawhorses near the TV. The granddaughter, whom Raven had met after showering yesterday, faced the Harbor's heavyset director. Both were gazing at a workbook.

An aroma of chile and meat filled the room. She could hear voices in the kitchen, something sizzling, and noticed the spokes of a wheelchair poised half out of the doorway.

"I'm up," Raven called after darting into the bedroom to toss toiletry bag and pajama top onto the lower bunk.

"*Hola!*" Kat's braid swung as she rose from her chair. "Feeling better?" She met Raven at one of the sofas.

"Smells delicious," the twenty-four-year-old said over the radio's sudden "Just Gimme Time to Haul These Old Boots On" that blasted from the country-and-western station Uni liked best. Raven drew the back of her fist across her nose.

"One of the refuge's regulars is showing our cook how to prepare *chiles rellenos piccadillos*. Stuffed with ground beef and pine nuts instead of cheese." Kat paused and pursed her lips. "Bruise on your throat's not so red. But you've just done a one-n-one, haven't you?"

"I can't go without it, Kat," Raven said.

Kat's jowls wobbled. "And I can't let you sleep here."

"Two more nights? Please? Monday I go to the cops with Q's daughter. She's flying back—you probably know that. Where are those two bums, anyway?"

"Lots of bums at Kat's."

"Q and Dirk, I mean. They gave me photos from last weekend to show the police. You know what I'm talking about?"

"The whole story. Twenty minutes ago I sent them to Wild Oats with a grocery list."

"Kat, only two more nights?"

"No can do."

"I want you to help sign me into rehab."

"Heard it a million times, girl."

"I mean it!" Raven dried her nose, stuffed the tissue into her yellow knit's pocket, and reached both hands to grasp one of the director's—tiny compared with Kat's bulk. The hand felt damp and Raven let go.

"I do know the head guy at Brighter Days out on Airport Road."

"I'm begging you, Kat." Raven sank to her knees.

"Hey there, get up!"

Beatriz looked over. "What's she doing, Abuelita?"

"Can't stay here high, *mija*. Says she wants to get clean, make herself beautiful again."

"No way I'm going through cold turkey on my own, Kat."

"There's a mattress in the garage," Beatriz said.

"Yes!" Raven launched her fist.

Bea came running. The tails of the long pink sash she'd strung through her belt loops flapped. She gazed up at the woman who looked Vonnie's age, though the flesh cushioning Raven's eyes was dark. "I'll carry a fan and the covers out, okay, Grandma?"

"Please, Kat?"

"It's a possibility."

"And I'll bring food if my abuela won't let you eat with us."

"You can bet I won't," Kat said.

Beatriz stamped her sneaker. "All your damn rules!"

"Enough, Bea."

Raven couldn't help herself—she gripped Kat's cheeks and kissed her on the mouth, then knelt again and kissed the little girl.

The eleven-year-old grinned and started to dance, pounding her feet and pumping her arms.

"I'm gonna go phone Frank Montoya," Kat said, disgusted at having let a sociopath like Tish homeschool her granddaughter. And to hell any more thinking she needed Flasher's thousand a month. Ask Marta's help? Kat was placing the Harbor into God's hands.

"How much coke have you in the room?" she asked Raven.

"The dozen quarter-grams I bought last night—less one. Who's Frank Montoya?"

"The Harbor and refuge are part of his beat."

"You're planning to rat on me?"

Kat wagged her head. "Brighter Days usually means a wait. Maybe Frank can speed up your getting a bed. And I want to find out what he's gonna do when I tell him about Tish and Flasher trying to kill you last night. It's way past time to pull the plug on them."

Raven watched the visible halves of spoked tires disappear into the kitchen. "Who's in the wheelchair?"

"Reuben Lightningfeather's daughter. Crippled with arthritis. C'mon along, Bea, we'll go move Raven into her quarters."

"Do I rate visitor privileges?" the sex facilitator asked.

"Hisi first!" Beatriz blurted. "You'll love her—I'll roll her in."

Kat scratched the spider bite on her neck, lumbered to the phone beside the TV, and punched in seven numbers she knew well. "Officer Montoya," she said.

After a few moments she hung up. "Gambling with his wife at Green Valley Ranch outside Vegas. Back Monday. His first break in three years." She vised her hips. "Bea, you recall the plan? If the Josephs show up—you know their silver car—squeeze like a bunny under the fence and across to Marcellina's to phone nine-one-one. Which I'll already, believe me, have done here."

OUTFOXED

Monday 24 September 2007

Jock had shaved off his stubble for the ten o'clock appointment at police headquarters. He sat in the conference room in running shoes, thigh-length khakis, and a short-sleeved, blue button-down at the end of an outsized table. Germaine, Raven, and officer Frank Montoya sat with him.

Floor-to-ceiling law books bound in black and gold lined the wall behind them; two mullioned windows opposite looked on the rental sedan the three had come in. Raven—after bringing the Hacienda's van out of hiding—had spent the night on the sleeper couch in Germaine's and Jock's suite at the Hotel Santa Fe.

"Apologies," Frank said in his high-pitched voice. Near his elbow rested a microcassette. He pushed bare forearms against the oval table's edge. "We'd be more private in my office but new Internet lines are being installed throughout the building."

Jock scratched his scalp—how strange to listen to this cop's childlike voice and see the biceps muscling from the elbow-length sleeves of his black shirt and American-flag shoulder patches.

Frank glanced at his watch. "Kat says you've got photos."

"Germaine?" Jock asked.

What surprised her most, as she dug into her shoulder bag, was the absence of smoke. She'd fantasized that whatever room they met in would stink of tobacco. But, ten degrees cooler than outside, in here the air felt crisp, like that surrounding a stream. And she'd dressed as if for a hike: khaki shorts like Jock's, sneakers thicker-soled than his and whiter, and a light pink, insect-repellent shirt. She gave the two-dozen photos to Jock and plunked down a small, brown bottle. Jock passed the photos to Frank.

The officer flipped through a few images, then turned to Raven on his left. Even she, buoyed by a hit twenty minutes ago in Germaine's and Jock's bathroom, looked spruce in capris and russet-swirled tunic she'd washed at Kat's. She snuffled and gazed through her glasses at Frank, relishing the sweetness that still trickled down her throat.

"You're Raven," the cop said.

"Yes, sir. Excuse me." She extracted a tissue from her burlap satchel, blew, and snuffled again.

"Head cold?" he asked.

"Allergies," she lied.

"Brighter Days has a bed waiting for you. They're expecting you by four. You can make that?"

"Yes, sir."

"You know where the rehab's located?"

Raven shook her head. The black topknot she'd secured with the silver knitting needle gifted by a former lover wobbled, dislodging a wisp that fell past her ear.

"Kat can explain. You've got wheels?"

Raven nodded and bit her upper lip, thankful—so close to this round-shouldered hunk with cropped hair as black as her own—that Germaine had suggested a double swipe of deodorant.

Frank fanned the photos across the table's glistening mahogany. "There's something going on, that's obvious. Who took these?"

"My fiancée's father and a friend."

"Fiancée!" Germaine exclaimed, and felt the throbbing in her right temple begin.

"Mucho congrats," Raven said.

Jock placed a beefy hand on Germaine's. "I bought the ring two days ago at Shreves, princess. Had planned to show you last night but wanted to wait till we were alone."

"Goddamn it, you should have told me you needed time together!" Raven exclaimed.

"Taking care of you seemed more important," Jock said.

Germaine said nothing because anger was overcoming her excitement.

"Sex retreats are springing up all over the country," Frank said. "This morning in the *Times*, cops raided a split-level in Duncanville, Texas, wherever that is. The house drew a hundred swingers a weekend. Your Beautiful Tomorrows is the first example we've come across in Santa Fe. You got anything else?" he asked Germaine. "Video? Audio?"

"Videos," Raven said. "But I couldn't sneak them out of the Josephs' den."

"We'll get a search warrant started. Finding the judge to sign it might take some time. We'll need your willingness to testify, Raven." Frank arced his arm toward Germaine. "Yours, too. Kat phoned me we've got blackmail to deal with, plus Flasher's possession with intent to distribute." He turned to Raven. "We're also talking about an attempt on your life—two attempts, I gather. Did I hear that right?"

"Yes, sir."

"It's all true, officer," Germaine added.

Frank cracked his knuckles. "Possession-with-intent is a felony." He faced Raven again. "You haven't been a saint either, *chica*. You may be looking at doing time, too. Have you lined up a lawyer?"

Raven shook her head.

"This," Germaine said and lifted the brown bottle. "Full of barbiturates the Josephs tried to overdose her with. Who should I give it to?"

"That comes to me." Frank reached out. "Kat probably knows a lawyer. Right now she's more concerned about Flasher and Tish. You're acquainted with them?"

Germaine felt her headache worsening. "Raven told us everything last night at the hotel."

"Okay. The refuge is mostly empty during the day. We'll pick those two up tonight, if they haven't already scrammed." Frank scratched his jaw with the back of a thumbnail. "We'll find them sooner or later. Kat says she's got Tish's revolver."

"I certainly hope so! Jock and I had planned to try to find my father this afternoon and get him out before dark." Germaine managed to swallow the acid welling into her throat.

"Kinda dangerous. Let us talk to him."

"He may not want to leave," Jock said.

"Why not?"

"He owes rent back east. Plus credit-card debt, other complications," Germaine said.

Frank pressed his thumbnail to his lower lip. "If you and your fiancé's willing—"

"He's not my fiancé, officer."

"Not yet, I guess," Jock said.

"Nobody's asked what *I* want," Germaine said.

"I thought…"

"Later, Jock."

Frowning, he turned to stare through the glass door at the gumball machine in the foyer.

"The Chief's calling for a roundtable in this room at eleven on domestic violence," Frank said. "Let's keep moving."

"Flasher's looking at a big payday when I'm pushing up daisies," Raven said. "After Germaine's gone poof, too, I suppose."

Frank faced the editor. "Tell you what. Kat says that your father and his friend plan to be in their campsite working on music and waiting for you a half hour before Flasher's curfew. If you and your boyfriend—or fiancé or whoever he is—get to the sofa by six thirty, another cop and I will have entered the creek bed from the north—and planted ourselves in the willows where Flasher hides the outhouse. If Tish shows the clothesline, start screaming. We'll be there in seconds."

"Officer? It all sounds pretty pie-in-sky," Jock said. "Princess?"

"I agree." Germaine tried to swallow, failed, moistened her lips.

"I'm not saying do it like this. Only saying we'll be making our move at seven, irregardless. If Tish or Flasher threatens you tonight, we'll be there. If you decide to look for your father this afternoon, we won't. I'm going to turn this gizmo on now."

Frank hit a button, stated the date and time, and pushed the microcassette in front of Raven. "You start."

Jock, who had been scanning the vents and fluorescent panels, jerked his head down. "Are you going to marry me?"

Germaine's elbow clamped her shoulder bag. "Jock, please."

"Are you?"

"I think so."

"I've bought the engagement ring."

"You've told us."

"And?"

"I need time, Jock."

"Folks? You've been taped, I'll mail you a copy for a wedding present. Can we get this other chore under way? Raven, go ahead. How the scam worked, how you got your coke, the Josephs' attempt on your life, Tish's near miss."

———

"I can't hear any music, can you?"

Jock put his forefinger to his lips, listened, and wagged his head.

"It's so damn quiet," Germaine said.

"Except for that churring—cicada? And the traffic grinding past that old graveyard along the road we came into town on yesterday."

After Raven had driven the van from the hotel back to Kat's and hidden it, Germaine and Jock—following much talk—had decided to risk going along with Officer Montoya's suggestion. They stood half an hour before sunset outside the wire gate to the refuge, gawking at the nearly full moon playing peekaboo with elm leaves as it rose to the northeast above the Sangre de Cristos. Behind them, the Stars and Stripes above Kat's Harbor rippled as the sun dyed a bank of clouds magenta.

An aluminum garbage can spilling empties of Bud Light lay against the chain-link fence closing off the PNM substation from the refuge's three-quarter acre. A gust blew clumps of hairy-leafed kochia and blades of cheatgrass around them.

Jock hauled out his pocket watch. "Montoya and his sidekick must be lying low up there somewhere, you think? Across from all that brush?"

Germaine drew her fingers through her curls. "Look, Jock, three daisies pushing through the weeds. No wonder Dad feels sentimental about this implausible place."

Jock opened the gate beside the *No Trespassing* sign. "You think your father'll leave?"

"The Red River Festival music director—I've told you she lives in Taos—confirmed on the phone this afternoon that she doesn't need to meet Dad. They can e-mail each other about the residency, same thing she said when I called from New York. Mostly I care that Dad's proud of me for helping to put the Josephs away. Flasher and his sister, too. At least Raven's safe."

"So Kat thinks. Good luck kiss?" An inch shorter than Germaine, Jock lifted his lips. She lowered her chin to meet them.

"I'm proud of *you*, princess. God, the danger. For my next book after

Moderate Muslims, sign me for an account of what you've been through—and what we're about to do now? Readers'll think I made it up."

"We'll call it creative nonfiction."

"Good! Guess we ought to whisper. I read Marcel Marceau died today—can we pull off our own mime act?"

"Else we go home feet first."

He laughed. "Princess, listen, thanks for giving my ring a try to see if your finger can stand the weight."

"I'm sorry I'm so skittish." She raised her hand from alongside her shorts and kissed the lozenge-shaped diamond and attendant chips. "I told Raven that sex changes intimacy to dependence, therefore I must hate you. How much more complex than that everything is."

She started onto the path leading to the sofa.

"Look at that red hair!" he breathed behind her.

"Tish, the sister girlfriend."

"Bow wow wow!" Reeking of Chanel No. 5, Tish stood in camouflage shirt and Levi cutoffs, knees slightly bent. The heel of a boot had skewed outward, making her seem clubfooted. "Halt there."

"Hello, Tish. Remember me? Q's daughter? This is Jock. We'd like to see my father."

"Dirky's with him," Tish said.

"All right! Then he's here," Germaine said.

"I'll take you to them."

"It's this path to the left, isn't it?"

"Rules say I take you."

"That's fine."

Tish flicked the hair sprouting from her mole and squinted under her rolled sombrero. "Girlies first."

Germaine's stomach rumbled. "Sure," she said as lightly as she could. A shiver shook through her though the evening's temperature hovered above seventy.

She pushed aside a clump of suckers arcing across the path that led through Reuben Lightningfeather's campsite to her father's beyond. She held the suckers back for Jock, then dodged under the thorned branch of a locust. Near a sprig of buffalo grass her sneaker crushed a dandelion braving the gloom. In the clearing ahead, close to the creek bed, she spotted a part-husky roped to the back of a wheelchair. It held a girl whose lush black hair covered the chair's back. The dog jumped up and started to bark.

"Ruff ruff," Tish shouted behind Jock. "Clam it, you big nobody."

"Hey!" Jock blurted as Tish bumped him.

"Boogie-woogie."

Germaine led the trio toward the clearing's far side, sucking in breath under the canopy of branches. Tell me the cops have showed up, she prayed. Reuben's wife, Wilda, nursed an infant in front of a lean-to like that Germaine had seen at Headquarters a week ago.

The crippled Hisi sat watching, holding her teddy bear against her tummy and the part-husky by its rope collar. "I want to go see!" She jerked her head toward her mother and gripped a wheel of her chair to turn it toward the path.

"You'll stay there," Wilda said.

"Betcher buttons, bitch kitty," Tish added.

Germaine began to feel sick. She paused and looked around.

Throwing his arms sideways, Jock stopped, too, causing Tish's breast to squash against his shoulder.

"Hey!" he blurted.

"Said that before, din cha?"

"Princess? Should we sound the alarm?"

"What alarm, clownface?" Tish sealed off a nostril with her thumb and snuffled air through the other. "You wanna see the composer, doan cha?"

A black-striped lizard skittered across dry leaves as Germaine broke through a column of gnats swirling in a sunbeam. Jock and Tish followed.

Jock's nose twitched at the turpentine scent of rabbitbrush. He dipped his head to miss a pair of brown shoes looped over a charred limb. Their soles had curled free.

The light filtering through the locusts and elms grew scant but glowed yellow-white in the clearing ahead.

In the instant that Jock saw two old men gagged and bound in beach chairs outside their lean-to—and heard Germaine's startled yelp ahead— he felt two arms pin his own. A clothesline softened by a rag tightened around his throat and the red-frizzed Tish shoved him past Germaine. He twisted to see Tish grin, and behind her, a man under a Capital Motors cap holding Germaine. A bald woman wearing an orange neckerchief drew a cloth between the lips of his hoped-for fiancée, cinched it, and secured its ends.

Jock's gut locked as Tish tightened the garrote. The pigtailed, tattooed Native American who had vised his arms wore a forest-green muscle shirt exuding the stink of rotting leaves. He wrapped a cloth across Jock's mouth and knotted it at the back of his neck.

"Attention!" Tish called out. "Remember those Josephs came by with more bills and that ever'body gets some if you follow orders. On your mark, get set, hoof it."

Reuben Lightningfeather guided Jock toward the tied-up Quentin and Dirk. Tish followed, holding the garrote's handles like reins. The Native American's thick lips touched the rim of Jock's ear. 'Sitcom,' is the word Jock thought he heard whispered.

The procession stopped among branches Quentin had lopped off nine days ago while raging that Byron planned to fly east. Stormy's enormous packing crate had vanished. The former marine, bare-chested, shirtsleeves wrapped around his waist, was tying Germaine's wrists behind her. Universal Cosmic Divinity in his chef's hat stood nearby between the toothless African American, Chiffon, and the cleft-chinned Flasher. His French Legionnaire's beret slanted rakishly. Twine Tish had sewn through each leg of his dungarees pulled them taut under his combat boots.

Jock's chest strained against the Native American's arm as Tish removed the garrote. She stuffed it with its rag into her beltless waistband, then roped his wrists. Where were those cops? "Umpf," he sounded as loud as he could, glancing past the lean-to toward the embankment where tops of the willows fluttered.

Flasher stepped close and slapped him. "We'll get the gorgeous hooker, too," he said. "Uni's heard where Kat took her."

Germaine's intestines were rioting. With fabric crammed between her jaws, she could no longer swallow the gastric juices that burned the back of her tongue. Her eyes swept across the overturned box marked *Grapefruit*, bearing cotton rags and lengths of hemp, to stare at Dirk tied in his chair.

He held his head high, thinning hair blowing. She watched his cracked lips try without success to close around his gag.

At last her gaze fastened on her father, face black in the dusk. Five furrows deepened under his rain hat. Quentin tried to speak but could only grunt.

Flasher doubled in a fit of coughing, then snatched up his beret, ran forward, and smacked the composer above the ear with the heel of his hand.

Germaine groaned.

"Clam it," Flasher squeaked. "Tisher, go grab a couple of ropes. Storm Born an' Reuben, prepare the grandpas."

Five minutes later the group stumbled toward Headquarters, Tish leading, Dirk limping along, Reuben in his black shorts, Quentin, Chiffon and Clara, Germaine, Uni, Jock, Stormy Weathers, and Flasher, a secondhand Silver Star bouncing among armed-service bars on the camouflage shirt that matched Tish's.

Just ahead of Stormy, Jock yelled into his gag as a stump's stub cut into his calf. Feeling the hot ooze of blood, he glanced to his left, saw in the moonlit gloom that the undergrowth of saplings and ragweed seemed particularly dense, and calculated that if the policemen had arrived, they were probably close down the brush-covered slope. He decided to attempt escape.

But the badger's den that Raven had almost stumbled into two weeks ago lay ahead. Jock's running shoe, as he threw his foot out to bolt, caught toe-down. Wrists roped, he pitched onto his shoulder into a patch of blue-green stems. Their bristly flowers raked his cheeks. Though his ankle smarted, he'd been able to kick his foot free in time to prevent a sprain. His torso spasmed as he sneezed, and sneezed again.

"C'mon up." Stormy's fingers gripped Jock's armpits from behind.

"That fairy canary—can he walk?" Flasher asked.

"Don't know yet."

Stormy and Flasher lifted Jock to his feet while Uni wrapped his arms around Germaine to keep her staying put.

"Move it, Tisher, we've got work to do," Flasher shouted, and punched Jock between the shoulder blades.

Jock discovered that he could limp.

They resumed their forward march. Seven people ahead, Dirk slumped to the right while Jock dipped to the left, pain lancing his leg at each step.

Moonlight guided them into Headquarters. What they could see of the western sky had become a jumble of magenta. A raven glided across. To the southeast, headlamps streaming north on Cerrillos winked through the foliage, crossing the red dots of taillights disappearing toward the freeway. The vehicles' purr abraded the constant hum of the substation's transformers south of the sofa.

The packing crate, large enough to sleep two under its polyethylene roof, sat beside the open hole next to the pen fenced for Uni's mongrel. The dog began to yip at seeing the nine homeless regulars and two fresher-smelling strangers.

"Quiet, Esmee, shhh." Uni tapped his lips.

"Little thing!" Tish arced a field mouse up by its tail. An eye had been eaten out. She shook the corpse to dislodge the ants and carried it to four shovels resting on the loose dirt, still damp from Friday's rain, that lined an edge of the pit. She dropped the mouse onto one of the shovels' blades. A pair of black-chinned hummers sipped their evening meal, accompanied by the clank of hubcaps dangling from Flasher's and Tish's lean-to.

"Storm Born," Flasher said, "you an' Uni an' Reub Boob take the prisoners to the site. Have 'em lie head-to-toe to see if four'll fit."

Quentin and Dirk staggered close to Jock and Germaine, who waited next to the stolen barber pole. Rags torn from someone's red-and-black-checked shirt draped the pole's top. The editor motioned to her father to take one of the directors' chairs.

Dirk lowered himself to the overturned US Postal Service bin.

"Sit-down strike?" Flasher guffawed. "Haul 'em up, Reuben."

The big Native American pushed Jock's elbow. "You all gotta hurry along."

They trudged toward the hole.

"Lie flat," Flasher commanded.

Jock, sneezing, clambered into the five-foot-deep grave.

"Face up," Flasher said.

Jock shivered as the dampness of the dirt seeped through his shirt. His bare calves cooled. What was biting into his neck? He managed to turn his head enough to spot a crumpled beer can, then stared at the moon glowing through leaves arching over the clearing. His buttocks squashed his fists.

"Next," Flasher called out. "Head-to-foot."

Reuben helped Quentin in, Germaine, Dirk. "Sitcom," he whispered again.

When the editor stretched herself out, she felt her cheek pressing her father's boot. It smelled of scat. Don't let me throw up, she prayed.

"Okeydokey, prisoners, you fit jus' dandy. Now sit up against the side where there's no shovels."

They struggled to obey, finally managing to lean against the pit's edge, where they faced Clara and Chiffon and the path they'd come in on.

"Blindfold 'em, Reub Boob, Stormy—you, too, Uni-roonie."

Clara handed them the red-and-black-checkered rags. Reuben strode past the mongrel gazing through her chicken-wire fence to veil Jock's and Germaine's eyes and knot the rags' ends. Uni and Stormy blindfolded Dirk and Quentin.

The composer started making gurgling noises. Uni pried open his nostrils with his pinkies so he could breathe better.

"Flasher?" Stormy asked, shifting his cap so the bill faced backward. "I'm gonna need a hit before we keep going."

"Serious? You ever done coke?"

"No Bacardi handy. Anyways, I stopped drinking. Whadda you charge?"

"Me, too, Nate, sure could use a touch," Tish said. "I never snuffed out four persons at a time."

"Be dark in half an hour, dingheads!"

"Hoo boy, Papa, we got ourselves a moon to see by," Tish said.

Chiffon, the hem of her red dress eddying, and Clara in her flowered bra and chartreuse capris, stayed mum. They'd perched back-to-back on the postal bin set next to the carton marked *Artichokes*. The soles of their sandals smeared mud on the Business section of the *Courier* that Flasher had tossed away earlier.

"Nate," Tish told her brother, "you make me do the deed, you gotta give me blow. Else someone else works the clothesline."

"You want me to leave off the rubber tonight?"

"Fuck me however you like, fartface. We're gonna be buying us a home."

"You'll be wanting my help with the shovels, Flasher—how much you charging?" Stormy asked again.

"Aw, shit."

Flasher flung his beret onto the plywood sheet fronting the lean-to and stomped in. Reuben, Uni, Stormy, Clara, and Chiffon watched him throw aside the camp stool, lift off the small square of plywood it had rested on, and reach into the cavity he'd uncovered.

Seconds later he carried out two bindles and half straws. "Get the windowpane ready," he told his sister. "Off the throne, bimbos."

Clara and Chiffon rose from the bin and helped Tish place the jagged piece of glass.

Flasher reached for a knife taped under one of the directors' chairs and approached.

A hundred yards to the east, past the old railroad right-of-way, sodium-vapor security lights loomed along the School of the Deaf's fence, topped by barbed wire. The lights popped on, yellowing the moonlight that brightened distant foxtails and ragweed.

"How much you get for that coke?" Stormy asked for the third time, stationing himself before the opening in the huge packing crate that he and Clara planned to keep house in.

"None a your beeswax."

Tish sidled close to her brother, tugged the garrote and rag buffer from her waistband, and hung them around her neck. The vinyl-loop handles dangled like braids.

"I want to buy some!" Stormy demanded.

"You've got no bread." Flasher handed Tish the knife. Kneeling on tufts of cheatgrass, she began to chop the coke's white grains.

"I'll have plenty of cash once we get this over with, thanks to you and Tish and our sex-scam benefactors," Stormy said.

Uni and Reuben had drifted behind Flasher, near where Chiffon and Clara waited a couple of steps from Tish.

Ten yards away, slumped against the grave, Jock ground his teeth, hoping to chew through the cotton gag.

Flasher smacked his gemstone rings to his mouth to muffle a coughing fit, then said to Stormy, "Ask me nice."

"Those two bindles. How much you charging?"

"One's mine!" Tish blurted.

"Oh, shut up." Flasher spread his boots and locked his fingers to his hips. "Same price I gave the Josephs' whore."

"And what's that?" The scent of Flasher's cologne was making Stormy dizzy.

Tish, having snorted the bindle's contents, leaned backward on her haunches and moaned, mocking Uni's bitch.

"Hunnerd bucks a gram."

Done! Price is what Frank Montoya had told Kat the group must hear before abandoning their sham. Clara and Chiffon leapt onto Tish, tumbling her into a stand of kochia. Chiffon grabbed the knife from the redhead's fist.

Flasher jerked as if unseen guards had electrified his balls. He high-stepped through kochia piled next to the packing crate and dashed toward the railroad bed. But Uni, somersaulting over the brush, bounded onto Flasher's back and wrestled him down.

Flasher, the hand bearing his rings immobilized, sank his teeth into Uni's palm, causing the street performer turned would-be sous-chef to scream.

Reuben came lumbering toward them.

But Uni's mongrel reached them first. She had clawed herself over the chicken wire strung along the green metal stakes, and sunk her own teeth into Flasher's cheek.

"Oh, Jesus, Joseph," he bawled, thrusting her head away. "She slobbered on my medals."

"Clara, go find the cops!" Stormy called out as Reuben set his hulk on Flasher's perspiring back and Uni persuaded Esmee to back off.

Clara scurried under the branches, the ends of her orange scarf flapping.

"Help the nigra," Stormy told Uni.

Uni grabbed his chef's hat from the dirt, crammed it on, dashed over, and lowered himself to Tish's buttocks. Chiffon had perched on one of the redhead's shoulder blades.

"I can't breathe," she gasped, chin and nose pressing the ground.

Chiffon yanked Tish's head to the side and sat on her ear.

Nearer the path to the sofa, all four of the gagged, blindfolded, and bound Anglos had assisted each other to stand. Weaving, they faced the shovels.

Never seen it; my old pop'd never believe it, Reuben thought. He couldn't help himself—he started to guffaw, breasts bouncing under the muscle shirt. He stretched out his tattooed forearms to untie the editor's blindfold. He'd never watched a woman heave her shoulders like that, even after lovemaking.

But he couldn't budge the knot.

"All this been planned," he told Germaine. "Had to catch 'em with their pants down, see Tish uncoil the noose, hear what Flasher's charging."

Reuben crouched to unsnap the knife that Flasher had forgotten to take from Dirk's belt. Still bent, the Native American cut the cloth from the editor's eyes and mouth. He used the knife's tip to pry loose the knot that bound her wrists.

"Daddy! Jock!" Germaine jiggled the blindfold from her father's eyes. "Help me untie him," she begged Reuben. The big man cut the rope while she pulled the mud-stained gag from Quentin's mouth and slid it down his neck. "Oh, Daddy!" She shook her arms to restore their circulation, flung them around Quentin, let go, and turned to Jock.

Meanwhile, Stormy had taken from Reuben the rope that had held Germaine's wrists and was tying Flasher's hands behind him.

Reuben now threw Stormy the rope he'd removed from Quentin's wrists. The Iraq veteran tied up Tish.

"Thank Kat and her cop friend for the whole scenario," Reuben told the prisoners, cutting the rags from Jock's and Dirk's faces. Germaine hugged Jock's head against hers.

"Never thought," he said to Quentin in deadpan, "that I'd want to lay eyes on you. Now I find myself asking in person for your daughter's hand."

Quentin—gagless but shocked silent still—merely blinked.

"They're here!" came Clara's shout. Frank Montoya and a skinnier cop, their .45s drawn, charged past her into the clearing.

"We got 'em," Frank said into his radio.

Stormy climbed off Flasher, as did Uni and Chiffon from Tish. Frank handcuffed the dealer while his buddy handcuffed Flasher's sister.

"Get on up, you two."

"Frankie," Tish begged the policeman, "you're not gonna—"

"Sure am. It's over. Flasher, where's your payoff money and the stash?"

"Why don't you stick it up—"

"Flasher, friend? Make it easier on yourself and her. Nasty wound, there."

Flasher hunched a shoulder toward the blood oozing from his cheek. "Uni's mongrel bit me."

"We'll stop at the ER for stitches and a look at rabies. Where's the money and inventory?"

The refuge's' once-arrogant leader slouched toward the lean-to, thighs lifting as if filled with concrete. Frank and the other officer ducked inside, under the hubcaps and feeders. Flasher dropped his chin toward the safe in the cavity he'd dug, its lid raised. "Feast your peepers, assholes. Scale, grinder, a hundred Jacksons, an' rocks of nose candy you can't barely see."

¡HASTA LA VISTA!

Tuesday 25 September 2007

If, the next morning, you'd been cruising by the sprawling home at Columbia and Ybarra Lane, you'd have supposed the trucks and equipment meant its owners were planning to sell.

That's correct.

But there's no way you could have seen what Arlene and Fritz Joseph were doing on their knees upstairs in the bedroom.

Not praying. Though perhaps they were doing that, too.

Three pickups had grouped in front under a cloudless sky. The first, white with four rear tires—its grille inches from the garage—held tubs of adobe-colored granules, rolls of black roofing paper, and tanks of propane. Welders' gloves and a pair of tar-spattered boots rested beside a tire.

A twin-fendered, rectangular 'tar pot' sat hitched to the truck's hind end. Smeared with asphalt, the red lid of the vat tilted skyward. A burner under the pot's belly kept the tar bubbling at four-hundred degrees. The air stank with its smell. On the pot's spigot hung a bucket. A ladder next to the Hacienda's broken window led to the living-room's roof.

On the graveled drive's south side, a second pickup, marked *Renewal by Anderson,* had parked by the curb. Strips of carpeting padded an aluminum A-frame rising from this pickup's bed. A strap secured two windows—a glider and a double-hung—to the A-frame's struts. Scraps of wood kept the windows apart. A pre-framed casement window leaned against the truck's bumper and raised tailgate. The two workmen indoors had cushioned its bottom rail from the street with carpet.

The third pickup, the words *Tile of Enchantment* emblazoned in yellow across its door, hugged the curb on the drive's north side. A front tire run over the curb had flattened the ground cover of lavender vinca. A so-called 'wet saw' sat on an X-shaped iron stand between the truck's grille and the drive. Two fifty-pound sandbags kept the stand from tipping. Water pumped from a two-foot-by-three-foot tray underneath cooled the circular blade. Nearby rested a carton of pre-sealed Saltillo tiles. A red extension cord snaked up the drive under the garage's lifted door and rose to an outlet beside Arlene's beautiful Cashmere Silver 135i BMW upholstered in Coral Red leather.

The living room's interior smelled of sawdust and old mortar. Last night the Josephs had carried chairs to the walls and rolled the throw rugs against them.

A man crouched on pads strapped to his knees beside a heap of broken Saltillos. Accompanying them were a second carton of new tiles, a sack of Permabond adhesive, two buckets—one half filled with water—and an electric drill sprouting a long shaft and mixing paddle. The lapels of the blue shirt hanging over the worker's belt were frayed, but gold links closed his cuffs. He was singing to himself in Spanish and cold-chiseling grout free, tap-tap-tapping with a hammer. A wax pencil and rubber mallet lay behind the soles of his high-topped sneakers.

The Josephs' wraparound sofa now jutted into the vestibule; the cabinet emptied of Arlene's grandmother's dishes rested next to the unicorn on its side.

Near the window that Quentin and Dirk had crashed through more than a week ago stood the two carved doors Arlene and Fritz had used to close off the jagged hole. The hiss and stink of boiling tar drifted through the opening.

A couple of Anglos—one goateed—in matching forest-green caps and *Renewal-by-Anderson* shirts, stood on a blue tarp. They used pry bars and claw hammers to loosen the broken window's frame from the wall's permanent jambs, head, and sill.

Upstairs, the Josephs—half-straws in their noses, upper arms touching—bent over powdered cocaine laid out on a low, circular table. The emptied bindles sat crumpled near the table's wooden rim. No conditioned air hummed through the vents.

Fritz hadn't shaved but both seemed dressed for partying. Five points of a purple hankie sprouted from a shirt splashed with hibiscus blossoms, and Arlene had decked herself in horned toads, cows, snakes, and goats capering over green silk.

She'd felt queasy ever since indulging in an extra half of Fritz's breakfast burritos. The coke was bound to help. "Oh, God, yes," she sighed, rocked back—belched and farted at the same time. "Sorry, Doctor, yummy yum. You cook good." She threw her fingers into the air and fluttered them. "Freedom! We're going to be all right, once that racket stops."

The tile installer had poured dry Permabond, then water, into the empty bucket and was mixing the result to a toothpaste consistency. His drill's whine edged under the upstairs-bedroom door.

Arlene grabbed Fritz's wrist.

"What're you doing?"

"We gonna be happy, Doctor." She keeled onto her side, belched again, snuffled, and grinned.

Through dilating pupils Fritz stared at this wife of fifteen years. Flab hung from the arm draped along her skirt, cellulite puckered the exposed thigh, turkey wrinkles climbed her neck. The flesh pressing his while they'd snorted their one-n-ones had felt like mud; the fingers that had gripped his wrist had felt like the legs of a giant spider.

Oh, but the coke, trickling like honey down his throat—Raven, he thought, I want you! "Babe?" he said aloud.

"You called?" Arlene asked.

The purple aster she'd plucked from the balcony's flower box dangled over the upper half of her ear.

"We should go see if Flasher and Tish and their ragtags did what we paid them to," he said.

"You think?"

"Before we head south for our two days off." He leaned back against the table's edge.

"Pretty crowded in the backseat, Fritz-o. And the trunk's full of videos to dump. You see? I don't mind your calling me Babe anymore."

"Huh?"

"Cat got your ear?"

He glanced out at the cottonwood's canopy of seeming green gauze, wincing at the sounds of scrapers and the blowtorch that drifted off the roof.

"Losing it, Fritz?"

"What are you saying?"

"There's no room for her in my comely wagon and I made no extra reservation at the B and B."

"For whom?" Fritz asked.

"Our sweet slut."

"You gotta be dreaming. Raven's at Kat's. And yesterday Flasher promised to do her in before the police show up."

"After we've watched the roadrunners and duckies at the Bosque long enough to settle on long-range plans—and sit with the Realtor you phoned this morning—maybe our coke whore will sprint down to Guanajuato with us, Fritzy. If Kat can keep her kicking."

Fritz wrinkled his nose at the lingering smell of his wife's fart.

"We'll make her our sex slave, why not?" Arlene sniffled, rolled over, and grabbed one of his veined ankles, bare above the moccasin. "I wanna play nurse and doctor."

"Huh?"

"Stop saying that!" She belched and threw a fist to her lips. "Bring out that medicinal dong."

He reached to pull her fingers off. From downstairs came the din of an Anderson man's reciprocating saw and Fritz clapped his palms to his ears, then twisted and pressed a palm to the rug. He tried to heave himself up but sank back. "Oh, boy."

"I'm your bride, Doctor. Not your boy. That slipped your mind?"

The vision of Raven easing amethysts from his ass accompanied a spreading euphoria, in spite of the saw's roar.

Arlene's voice grew snarly as she rose to her elbow:

"Forgotten I've put up with your frittering away the fortune this business has been? Kiss off our being able to settle south of the border next year."

"Frittered?" He swallowed a sweet gob of phlegm as anger crowded out the coke's assurance of well-being.

"Money wasted on misfits, Wishy-Wash. Ragpickers. Addicts. Alcoholics. The unclean. Mental midgets." This time she did not apologize for the blast escaping her bowels. "I want to go see Raven."

"That's nuts."

"More than your wanting to hunt down Flasher?"

What he wanted was to grab her head and twist until it spun off, like the lid of a jar. The sun's heat was causing his armpits to wet. "Let's go. Get up."

"Don't tell me what to do!" But she followed his lead and in golden flats followed towards the door.

"You forgot your purse," he said.

"And you, sir, forgot our bag." She patted her ducktails. Somehow the flower stayed put. "You're the husband here." She steadied herself against the doorknob.

Clamping his jaw, he marched to the dresser, lifted their suitcase clad in tapestry, and grabbed her sequined purse—weighted by the derringer— off the dresser's top.

Arlene stepped out to the landing.

How he wished he'd followed through with his plan two weeks ago to bolt with Raven. *Damn* that he'd ever married. At least Arlene had soon abandoned the try for children. He walked out and stopped behind her. They planned to skip to Mexico after signing with a Realtor here? Didn't they need a passport?

Arlene stood gazing at the workers below. Her hold on the railing remained as, hearing him breathing, she turned and said, "Fix me a tequila sunrise downstairs, will you? Fix a whole bunch."

She threw her hand into the air as if proposing a toast and twisted back to look down. By now the tile installer had freed all loose Saltillos, opening up a twelve-foot square. His chisel clinked against the mortar remaining stuck to the exposed concrete slab. "Look at him in that ridiculous bowl cut. Can you imagine what animals these people are in bed? The odor, Fritz!"

One of the Anderson Windows men had laid aside his saw and was pushing scraps of sash and the former frame out through the opening where the window had been, and onto the front path.

Arlene lowered her foot to the stairway's first tread.

Did she really fart a third time? Fritz was never sure. He remembered blurting, "Ugh!" and though he considered a push, instead thrust his right knee between her buttocks and catapulted her up.

"Whah!" Cows and horn toads tumbled. The purple aster flew off her ducktail, landing on the wire-mesh head of the nude riding the unicorn below.

Neither the tile installer nor the Anderson men let her body's thumps divert their focus. Perhaps they just didn't hear. In any case, Arlene bounced over the lips of the treads until she lay huddled on a Zuni throw, a ducktail jutting into the air.

Fritz had never felt so alert. His heart seemed a ship's engine though his vision stayed blurry. Raven! I did it! He snuffled back phlegm, clamped Arlene's purse between elbow and ribs, hoisted the suitcase, grabbed the iron handrail, and started descending.

She lay curled on her hip opposite the unicorn, hugging a raised knee with her left hand and clutching the leg's ankle with her right. The brows she arched forced a deep frown from Fritz as he dragged the suitcase across her. She shuddered and her chest heaved but she made no sound.

The goateed Renewal-by-Anderson man was pulling together the corners of the tarp. He noticed Fritz heading toward the glass slider and waved. "Out of your hair in a couple hours," he called. "Our stucco man and the plasterer will be on board this afternoon. Mind if we grab ourselves a glass of water?"

"Go for it. Through the dining room. Mugs above the sink."

"'Preciate it."

"No problem."

"The missus there, she all right?"

"Slipped," Fritz said. "Resting up. Thanks."

The worker saluted, grazing the green bill of his cap, and strode into the vestibule. His companion followed.

Fritz paused beside the tile installer, who had dipped his trowel into the bucket and was screeding the now-glutenous Permabond onto the slab he'd cleaned. Fritz aimed his thumb back at Arlene. "If you need anything, ask her."

"¿Qué dices?" He scratched a long sideburn.

"She'll be the one to pay you."

The installer threw out his arms and grinned, showing a chipped tooth—knelt, dipped his trowel, and screeded adhesive onto the back of a new tile.

Fritz hung the purse on his elbow, rolled the suitcase to the slider that opened to the garden, heaved it back, and walked across yellowed cottonwood leaves—past the bed of iris—to the garage's rear door.

The scent of boiling tar drifted in. Coughing, he opened the sports coupe's door, hefted the suitcase to the backseat, and lowered himself to the soft leather, feeling it settle around his kidneys. "Calm down," he said aloud, yanked the seat belt around his chest, and reached to push a button on the mirror.

As the garage door ground up, revealing the hood of the roofers' pickup parked catercorner on the drive, Fritz searched the purse until his fingers touched the BMW's electronic key. He jammed it into the slot below *Start*.

Arlene had let him captain her forty-five-thousand-dollar prize only twice. On neither occasion had the image of a panther leaping at him from a low branch accompanied the roar and purr of the 135i's three-hundred-horse-power, turbocharged engine.

He raised the windows, hoping to ease the stink of tar, found dark glasses in the glove compartment, and shoved them onto his nose. He levered the seat back an inch, then tilted it until the cushion felt snug under his knees.

What comforting fragrance this dimpled leather had! He lifted his eyes to the mirror to stare at the roofers' truck, the installer's wet saw, and his home's new window leaning against the tailgate of the Renewal-by-Anderson pickup—then to the honeysuckle that crowded the coyote fence bordering the driveway across Ybarra Lane. Bye-bye, Santa Fe, he thought, and slammed on the air conditioning.

His sweaty hands grasped the padded wheel. Where should he head? Kat's Harbor to try to find Raven? The hundred and seventy miles to the Casa Blanca B & B north of the Bosque del Apache, where Arlene had made reservations? Keep going another two hundred miles till he crossed into Mexico?

No passport, remember?

Huh? What would his mother and father say if they could peer inside his mind? He'd funded their moving to an assisted-living Shangri-la in New Haven two years ago and last talked with them at Christmas, after Arlene, Raven, and he moved here last November. His father's emphysema had sounded worse and his mother's sobbed pleas to return to New York had decided him not to call again.

Wherever he headed, he suspected himself soon done for, though preferred to die than be caught.

Taos! Sail the coupe into the Rio from the picnic grounds at the west end of the bridge. He wiped his eyes with the back of a hand and shifted into reverse.

His chin jerked as the coupe leapt over the gravel. He wrenched the wheel to aim the 135i—its silver skin sparkling—toward Columbia and then north on St. Francis and the freeway.

A white police car parked at the corner faced him, red light off.

His heart felt like a club whacking his chest as he tore across Ybarra into the honeysuckle-lined drive, and swung the wheel to head down to the Bosque.

A second police car eased into the street from behind the Anderson pickup.

In the mirror Fritz saw the white car, red light now revolving, leave the corner and roll toward him.

A third cop nosed out of a drive on the far side of the honeysuckle.

Fritz fumbled the derringer out of Arlene's purse, screeched into the neighbor's drive, and floored the pedal. His head flew back as he plunged forward across Ybarra. But his arms seemed palsied and he couldn't spin the wheel. A corner of the wet saw's iron stand gouged a groove into the coupe's opposite door as the 135i rushed headlong into the hamper of tar. Like lava, the hot mix leapt from its vat onto the hood and drenched it. Fritz clutched the wheel and, engine racing, the silver streak smashed into the replacement window propped in the street on scraps of carpet.

Splinters of glass tinkled down, bristling the tarred hood as if feathering it. Black drops speckled the windshield.

A roofer appeared at the top of the ladder. He pushed his sombrero back and started down. A second man carrying a scraper followed as the clean-shaven Anderson worker led his companion and the tile installer out the Hacienda's front door at a run.

Fritz grabbed the derringer, jammed its barrel against his temple, and cocked the hammer. But Frank Montoya had yanked the passenger door wide. Fritz squeezed the trigger while Frank was wrenching the pistol away. The bullet turned the driver's side of the windshield into a spiderweb darkened by flies.

— — —

"Explain to me again, Abuelita?"

An hour before noon, Beatriz had settled into the lap of Kat's former lover. Marta and the eleven-year-old occupied the sofa placed catercorner to the upright piano near the Harbor's front door.

Kat, Quentin, Dirk, Germaine, and Jock sat at a door laid on sawhorses nearer the kitchen, where Universal Cosmic Divinity continued shaving spines from *nopalitos* for the farewell salad. A bowl of oranges under a cabinet awaited his knife while black beans and sliced chorizo sat on the stove in a pot. A fan whirred to the right of the window that looked out on the apricot tree and Kat's truck.

The Harbor's director had dressed for the parting in her blouse embroidered with bracts of bougainvillea. A scarlet bow brightened the braid that hung to her waist.

"Raven's well taken care of. For a month, anyway," Kat told Bea. "And we don't worry about the Lightningfeathers. Vonnie found subsidized housing for them and their mutt."

"I know all that!"

"Do you also know that, by popular vote, Stormy and Clara are the refuge's new leaders? Planning to live in Flasher and Tish's lean-to, and rent out the crate like a B and B for five dollars a night?"

"Dirk explained it—can't you get to what I asked?" Beatriz placed her fingers, nails painted violet, on Marta's cheek. "Abuelita gives me a headache, Marta."

"Patienth, Bea." She wrapped her arms tighter around the girl's thick, pinafore-draped waist.

"*No te preocupes, mijita.* Your Marta's coming back! Leasing her house and hiring a manager for the café, like I said. With her financial help, and her friend's at the McCune Foundation, we remodel the garage and put in a bath so Uni and a couple more men can take up quarters. Chiffon finishes her stay here in the women's guest room. But you leave my room for the room with the skylights where you used to sleep. Marta paints her landscapes while you're at school. It should work, no?"

"It'll work, it'll work!" Beatriz kissed Marta's bony shoulder.

"Of courth it will."

"But what are we going to do about our renegades?" Kat glanced at Quentin, then over at Dirk. "These two—loco!"

"Give them their presents," Beatriz urged.

Wrinkled pink tissue enlivened bundles on the table, ringed by the seven napkins Bea had folded into triangles. She'd tied the surprises with ribbon and curled the ends with a knife.

Germaine clutched her father's elbow. "The Red River Music Festival's Director said you don't even need to meet. She's been following your career for years."

"You told me that yesterday."

"This is crazy, Daddy. At least let Jock and me drive you and Dirk to Taos. It's seventy miles, Dirk says."

"We want the adventure, sweetheart."

"Who knows?" Dirk added. "Red River may install us in its Hilton or equivalent as composer-in-residence and his keyboard whiz. Or we'll hitch our way back to the trailer I locked up south of Socorro."

"Presents, presents!" Beatriz yelped.

Jock was reaching toward the center of the table when three raps sounded on the screen door.

Bea hopped off Marta's lap and ran to hide behind her grandmother. "They stood in line for Monday'th lunch," Marta said.

The couple whom Quentin and Dirk had seen outside Wild Oats on Friday, before Quentin encountered Milt, waited outside in knit caps rolled above their ears.

The boy smelled of hot sauce. "Your cook told us to ask about a place to flop."

"Would need to do a Breathalyzer and UA first," Kat said.

"UA?" A rash had sprung across the girl's forehead.

"Urine analysis. And we'd have to separate you."

"Can't be done," the boy said.

"Try Saint Elizabeth's—well, they'd split you up, too."

The couple stepped away as Kat pushed past the screen and arced her forefinger. "See that chain-link fence half a block down? Ignore the *No Trespassing* and head through the gate toward a moth-eaten sofa. You may find someone to talk to about accommodations."

Kat wiped her double chin with her wrist, let the door close, ducked to kiss Marta's ear, and had reached her chair when the phone jangled.

"Kat's Harbor," she growled, stopping next to the TV. She held the receiver against her ear. "*¡Dios mío!*"

"Frank Montoya," she said a minute later, after settling at the head of the table. "The judge gave Fritz Joseph a cash-only, quarter-million-dollar bail. His wife's under guard in the hospital with a broken ankle and cracked ribs."

Beatriz and Marta now squeezed in together at the table's other end.

"Open them up, hombres." Kat pushed one package at Dirk and the other at Quentin.

For the occasion Dirk sported a T-shirt reading *Captain Marvel*. He pulled the stem of his hearing aid and smoothed down hair as white as his overalls. "Pissant, Kat, I don't mean to seem ungrateful, but why did you and Montoya have to concoct a scheme to catch those bastards that involved so much pain for us?"

"Frank said that playing charades until witnesses could hear Flasher name a price and see Tish pull out her clothesline was the best way to ensure a case. I'm sorry."

"Now that we're forever spooked," Dirk said.

Quentin and Dirk unwrapped their presents in silence, except for the swish of pink tissue and Uni's clanging in the kitchen.

"See?" Beatriz said of the red-and-gray backpacks. "Marta and I bought them. See, straps for your bedrolls underneath? Sleeping bags on top, just like with your old ones."

She scampered over to wedge herself between Quentin and Germaine. "Flaps cover the zippers for when it rains. See the pockets for water bottles? And in this pocket, see? Marta bought a cell phone and paid for a month. I wish we could go with you!"

Germaine began to cry. Uni poked his face out from the kitchen, disappeared, then hurried behind Quentin to give the editor a dish towel. He laid a hand on her shoulder.

"You guys are braver than I am," Jock commented.

"Senility or second childhood." Dirk scratched his hair. "But oh, what a snipe hunt this could turn out to be."

"Bea and Marta, we're overwhelmed. So grateful," Quentin said.

"Take this." Jock pulled an envelope bulging with twenties from between his shirt and chest.

"What is it?"

"Daddy? Darling? Zip the lip."

— — —

As the evening sun silvered Kat's flagpole a hundred yards distant, Germaine and Jock in their khaki shorts, Kat, Bea, and Marta stood behind the lean-to on the bank of the creek bed, where willows sheltered the outhouse. The homeless stood with them—Stormy, Clara, Uni, Chiffon, Reuben and Wilda and their children, Hisi bareheaded in her wheelchair, the part-husky roped beside her.

Two hidden finches chirped on the branch of a thorned locust as unseen traffic rumbled along Cerrillos east of the substation. One of its insulators gleamed through the top of an elm. A sphinx moth's two-inch wings beat past Germaine's face. Recoiling, she flapped her fingers at it. Reuben kicked a rusty beer can full of dried mud down the slope.

"Time to start north," Dirk said, waiting beside Quentin a little way off, both men harnessed in their going-away gifts. A saucepan dangled from Quentin's belt; Mahdi hung through a loop at Dirk's hip.

"Remember: Dynamic Duo of four-handed piano when you get back," Stormy said.

Quentin smiled. Freshly shaved, he held out his arms and Germaine broke rank to run into them.

"You'll topple me," he laughed. "You've got the cell number?"

She nodded.

"I'll keep the phone on."

"Don't forget that Flavio up in Española has a meal and shower and bunk waiting if you want them," Kat said.

Dirk grabbed a stump to help him negotiate the four-foot descent to the creek bed, and waited for Quentin between a pile of wire hangers and an empty of peppermint schnapps.

On the way down the composer's boot caught on a clump of kochia and he stumbled.

"Daddy!"

"No, no, I'm okay." He took the hand Dirk stretched out and joined him.

"¡Hasta la vista!"

The two friends began their tramp over the sand.

READERS GUIDE

Who is your favorite character? Why?

Do you find it believable that Quentin became active as a gay man after his divorce? Have you acquaintances, women or men, who have done the same? What do you think motivates them?

Frigidity is a problem many women face. Does Germaine's seeking help from a supposedly legitimate sex retreat seem likely? Why or why not?

Why do you think a few years ago that *Top Ten Reviews* reported forty-three percent of all Internet users view pornography? Might loneliness be a cause? What others come to mind?

Does the reconciliation of Germaine with her father seem likely, given that she's an incest victim? How have incest victims you've known handled their relationships with their parents?

Why does Germaine, a top book editor, become so attached to Jimmy, a real estate developer? What likes, what needs have they in common?

In the preface ("Backdrop") the author states that "a small share [of the homeless] opts permanently to depend on shelters, soup kitchens, Medicaid, and their wits." What reasons can you give, perhaps from your own experience, that anyone would choose such a lifestyle?

Does it seem reasonable to you that none of the sex-hacienda's blackmail victims report Fritz, Arlene, and Raven to the police until Germaine does? How has the author tried to persuade you the victims have been too frightened?

Drug dealers often keep no permanent address for their transactions. Why do you think Flasher has decided to keep one?

When you finished the story, which two characters would you most like to have lunch with, or visit in prison, to ask questions about their experience? Why these two people?

CPSIA information can be obtained at www.ICGtesting.com
Printed in the USA
LVOW10s0841150913

352500LV00003B/160/P

9 780865 349643